THE WAY EARTH CHANGED

ERFAN FIROUZI

BlueRose ONE

First Published in March 2023

ISBN: 978-93-5741-066-3
Ebook ISBN: 978-93-5741-060-1

BLUEROSE PUBLISHERS
www.BlueRoseONE.com
info@bluerosepublishers.com
+91 8882 898 898

Cover Design:
Yash

Distributed by: BlueRose, Amazon, Flipkart

Contents

The Opportunity to Change

Aerial view an abandoned Ferris wheel stands on a public space overgrown with trees in the former city Centre of Pripyat, Chernobyl, Nearly 30 Years Since the Catastrophe (©Sean Gallup/Getty Images)

The world we see around us today is a complex interconnected system, that is a result of nature's many years of experimentation, evolution, and diversification of life. This allowed species like us to develop culture and break the boundaries of many of the creatures before us. It was Nature that allowed us to dominate this world.

Our living planet runs by nine planetary boundaries that if crossed trigger irreversible changes that would send the whole earth as we know it to extinction. The problems we have blindly brought for nature to deal with, are more than one and they work together, silently as they destroy our planet's stability.

Yet we have had similar environmental catastrophes before as well, but nature turned the tables and showed that although we might dominate the world, we still depend on nature and that nature's ability to recover in the worst scenarios is truly a marvel to behold.

The Ukrainian town of Pripyat seems to have all the comforts that we as humans have created for a happy and comfortable life. The flats are located all around the town's cultural and commercial hub. There are 160 towers, each one constructed at a specific angle to a well-planned grid of roads. Each largest buildings, which are nearly 20 stories high, is capped with a massive iron hammer and sickle, the town's founders' seal. The Soviet Union constructed Pripyat during a bustling construction phase in the 1970s. It was the ideal home for approximately 50,000 people.

But today, nobody lives in Pripyat. Almost everything is frozen in place. Its architecture and accessories are so well-known that you are aware that their deterioration cannot be attributed to the passage of time alone. Only humans on Earth possess the power to both create and destroy entire universes. The neighbouring Vladimir Ilyich Lenin Nuclear Power Plant's reactor number 4, now universally known as "Chernobyl," exploded on April 26, 1986. Human mistakes and poor planning led to the explosion. The reactors at Chernobyl were poorly designed. The operating crew was negligent in their work and unaware of these issues. It infiltrated the soils and streams of numerous countries as it descended from the sky as rain and snowflakes. In the end, it entered the food chain. In fewer than 46 hours, more than 100,000 individuals were evacuated, never to return. The area was deemed uninhabitable for the subsequent 20.000 years. Though estimates go into the hundreds of thousands, the exact number of premature deaths brought on by the incident is still debated. Chernobyl has often been referred to as the most catastrophic environmental disaster in history. Sadly, that is not the case. There is a global disaster. Its effects could ultimately result in the destabilization and collapse of everything we depend on, which would be considerably more devastating than the pollution of soils and waterways in a few unfortunate countries. The accelerating loss of biodiversity on our planet is the great tragedy of our time.

There needs to be a vast diversity of life forms for the earth to support true life. The earth can only function effectively if billions of distinct individual organisms make the most of every resource and opportunity they come across and millions of species lead interdependent lives that support one another.

All species on Earth, including us, will be more secure when higher the biodiversity. But now that we are aware of this, we must choose the right path. We may continue leading contented lives, rearing our children, and occupying ourselves with the moral pursuits of the contemporary society we have established, preferring to ignore the catastrophe that is just around the corner.

The massive nuclear power plant that would one day end their lives was the first thing the residents of Pripyat saw every morning when they pulled back the curtains in their flats. Now, we are all Pripyat residents. We enjoy a nice existence while a catastrophe that we caused looms overhead. The exact things that allow us to live our luxurious lifestyles are causing that catastrophe.

Radioactive Red Fox, in the Ghost town of Pripyat, near the Chernobyl nuclear reactor. (©Netflix Our Planet)

As a kid, I remember museum experiences that inspired me to want to go see the creatures that I could not see in my backyard, but I knew they existed. It is indeed in such museums that studies of countless specimens have proven that our climate is changing and that we are losing our biodiversity. It was these museum experiences that made me want to act and so during my own adventures and research that I began when I was just 10 years old, I started collecting animal specimens that I used to find, already dead due to natural causes or in some cases their death was due to human interactions.

I grew up in the 21st century, at a time when the loss of biodiversity and climate was becoming very clear, and in just 17 years I have seen the natural world disappear all around me. Nature is declining globally at rates unprecedented in millions of years. The way we produce and consume food and energy, and the blatant disregard for the environment entrenched in our current economic model, have pushed the natural world to its limits. COVID-19 is a clear manifestation of our broken relationship with nature. It has highlighted the deep interconnection between nature, human health and well-being, and how unprecedented biodiversity loss threatens the health of both people and the planet. It is time we answer nature's SOS. Not just to secure the future of tigers, rhinos, whales, bees, trees and all the amazing diversity of life we love and have the moral duty to coexist with, but because ignoring it also puts the health, well-being, and prosperity, indeed the future, of nearly 8 billion people at stake. I have also seen the loss of wildlife myself. From giant 14-inch crayfish found in the 7 lakes (Barm) of shiraz to the Arabian Oryx. I was always in love with the natural world, curious about what happens all around us, and yet listening to my grandfather's childhood experiences, the loss of nature becomes even clearer. I will be talking about these stories here as well.

We have indeed lost an average of 68% of the population sizes of mammals, birds, amphibians, reptiles and fish between 1970 and 2016. That's because in the last 50 years our world has been transformed by an explosion in global trade, consumption, and human population growth, as well as an enormous move towards urbanisation. Until 1970, humanity's Ecological Footprint was smaller than the Earth's rate of regeneration. To feed and fuel our 21st-century lifestyles, we are overusing the Earth's biocapacity by at least 56%.

Tigers, pandas, and polar bears are well-known species in the story of biodiversity decline, but what of the millions of tiny, or as-yet-undiscovered, species that are also under threat? What is happening to the life in our soils, or in plant and insect diversity? All of these provide fundamental support for life on Earth and are showing signs of stress.

Since the industrial revolution, human activities have increasingly destroyed and degraded forests, grasslands, wetlands, and other important ecosystems, threatening human well-being. Seventy-five percent of the Earth's ice-free land surface has already been significantly altered, most of the oceans are polluted, and more than 85% of the area of wetlands has been lost. This destruction of ecosystems has led to 1 million species (500,000 animals, plants and insects) being threatened with extinction over the coming decades to centuries, although many of these extinctions are preventable if we conserve and restore nature.

Globally, climate change has not been the most important driver of the loss of biodiversity to date, yet in the coming decades it is projected to become as, or more, important than the other drivers. Climate change adversely affects genetic variability, species richness and populations, and ecosystems. In turn, loss of biodiversity can adversely affect climate – for example, deforestation increases the atmospheric abundance of carbon dioxide, a key greenhouse gas.

Therefore, it is essential that the issues of biodiversity loss and climate change are addressed together.

If nature can recover from a disaster as disastrous as Chernobyl without our help, surely if we work with nature we can once again REWILD the world. That is why, I have written this book. This book is a detailed version of my TEDx speech, as I shared my experience and showed how we can REWILD the world. There is still time to switch off the reactor. This book is the story of life on our planet, how we came to dominate the world, and in doing so destroyed the life support systems that allowed us to dominate the earth in the first place, my experiences as a young naturalist in the 21st century and how we can REWILD the planet.

Me and my Grandfather during a climb to the top of a cliff in the Rainforests of Iran, Mazandaran Province. July 24, 2018

CHAPTER I

Beginning of Life

من لا يعرف ماضيه لا يستطيع أن يستفيد
من وجوده ومستقبله ، فنحن نتعلم من
الماضي

He who does not know his past cannot
make the best of his presence and
future, for it is from the past that we
learn.

H.H Sheikh Zayed Bin Sultan Al Nahyan

E arth is over 4.5 billion years old, and the third planet from the sun. It is, as far as we know it, the only planet with life. Life prospers here, thanks to extraordinary natural forces. First is the distance from the sun; Light from it reaches us in just 8 minutes, providing a source of food for plants and in doing so powering our world, and its daily, seasonal, and yearly rhymes shape the life of every living creature, including ourselves. Moreover, Earth is safeguarded from harmful solar radiation by its magnetic field and Ozone Layer, it is kept warm by a heatproof atmosphere, and it has the right chemical components like water and carbon. Next comes the Volcanoes, another powerful force and they are the architects of our planet, creating over 80% of the earth's Surface. From unforgiving storms to freezing winds, the weather is another force essential for life. As water evaporates, rain clouds form and powerful winds carry it around the globe, revitalizing the land. This system of weather has been stable for thousands of years and it is this reliability that life depends on. All these are the forces that shape our living planet. However, this system is very fragile, and today there is a new force, one so powerful it threatens all life on Earth, humans!

Over the Years of my research some 8 years so far, I have witnessed and reached a belief that life is all around us and it is not difficult to find it. Spend a night in the deserts of the UAE with a torch in hand, looking around Rimth (ريمث) Shrubs (Haloxylon salicornicum), turning over logs, looking beneath rocks or rather simply shining light over sand dunes and around, you will surely come across hundreds of different animals, from the Arabian Fox (Vulpes vulpes arabica), Or a herd of Mountain Gazelle (Gazella Arabica) to countless Beetles or even the elusive Ethiopian hedgehog (Paraechinus aethiopicus).

Just a few years back I visited a rainforest in the southern Caspian Sea of Iran, in the Mazandaran province and it was here, I realized the deep connections of life and that each creature no matter where it lives is part of an enormous global chain that connects all of us, and yet if any of it breaks, the whole planet falls out of balance. As we walked through the moist litter of leaves, snakes of all shapes and sizes slithered beneath our feet, and when night followed, just by simply shining a mercury lamp on a white cloth, and with a little patience you will find yourself surrounded with life.

Mosquitoes would initially be plentiful, but larger insects such as stink bugs, moths, spiders, beetles, and butterflies that looked like wasps, wasps in the shape of ants, leaves or sticks that, when touched, would walk and in some cases bite, and eventually open their wings and fly - would soon follow. The sheer number of animal species found in these greenhouse-humid, darkly light jungles is difficult to estimate. These unique habitats contain the richest variety of animals and plants.

Charles Darwin had a similar experience while travelling aboard HMS Beagle in 1832, a ship dispatched by the Admiralty in London on a surveying expedition around the world. Darwin's scientific passion was collecting insects. He also visited a jungle like this outside of Rio de Janeiro. He gathered 68 different species of Rove beetle (Staphylinidae) in a single day, and he was astounded by the diversity of these insects. Not all of the beetles that Darwin collected, however, were willing to give up without a struggle. With ground beetles like the bombardier beetle, Darwin witnessed one such defence firsthand: many of these insects produce unpleasant compounds to protect themselves, as he mentioned in his journal: "One day, on tearing off some old bark, I saw two rare beetles, and seized one in each hand; then I saw a third and new kind, which I could not bear to lose so that I popped the one which I held in my right hand into my mouth. Alas! it ejected some intensely acrid fluid, which burnt my tongue so that I was forced to spit the beetle out, which was lost, as was the third one." Shockingly, a creature so small had the power to create boiling chemicals that shoots out from its abdomen without hurting the beetle itself. But here the question appears, how did these beetles or indeed all life become so complex and interconnected?

The Galapagos Expedition is one of Darwin's most well-known expeditions. He was enthralled to learn that the Galapagos species have a basic similarity to those he'd seen on the mainland but differ in detail. It was here that Darwin proposed his evolutionary theories. He observed that the tortoises on each island differed, making it feasible to determine which island they belonged to. For example, in well-watered islands, the water allowed ground vegetation to flourish, resulting in tortoises with a slightly curved front edge to their shells just above the neck, allowing them to feed on the ground flora. In dry, arid islands, herbivores' only source of food is cactus branches or tree leaves, so tortoises have much longer necks and a high peak to the front of their shells, allowing them to stretch their necks upwards and reach those sources of food, and so he witnessed evolution that happened in this case over a few generations, but it's possible that major transformations occurred over millions of years.

In a summary, Darwin argued that no two members of the same species are alike. An Arabian gazelle, for example, with a smaller body, long legs, and a lighter coat, can flee from predators faster; its lighter coats mean it releases more heat; and its smaller body means it is more drought resistant since it requires less water, energy, and absorbs less heat. So, if there is a drought, this gazelle, and others like it will survive. So those best fitted to their surroundings will be naturally selected and will also transfer their characteristics to their offspring. Darwin spent twenty-five years collecting data to back up his hypothesis, and his book was published in 1859, when he was forty-eight years old, two years after another young naturalist, Alfred Wallace, presented a similar concept. Darwin called his book in which the theory section was

written in great detail, "On the Origin of Species by Means of Natural Selection".

We must seek two aspects to uncover evidence of evolution; one can be found in the genetic makeup of cells. Another isfound in sedimentary rocks. Although, once they die, most animals leave no evidence of their presence. Their flesh rots, their shells and bones disintegrate, and their bones become powder. However, one or two individuals out of a population of tens of thousands had a different outcome. A reptile dies after becoming stranded in a marsh. Its body rots away, but its bones become entangled in the mud. They are covered with dead vegetation that has drifted to the bottom. The deposit transforms into peat as the ages pass and more vegetation accumulates. Changes in sea level may cause the marsh to flood, resulting in sand layers accumulating on top of the peat. The peat is compacted and transformed into coal over a long period of time. The bones of the animal are still within. The great pressure of the overlying sediments and the mineral-rich solutions that circulate through them cause chemical changes in the calcium phosphate of the bones. They are eventually converted to stone, yet their outer shape is preserved as they had life, albeit sometimes distorted. In certain circumstances, the specimen is so well preserved that specific cellular architecture and, in extremely rare situations, even the colour of their skin and feathers may be seen under a microscope. My first fossil was that of a sand dollar, possibly 16 thousand years old, yet it revealed extraordinary details, of the most delicate structures like the Petalodium, these are tiny holes in this echinoderm's skeleton, through these emerge tube feet and it is through these feet that the animal breathes.

However, fossils will not assist us to understand how life began, since the origin of life requires the interaction of molecules, which leaves no fossil evidence. The Earth back then was very different from the one we live on now in many respects. Despite the presence of seas, the land masses had little similarity to present continents in terms of form or distribution. Volcanoes erupted everywhere, unleashing toxic fumes, ash, and lava. Hydrogen, carbon monoxide, ammonia, and methane clouds swirled throughout the atmosphere. There was very little, if any, oxygen available. This unbreathable combination allowed the sun's UV radiation to bombard the earth's surface at a level that would kill any modern animal. Lightning struck the land and the water as electrical storms raged in the skies.

All kinds of life on the planet today have a common method of conveying genetic information and instructing cells. Deoxyribonucleic acid, or DNA for short, is the chemical in the discussion. It has two crucial characteristics due to its structure: first, it serves as a blueprint to produce amino acids, and second, it can duplicate itself. Even the smallest of living species, such as bacteria, have these two features of DNA. Bacteria, in addition to being the most basic form of life, are also among the earliest fossils known. Because all living things share DNA, DNA sequences from various creatures may be compared to reveal how they are linked.

The bacteria in those early days fed on the numerous carbon compounds that had accumulated over millions of years in the ancient oceans, releasing methane as a by-product. Similar bacteria may still be found all over the world today. Then, over 2 billion years ago, bacteria began to create their own food within their cell walls, absorbing the energy needed to do so from the sun. Photosynthesis is the name for this process. Initially, photosynthesis relied on hydrogen, a gas released in large amounts during volcanic eruptions, but bacteria could not spread far as long as they were reliant on volcanic activity.

However, new forms subsequently developed, capable of extracting hydrogen from a far more common source - water. This finding would have far-reaching implications for all future life because when hydrogen is taken from the water, the only element left is oxygen. The creatures that performed this had a structure that is scarcely more complicated than that of bacteria. They were once known as blue-green algae because they looked to be near cousins of green algae, but we now know that they are more closely related to the ancestors of those algae, and they are now known as cyanobacteria or simply blue-greens. The chemical agent that they contain, making it possible for them to use water in the photosynthetic process, is chlorophyll, which also possessed by true algae and plants.

The emergence of the blue-greens represented a turning moment in the history of life. Over millennia, oxygen accumulated to produce the oxygen-rich atmosphere we are familiar with today. It is essential to our survival, as well as the survival of all other species. Not only do we need it to breathe, but it also protects us. The ozone layer, which is formed by oxygen in the atmosphere, blocks most of the sun's UV radiation. For a long time, life remained at this stage of evolution. Then, some 2 billion years ago, a single-celled living form became stuck within another due to a completely random meeting. Simply by taking a drop from a pond and looking at it through a microscope, you can see swarms of tiny organisms, some spinning like rotifers, some crawling like Nematode worms, some whizzing across the field of vision like rockets and pretty hard to get a look at, like coleps, and now they are a key part of a freshwater system, some breaking down organic matter, some filtering the water, making it cleaner, and some food for others, so from here the relationships and the bond of life on earth were starting to form.

They are collectively known as protozoa, or protists - the word meaning 'first creatures.' They are all solitary cells with significantly more intricate structures within their cell walls than any bacteria. The nucleus, which is full of DNA and believed to represent the cell's organizing power, is one of the core packets. The mitochondria are descended from a trapped single-celled creature

2 billion years ago, whereas the chloroplasts are descended from a trapped blue-green.

There are around 50,000 different types of protozoans. Some animals, such as coleps, have a coat of flailing threads or cilia that move with a synchronized beat that propels the creature through the water.

Others, like the amoeba, move by extending fingers from the main body and flowing into them. Many creatures that dwell in the water create shells with the most complex silica or calcium carbonate structures. These tiny, microscopic shells may be found if you collect a little sample of sand from the shore, and they are among the loveliest artefacts that a researcher carrying a microscope will ever encounter. Some look like tiny snail shells, while others are beautiful vases and flasks. Long threads are extended into the pores of these shells by the residents, trapping food particles. Other protists feed in a different way, using their chlorophyll packets to photosynthesize. These can be classified as plants, while the rest of the group, which feeds on them, can be classified as animals.

At this level, however, the difference between the two does not have as much relevance as such labelling may imply, because many species can employ both techniques of eating at various times. Some protists are large enough, that they may be seen with the naked eye. However, the expansion of a single-celled species has a limit, since as the cell grows larger, the chemical reactions inside it become more complicated and inefficient. Size, on the other hand, can be gained in a different way: by forming an organized colony of cells. When sponges formed between 800 and 1,000 million years ago, this sort of coordination between constituent cells in a colony was carried a step further. Sponges can grow to be rather large, perhaps like the present Giant Barrel sponge (Xestospongia muta). With the aid of flagellums on each cell, the sponge feeds by filtering particles as a stream of water travels through its body. If a sponge is torn down into distinct cells and squeezed through a tiny gauze sieve, the cells will gradually reorganize themselves into a new sponge, with each kind of cell finding its proper location inside the body. Some sponges make a soft, flexible material that surrounds their cells and help them to maintain the entire organism. This is what we use in our baths once the cells have been destroyed by boiling and rinsed away. Other sponges produce spicules, which are small needles made of calcium carbonate or silica that mesh to form a framework on which the cells are placed.

Even though sponges can create such amazing complexities, they are not like other animals. They are devoid of a nervous system and muscular fibres. Jellyfish and their cousins are the simplest organisms to have these physical traits. Unlike sponge cells, their cells are unable to survive on their own. Some have been adapted to conduct electric impulses and are connected into a network that resembles a primitive nervous system; others may contract in length and are therefore classified as simple muscles. The jellyfish tribe's unique belongings are stinging cells with coiled threads inside of them. When food or an opponent approach, the thread, which is equipped with spines like a little harpoon and frequently filled with poison, is discharged by cells called the nematocyst. A blue blubber jellyfish (Catostylus mosaicus) contains these cells in its tentacles that will sting you if you brush up against it while swimming; I had several similar encounters at Dubai's AL-Mamzar beach. Although this sting will not kill you, it will cause you to itch for a long time, giving you an enticing and irritating sensation. Jellyfish have no heart, no blood, and no brain. They are incapable of making decisions or even cooperating, and they reproduce by releasing eggs and sperm into the water. The fertilized egg does not grow into another jellyfish, but rather into a free-swimming organism with characteristics distinct from its parents. It finally settles on the seafloor and develops into a little flower-like creature known as a polyp. This grows into additional polyps in certain species through branching branches. With the help of tiny beating cilia, they filter-feed. The polyps eventually bud in a different way, producing small medusae that detach and crawl away to resume swimming life, and as a result, they have lived on Earth for at least 600 million years, and can now be found in every ocean and depth, having survived five mass extinctions.

True jellyfish spend most of their existence as free-floating medusae, only clinging to the rocks for a brief duration. Others, such as sea anemones, do the opposite. They spent their whole adult lives as solitary polyps, stuck to the rock with their tentacles waving in the water, ready to catch any prey that came by. The third type of polyp colony is one that has, perplexingly, abandoned its connection to the seabed and sailed free like medusae. One of these is the Portuguese man of war. Polyp chains dangle from a float that is filled with gas. Each chain has a distinct purpose. One kind produces reproductive cells; another absorbs sustenance from captured prey; another, heavily armed with particularly virulent stinging cells, trails behind the colony for up to fifty meters, paralyzing any fish that blunder into it.

Their relatives, stony corals, typically develop alongside them and are colony organisms as well. An organism that develops a stone skeleton and lives in an environment with ooze and sand deposits is an excellent candidate for fossilization. Huge thicknesses of limestone in many regions of the world are nearly completely made up of coral remnants, providing a precise record of the group's evolution. The skeletons of coral polyps are secreted from their roots. Each neighbour is linked to the others via strands that stretch laterally. The first time I saw these intricate structures was through my own brain-coral specimen, (Pseudodiploria strigosa), and it is extraordinary to see that such minute organisms can create such unique designs. New polyps arise as the colony grows, frequently on these connecting parts, and their skeletons grow over and suffocate previous polyps. As a result, the limestone the colony constructs are riddled with microscopic cells that originally housed polyps. Only a thin layer of live organisms' forms on the surface. Each coral species has its own unique pattern of budding and so erects its own distinctive monument. Corals have extremely stringent environmental needs. They will die if they come into contact with dirty or fresh water. Because they are dependent on single-celled algae that grow within their bodies, most will not develop at depths beyond the reach of sunlight. zooxanthellae are algae that photosynthesize food for themselves while also absorbing carbon dioxide from the water. This aids the corals in the formation of their skeletons and releases oxygen, allowing them to breathe. The first time you dive on a coral reef is an unforgettable experience. The sense of swimming freely in three dimensions in the clean, sunny water that corals prefer is enthralling and otherworldly in and of itself. There are domes, branches, fans, antlers with delicate blue tips, and clusters of blood-red thin pipes. Some appear to be flowery, but when you touch them, they have an odd stone scrape.

On a visit to Al Bastakiya in Dubai along with Al Shandiga, one of the oldest residential areas in the city of Dubai, we came across extraordinary architecture and witnessed that people were so connected to the sea that even their homes were built of coral. Its walls not only record the narrative of the people who lived in the area, but also the history of the sea. Its homes, mosques, and courtyard are made up of almost 11.97 million pieces of sunbaked coral, each one revealing something about the Gulf's marine heritage. Since the 1550s, the reefs' composition appears to have remained relatively unchanged. To date, 11 distinct genera of coral have been discovered from the village walls, with diversity and composition comparable to today. Brain coral was by far the most common on the houses in Jazirat Al Hamra, and it was here that I obtained my football-sized brain coral specimen. On Ras Al Khaimah's reefs, the brain coral is still the most abundant. The corals in the structures ranged in size from fist-sized pieces to large slabs of brain coral utilized as fundamental blocks. They were mined, sifted by size in fresh water to kill off the organisms, and then dried for a year on the beach. The porous blocks provided excellent insulation and were one of the few locally available construction materials. As a result, coral was employed in many of the UAE's ancient structures. People would have only had coral as a hard material. Cement soon replaced coral stone, and the community was entirely abandoned by the 1970s.

If you just walk along these old towns or if you just swim during the day, though, you will rarely observe the organisms that have produced this magnificent landscape. At night with a torch in hand underwater, however, You will find the coral transformed: Hundreds of millions of microscopic polyps have emerged from their limestone cells at night to stretch out their small arms and scavenge for nourishment. Coral polyps are only a few millimetres wide, yet when they work together in colonies, they create the most incredible animal structures the world has ever seen, long before humans arrived.

However, some 600 million years ago, many distinct types of creatures began to secrete shells, which served as records of their abundance. Back on the reef, we may look for some live hints. Flat leaf-shaped worms flutter over coral heads, hide in nooks, and cling to the undersides of rocks. They don't have gills and breathe via their skin. Their undersides are coated with cilia, which allow them to glide gently over surfaces by beating. The animal's front end features a mouth below and a few light-sensitive patches above,

Barjeel towers of traditional desert homes (© Culture Trip)

like the beginnings of a head, these are flatworms, and there are over 3,000 different flatworm species in the world today.

Between 600 and 1,000 million years ago, when these early marine creatures were emerging, the continents were eroding, leaving vast stretches of mud and sand on the seabed surrounding the continental borders. The flatworm's form, on the other hand, isn't ideal for digging. A tubular form is far more effective, and worms with this shape ultimately developed. Some of the burrowers became more active, tunnelling through the mud in quest of food particles. Others lived half-buried, their front ends poking out from behind the silt. Cilia produced a stream of water around their lips, which they used to filter their food. Some of these species were protected by a tube. These can be seen today as organisms like blue tube worms, and once they die, they leave their hard tubes behind, and this allowed me to obtain yet another specimen of a whole community of these creatures. The shape of the top of this creature was eventually changed into a collar with slits. They finally came up with a two-part protective casing for the front end. The first brachiopods were these. It has a mouth within the shell that is encircled by tentacles. They are coated in cilia that beat, creating a current in the water. The tentacles catch any food particles in them and then transport them down to the mouth. While doing so, the tentacles serve another crucial purpose: the water contains dissolved oxygen, which the animal requires to breathe. The tentacles absorb it and turn into gills as a result. The tentacles are protected by a shell that not only protects them but also focuses the water into a continuous stream that passes more effectively across them.

Molluscs are found in roughly 80,000 distinct species now, with nearly the same number known from their fossils. Snails and slugs are two of them that can be found in your garden. The lower part of the molluscan body is called the foot. The single-shelled molluscs feed via a radula, a ribbon-shaped tongue coated in rasping teeth, rather than tentacles within the shell like the brachiopods. Some individuals use it to scrape algae off of rocks, and these snails may be found not just in ponds or lakes, but even in pet stores. Species have developed a stalked radula that can extend outside the shell and be used to bore through the shells of other molluscs. They push the tip of the radula through the holes they've dug and suck away the flesh of their victim. Cone shells feature a stalked radula as well, but it has been transformed into a kind of gun. They stretch it surreptitiously towards their target — a worm or perhaps a fish - and then fire a small, glassy harpoon from the end. As the tethered victim struggles, they inject a venom so potent that it instantaneously kills a fish and can even kill humans. They then drag the prey back to the shell, where it is slowly consumed. When actively foraging, a heavy shell must be a hindrance, and some carnivorous molluscus have abandoned it entirely, reverting to the lifestyle of their flatworm-like ancestors.

These are sea slugs (nudibranchs), which are among the most colourful and fascinating invertebrates in the ocean. They are not completely defenceless, though, because some have obtained second hand weapons. These species, such as the modern sea swallow (Glaucus atlanticus), hunt jellyfish by floating near the surface of the water on their fluffy extended tentacles. This little slug, on the other hand, will attack colonies of floating cnidarians. This includes the Portuguese man-o-war, a colonial open-sea animal closely related to jellyfish whose sting can be lethal to humans. The stinging cells of the victim are absorbed into the gut of the sea slug as it slowly eats its way through its floating helpless prey. These eventually move through the sea slug's tissues and end up in the tentacles on its back. They provide the same level of protection to their new owners as they did to the jellyfish who gave birth to them. Other molluscs, such as mussels and clams, have shells that are separated into two valves, like those of a brachiopod, and are hence called bivalves. These species aren't as mobile. They utilize the protrusion on their foot to drag themselves down into the sand. They're mostly filter feeders, with valves agape and water drawing in at one end of the mantle cavity and squirting out via a tube siphon at the other. Because they don't have to move, their size isn't an issue. On the reef, giant clams may grow to reach a meter long. Their mantles are totally displayed in the coral, a zigzag of vivid green skin with black spots that pulsates softly when water is pumped through it. They can certainly be large enough for a diver to step inside, but he would have to be extremely unlucky to become trapped. Even with its powerful muscles, the clam's valves cannot be slammed shut.

Some filter feeders, such as scallops, can migrate by convulsively slapping their valves together and leaping through the water in curved jumps. Adult bivalves, on the other hand, tend to spend rather static lives, and the young are responsible for spreading the species to new areas of the seafloor. The young are the ones who carry the species to far-flung places of the bottom. The molluscan egg develops into a larva, a tiny living globule patterned with cilia that are carried by ocean currents far and wide. After a few weeks, it takes on a new shape, develops a shell, and settles down. During this stage, It is at the mercy of all types of hungry creatures during its floating period of life, from other stationary filter feeders to fish, mollusks must produce large quantities of eggs in order for their species to survive. It does. A single individual can release up to 400 million of them.

Early in the history of the molluscs, one branch discovered a means to become very mobile while maintaining the protection of a massive and heavy shell — they constructed gas-filled floating tanks. Around 500 million years ago, the first organism of this type arose. Its flat-coiled shell, unlike that of a snail, was not entirely filled with flesh but had its back end walled off to create a gas chamber. New chambers were added as the animal matured to give enough buoyancy for its growing weight. The nautilus was this creature, and we can get a good picture of how it and its family lived since a few nautilus species have survived to the current day, such as Lingulella and Neopilina. A tube connects the back of the body chamber to the rear flotation tanks, allowing the animal to flood them and change its buoyancy to float at whichever level it desires. The nautilus eats not just carrion but also live animals like crabs. It moves by squirting water via a siphon in a version of the current-creating approach used by its filter-feeding cousins. With the use of minuscule stalked eyes and taste-sensitive tentacles, it hunts for its meal. It possesses ninety long gripping tentacles on its molluscan foot, which it uses to grapple with its food. It possesses a horny beak fashioned like a parrot's and is capable of delivering a fatal, shell-cracking bite in the centre of them. The nautiluses gave rise to the ammonites, a variation group with many more flotation chambers per shell, some 400 million years ago, following approximately 100 million years of evolution. These were far more successful than their nautilus ancestors, and their fossilized shells may now be discovered in such dense layers in the rocks that they form solid bands. Some species developed to be as large as lorry wheels.

The ammonite dynasty began to fade about 100 million years ago. Perhaps environmental changes have an impact on their egg-laying patterns. Perhaps new predators had emerged. In any case, many species became extinct. Except for the pearly nautilus, all shelled creatures eventually vanished. However, certain shellless molluscs, such as squids, cuttlefish, and octopuses, survived and evolved into the most sophisticated and intelligent of all molluscs. Cephalopods are what they're called. Deep within it, vestiges of the cuttlefish's ancient shell can be found. The cuttlebone is a flat leaf of powdered chalk that is frequently washed up on the beach and may also be found in pet stores because it provides calcium for birds such as parrots. The octopus has no evidence of a shell even within its flesh, but one species, the argonaut, secretes a wonderful paper-thin replica structured like a nautilus shell but without chambers from one of its arms, which it uses as a delicate floating chamber in which to deposit its eggs.

Darwin's first stop on the Beagle journey was Cape Verde, off the west coast of Africa, where he left home at the age of 22. One of the first items Darwin gathered was an octopus. The octopus' capacity to generate clouds of dark ink, fit through crevices, spray water at him, and change colour fascinated Darwin. He thought he'd uncovered a brand-new species. 'This fact appears to be new, as far as I can find out,' wrote the young Darwin. Darwin's letters are full of beautiful descriptions of the octopuses and other cephalopods he saw in the area 'While looking for marine animals, with my head about two feet above the rocky shore, I was more than once saluted by a jet of water accompanied by a slight grating noise,' he wrote. 'From the difficulty which these animals have in carrying their heads, they cannot crawl with ease when placed on the ground. I observed that one which I kept in the cabin was slightly phosphorescent in the dark.' Before preserving the animal in alcohol, Darwin carried it live on board the Beagle, where it would have perished soon after. It seemed to glow in the dark at night, he noticed. Although many deep-sea organisms emit bioluminescence, typical octopuses like this one do not. I believe Darwin gathered seawater to keep the octopus in the container, and that there were maybe some phosphorescent algae or some creature in the water that shone when the octopus moved around and disturbed it.

Squids are the most mobile of the three species, with lateral fins running along their sides that undulate and push the animal through the water. Cephalopod eyes are extremely detailed. They're even better than ours in several aspects because squids can discern polarized light, which we can't, and their retinas have a finer structure, implying that they can almost likely identify finer detail than we can. They have large brains and rapid responses to deal with the messages provided by these sensory organs. Squids may grow to be enormous. Like the deep-sea giant squid believed to fight with sperm whales in the debts as enormous beaks of these giants have been found in the stomach of whales. All cephalopods – octopus, squid, and cuttlefish – are noted for their intelligence. Octopuses have been seen hiding from an oncoming opponent by covering themselves with shells or by picking up two halves of a coconut and sheltering inside. Many creatures in all three categories have the capacity to alter their colour and form in amazing ways. On a small research journey, I and my friend Zayaan witnessed the same colour-changing ability. A cuttlefish feeds on Crabs and is active at night, so with a torch in hand we witnessed this cuttlefish changing to vibrant colours in order to hypnotize the crab itself. However, once we approached it, it had blended in with its surroundings or indeed they can blend practically with any surroundings and communicate with each other via patterns and forms that sweep across their body. This ability to change colour has been made possible by organs present in the skin called chromatophores which contain pigment sacs that become more visible as small radial muscles pull the sac open making the pigment expand under the skin. Octopus and squid, are two of the most intelligent organisms in the ocean that have the least resemblance to humans, and appear to be among the few that can compete with mammals in terms of intelligence. But what about the second large group of backboneless creatures, the flower-like crinoids that may be found in ancient rocks? Each contains a central body, the calyx, that rises from a stem like a poppy seedhead. Five arms develop from here, with some species branching many times. The calyx, like the stems and branches, is made up of calcium carbonate plates that fit together tightly. The stems seem like shattered necklaces lying on the rocks, their individual beads scattered here and there, sometimes still in loose snaking columns, as if their thread had just snapped. Occasionally,

A Picture of myself as I introduce a Glittering Cuttlefish to the camera, as we researched on their colour-changing abilities. (Al Mamzar Beach, 15 August 2021)

A Glittering Cuttlefish ensnared within our net, as it is brought out from the water. (Al Mamzar Beach, 1 August 2021)

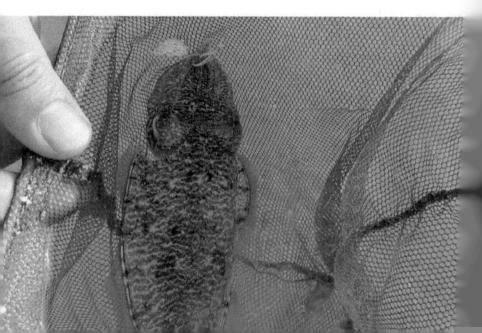

massive specimens with 20-meter-long stems are discovered. These animals, like ammonites, have had their day, but a few species, known as sea lilies, may still be found deep inside the ocean.

The calcium carbonate plates of sea lilies are implanted just beneath the epidermis in life. Their surface has a strange prickly sensation to it as a result of this. Echinoderms, or spiny-skins,' are organisms that have spines and needles connected to their skin and are linked to the crinoids. The echinoderm body is formed around a fivefold symmetrical fundamental module. The calyx has pentagon-shaped plates. It has five arms, and all of the internal organs are arranged in groups of five. Their bodies operate by uniquely utilizing hydrostatic principles. Tube feet wave and curl in rows down the arms, each a thin tube ending in a sucker and maintained hard by the pressure of water within. This system's water circulates independently from that of the bodily cavity. It is pulled into a channel encircling the mouth through a pore and distributed throughout the body and into the countless tube feet. When a stray food particle lands on an arm, tube feet grab it and transport it from one to the next until it reaches the gutter that runs down the upper surface of the arm to the central mouth. Though stalked sea lilies were the most common crinoid in prehistoric times, feather stars are the most frequent now. They have a clump of curling roots that they use to attach themselves to coral or rocks instead of stalks.

Both starfish and their more vivacious cousins, brittle stars, have them. These animals appear to be crinoids with no stalk or rootlets, lying inverted on the ground with their mouths on the ground and five arms extended. Sea urchins are also clearly connected. They appear to have coiled their arms up as five ribs from the mouth, then joined them with other plates to form a sphere. Echinoderms, like the sausage-like sea cucumbers that spread over sandy sections of the reef, have shelly internal skeletons that are reduced to microscopic structures beneath the skin in most species. There is an opening termed the anus at one end, though the phrase isn't accurate because the animal utilizes it not only for excretion but also for breathing, pulling water in and out softly over tubules slightly within the body. The mouth, which is located on the other end, is encircled by tube feet that have grown into short tentacles. These wriggle about in the mud or sand. Particles stick to them, and the sea cucumber folds them back into its mouth, sucking them clean with its velvety lips. Picking up a sea cucumber should be done with caution since they have a unique defence mechanism. Internal organs are simply extruded by them. A steady but relentless flow of sticky tubules flows out the anus, tying your fingers together in a tangle of strands. When a curious fish or crab spurs them into action, it becomes caught in a web of filaments, while the sea cucumber gently moves away on its tube feet. It will gradually sprout a new set of entrails during the next several weeks. On the reef, a starfish may crawl across a clam, fastening its tube feet on either side of the clam's gape and gently wrenching the valves open to eat the flesh within. The crown-of-thorns starfish can occasionally become an epidemic, wreaking havoc on large regions of coral. Thousands of crinoids are caught in trawls from the deep sea at a time.

Those with segmented bodies make up the third group of organisms on the reef. The spherical larvae of segmented worms have a cilia belt around their middles and a lengthy tuft on top. These are nearly similar to the larvae of some molluscs, indicating that the two groups descended from a common ancestor. The larvae of echinoderms, on the other hand, is highly unique, with a twisted structure and spiral bands of cilia all around it. This group must have broken from the ancient flatworms very early on, much before the molluscs and segmented worms split. Geneticists have recently confirmed these inferences by examining the DNA of each of these groups, revealing that there are two primary groups of bilaterally symmetrical animals. Echinoderms, tunicates, and all backboned creatures make up one category, while octopuses, crabs, and flatworms make up the other.

We will never know how many different species of creatures existed in the primordial oceans. Conditions enabled for a disproportionately big chunk to be preserved, yet even this is merely a fragment of what must have been previously. Their body armour was made largely of calcium carbonate and reinforced with chitin, a horny substance that forms the exterior skeletons of insects. However, because chitin cannot extend like skin, any animal with such an exterior chitinous skeleton must shed it on a regular basis in order to develop — as insects do today. Many of the trilobite fossils we uncover are actually empty armour suits. As far as we know, trilobites were the first organisms on the planet to evolve high-definition eyes. They're mosaics, a collection of individual components, each with its own crystalline calcite lens oriented in the exact position where it transmits light most efficiently, similar to the eyes of today's insects. One eye may have had 15,000 components, giving its user a nearly hemispheric field of view. A basic calcite lens in contact with water, on the other hand, has optical qualities that allow it to disperse light and not bring it to a finely focused point. A two-part lens with a wavy surface at the junction between its two parts is required for this. And this is how these trilobites came to be. Trilobites developed into a large number of species as they spread over the world's waters. Their dynasty came to an end two hundred and fifty million years ago. The horseshoe crab is the only relative that has survived. It's a deceptive title because it's not a crab and just half of its shell looks like a horseshoe. It is several times larger than other known trilobites, measuring 30 centimetre or more wide, and its armour no longer exhibits any traces of segmentation. Its front part is a massive domed shield with two bean-shaped compound eyes on the front. A sharp spike of a tail protrudes from a roughly rectangular plate attached to the back of the shield. The animal's segmentation is visible beneath its shell. It features numerous pairs of jointed legs with pincers at the ends and plate-like gills behind them that are big and flat like book leaves.

Despite their popularity, trilobites were far from the first armoured organisms to emerge from segmented worms. So did a group of sea scorpions, technically known as Eurypterids, which must have been among the most terrifying of all marine monsters. They vanished at the end of the Permian epoch, just as the trilobites. However, one trilobite-related group survived and is now exceedingly successful. They were distinguished by one apparently insignificant but nonetheless diagnostic feature. They have two pairs of antennae on their heads, not one. For hundreds of millions of years, they coexisted peacefully with the trilobites, and when the trilobite dynasty came to an end, it was they who took control. Crustaceans are what they're called. Crustaceans now number over 40,000 species, which is seven times the number of bird species. Crabs, shrimp, prawns, and lobsters are among the most common creatures found on the rocks and reefs. Barnacles, for example, have adopted a sedentary lifestyle. Others, such as the krill that whales eat, swim in enormous shoals. For specific functions, each crab species alters the form of its numerous paired legs. The exterior shell, on the other hand, poses the same challenge for crustaceans as it did for trilobites. It won't expand, and because it totally encloses their bodies, the only way for them to grow is to shed it on a regular basis. As the time for molting approaches, the animal takes a significant amount of calcium carbonate from its shell into its bloodstream. Underneath the shell, it secretes a new, delicate, wrinkled skin. The animal drags itself out of the shell, which is more or less complete, like a transparent ghost of its previous existence, while the overgrown armour cracks at the back. The animal must now hide since its skin is delicate, but it grows quickly and the animal swells its body by absorbing water and stretching out the folds in its new carapace.

This hardens over time, allowing the animal to return to a hostile environment. The hermit crab partially avoids this difficult and dangerous procedure by having a shell-less rear section and sheltering it with a discarded molluscs shell, which it replaces as it grows and slips into in a minute or so. One unintended feature of the external skeleton has had far-reaching consequences. Mechanically, it functions almost as well on land as it does in water, so there's little stopping a creature from walking right out of the sea and up the beach if it can find a method to breathe. Many crustaceans have done so, including sand shrimps and beach hoppers, which live near the sea, and pill bugs and penny sows, which have colonized damp ground all throughout the land.

The robber crab is the most stunning of all these land-dwelling crustaceans. It may be found on islands in the Indian Ocean and the Pacific's western parts. There is an opening to an air chamber lined with wet puckered skin near the back of its primary carapace, where it meets the first section of its belly, through which the animal collects oxygen. This creature is so large that it can hold a palm tree's trunk between its spread legs. It climbs easily and, once at the palm's peak, chops down the immature coconuts with its massive pincers. It must return to the water to deposit its eggs, but other than that, it is quite at ease on land. Other marine creatures' descendants have also departed the ocean. Snails and shell less slugs are among the molluscs, however, they just emerged from the sea lately in the group's history. Millipedes, descendants of segmented worms, were most likely the first to migrate on land. They were followed by pioneers who, according to modern DNA analyses, were crustaceans. And some of them thrived in their new environment to the point that they gave rise to the most numerous and diversified group of all terrestrial creatures – insects.

The earliest volcanoes to arise on the cooling planet erupted on a far larger scale than those we are familiar with today, forming entire mountain ranges of lava and ash. Wind and rain have annihilated them over millennia. Their rocks deteriorated and became clay and sludge. Streams carried the debris, particle by particle, and strewn it across the seafloor beyond the land's edge. The sediments compressed into shales and sandstone as they accumulated. The continents were not fixed in place. They moved slowly over the earth's surface, propelled by convection currents deep inside the mantle. The sedimentary layers surrounding them were compressed and rucked up as they met, forming new mountain ranges. The land remained barren while geological cycles repeated themselves over three thousand million years, and volcanoes burst and exhausted themselves. Life, on the other hand, flourished in the water. Some marine algae may have survived on the sea's edge, rimming the beaches and boulders in green, but they couldn't have spread far beyond the splash zone, since they would have dried out and perished. Then, between 450 and 500 million years ago, certain species evolved a waxy coating called a cuticle that protected them from drying out. This, however, did not completely free them from their dependence on water. They couldn't leave because it was necessary for their reproductive processes.

Algae reproduce in two ways: by simple asexual division and through sexual reproduction, which is very important in the evolutionary process. The generation that produces the sex cells is the well-known green moss. Each giant egg remains connected to the stem's top, while the smaller microscopic sperms are discharged into the water and wiggle their way up to fertilise it. Plants like this are extremely likely to have been among the first to colonize the land's damp borders, although no undoubted moss fossils have yet been recovered from this time period. Simple leafless branching strands that exist as carbon filaments in the rocks are the first terrestrial plants we have identified, going back over 400 million years. They didn't have roots, like mosses, but when their stems are properly prepared and inspected under a microscope, they reveal characteristics that no moss has — long, thick-walled cells that must have carried water up the stem. They were able to stand several centimetre tall because of these structures, which provided them with strength. That may not seem impressive, but it was a significant step forward in life's colonization of the land.

These plants, along with primitive mosses and liverworts, produced green tangled carpets, tiny forests that extended inland from the borders of estuaries and rivers, when the earliest animal colonists from the sea crawled in. They were segmented organisms, ancestors of today's millipedes, with chitinous armour that made them ideally suited to ground mobility. They probably stayed near the water's edge at first, but wherever there was moss, there was wetness, vegetable detritus, and spores to consume. The word millipede, which means 'a thousand legs,' is a bit of an exaggeration. There are no living animals with more than 200 legs; some have as few as eight. The millipedes' exterior skeleton, which they inherited from their water-dwelling forefathers, required little adaptation for life on land, but they did need to learn a new way of breathing. The feathery gill linked to a stalk beside the leg that had previously served their watery ancestors, crustaceans, would not function in the air. In its place, millipedes developed the tracheae, a system of breathing tubes. Each tube starts at an opening on the shell's flank and branches internally into a fine network that eventually leads to all of the body's organs and tissues, with the tips even entering individual specialized cells known as tracheoles that deliver gaseous oxygen to the surrounding tissues while also absorbing waste. These tubes can be clearly seen in the abdomen of modern locusts too. On the other hand, millipedes have difficulty reproducing outside of water. Their oceanic ancestors, like the algae, relied on water to get their sperm to their eggs. On land, the solution was obvious: males and females must meet and transmit sperm straight from one to the other because they are both mobile. Millipedes do precisely this.

The reproductive cells of both sexes are stored in glands near the base of the second set of legs. During the mating season, the male and female get entwined. The male reaches forward with his seventh leg, grabs a sperm bundle from his sex gland, and then clambers alongside the female until the bundle is beside her sexual pouch, where she can take it in. Millipedes eat nothing but vegetables. Fiercer invertebrates, who had come to the moss jungles to feed on this grazing population of millipedes, were unable to form such trusting bonds. Centipedes, scorpions, and spiders are three groups of predatory organisms that still exist today. They belong to the segmented group of animals, like their prey, albeit the degree to which their bodies have retained divisions varies greatly.

When these predators mate, however, there's a good chance it'll be mistaken for food rather than a mate. So, for the first time among the species that have appeared in this history, scorpion mating needs ritualized precautions and placations of courting. The male scorpion approaches the female scorpion with caution. He grips her pincers with his own. The duo procced to dance once they have been bonded and her weapons have been neutralized. Their tails are held straight and sometimes even entangled as they travel backward and forward. Their shuffling movements had cleared the dancing ground of much of the debris after some time. The male then extrudes a package of sperm from underneath his thorax's genital hole and drops it on the ground. He pulls and heaves the female-forward, still clutching her by the claws, until her genital opening, which is also on her underside, is brought directly above the sperm package. She accepts it, and the partners separate and go their own ways. The eggs hatch within the mother's pouch, and the babies climb out and up onto her back. They stay there for about a fortnight until their first molt is complete and they can fend for themselves.

Spiders, too, must practice extraordinary caution when courting. The male's situation is rendered considerably more dangerous by the fact that he is almost invariably smaller than the female. Long before he meets his partner, he prepares for their encounter. He weaves a small silk triangle a few centimetre long and drops a sperm-drop onto it from a gland beneath his abdomen. He then sucks it into the pedipalp's hollow first joint, a peculiar limb at the front of his body. He's all set now. Jumping spiders and wolf spiders use their exceptional eyesight to hunt mostly by sight. As a result, the courting male depends on visual cues to alert the female of his presence and purpose. His pedipalps are vividly coloured and patterned, and he begins to signal with them in a manic semaphore as soon as he sees a female. In order to discover their food, nocturnal spiders rely heavily on their incredibly sensitive sense of touch. They cautiously touch one other's lengthy legs when they first meet, and only after much hesitation do they go closer together. Web-making spiders are sensitive to vibrations on their silken strands, which indicate when a victim has become caught in the web. When a male of such a species approaches a female who is hanging, huge and frightening, on her web or lurking nearby, he signals her by twanging the threads at one side in a specific and important way that he trusts she will recognize. Bribery is a strategy used by other species. The male captures an insect and wraps it in silk with great care. He gently approaches the female, holding this in front of him, and delivers it to her. He immediately scuttles over her and binds her to the ground with silk ropes while she is examining the gift. Only then does he take a chance on an embrace. After surviving every risk, the male inserts his pedipalp near the female's genital entrance, squirts out the sperm, and quickly flees. It should be noted that, despite his best efforts, he occasionally fails to make his escape in time, and the female consumes him as a result. However, the male's misfortune

A pair of Tanzanian Earthworm Millipede mating rituals. (© Puripatch Lokakalin/Getty Images)

A Male spider as it tries to motivate a fema[...] (© Colin Ewington/Getty Images)

A Male Scorpion as he grips the female's pincers with his own. (©Austin Simon/Getty Images)

had little impact on the transfer of his genes because he died after, not before, completing his duty.

Plants were altering at the same time as the early segmented animals perfected their adaptations for surviving on land and away from dampness. The ferns had created a particular protein to defend themselves against UV light damage early in their evolution, which had not been a concern for their forefathers because they lived in water where such wavelengths could not reach them. This chemical began to transform into lignin over time. This is the foundation of wood, and it provided the stiffness that allowed them to grow tall. As a result, plants evolved a new type of competition. All green plants rely on light to power the chemical reactions that allow them to synthesize their body components from basic elements. As a result, if a plant does not grow tall enough, it risks being overshadowed by its neighbours and condemned to shade, where it will perish from a lack of light. As a result, these early groupings took use of their newly acquired stem strength to grow extremely tall. They grew into trees. The club mosses and horsetails were still mostly swamp inhabitants, and they now stood in thick clumps thirty meters tall, some with two-meter-wide wooden stems. Coal is made up of the compacted remnants of their stems and leaves. The large widths of the seams are stunning evidence of the early woods' richness and durability. Other species from each of these groups also moved inland, mixing with ferns. True leaves had evolved, enormous spreading structures that gathered as much light as possible. Like the tree ferns that still survive in tropical rainforests, they grew tall with curved trunks.

The forest floor was thinly vegetated at best, and large portions may have been completely devoid of any live leaves. Climbing up the trunks was how some of the multi-legged vegetarians got their food. Another force might have compelled these organisms to flee the earth. Around this period, a whole new kind of animal joined the land's invertebrates. They possessed four legs, backbones, and moist skins. They were the earliest amphibians and carnivores as well. These came from fish that began to evolve around 530 million years ago, as they formed muscular fins and could stand moving onto land.

Body temperature has a significant impact on insects, as it does on other creatures. The faster their body's energy-producing chemical processes can run, and the more active they can be, the warmer they are. They could probably warm themselves efficiently and quickly in the sun if their blood was pumped via thin flaps extending laterally from the back. These flaps may also be turned to face straight to the sun's rays if they possess muscles at their base. Insect wings do start out as flaps on the back, and they do have blood running through their veins at first, so this explanation sounds reasonable. However, this may be, insects with wings appeared some 350 million years ago. Dragonflies are the earliest known insects. There were various species, most of which were around the same size as those alive now. However, due to a lack of competition, certain early forms grew to huge proportions, and dragonflies with a wingspan of 70 cm became the world's biggest insects. Such flamboyant forms vanished as the atmosphere got more densely occupied. Dragonflies have two sets of wings, each with basic joints that allow them to only move up and down and cannot be folded back. Because of their reliance on sight, most dragonflies do not fly at night. Instead, they hunt during the day, flying with their six legs curved in front of them to form a little basket in which they collect smaller insects like flies or mosquitoes indeed their larvae too, feed on mosquito larvae. That characteristic alone indicates that they must have been preceded into the air by other herbivorous creatures, most likely cockroaches, grasshoppers, locusts, and crickets, based on the rudimentary nature of their anatomy. The existence of these vast numbers of insects, whirring and buzzing through the air of the old woods, was to play an essential role in the plant revolution that was taking place.

Fertilization takes significantly longer in a pine forest. The pollen tube takes a year to grow down to the egg, but once there, it hits the egg cell directly, and the male cell does not tarry in a drop of water after descending the tube but instead fuses immediately with the egg. Conifers have finally gotten rid of water as a mode of conveyance for their sexual processes. Conifers use a particular sticky material called resin to protect their trunks against mechanical injury and insect assault. It is runny when it first runs from a wound, but the more liquid element, turpentine, rapidly evaporates, leaving a sticky lump that successfully heals the incision. In addition, it serves as a trap. Any insect that comes into contact with it becomes irreversibly stuck and is frequently buried as additional resin pours around it. These lumps have shown to be the best fossilizing material available. In their translucent golden depths, they hold ancient insects thatpersist as amber bits. When the amber is meticulously sectioned, mouthparts, scales, and hairs may be seen via a microscope with the same clarity as if the insect had been entangled in the resin only the day before. Scientists have even identified microscopic parasitic insects called mites that adhere to the legs of larger animals. However, extracting DNA from a blood-sucking arthropod appears to be science fiction. The oldest amber fragments recovered so far date from roughly 230 million years ago, a long period before conifers and flying insects evolved.

The dragonflies' two wings beat in unison, with the front pair lifted and the back pair lowered. This, on the other hand, produces significant physiological complications. Even though their wings do not generally come into contact, there are issues when the dragonfly makes quick turns. The fore- and hindwings then beat against one another as they bend under the added effort of the turn, producing a loud rattling that you can readily hear as you sit watching them do their circuits over a pond or a grass field being watered. Later insect groups appear to have discovered that flying with just one pair of beating membranes was more efficient. Bees and wasps, flying ants, and sawflies all use hooks to join their fore- and hindwings to create a single surface. The wings of a butterfly overlap. Hawkmoths, which can fly at speeds of up to 50 kilometre per hour, have drastically decreased the size of their hindwings and attached them to the long, thin forewings with a curled bristle. Beetles use their forewings for a very different function. These insects are the insect world's hefty armoured tanks, and they spend a lot of time on the ground, barging through the vegetable litter, scrabbling in the dirt, or chewing into the wood. Such actions have the potential to harm sensitive wings. Beetles defend theirs by transforming the front pair into thick, hard coverings that fit over the top of the abdomen. The wings are neatly and cleverly folded and hidden beneath. There are sprung joints in the wing veins. The joints unlock and the wings spring open when the wing coverings are lifted.

Insects were the first species to explore the air, and they had it all to themselves for nearly 100 million years. Their lives, however, were not without danger. Spiders, their old enemies, never evolved wings, yet they didn't let their insect victims completely escape. They proceeded to take a toll on the insect population by laying silk traps across the flyways between the trees. Plants began to use the insects' ability to fly for their own benefit. In biological terms, their dependence on the wind for the dispersal of their reproductive cells was always random and costly. Spores do not need to be fertilized, and they will grow wherever they fall if the earth is wet and fertile enough. As a result, the pine tree must generate massive amounts of pollen. A single little male cone may generate millions of grains, which fall out in such large quantities that they form a golden cloud when tapped in the spring. Insects may be able to provide a far more efficient mode of transportation. They could transport the little amount of pollen required for fertilization and deposit it in the exact position in the female section of the plant where it was required if appropriately encouraged. If both pollen and eggs were planted together on the plant, this courier service would be the most cost-effective. The insects would thus be able to make both deliveries and pickups in one call. As a result, the flower developed. They first appeared 100 million years ago. Each egg is covered by a green covering with a receptive spike on top called a stigma, on which pollen must be put if the eggs are to be fertilized. Many stamens generating pollens are clustered around the eggs. The entire structure is encircled by brilliantly coloured modified leaves, the petals, in order to draw the insects' attention to these organs. Beetles had been feeding on the pollen of cycads, and they were among the first to notice the early blooms, such as magnolias and waterlilies. They acquired pollen meals as they went from one bloom to the next, and they paid for them by being covered with surplus pollen, which they inadvertently carried to the next flower they visited. One risk of combining eggs and pollen in the same structure is that the plant would pollinate itself, avoiding cross-fertilization, which is the whole point of all these intricacies. The magnolia, like many other plants, avoids this danger by having eggs and pollen that mature at distinct periods. As soon as the flower opens, the stigmas of Magnolias receive pollen. Its own stamens, on the other hand, do not generate pollen until later, by which time its eggs have most certainly been cross-fertilized by wandering insects. Insects, unlike humans, can detect ultraviolet light, which gave them an edge when looking for pollen. Many flower patterns are invisible to humans. Only animals, like bees, can see these Nectar "bulls-eyes." The emergence of flowers changed the world's landscape. As the plants announced the joys and benefits, they had to give, the green forest burst with colour. The first blossoms were available to anyone who wanted to land on them.

Such blossoms attracted a variety of insects, including bees and beetles. However, the diversity of visitors is not an indisputable benefit, as they are equally likely to visit a range of unspecialized flowers. Pollen from one species deposited in the blooms of another species is pollen that has been wasted. As a result, there has been a tendency for specialized flowers and insects to grow together throughout the evolution of flowering plants, each catering precisely to the needs and tastes of the other. Insects have been visiting the tops of trees to harvest spores as food since the time of the big horsetails and ferns. Pollen was nearly the same diet, and it is still a prized possession. Bees gather it in large baskets on their thighs and return it to their hives to eat it right away or make it into pollen bread, which is an important diet for their developing young. Some plants, such as myrtle species, generate two types of pollen: one that fertilizes their blooms and another that is especially pleasant but has no other use. Other flowers came up with a brand-new bribe: nectar. The primary goal of this delectable liquid is to delight insects so much that they spend all of their time gathering it throughout the flowering season. The insect is equipped with marks on the petals as it approaches, indicating the exact location of the prize they seek (The nectar bulls-eye) enabled by the insect's ultraviolet Vision.

The aromas that attract insects, such as those generated by lavender, roses, and honeysuckle, usually appeal to us as well. This isn't always the case, though. Some flies are drawn to rotting meat because it provides food for them and their larvae. Flowers that attract them as pollinators must conform to their preferences and generate a scent that is identical to theirs, and they frequently do it with a precision and pungency that are beyond the human nose's endurance. The maggot-bearing Stapelia from southern Africa has blooms that smell awfully like carcasses, but it also has wrinkled brown petals coated in hairs that appear like the rotting skin of a dead animal, which adds to its allure to flies. To enhance the illusion, the plant emits heat that is eerily similar to that caused by corruption. The overall picture is so realistic that flies delivering Stapelia's pollen not only visit blossom after flower but also

complete the activity that they undertake when they visit genuine carcasses - depositing their eggs on the flower, precisely like they do in a corpse. When these hatches, the maggots discover that instead of decaying flesh, they are given an inedible flower as a diet. They starve to death, but the Stapelia have been fertilized. The most unusual of such blossoms attracted a variety of insects, including bees and beetles. However, the diversity of visitors is not an indisputable benefit, as they are equally likely to visit a range of unspecialized flowers. Pollen from one species deposited in the blooms of another species is pollen that has been wasted. As a result, there has been a tendency for specialized flowers and insects to grow together throughout the evolution of flowering plants, each catering precisely to the needs and tastes of the other. Insects have been visiting the tops of trees to harvest spores as food since the time of the big horsetails and ferns. Pollen was nearly same diet, and it is still a prized possession. Bees gather it in large baskets on their thighs and return it to their hives to eat it right away or make it into pollen bread, which is an important diet for their developing young. Some plants, such as myrtle species, generate two types of pollen: one that fertilizes their blooms and another that is especially pleasant but has no other use. Other flowers came up with a brand-new bribe: nectar. The primary goal of this delectable liquid is to delight insects so much that they spend all of their time gathering it throughout the flowering season. The insect is equipped with marks on the petals as it approaches, indicating the exact location of the prizes they seek (The nectar bulls-eye) enabled by the insect's ultraviolet Vision.

The aromas that attract insects, such as those generated by lavender, roses, and honeysuckle, usually appeal to us as well. This isn't always the case, though. Some flies are drawn to rotting meat because it provides food for them and their larvae. Flowers that attract them as pollinators must conform to their preferences and generate a scent that is identical to theirs, and they frequently do it with a precision and pungency that is beyond the human nose's endurance. The maggot-bearing Stapelia from southern Africa has blooms that smell awfully like carcasses, but it also has wrinkled brown petals coated in hairs that appear like the rotting skin of a dead animal, which adds to its allure to flies. To enhance the illusion, the plant emits heat that is eerily similar to that caused by corruption. The overall picture is so realistic that flies delivering Stapelia's pollen not only visit blossom after flower but also complete the activity that they undertake when they visit genuine carcasses - depositing their eggs on the flower, precisely like they do in a corpse. When these hatches, the maggots discover that instead of decaying flesh, they are given an inedible flower as a diet. They starve to death, but the Stapelia has been fertilized. The most unusual of all the impersonations are those of certain orchids that use sexual impersonation to attract insects. One develops a flower that nearly mimics the shape of a female wasp, complete with eyes, antennae, and wings, as well as emitting the odour of a female wasp in the mating phase. Deceived male wasps seek to copulate with it. They deposit a load of pollen within the orchid flower when they do so, and get a fresh batch to deliver to the next fake female shortly after. These orchids don't make any nectar. They don't give their insect pollinators sex, but they do give them the illusion of it.

The number of individual insects in the globe appears to be beyond calculation, but someone has attempted it and calculated that there must be something of 10 billion at any given time. To put it another way, there are nearly a billion insects for every human living – and these insects would weigh around 70 times as much as the typical human. Insects are considered to have four times the number of species as all other types of living beings combined. We've characterized and identified over a million of them so far, but there are likely three or four times that number remaining nameless, and maybe much more awaiting the attention of anyone with the time, patience, and knowledge to sit down and do a systematic study of them. Despite their abundance, insects plays an important role in the web of life and any ecosystem. Sometimes they act as prey, and other times they act as decomposers or something else entirely. All of these different forms, however, are variations on one basic anatomical pattern: a body divided into three distinct parts - a head bearing the mouth and most of the sense organs; a thorax filled almost entirely with muscles to operate the three pairs of legs beneath and, usually, one or two pairs of wings above; and an abdomen carrying the digestive and reproductive organs. An exterior skeleton formed mostly of chitin encases all three parts. As we've seen, the early segmented organisms, crustaceans, and most likely trilobites formed this brown fibrous substance approximately 550 million years ago. Chemically, it is similar to cellulose, and it is flexible and permeable in its purest form. The insects, on the other hand, coat it in a protein called sclerotin, which makes it very hard. This results in the beetles' hefty, rigid armour, as well as mouthparts that are sharp and robust enough to eat through wood and even cut metals such as copper and silver. Indeed, this also allows insects like rhinoceros beetles to lift up to 800 times their own weight, and you can experience this by simply holding an elegant rhinoceros beetle that appears in May in UAE, and here you can see that the beetle can with surprising power open your fingers in a painful digging manner.

The chitinous exterior skeleton is especially adaptable to evolutionary pressures. Its exterior may be sculpted without damaging the anatomy underneath. Its proportions may be tweaked to create various forms. Thus, the chewing mouthparts of early cockroach-like insects have been transformed into siphons and stilettos, saws and chisels, and probes that are as long as the entire body when unreeled. Legs have evolved into catapults capable of propelling an insect 200 times its own body length, broad oars for rowing it through water, and thin hair-tipped stilts with a wide stride that allow their owners to walk on the surface of pools. Many limbs are equipped with chitin-based equipment, including pollen pouches, combs for cleaning compound eyes, spikes to function as grappling irons, and notches to play a melody. An exterior skeleton, on the other hand, is an impenetrable prison. Trilobites in ancient waters moulted to get around the restrictions. The insects' solution is still the same. The procedure may appear wasteful, yet it is carried out efficiently. Underneath the old chitinous shell, a new one grows, greatly wrinkled and squeezed. A layer of liquid separates the two, absorbing the chitin from the old skeleton and leaving just the thinnest of tissues connecting the hard sclerotinised sections. The chitin-rich liquid is subsequently absorbed back into the insect's body through the still permeable new skeleton. The old plates break apart along a line going along the back, and the bug crawls out. As it does so, its newly freed body swells, filling the folds in the new skin. The chitin hardens and becomes reinforced by additional sclerotin deposits in a short period of time. Bristletails and springtails, for example, are primitive insect cousins that do not alter form significantly as they mature. They just moult as they become larger. They may continue to moult even after they have begun to reproduce. Cockroaches, cicadas, and crickets, which are ancient winged insects, grow in a similar fashion, with their early stages resembling adults but without wings. Even though these insects dwell in a significantly different environment for the early portion of their life, they do not drastically alter their appearance. Cicada larvae that sit shrieking on trees spend their lives sucking sap from roots below ground. Larval dragonflies use their large protruding mouthparts to catch worms and other tiny organisms near the pond's bottom. The image of the adult may be seen in both the cicada and the dragonfly. More evolved insects, on the other hand, go through such drastic transformations that there's no way to tell the difference between the larva and the adult except by witnessing the organism change. Maggots transform into flies, grubs transform into beetles, and caterpillars transform into butterflies. A grub, a maggot, or a caterpillar's only function is to eat. Its entire body is committed to this one goal. It has no sexual equipment because it will not breed in this form nor does it need a reason to attract a mate, it needs no mechanisms to send out call signals whether by sight, smell or sound, nor any sense organs to receive such messages; and as its parents have gone to considerable trouble to ensure that when it hatches it is surrounded by great quantities of the particular food it requires, it needs no wings.

Many insects spend practically their entire lives as larvae, becoming larger and accumulating food reserves. Beetle grubs may bore into wood for up to seven years, obtaining nutrients from the most indigestible of compounds, cellulose. Caterpillars eat for months, saving their favourite leaves until the end of the season. But, sooner or later, they all attain full size and reach the end of their allotted span of their larval existence'. The first of two extremely dramatic shifts is about to begin. Silk glands are only found in insect larvae. They've already utilized them to make community tents, extrude lifelines to guide them across plants, and use them as ropes to let themselves down from one twig to the next. Many individuals now weave silk to keep themselves hidden from the world. The silk moth larva wraps itself in a fluffy bundle of threads, the moon moth spins a gleaming metallic cocoon, and the ermine moth spins a beautiful lacy net casket. Many butterfly larvae do not create any kind of covering. They just spin a silken sling and fasten it to a twig using it. They take off their caterpillar costumes as soon as they've settled in. The pupa is revealed when their skin cracks and rolls down, revealing a smooth, brown hard-shelled item. The only movement it makes is a twitch of its pointy tip every now and then. It has spiracles on its sides that allow it to breathe, but it does not eat or excrete. Its existence appears to have been halted.

Internally, though, the most significant changes are occurring. The larva's body is being dismembered and reconstructed in large parts. The actual emergence is generally done in the dead of night.

The pupa of a butterfly begins to tremble as it hangs on a twig. At one end of the pupa, a head with two enormous eyes and antennae pushed over its back pushes through. Legs break loose and begin clawing in the air madly. The bug drags itself out slowly and laboriously, pausing frequently to regain strength. The thorax emerges, with two flat crumpled items on its back, its wings, wrinkled like a walnut kernel. The bug rips itself free and hangs nervously on the empty pupa case. Then it starts pumping blood into a network of veins within the baggy wings with convulsive shudders. Within half an hour, the wings have fully expanded to the point where the two sides of the bag meet flat against one another, trapping the veins. The veins themselves remain pliable. It would ooze blood if the tip of one of them was wounded right now. However, blood is taken back into the body over time, and the veins harden into stiff struts that give the wing its strength. Butterflies, unlike their larvae, have superb compound eyes - the males are usually larger than the females, as he is the one who conducts the seeking. Butterfly wings, like flowers, contain more intricate patterns than our ultraviolet-blind eyes can discern because their eyesight is sensitive to sections of the spectrum that we can't see. Pigments or, more often, the effects of microscopic structures that divide the light falling on them and reflect just a part of its back generate the colours and designs formed by small scales overlapping like tiles on a roof. I had seen these structures under the microscope from the wings of a Lime Butterfly (Papilio demoleus) Specimen. Other insects use different methods to communicate across large distances and send equally intricate and powerful signals. Cicadas, crickets, and grasshoppers all communicate through sound. Because the majority of insects are deaf, they have had to develop not only voices but also ears. Cicada eardrums are circular and located on either side of the thorax. Grasshoppers listen with their legs. There are two slits on the first pair of thighs that lead to deep pockets. The common wall between these two is a membrane that looks like an eardrum.

Cicadas, the noisiest of insect singers, have a considerably more sophisticated system. There are two chambers in their abdomen, one on each side. Each chamber's inner wall is firm, and as it is pushed in or out, it generates a clicking sound, similar to that of a tin lid. A muscle in the rear of the abdomen may pull the wall back and forth up to 600 times per second. Because much of the belly behind the vibrating plate is hollow, and two huge rectangular pieces of the abdominal wall are stiffened to create resonators, the noise produced is substantially magnified. These are covered by flaps that protrude from the lower border of the thorax and may be opened and closed like organ shutters to augment or decrease sound. Each species has its own distinct vocalization. However, as larvae, they spend somewhere between 7 to 12 years underground emerging like zombies and transforming ecosystems.

Other insects use the third of the five senses, scent, to attract their mates. Some moths' females emit an odour that males may detect with their big feathery antennae. These organs are so sensitive, and the fragrance is so distinct and potent, that a female has been reported to summon a male from eleven kilometre away. Even if there is just one molecule of fragrance in a cubic metre of air at such a distance, it is enough to trigger the male to fly in search of its source. To achieve this, he'll need both antennas. He can't determine the direction with only one, but with two, he can evaluate which side has the strongest scent and hence fly steadily towards it.

Things were shifting in the ocean as well. Fish began to lift themselves out of the water and colonize the land as the first backboned organisms. They, like the early terrestrial invertebrates,

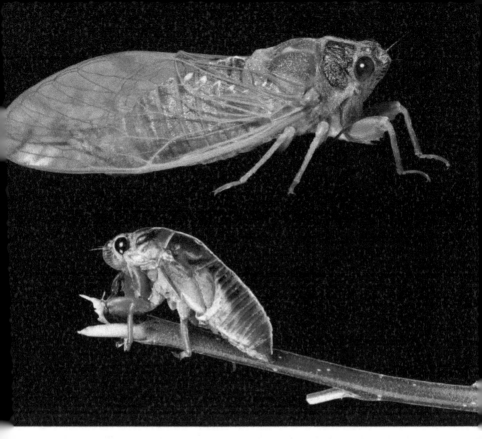

(Top to bottom) An image of an Adult Cicada and a Juvenile Cicada. (© KirssanovV/Getty Images)

(Left to right) An image of myself holding an Adult Oasis Skimmer Dragonfly (Orthetrum sabina) while researching on these ancient insects at Al Qudra Lakes. A closeup shot of a Dragonfly nymph.

had to overcome two challenges in order to breach this barrier: first, how to move around outside of water, and second, how to collect oxygen from the air. The mudskipper is the only fish living today that can perform both of these things. It is not closely related to the fish that first landed on land, so any comparisons must be made with caution, but it can nevertheless provide insight into how that historic shift was done. Fins with muscled fleshy bottoms, which mudskippers have developed lately in evolutionary history, were also seen in a diverse collection of ancient fish that lived between 450 and 70 million years ago. One of the most prevalent was the coelacanth family. So, when a living coelacanth was discovered off the coast of South Africa in 1938, evolutionary experts were thrilled. This was an opportunity to learn about the flesh and internal structure of these ancient fish in ways that no fossil could. The fisherman, however, had already gutted the fish and thrown away the vital entrails. A second coelacanth was discovered in 1952. It was captured this time in the north of Madagascar, off the coast of the Comoro Islands. The locals did not appear to place a great value on these unusual creatures. However, extensive anatomical examinations, including genetic research, finally led scientists to the conclusion that, while the coelacanths are clearly an old group, they are not as closely connected to the earliest backboned creatures to colonize the land as previously assumed.

Tiktaalik is unlike any other fish — or anything else - living today. It was around two meters long and had a giant flattened head with a pair of eyes on its upper portion, similar to those of a crocodile. It possessed the beginnings of a neck and was protected by fishlike scales. Its limbs, however, are crucial in evolutionary history. As one might anticipate from a fish, those in the front were each fringed with a fin. Their fleshy base, on the other hand, included bones that were joined at the elbow and wrist. This was certainly a limb that might have assisted its owner in getting out of the water.

But why should it have done so in the first place? Perhaps it was to gather food, such as the remains of dead sea creatures washed up on the shore, or to catch some invertebrates that had established themselves farther inland. But how could it breathe while it was submerged in water? The mudskipper accomplishes this by keeping water in its mouth and swilling it over the lining of its mouth while rotating its head to extract oxygen. It also takes some from the air directly via its wet skin. However, these technologies only allow it to stay out of the water for a brief period of time. Within a few minutes it has to return to wet its skin and take a fresh mouthful of water, yet one fish, the lungfish, manages to live in them all year round and survive the dry season by breathing air. The lungfish burrow into the mud at the bottom of the ponds as they diminish. It curls into a ball and secretes mucus to fill its hole, wrapping its tail around its head. The mucus turns to parchment as the sun bakes away the remaining traces of moisture in the dirt. Other primitive freshwater fish, like the bichir, have a pouch opening from their gut that allows them to breathe. Yet they are also the primary suspects of the first fishes to leave the water and walk onto land. You can try an experiment I made with a Senegal Bichir I had in my tank if you have a Bichir at home, possibly as a pet. Take a straight smooth surface and release the fish on it; you'll be able to witness the fish's incredible ability to crawl like a snake, despite the fact that it utilizes its two-side fins to maneuver laterally. These organs are primitive lungs, and the lungfish may survive out of water for months, if not years, with their help. When the rains return and the pond fills up again, the fish springs to life within a few hours wriggles free of its cocoon and the re-softened mud and swims away. It now breathes through its gills, just like any other fish, but it also utilizes its lungs, rising every now and then to suck air from the surface, a skill that is especially useful when the water in the pools gets tepid and loses most of its oxygen.

The link between lungfish, coelacanths and land-dwelling four-legged creatures known as tetrapods has long been a point of contention. Molecular genetics has once again provided an unequivocal explanation. Lungfish possess the biggest known genome of any vertebrate (about 10 times the size of a human genome), which makes sequencing difficult. However, examinations of the lungfish's protein-producing genes have proven that it is more closely linked to Tetrapods than to coelacanths. These analyses also suggest that roughly 380 million years ago, just after Tiktaalik's period, all three lineages split quite quickly. Tiktaalik was either our ancestor or a distant relative, according to scientists. Whatever the case, Tetrapods had evolved into real land dwellers within a few million years after Tiktaalik waddling through the mudflats. Horsetails and club mosses, both of which had grown to the size of trees, covered the marshes they lived in. Their fallen trunks accumulated in the swamps and ultimately fossilized and converted to coal, so it's no surprise that scientists first discovered the bones of those earliest vertebrate land-dwellers, the frogs, in coal mines. It had to be terrible for some of them. Their jaws were studded with lines of cone-shaped teeth, and they grew to be three or four meters long. For the following hundred million years, they ruled the earth. However, some 200 million years ago, life on this planet was wiped out by a worldwide disaster analogous to the better-renowned one that wiped off the dinosaurs. Approximately half of all species on the planet vanished. The last of the huge frogs lived around 110 million years ago in what is now Australia, and it was a five-meter-long monster. The gigantic salamander, for example, is a living amphibian that can offer us a hint of those early forms. The Japanese amphibian reaches a length of around a meter and a half, which is just a fraction of the size of its forefathers but unusual for modern frogs. The majority of salamanders and their cousins, newts, are rather small. The legs of a newt, while advanced in comparison to the fins of a coelacanth or a mudskipper, are inefficient. It can't get too far away from water, though. For one thing, its skin is porous, and in a dry environment, the animal soon loses its bodily fluids and dies. To make matters worse, newts, like other amphibians, lack the ability to sip with their mouths. All of the fluids it requires must be absorbed via its skin. It also needs to keep its body wet in order to breathe. Because its lungs are simple and insufficient for its needs, it, like the mudskipper, must supplement its oxygen intake by absorbing it via its moist skin. Both of these characteristics limit it, as well as other amphibians, to damp environments. However, it has a third requirement that binds it to water: its eggs, like those of a fish, do not have waterproof shells, so when it is time to reproduce, it must locate water for them. After a long time, some 70 million years ago, the amphibians developed watertight skins and leathery eggs, transforming them into reptiles.

Reptiles and amphibians do not create their own heat; instead, they obtain it from their surroundings. Due to the permeability of their skins, amphibians cannot be exposed to the light directly, thus they must stay chilly and sluggish. The reptiles, on the other hand, have no such issues. The term "cold-blooded," which is frequently given to reptiles, is clearly deceptive. Ectotherms, as opposed to endotherms, such as mammals and birds, they gather heat from the environment. Endotherms offers several benefits. It enables the growth of delicate and sophisticated organs that might otherwise be destroyed by temperature variations. It enables those who possess it to remain active even after the sun has set. It even allows species to dwell in extremely cold environments where no reptile can survive. However, such advantages come at a very steep cost. For example, almost 80% of the calories in our diet are used to keep our body temperature steady. Ectothermic reptiles can survive on 10% of the food that a mammal of similar size would require since they don't have to waste as much energy on maintaining body temperature.

The reptiles not only survive but also reproduce in arid environments, implying that their eggs, like their bodies, must be impermeable. It is not difficult to make them so. As the egg travels down the oviduct, a gland in the bottom section of the oviduct secretes a parchment-like shell around it. Because the embryo needs to breathe, the shell must be somewhat porous to allow oxygen and carbon dioxide to flow through. As a result, fertilization must occur within the female's body before the shell is implanted. The male is equipped with a penis to deal with this difficulty. The shape of this organ varies greatly among reptile species. Only one reptile now lacks such an organ: the tuatara, which achieves internal fertilization in a similar way to salamanders and frogs. When the couple comes together, their genital openings are squeezed close together, allowing the male's sperm to flow actively into the female's oviduct. Surprisingly, the tuatara possesses another feature that is similar to that of frogs. It can survive in temperatures as low as 7°C, which is well below what any lizard or snake would choose. It appears to be a very primitive reptile, as evidenced by the anatomy of its skull, which matches those of the oldest known reptile fossils in crucial respects. Bones of a very similar species have been discovered in rocks dating back 200 million years. The tuatara, therefore, stems back to a period in reptile history when, if not to the time when reptiles originally split from amphibians, then at least to a time when, at the dawn of their golden era, reptiles were beginning to diversify into a wide range of forms. The continents that we know today were merged into one huge landmass called Pangaea by geologists, and the four-legged, tough-skinned, egg-laying ectothermic reptiles had spread throughout it. The dinosaurs, which varied in size from chickens to monsters weighing more than 30 tonnes, controlled the dry ground. Others, such as the ichthyosaurs and plesiosaurs, went back to the water and had their limbs changed into paddles. Pterosaurs, for example, evolved an area of skin on each arm that stretched between one massively expanded digit and the remainder of their body, allowing them to fly. As a result, the reptiles began their reign of terror over the world, which would continue for the next 150 million years.

After a few years, scientists uncovered fossils of feathers, not scales or fur. The feather is a remarkable device. Few substances can compare to it as an insulator, and none can outperform it as an aerofoil, weight for weight, whether man-made or animal-grown. Keratin is the main component. A reptile's scales and our own nails are made of the same horny substance, but a feather's unique attributes derive from its precise architecture. Almost all of the qualities that separate birds from other animals can be traced back to the advantages provided by feathers in some manner. Indeed, in today's world, just having a feather is enough to classify a creature as a bird. In 1861, an almost complete skeleton of a feathery creature the size of a pigeon was unearthed. It lay sprawled on the rock, its wings spread, one long leg disarticulated, the other still linked with four clawed toes, and the distinct impression of its feathers all around it, dramatically and unmistakably. It felt appropriate to refer to it as an "old bird," but it was unlike any other live bird. It possessed claws on both its feet and the three digits of its feathered forelimbs, and a bony extension of its spine supported its long-feathered tail that stretched out behind it. It was almost as much a reptile as a bird, and its discovery just two years after Darwin's book The Origin of Species was a fortunate validation of Darwin's theory that one group of creatures evolved into another through intermediate stages. Some of its features are plainly reptilian, such as a skull with bony jaws studded with teeth, distinct fingers equipped with sharp curved claws on the rear limbs and forelimbs, and a long bony rod in the tail. It does, however, have feathers that cover its entire body. It was known as

Archaeopteryx. It had to have made its way through the trees of its dinosaur-infested woods. The feathers of Archaeopteryx, on the other hand, have never been observed previously on such a prehistoric organism.

In the 1980s, China provided new and seemingly astonishing proof. Dinosaur skeletons were unearthed that were certainly ground-dwelling yet were still clothed in feathers. Some belonged to Theropods, tiny, flesh-eating dinosaurs. The group had already made a name for themselves. In other places, near-perfect skeletons have been discovered. Only in the Liaoning deposits, however, were the circumstances for fossilization so ideal that remnants of feathers were retained. The entire body was covered with feathers. Their major purpose was to insulate the body and keep it warm during high-intensity activities. As a result, feathers did not evolve for the purpose of flight and do not characterize birds. They were passed down from feathered forefathers to the birds. As a result, it's possible that not all dinosaurs were wiped off when an asteroid slammed into Mexico 66 million years ago. Some of the individuals who had feathers made it out alive. As a result, dinosaurs may now be seen soaring through our lawns. However, many significant changes would have to occur in order for those little feathered dinosaurs to evolve into the highly efficient flying species we see today. They had to change their bodies to aid with the shift. The lungs of birds are stretched into air sacs that protrude into the bodily cavity, filling the space as lightly as possible. The hefty bony extension of the spine that supported Archaeopteryx's tail has been replaced with stout-quilled feathers that do not require any type of skeletal support. A large, tooth-laden mouth must have been a significant hindrance for any creature attempting to fly since it would unbalance the animal and make it nose-heavy. Modern birds have lost it and instead created the beak, a keratin-based lightweight structure. However, even the greatest beak is incapable of chewing, and most birds require to break up their food. They do so, as did some of their distant sauropod relatives, via a unique muscular section of the stomach called the gizzard. As a result, the beak's only job is to gather food. Similar differences in the beak of Galapagos finches were discovered by Darwin, who saw them as significant support for his natural selection hypothesis. Bird wings have a considerably more complicated role than aeroplane wings because they must also function as the bird's engine, propelling it through the air. Even still, a bird's wing shape follows the same aerodynamic laws that humans later found when creating planes, and if you know how different types of planes fly, you can anticipate how birds with comparable profiles will fly. The most magnificently caparisoned birds, on the other hand — peacocks, pheasants, and parrots - are those that are so self-assured, so unafraid of opponents, that they have no worries about exposing themselves in prominent places to flaunt their adornments. Given that their primary communication is visual, it's no wonder that such birds' sounds are often short, simple, and harsh. In the last 30 million years or more, intricate singing has developed three times in different bird lineages. This indicates that the first birds, as well as the feathered dinosaurs, would have croaked, growled, or hissed instead of singing softly.

However, another group of animals would soon take over, giving rise to the most powerful and intelligent living form on the planet. The skin of an incredible beast came to London around the end of the eighteenth century. It had arrived from Australia's freshly created colony. It belonged to a creature approximately the size of a rabbit, with fur as thick and silky as an otter's. It possessed webbed and clawed feet; a single back vent that served both excretory and reproductive duties, similar to a reptile's cloaca; and, most bizarre of all, a wide flat beak like a duck. The odd bill, which seemed to fit uncomfortably on the hairy skull and had a flap like a cuff at the junction, belonged to it. The similarity to a bird might be dismissed because it was malleable and leathery in life. Because a mammal's hairy covering insulates the body and allows it to maintain a high temperature, it follows that this new species must likewise be warm-blooded. It also apparently had a mamma, or breast, with which to milk its young, which is the third attribute of a mammal and the one that gives the group its name. There were several unique characteristics that prompted the creation of a memorable name, but the platypus, which simply means 'flat-footed,' was chosen. Soon after, it was pointed out that the name was already in use for a flat-footed beetle, so a new one had to be invented, and the animal was renamed Ornithorhyncus, which means 'bird-bill.' This is the name given to it by scientists. To the majority of people, though, it is still a platypus. It dwells in eastern Australia's rivers, as it does now. It is primarily nocturnal and swims vigorously and buoyantly, frequently cruising over the surface with its webbed forefeet paddling and steering with its hind. When it dives, it uses little muscular flaps of skin to seal its ears and tiny eyes. It uses its bill, which is rich in nerve endings and can detect minute changes in pressure and electrical impulses from its food, to feel for freshwater prawns, worms, and other tiny organisms as it scans around on the riverbed, unable to see. It is a capable swimmer as well as a vigorous and diligent burrower, building huge tunnels through the riverbanks that may be up to 18 meters long. It accomplishes this by folding the webbing of its forefeet into its palms, freeing the claws for work. The female builds an underground nest of grass and reeds at the end of the tunnel. If eggs were discovered in a platypus nest, they had to have been dropped there by another species. They were characterized as roughly spherical, marble-sized, and soft-shelled, indicating that they were most likely reptile eggs. Then, in 1884, a female was killed shortly after laying an egg. A second one was discovered inside her body, on the verge of extrusion. There's no way there could be any questions now. This was a mammal that really laid eggs. When these eggs hatch after 10 days, the young are not left to fend for themselves, as all juvenile reptiles must. Instead, the mature female develops a set of unique glands on her stomach. They have a structure that is comparable to the sweat glands that the platypus, like most mammals, possesses in its skin to help cool the body when it becomes too hot. However, the sweat produced by these enlarged glands is viscous and high in fat; it is milk. It seeps into the fur and is sucked from tufts of hair by the young. The platypus does not have a genuine breast since it lacks a nipple, but it is a start. Despite almost every mammal maintaining a body temperature of 36° to 39°C, the temperature of the platypus, however, is only 30°C and varies greatly.

The spiny anteater is the only other species on the planet with a similar mix of primitive mammalian and reptile traits, and it, too, hails from Australia. Its naming history is similar to that of the platypus. It was given the name echidna, which means "spiny one," by scientists, only to learn that the term had already been given to a fish. As a result, it was dubbed tachyglossus, which means swift-tongued.' But it was the first name that stayed this time too. The creature resembles a huge flattened hedgehog with an armoury of spines imbedded in a black bristly hair covering. Its snout and spines, like the bill of a platypus, are specialized features that help it adapt to its environment. They are recent additions in evolutionary terms. In many ways, the echidna and the platypus are quite similar. It has hair, a very low body temperature, a single vent, and a cloaca, and it produces eggs. It varies in one aspect of its reproduction. The female lays a single egg, which she stores in a brief pouch on her bottom rather than in a nest. The egg's shell is wet, and it adheres to the hair in the pouch. It hatches after seven to ten days. The hatchling suckles thick, yellowish milk that oozes from the mother's belly skin. It stays in the pouch for about seven weeks, by which time it has grown to around ten centimetres in length and has begun to acquire spines. The yolk of an egg, on the other hand, is the sole sustenance a reptile supplies for its young. The juvenile reptile must construct a body from this little yellow ball that is complete and strong enough to allow it to be completely self-sufficient as soon as it emerges from the shell. The echidna and platypus have ancient body designs, but we don't have any strong evidence to show which prehistoric reptiles were their forefathers. As a result, we have very few evidences that these organisms are related to any specific group of fossil reptiles. Nonetheless, it's a safe bet that certain reptile populations evolved the kinds of breeding strategies that platypus and echidna utilize today throughout their metamorphosis into mammals. The genes that make them may be tracked back to their origins. These findings show that mammals and reptiles diverged over 300 million years ago when various versions of the keratin gene arose. Keratin is the protein that gives reptiles and birds their feathers and scales. It produces hair in mammals in a somewhat different form. At the same time, glands developed at the roots of mammals' hair, resulting in sweat and milk glands.

Fully developed mammals first appeared 200 million years ago. A tiny mammalian fossil unearthed in China that dates from 160 million years ago, making it the earliest near-complete specimen yet identified. Rugosodon ('wrinkle-tooth') was a shrew-like species that was only around 17 cm long. Its teeth indicate that it was an omnivore capable of eating plants, insects, and worms and that it was warm-blooded and hairy. Despite being outnumbered in both numbers and size, the mammals survived thanks to their warm blood, which allowed them to remain active at night when the giant reptiles were likely to be dormant. These little warm-blooded organisms may have then emerged from their hiding places to search for insects and other small animals. Some mammals, such as the repenomamus, grew to be the size of cats and may have even devoured tiny dinosaurs. However, these early mammals effectively lived in the shadow of the reptiles. This state persisted for a long time – 135 million years – until the disaster that wiped out non-avian dinosaurs as well as much else. The small mammals, on the other hand, managed to survive and swiftly evolved into new species in order to reclaim lost habitat in the world's ecosystems. The first mammalian fossils that have been positively identified as marsupials.

The marsupials, it appears, were still emerging from the early mammal stock at this time. Meanwhile, on the northern supercontinent, rudimentary mammals were emerging. They were supposed to come up with a new technique to feed their young. Rather than moving them to an external pouch at an early stage, they were kept within the female's body and maintained by a mechanism known as the placenta.

However, the southern supercontinent's parts were drifting apart, and South America was slowly heading northwards. It eventually connected with North America by a land bridge in the Panamanian borderlands. The placental animals descended this corridor to contest the control of South America with the marsupial occupants. Many marsupial species vanished as a result of this conflict, leaving just the fierce, opportunistic opossums. As the Virginia opossum has done today, some of them entered the invaders' territory and colonized North America. The marsupials that resided in the southern supercontinent's central region, on the other hand, did not survive. Antarctica was formed from this massive patch of land. It floated over the South Pole, where it grew so frigid that it formed an enormous ice sheet, rendering life on the ground uninhabitable. However, geologists have discovered fossils that prove this was formerly marsupial territory. The species on the supercontinent's third portion, on the other hand, had it better. This was Australia, after all. It moved north and east into the void of the Pacific basin, being completely isolated from the rest of the world. As a result, over the past 50 million years, its marsupials have developed in isolation. Taking advantage of the diverse range of surroundings accessible to them, they evolved into a variety of various sorts throughout the course of this long era.

Platypus feeding on a worm underwater. (© John Carnemolla/Getty Images)

An Echidna, a species of egg-laying mammal. (© David Cunningham/Getty Images)

All mammals have discovered ways to provide considerably more than could possibly be packed into a shelled egg. Marsupials were among the first mammals to appear on the northern supercontinent. However, it is highly doubtful that they attained the same advanced levels of efficiency that Australian marsupials do now. The northern approach, on the other hand, permits the young to stay in the uterus for an extended period of time. It does so through the placenta, a flat disc that attaches to the uterine wall and is linked to the foetus via the umbilical cord. The placenta's connection with the uterine wall is extensively convoluted, resulting in a large surface area between the placenta and maternal tissues. The interchange between the mother and the foetus takes place here. Although blood does not travel directly from mother to child, oxygen from her lungs and nutrients from her diet, both dissolved in her blood, diffuse over the junction and into the foetus' blood. There's also traffic going the opposite way. The foetus waste products are absorbed by the mother's blood and subsequently expelled through her kidneys. All of this adds up to a lot of metabolic difficulties. The mammalian sexual cycle includes the creation of a fresh egg on a regular basis. A fresh egg is produced on a regular basis throughout the mammalian sexual cycle. The marsupial has no difficulty with this because the neonate emerges before the next egg is supposed to be generated in every species. The placental foetus, on the other hand, remains in the uterus for considerably longer. As a result, the placenta secretes a hormone that causes the mother's sexual cycle to be suspended for as long as the placenta is there, preventing any additional eggs from being generated to compete with the foetus in the uterus. There's another issue as well. Genetically, the tissues of the foetus and the mother are not the same. They have elements of their father in them. As a result, when it is attached to the mother's body, it has the same danger of immunological rejection as a transplant. The exact mechanism by which the placenta

69

prevents this is unknown, but it appears that a specific element of the mother's immune response is shut off at the start of pregnancy. As a result, whales and seals may bear their unborn offspring for months in frigid waters. No marsupial with a pouch full of airbreathing neonates could ever pull it off. This placental strategy would prove to be one of the most important elements in mammals' eventual success in colonizing the whole globe.

The reptiles' dominion lasted a long time. Around 250 million years ago, they ascended to rule. They'd rummaged through the woods and feasted on the swamp's rich flora. Plant-eating creatures had evolved into meat-eating ones, which preyed on the plant eaters. Then, 66 million years ago, all of these organisms, as well as many more, vanished in a global catastrophe.

Early on, a few insectivores specialized in consuming only one type of invertebrate: ants and termites. There's little doubt that a lengthy, sticky tongue is the greatest tool for the task. Many unrelated organisms have created such an organ on their own as a result of eating this diet. The numbat, an Australian marsupial anteater, possesses one. The echidna has done the same. Even anteaters, woodpeckers, and wrynecks have one that fits inside a specific compartment of the skull and extends around the eye socket in certain species. The tongue evolved by early placental animals is the most severe example of such a tongue. Pangolins are medium-sized animals with short legs and long prehensile tails that live in Africa and Asia. There are eight main types of pangolins. The largest of them can stretch its tongue 40 cm beyond its mouth. It is housed in a sheath that stretches all the way down the front of the animal's chest and connects to its pelvis. All of the pangolin's teeth have been gone, and its lower jaw has been reduced to two slivers of bone. The ants and termites gathered by the mucus on the tongue are eaten and then mashed by the stomach's muscular motions, which are horny and occasionally include stones to aid in the grinding process. The pangolin must be adequately safeguarded due to its lack of teeth and ability to turn quickly. It has horny scales on its armour that overlap like shingles on a roof. When the animal senses danger, it tucks its head towards its stomach and curls up into a ball, its powerful tail tightly clutched about it. A pangolin cannot be made to unwind after it has horny scales on its armour that overlap like shingles on a roof. When the animal senses danger, it tucks its head towards its stomach and curls up into a ball, its powerful tail tightly clutched about it. A pangolin cannot be made to unwind after it has been rolled, in my experience. The only way to see what it looks like is to leave it alone long enough for it to get enough confidence to pop its head out cautiously and then trundle away. The animal can close its nose and ears using specific muscles, yet it appears unconcerned with bug bites outside of these hyper-sensitive locations. The pangolin may occasionally lift its armour and entice ants to crawl in between its plates and onto its skin, allowing it to cope with parasites it can't scratch off. For an Art Exhibition, I created a 3D African pangolin out of cardboard with a group of creative students, and I also displayed my specimens there. Despite its extraordinary uniqueness, the pangolin is also the world's most trafficked animal, since it is killed for its flesh and the prospect of using its scales for medicinal purposes.

All of these species are scavengers of crawling insects. However, insects can fly as well. Put up a white screen in a tropical forest at night, illuminate it with a mercury vapour lamp that produces a light that is particularly attractive to insects, and the screen will be teeming with insects of an incredible array and in exceptional numbers. Insects took to the air 400 million years ago and had it all to themselves until the arrival of flying reptiles such as pterosaurs 200 million years later. We don't know if the reptiles flew at night, but given the reptiles' difficulty in controlling body temperature, it seems improbable. As a result, any creature who mastered the art of flying in the dark was in for a huge feast of nocturnal insects. This was accomplished by yet another insectivore variety. We think we know how the mammals got into the air. A strange species resides in Malaysia and the Philippines, and zoology has had to create its own classification system for it. The colugo is its name. It's roughly the size of a big rabbit, but its entire body is covered with a gently furred cloak of skin, beautifully mottled in grey and cream, from its neck to the end of its tail. This skin renders the animal nearly undetectable when it hangs beneath a branch or rubs against a tree trunk, and when it extends its legs, the cloak transforms into a gliding membrane.

In the same way, the marsupial sugar glider flies through the air. Two separate groups of squirrels have also developed the ability. The colugo, on the other hand, has the largest and most fully encompassing membrane horny scales on its armour that overlap like shingles on a roof. When the animal senses danger, it tucks its head towards its stomach and curls up into a ball, its powerful tail tightly clutched about it. A pangolin cannot be made to unwind after it has been rolled, in my experience. The only way to see what it looks like is to leave it alone long enough for it to get enough confidence to pop its head out cautiously and then trundle away. The animal can close its nose and ears using specific muscles, yet it appears unconcerned with bug bites outside of these hyper-sensitive locations. The pangolin may occasionally lift its armour and entice ants to crawl in between its plates and onto its skin, allowing it to cope with parasites it can't scratch off. For an Art Exhibition, I created a 3D African pangolin out of cardboard with a group of creative students, and I also displayed my specimens there. Despite its extraordinary uniqueness, the pangolin is also the world's most trafficked animal, since it is killed for its flesh and the prospect of using its scales for medicinal purposes.

All of these species are scavengers of crawling insects. However, insects can fly as well. Put up a white screen in a tropical forest at night, illuminate it with a mercury vapour lamp that produces a light that is particularly attractive to insects, and the screen will be teeming with insects of an incredible array and in exceptional numbers. Insects took to the air 400 million years ago and had it all to themselves until the arrival of flying reptiles such as pterosaurs 200 million years later. We don't know if the reptiles flew at night, but given the reptiles' difficulty in controlling body temperature, it seems improbable. As a result, any creature who mastered the art of flying in the dark was in for a huge feast of nocturnal insects. This was accomplished by yet another insectivore variety. We think we know how the mammals got into the air. A strange species resides in Malaysia and the Philippines, and zoology has had to create its own classification system for it. The colugo is its name. It's roughly the size of a big rabbit, but its entire body is covered with a gently furred cloak of skin, beautifully mottled in grey and cream, from its neck to the end of its tail. This skin renders the animal nearly undetectable when it hangs beneath a branch or rubs against a tree trunk, and when it extends its legs, the cloak transforms into a gliding membrane.

In the same way, the marsupial sugar glider flies through the air. Two separate groups of squirrels have also developed the ability. The colugo, on the other hand, has the largest and most fully encompassing membrane of the group, indicating that it adopted the habit early in mammalian evolution. It is unquestionably the most basic member of the group and appears to be a direct descendent of an insectivore ancestor. It has stayed uncontested – and unmodified – after perfecting a way of life. There is no connection to bats because their structure is vastly different, but it is a sign of a stage that certain early insectivores may have gone through on their path to flapping flight and becoming those really skilled aeronauts, bats. That development took place quite early, since fully grown bat fossils have been discovered dating back 50 million years. They most likely grew to occupy one of the empty aerial niches left by the pterosaurs' extinction, some of which were likely nocturnal. The bat's flight membrane runs along the extended second finger, not only from the wrist like the colugo's. Many of the adaptations produced by birds to reduce body weight have been adopted by bats. To sustain the flying membrane, the bones in the tail have been thinned to mere straws or have been eliminated entirely. Though they haven't lost their teeth, their heads are small and snub-nosed, allowing them to fly without being nose-heavy. They have one issue that birds don't have to deal with. Their mammalian ancestors had perfected the process of using a placenta to nurture their offspring. The evolutionary process is seldom reversed, and no bat has ever returned to producing eggs. As a result, the mother bat must fly while carrying the weight of her growing fetus. As a result, bat twins are uncommon, and just one young is usually produced each season in practically every case. This implies that the females must compensate by reproducing over a lengthy period of time in order to ensure the effective survival of their genes, and bats are astonishingly long-lived creatures for their size, with some having a life expectancy of nearly twenty years. All bats now fly at night, and this was most likely always the case because the birds had already claimed the day. The bats, on the other hand, had to evolve an effective navigating system in order to do so. It is based on ultrasounds produced by shrews and, most likely, many other insectivores. They're used by bats for sonar, an advanced kind of echolocation that uses frequencies that are well outside the range of the human ear. Most bats utilize sonar to fly and employ noises ranging from 50,000 to 200,000 vibrations per second. Echolocation developed more than once in bats, according to genetic research. Surprisingly, the same genes that cause echolocation in bats also cause it in the dolphin, which is the only other mammal with this capacity. Before generating the next signal, most bats wait for the previous signal to be echoed. The shorter the time it takes for an echo to return the the bat to an object, therefore the bat may increase the number of signals it transmits as it gets closer to its prey, allowing it to follow its target with greater accuracy as it moves in for the kill. Hunting success, on the other hand, might result in temporary blindness, as a bat's mouth cannot squeak normally while it is loaded with an insect. Some species sidestep this difficulty by squeaking through their nostrils, developing a range of bizarre nasal outgrowths that help to focus the squeak's beam and act as little megaphones. The ears are then able to detect the echoes. So many bats' faces are dominated by sonar equipment, which includes intricate transparent ears ribbed with cartilage and interwoven with an internal tracery of red blood vessels, as well as leaves, spikes, and spears on the snout to guide sound.

Bats don't all eat insects. Some have found that nectar and pollen are extremely nourishing, and have tuned their flying skills to the point that they can hover in front of flowers like hummingbirds, probing deep into the petals with their thin tongues to collect nectar. Some plants, like many others, have evolved to rely on insects as pollinators, while others rely on bats. Some cactus plants, for example, only bloom at night. These are huge, robust, and pale, as a colour has little significance in the dark. Their perfume, on the other hand, is heavy and intense, and the petals extend well over the stem's armour of spines, allowing bats to visit without hurting their wing membranes. Fruit is the only food for the largest of all bats. They are called flying foxes not only because of their size - some have a wingspan of one and a half metres - but also because their coats are reddish brown and their faces are long-nosed and very fox-like. They have huge eyes but only small ears and no nose-leaf, indicating that they are not echolocating flyers. Other bats have taken to eating meat. Some eat roosting birds, others frogs and tiny reptiles, while one is said to eat other bats. Even an American species manage to catch fish. It thumps up and down across ponds, lakes, and even the sea after dusk. Most bats' tail membrane reaches their ankles. It is fastened considerably higher up at the knee in the fishing bat, leaving the legs completely free. As a result, the bat may trail its feet in the water while folding

(Left to right) An image of a bat feeding on pollen from a plant. The Fruit Bat has excellent peripheral vision. This is necessary for it to employ in conjunction with its sense of smell to discover food sources. Its senses aid it in escaping from dangerous conditions. (© Ethan Tremblay/Getty Images)

Bats that feed on insects however depend entirely on their echolocation and thus don't depend much on sight. 70% of bats eat insects like moths, mosquitoes, and beetles. (© Paul Golley /Getty Images)

up its tail to keep the membrane out of the way. It has big toes that are furnished with hook-shaped claws. The bat takes the fish into its jaws and kills it with a strong crunch of its teeth as it strikes it. On the other hand, the vampire bat has evolved into a highly specialized creature. It has two triangular razors on its front teeth. It gently lands on a sleeping creature, a cow, or even a person. Its saliva includes an anticoagulant, so when its victim's blood emerges, it will seep for a long period before forming a clot. The vampire then sits down next to the wound and drinks the blood. They employ a very faint kind of sonar, and it is stated that dogs, whose hearing is tuned to extremely high frequencies as well, are rarely attacked by vampires since they can hear them approaching. This extraordinary adaptation and Characteristics have led to over 1,400 different species of bats.

Whales and dolphins, like humans, are warm-blooded, milk-producing mammals with a lengthy history, with fossils reaching back over 50 million years to the beginning of the great mammalian radiation. We have a group of fossils that demonstrate the evolution of these creatures in remarkable detail. Semi-aquatic creatures the size of a large dog were their oldest known ancestors. Animals with more paddle-like legs, around the size of sea lions, followed. The forelimbs have been transformed into paddles. Though there are a few tiny bones buried deep in the whale's body to suggest that the whale's ancestors did, at one point, have back legs, the rear limbs have been destroyed entirely. The action of fur as an insulator on air trapped between the hairs is what distinguishes mammals. As a result, it's of little use to a creature that never visits dry ground, and the whales have lost it as well, though there remain traces, such as a few hairs on the nose to show that they formerly had a coat. Whales, on the other hand, have evolved blubber, a thick layer of fat beneath the skin that keeps their body heat from escaping even in the coldest oceans. In the sea, mammals' need for air for breathing is a serious limitation, but the whale has overcome this by breathing even more effectively than most terrestrial animals. With regular breath, humans only clear roughly 15% of the air in their lungs. In one of its booming, spouting exhalations, the whale expels around 90% of its exhausted air. As a result, it only needs to breathe at extremely lengthy intervals. It also possesses a very high proportion of myoglobin, a protein that allows it to store oxygen, in its muscles. The fin-back whale, for example, may dive to a depth of 500 meters and swim for forty minutes without taking a breath using these strategies. But whales like land-dwelling animals, and each also has different diets. One type of whale, for example, has specialized in eating krill, which are small shrimp-like crustaceans that swarm in large clouds in the water. Teeth are useless to animals who eat ants, and they are useless to those who consume krill. As a result, like anteaters, these whales have lost their teeth. Instead, they have baleen, which are feathered horn sheets that hang like stiff, horizontal curtains from either side of the roof of the mouth. The whale takes a large mouthful of water in the midst of the krill shoal, half-closes its jaws, and then expels the water by thrusting its tongue forward, allowing the krill to be eaten while the water is evacuated. Baleen whales have grown to enormous proportions on such a diet. The blue whale is the largest of them all, reaching lengths of over 30 meters and weighing more than twenty-five bull elephants (200 tons). Their tongue alone can weigh as much as an elephant. Their hearts are as much as a car. Being huge has a good side to it for a whale. The larger you are and the smaller the ratio between your volume and surface area, the easier it is to maintain body temperature. The dinosaurs were influenced by this tendency, although their size was restricted by the mechanical strength of bone. Legs would just shatter over a certain weight. Whales aren't as hindered. Their bones primarily serve to provide stiffness. The water provides support for their bodies.

As a result, baleen whales have grown to be the biggest living creatures of any sort to have ever existed on Earth, weighing four times as much as the heaviest known dinosaur. There are also other whales that feed on a larger prey, these are the toothed whales The squid-eating sperm whale, the largest of all, is just half the size of a blue whale. The smaller whales, such as dolphins, porpoises, and killer whales, hunt both fish and squid and have evolved into extraordinarily fast swimmers, with some reportedly reaching speeds of over 40 kilometres per hour. When travelling at such speeds, navigating becomes crucial. The lateral line system helps fish, but mammals have lost it long back in their evolution, and toothed whales instead have sonar, a mechanism based on the noises employed by shrews and refined by bats. The larynx and the melon, an organ at the front of the skull, produce ultrasound in dolphins. They employ frequencies of roughly 200,000 vibrations per second, which are similar to bat frequencies. They may use it to not only detect obstructions in their way but also to determine the nature of the items ahead based on the quality of the echo.

The enormous whales have voices as well. Every spring, humpback whales, one of the baleen whales, assemble in Hawaii to give birth to their young and mate. Some of them even have the ability to sing. A series of yelps, growls, high-pitched squeals and long-drawn-out rumbles make up their song. Humans can recognize each individual whale by its song, and if we can, then whales should be able to as well. Because water transmits sound better than air, it's possible that parts of these songs, particularly the low-vibrating notes, can be heard by other whales twenty, thirty, or even fifty kilometres distant, telling them of the community's whereabouts and activities.

Aside from insects, fish, and krill, plants were another source of nutrition to be exploited. Some grass-eating species emerged, and they began to migrate from the forest to the plains to graze. They were pursued by flesh-eaters, and the two interdependent societies evolved side by side in the open, each increase in hunting efficiency prompting defensive responses from the prey. The leaves of a second set of critters were discovered high in the treetops. Each group requires its own chapter, the first because they are so numerous, and the second because of our egocentrism — after all, those tree-dwellers were our ancestors. We may witness some of these transitions in our great ape cousins, from those who utilize tools to those who communicate via sign language.

The story of evolution is ever more diverse and challenging to understand, new discoveries are changing our understanding of evolution every time, and so life still to this day continues to evolve.....

CHAPTER II

The Holocene & The 6th Mass Extinction

""

 في الأرض وفي البحر ، عاش أجدادنا ونموا في هذه البيئة. لقد تمكنوا من القيام بذلك لأنهم أدركوا الحاجة إلى الحفاظ عليه ، وأن يأخذوا منه فقط ما يحتاجون إليه للعيش ، وأن يحافظوا عليه للأجيال القادمة.

On land and in the sea, our fore-fathers lived and
survived in this environment. They were able to do so
because they recognized the need to conserve it, to take
from it only what they needed to live, and to preserve i
for succeeding generations.

H.H Sheikh Zayed Bin Sultan Al Nahyan

As we began to evolve, our brains began to increase in size at such a rate that we were acquiring one of our most characteristic features–a capacity to develop cultures to a unique degree. To an evolutionary biologist, the term 'culture' describes the information that can be passed from one individual to another by teaching or imitation. Only a handful of other species show any signs of having a culture. Chimpanzees and bottle-nosed dolphins are two of them. Culture transformed the way we evolved. Whereas other species depended on physical changes over generations, we could produce an idea that brought significant change within a generation. Tricks such as finding the plants that yield water even during a drought, crafting a stone tool for skinning a kill, lighting a fire or cooking a meal, or even using herbs to heal wounds that we had got during a hunt, could be passed from one human to another during a single lifetime. Our ancestors' brains expanded at an extraordinary speed, enabling us to learn, store and spread ideas. But, ultimately, the physical changes in their bodies slowed almost to a halt. By some 200,000 years ago, anatomically modern humans, Homo sapiens–people like you and me–had appeared. We have changed physically very little since then. But, despite our ingenious culture, our lives were not easy. The environment was harsh and, more importantly, unpredictable. The world, in general, was a lot colder than now. The sea level was much lower. Freshwater was harder to find, and global temperatures fluctuated greatly within relatively short periods of time. We may have had bodies and brains very similar to those we have now, but because the environment was so unstable, it was hard to survive.

But then, approximately 10,000 years ago, something truly remarkable happened. The climate stabilized. The natural system that we were living in, was filled with billions of individuals, and millions of different plant and animal species. They had evolved into something extraordinarily complex, yet interconnected. Leading their own lives. But lives that are connected intimately to the lives of others around them. The astonishing development of the web of life as we know it, was made possible by nature's many years of experimentation, evolution and diversification of life. From the largest to the smallest organisms in the environment, this web binds them all together. Each habitat was also a part of a bigger system, the web of ecosystems that made up the biosphere. This extraordinarily interconnected diverse system was able to supply us with fresh water, abundant fish and meat, timber to build our homes and to keep us warm, fertile land, pollinators for our crops, even able to regulate the seasons, and bring dependable weather. By working so efficiently in absorbing carbon from the atmosphere, recycling nutrients and water the bewildering variety of life helped to bring stability to our restless planet. This was the Holocene, an Epoch that began 12,000 to 11,500 years ago at the close of the Paleolithic Ice Age and continues through today. The glaciers of the late Paleolithic retreated as Earth began to warm. Forest replaced the tundra. The extremely huge mammals that had adapted to harsh cold, such as mammoth and wooly rhinoceros, became extinct when the temperature changed. These "mega animals" were a major source of food for humans, but with their decline, we began to rely more on smaller wildlife and increased our collection of plant resources to supplement our diet. These dependable conditions made the ecosystems resilient, and gave us the services of nature that we rely upon. It was these stable conditions that also led to the evolution of the largest animal ever to live on earth; an animal whose size is half of the length of a football field, and weighing up to 200 tons, it tongues alone can weigh as much as an elephant, their hearts as much as an automobile, the blue whale.

So, the flourishing biodiversity of the Holocene helped to moderate the global temperatures of Earth, and the living world settled into a gentle, reliable annual rhythm-the seasons. On the tropical plains, dry and rainy seasons alternated with clockwork regularity. In Asia and Oceania, the winds changed direction at the same time each year, delivering the monsoon on cue. In northern regions, the temperatures rose above 15°C in March, triggering spring, and then stayed high until October when they dipped and brought autumn. The Holocene was our Garden of Eden. Those early humans moved from Africa to the middle east. Traveling from Africa to Arabia today means crossing the red sea. Around 130,000 years ago, the Red sea was much lower than it is today. This means that crossing from Africa to Arabia would have been like crossing a small river. We now know from Jebel Faya, in the UAE that this is one of the routes that humans took into Arabia. During this time, there was also more rainfall in Arabia than there is now. The humans arriving in Arabia found grasslands and large numbers of Wild animals. The newly arriving humans kept on the move. One group moved to Jebel Faya and left their distinctive stone tools. Almost as soon as the environment stabilized, groups of people living in the Middle East began to abandon gathering plants and hunting animals and take up to a completely new way of life. They started to farm.

Farming transformed the relationship between humankind and nature. We were, in a very small way, taming a part of the wild world-controlling our environment to a modest degree. We built walls to protect plants from the wind. We shaded our animals from the Sun by planting trees. Using their manure, we fertilized the land where they grazed. We ensured that our crops flourished in times of drought, keeping them watered by building channels from rivers and lakes. We removed plants that competed with the ones we found useful, and covered whole hillsides with those we particularly favored. Both the animals and the plants we selected in this way also began to change. As we protected the grazing animals, they no longer needed to guard against attacks from predators or fight for access to females. We weeded our plots so that our food plants could grow without competition from other species and get all the nitrogen, water and sunlight they needed. They produced larger grains, and bigger fruits and tubers.

The farmers' work was hard. They suffered frequent droughts and famine. But eventually they were able to produce more than they needed for their own immediate requirements. Compared to their hunter-gathering neighbors, they were able to raise bigger families. After feeding the family, the farmers were able to use any surplus to trade for other goods, from carpenters or fishermen. As the number of traders increased, the markets developed into towns and then cities in many of the fertile river valleys. Civilisation had started. Water power, steam power, electrification was invented and refined–and eventually all the achievements with which we are familiar today were established. But each generation, in these ever-more complex societies, was able to develop and progress only because the natural world continued to be stable and could be relied upon to deliver the commodities and conditions that we needed the most. The benign environment of the Holocene, and the marvellous biodiversity that guaranteed it, became more important to us than ever.

Before the Holocene, the human population was essentially constrained by the same forces that limit other living organisms. Natural population balances are produced by limiting elements in the environment, such as the availability of food, water, and shelter, evolutionary interactions like predator/prey ratios, or the existence of viruses. A population will typically grow until it achieves its carrying capacity, or the amount of organisms an environment can sustain without suffering negative consequences, after which it will level out. Continuous growth that exceeds the carrying capacity typically leads to a crash (a rapid decline to a level far below the carrying capacity). The population might rebound if there is still enough genetic variation, but it potentially might go extinct. However, the Holocene changed all that for us. We have moved from a small species on a big planet, to a species so dominant that our impacts rival the forces of nature.

The Holocene gave us stability, allowing Humans to get around those limitations. We were the first animals to expand the carrying capacity of our existing habitat; we began to farm and agriculture was able to expand the number of people that the ecosystem could sustain. Population growth commenced gradually. At the end of the first century, there were roughly 170 million people on Earth; by 1800, there were more than 1 billion.

For the first time in the history of the planet, the nine planetary boundaries were all in harmony and within the safe zone during the Holocene, which was our ideal world. Earth is a living planet that functions similarly to a living, breathing organism. Its habitats, which are home to many species, function like its organs. Each having a particular responsibility for maintaining the health of the earth. The poles of our globe deflect sunlight away from it, keeping the earth cold like an air conditioning system. The sea ice acts as a soil, preserving algae that support the extraordinarily productive food chains in the frigid oceans. Similar to the arteries and veins in the human body, freshwater networks crisscross the surface of the environment, distributing life-giving water and nutrients. Globally extensive forests and the billions of microscopic floating plants that cover the surface of our oceans help to keep the atmosphere stable by storing carbon and releasing oxygen. Mangroves and coral reefs along the coast serve as breakwaters, shielding the land behind from eroding waves and providing the ideal habitat for young fish. And in order to absorb as much of the sun's energy as possible, jungles stack one plant on top of another. This process generates water and oxygen that are used well beyond the forests. Each of these biomes needs the plants, animals, fungi, and bacteria that live there to function properly. Only as an ensemble can the living world work its magic. Biodiversity equals stability. And no species on Earth has benefited more from this fact than us humans.

We wasted little time in establishing our dominance over the world; we quickly established ourselves, and our populations grew. We mechanized our societies after discovering fossil fuels. Human

populations were able to increase dramatically thanks to the Industrial Revolution of the 19th century. Death rates decreased as a result of industrialization, better sanitation, and medical treatment, while birth rates in much of the world continued to rise. Thanks to science, we have continued to enhance the planet's carrying capacity, but not its size,. In 1955, three billion people live on Earth . We are still a small world on a large planet since we have not yet had any impacts on a planetary scale. Ten years after the end of World War II, trust, reasonable peace, and technology all became available. At that point, the Great Acceleration began. The Great Acceleration, which is still going on now, has brought about unprecedented change. We have accomplished a great deal in this period. Technology is the global force behind advancements. More than ever, our globe is becoming interconnected. Additionally, business has expanded significantly. There has never been a time when production and growth were this high. However, industrialisation and so-called technology may soon be the main factors contributing to the extinction of humanity and the earth.

Biodiversity was already declining when I was born in 2004, although the amount of carbon in our atmosphere was just 376.8 ppm, much lower than today. My grandfather, on the other hand, spoke of his own childhood experiences, which clearly indicated a time when nature determined our survival. Mohammad Khaledi, born in 1954, is the name of my grandfather. His life was full of unique wildlife adventures back then, most of which happened by chance. He used to go to the desert with his father when he was about 5 years old; his father had a truck, and around the city of Shiraz back then, there were many types of wild animals, including leopards, wolves, bears, hyenas, and so on; they are still there, but their numbers have declined, and they can only be seen in the protected areas.

When he was a child, they had stopped for the night near a waterhole around evening time. Here he saw a very beautiful mammal, one with sky blue eyes, a light sandy colored body, and spots, it was the baby of a now elusive Persian Leopard (Panthera pardus tulliana), as soon as he saw it, he quickly ran to his father and said "come and look at this baby leopard, let's catch it, and take it with us," his father then stopped him and said "what do you mean catch it, you may not know it, but it's mother is looking at us from somewhere, and She can attack with the smallest movement from us." Such experiences are now only possible if you have a special permit to visit the protected areas, and even then, you cannot get so close to them. "The leopard was so beautiful and majestic," my grandfather said, "that I became trapped and mesmerized by its beauty." Although he begged his father as a child to capture and take the leopard, his father refused. On the other hand, his father was correct, in the case of wild animals, either the mother or the father watches over and protects the offspring from a distance. My grandfather was a witness to many of these breathtaking moments as a child.

However, while there may have been over two to three hundred of these leopards and other wildlife found at the time, they are now all on the verge of extinction, with only a few, possibly a population as small as the fingers on your hand, remaining.

Previously, there was a population of big cats in Iran's Mazandaran province. When my grandfather was on another trip around the rainforest with his father, a majestic, yet elusive of these striped cats was crossing the road, it was a Caspain Tiger (ببر مازندران), this male he saw in 1966 was possibly the last of these majestic cats, which sadly none remain today due to hunting and habitat loss.

The wildlife all around became increasingly difficult to find as time passed, but my grandfather witnessed the extraordinary wildlife of the Holocene on the outskirts or sometimes within the town.

Another memory he mentioned was a terrifying experience he had in his old house. There were snakes here that lived and thrived in the environments outside the house while causing no harm to anyone. He recalls seeing an enormous snake emerge from a hole and move across the roof of a house, possibly a Chernov Blunt-nosed Viper (Macrovipera lebetina cernovi), its head bent and tilted towards the neighbor's house to feed on sparrows or their chicks within a nest there. He had an axe with him when he saw the snake and brought it to scare it away. But this snake was so huge and terrifying that he described it as "some 30 to 35 mm wide and as long as nearly 2 meters long." It seems to have a yellow body with brown spots. The snake was too busy with its head in a sparrow nest to notice my grandfather, but as he brought his axe up to scare it, he was terrified and didn't dare bring his axe down, so he left it to continue living its own life. It later caught a sparrow, which it began to swallow, and my grandfather gradually moved away from it, as it was very frightening due to its sheer size.

Unfortunately, snakes like these can no longer reach these sizes. Even if you find one alive, it is said that you are extremely fortunate. I nearly searched everywhere in July 2022 for even one snake to study, but their numbers are far too low. I heard of people seeing them, but they were either intentionally squashed by cars or killed in other ways. During my time in Iran, I heard of a one-meter-long snake being killed by a factory's workers simply because it was feeding on a sparrow, they had hit it so hard that its head was squished. This is all due to a lack of education and unnecessary fear; snakes are not out to get us, nor are they dangerous unless irritated or in a fight-or-flight situation; nevertheless, they play one of the most important key roles in the ecosystem, providing food for local Indian mongooses, birds of prey, and much more, as well as keeping the population of invasive rodents under control. Unfortunately, when people see these unique serpents, the first thought that comes to mind is to kill them. However, there are far

Since the very beginning, my grandfather has been my supporter and inspiration. He himself is a wonderful animal enthusiast, an electric engineer and a Botanist.

more human options; if they are in the wild, let them survive, they won't mind you until you try to get them, enjoy them as they are and if they are in other places, such as houses, call animal rescue centers to relocate them, remember that now even if you see a snake, you are very fortunate.

So, wildlife was not as elusive and rare as it is today, and it nearly flourished everywhere. My grandfather also owned a farm land on the outskirts of town. During the winter, you might see Indian wolves (Canis lupus pallipes), which travel in smaller packs and are less vocal than other grey wolf variants. However, the Indian wolf is one of the world's most endangered grey wolf populations. During the spring, you could see herds of wild boars (Sus scrofa) or wild pigs. My grandfather had planted corn on his farm, and wild boars have a habit of rolling over the corn, causing extensive damage. The wild boar is an intelligent animal, though its sense of smell and hearing is acute, its eyesight is poor.

Many animals came to the farm, some as one-time visitors and others as permanent residents. An Indian crested porcupine (Hystrix indica) is one example of an animal that has made a permanent home here. A section of the farm was devoted to the cultivation of sweet melons, and every night a porcupine came to eat these melons. The Indian crested porcupine has multiple layers of modified hair known as quills, with longer, thinner quills covering a layer of shorter, thicker quills. The quills are brown or black with white and black bands that alternate. They are keratin-based and relatively flexible. Because each quill is connected to a muscle at its base, the porcupine can raise its quills when threatened. My grandfather had tried numerous times to catch it, but he didn't want to end up full of quills because, while they go in smoothly, they have microscopic bars that latch onto flesh, making them painful to remove, so whenever this porcupine was threatened, it rattled the quills to produce a warning sound. Many of them are hunted for their flesh, believing that they serve some medical purpose, but contrary to popular belief, they cannot shoot their quills. So, with its incredible sense of smell, this porcupine would find those melons every night and eat them by opening them with its chisel-like incisors. So, my grandfather set traps, an enormous trap door cage with a melon as a lure, the porcupine, with curiosity and hunger, ventured inside and was caught. It was later released far away from the farm, in a better natural habitat, so it wouldn't harm the crops, as they don't feed on the entire melons and only eat a little while moving to the next melon.

So, despite being a simple farm, the wildlife was so abundant that it came into direct contact with humans. My grandfather had three little dog pups on his farm. These are rather tasty meals for a mammal whose African cousins are even feared by lions; it is well adapted to anchoring exceptionally strong jaw muscles that give it enough bite-force to splinter a camel's thigh bone. They are a smaller primitive hyena species known as the striped Hyena (Hyaena hyaena), whose muscular body and striped body frighten many animals, including humans. Although a scavenger they feed on whatever they can overcome, among their favorites seem to be dog flesh. One of these nocturnal beasts had visited my grandfather's farm once, and the three puppies had vanished the next day. Most animals fear dogs, not only for their strength, but also for their ability to make friends with the most dangerous animal on the planet: humans. Hyenas are feared for their strength and savage behavior, despite being one of the most effective decomposers and scavengers in an environment. They are so effective at what they do that they can eat whole bones or break them down into smaller pieces that can later be swallowed, which no other animal can do in a matter of days. Similarly, another trap cage was set, but the hyena would pass by the trap and not enter, so many attempts failed. However, once its thigh became stuck in the cage's door, and in its fear and struggle to escape, the beast savagely removed its own foot, escaping while leaving the foot behind. Many weeks later, the same hyena was seen with three legs near a road at night.

A book could be written to discuss all of my grandfather's experiences. However, I was born in the midst of Naturedecline. Nonetheless, most, if not all, people do not believe in climate change. I also had no idea about the alarming loss of nature until I experienced it for myself. I'm not sure if I was lucky or unlucky to be born during a period of nature's decline, because the chances of becoming someone like David Attenborough in the future are slim, because no one knows if there will be any nature left by then. However, it is unfortunate that people refuse to acknowledge the importance of nature and how much we rely on it. Being a young naturalist in the twenty-first century is difficult, not only because of nature's loss and disappearance, but also because nature now only flourishes outside of cities, and most of us are so connected to the civilized world that we forget nature. We must remember that the natural world exists alongside us and is the foundation of our own lives. They are living these lives all around us while we go about ours, and we are completely unaware of it.

Since the beginning of the industrial revolution, we have emitted 2400 billion tonnes of carbon dioxide. This is just one way that we have damaged the planet, we have so far sent many animals towards extinction, and once a species becomes our target, there is no place on earth that it can hide. When it first arose, the human species was unique. It was so intelligent and deft that it didn't need to adapt its physical appearance to live on the African plains, where it initially originated. It didn't require a body built for high-speed sprinting or slicing teeth to catch and kill other animals for sustenance since it could manufacture weapons to do it. It also didn't have to adapt physiologically to colonize environments that were cooler than the African plains. It could stay warm by wearing garments produced from the skins of the animals they slaughtered. With time, these bright, resourceful individuals grew in number

(Top to bottom) Image of a male Persian leopard (Panthera pardus tulliana) , captured from a camera after marking its territory, Shiraz Iran. An Image of a striped Hyena (Hyaena hyaena) , they have an cultural reputation as child killers, witch transporters, grave robbers, and other absurd accusations. result, they have been persecuted on a larger level by humans in many regions (©Sanjeev Kumar /C Images). An Image of an Indian Crested porcupine (Hystrix indica) with erect spikes. (©MaZikab /C Images).

96

and dispersed around the globe. As the end of the Ice Age neared 40,000 years ago, individuals in Europe undoubtedly had a role in the extinction of the large cold-adapted creatures – huge cattle, sabre-toothed cats, and mammoths - as the planet warmed. The first species of animal that humans eliminated in history lived in Madagascar; it was thought that these birds, while being dangerous since they had a kick similar to an ostrich, that could open a man's stomach, yet they stood almost twice the size of an ostrich and weighed almost 4 times. They went extinct as a result of humans taking their massive eggs. These were Elephant birds, and their eggs could feed a whole family, and they went extinct sometime between 1000 and 1200 CE, and their egg shells still lie in Madagascar, graveyards showing the effect of humans, but they weren't alone; on the island of Mauritius in the Indian Ocean, Portuguese sailors arrived at the beginning of the sixteenth century, they discovered large flocks of flightless pigeons. Because the large lumbering birds were easy prey, the sailors nicknamed them dodos, which allegedly means "comic or foolish." The sailors slaughtered and ate a large number of them. The flesh was rough and unpalatable, according to all reports, but fresh meat of any type was what the seamen sought. Ships from all over the world began to visit the island on a regular basis, hoping to get a piece of the action. By 1690, the last dodo had been hunted down.

Europeans had already begun to settle in the lush areas of southern Africa at this time. They saw immense grasslands teeming with herds of blaubok, a large antelope, and quagga, a near relative of the zebra named for the sound of its barking cry. The quagga had striped forequarters like its zebra relatives, but plain brown hindquarters. Both species were hunted by the colonists for fun and because the wild herds grazed on the grass they needed for their tamed animals. Both the blaubok and the quagga were extinct by 1883. Around the same time as the Dutch were attacking large game in South Africa, British farmers in North America were dealing with the passenger pigeon, which was thought to be the most numerous birds at the time. Its flocks were so large that they clouded the sky, obliterating the sun and requiring days to pass. Their weight was so immense that branches snapped beneath them when they roosted in trees at night. Despite being murdered in large numbers, they appeared to be invulnerable. Entrants in competitive hunts had to kill at least thirty thousand birds in order to qualify for a reward. The flocks roamed the countryside in quest of nourishment. Occasionally, several years might pass without a visit to a certain location. Then, all of a sudden, people realized that the birds had not only failed to return for several seasons, but had also gone forever. In 1914, the final survivor, a female named Martha, died in a Cincinnati Zoo cage. We began eliminating species all over the world. Until a little over a century ago, Australia had a huge native carnivore. It looked like a striped dog, but it held its offspring in a pouch like kangaroos and other marsupials. It was given the scientific name Thylacinus cynocephalus, which means 'pouch-bearer with wolf head,' but most Australians nicknamed it the Tasmanian tiger and drove it to extinction because it destroyed their sheep. Living specimens were shipped all over the world to be seen and marvelled at as scientific marvels. However, their numbers decreased until only one survived, at Hobart Zoo. It died in 1936. These are only a few of the species that have been extinct since the dodo.

Since 1500, it is estimated that 900 species have gone extinct. This comprises 85 mammal, 159 bird, 35 amphibian, and 80 fish species that have been wiped out by hunters or animal predators that humans have brought with us as we moved over the globe. The Splendid Poison Frog (Dendrobates speciosus) was the most recent species to become extinct. It wasn't until the turn of the twentieth century that people realized the magnitude of the harm we're doing. European big-game hunters, ironically, were among the first to try to put a stop to it. They have competed with one another to obtain the largest horns borne by any given species since they first began exploring the wilder portions of Africa. However, no matter how daring and skilled the chase was or how precise and lethal the guns they had, previous records were proving hard to duplicate, much alone exceed. The hunters gradually realized what was going on. They were annihilating the same creatures they cherished. The wilderness was not limitless.

One species that big-game hunters treasured had nearly vanished from the wild by the 1950s. The Arabian oryx was an antelope with long, straight horns of unrivaled grace and grandeur. It is the UAE's national animal, and with that I have had the opportunity to work and witnesssomething absolutely spectacular for their species. Despite the fact that their numbers had declined, a few captives remained in zoos and private collections around Europe. All of the captive individuals were brought together in the Phoenix Zoo in Arizona, where the climate was similar to that of the species' natural habitat, and captive breeding commenced. Because the animals were acquired from various locations around Arabia, the new herd was genetically diverse, posing little risk of inbreeding. The number of animals soon grew, and by 1978, there were enough to risk returning to Arabia and releasing some. However, the major influence was made in the UAE by His Highness Sheikh Zayed. The Arabian Oryx was in danger of becoming extinct. He realized that such animals will suffer several threats as a result of increased urbanization, the use of contemporary technology, and non-sustainable human activities. In Al Ain, Sheikh Zayed established a captive breeding program for the endangered Arabian Oryx in 1968. Four Arabian Oryx heads (2 males and 2 females) were transported from Al Ain to Sir Bani Yas Island in 1978. This was the true start of the breeding effort on this island, and many other triumphs followed. In February 1999, there were 311 Arabian Oryx on the island, and by the end of 2011, there were 450 Arabian Oryx. Sheikh Zayed's program resulted in the release of Arabian Oryx both inside and beyond the UAE. I was a witness during this shift; in 2007, there were just 160 individuals in the UAE herd, but now there are over 6900, making it the world's biggest population, Thanks to His Highness Sheikh Zayed's efforts. Today, approximately a thousand Arabian oryx wander the desert that formerly served as their habitat. The conservation movement had begun. The giant panda, which was dangerously endangered at the time, became a symbol of the pressing need for conservation. Attempts by zoos in Europe and the United States to breed them in captivity failed miserably, and it appeared that the species was on the verge of extinction. However, Chinese zoologists studying captive animals figured out the species' complicated breeding cycle and began raising them in large enough numbers that some of them could be released back into the bamboo woods where they originated. The Birds, too, were in desperate need of assistance. The kakapo, New Zealand's huge flightless parrot, was previously widespread over the two major islands. However, Europeans arrived in the nineteenth century, bringing with them cats, dogs, stoats, and rats, all of which found the giant flightless birds easy prey. The species was on the verge of extinction by the 1980s. However, in 1987, the survivors, numbering 37 in all, were captured and released on three tiny offshore islands free of land-based predators. Its rehabilitation has been difficult due to the bird's rarity. Even under ideal circumstances, it does not reproduce every year, and even then, it only produces one or two eggs every season. So, despite the fact that its numbers are increasing, its survival is still uncertain.

So with humans came destruction even the largest habitat and the so called unlimited ocean were not safe. When we stand on land and we look out at the sea, you know, it's just this flat blue thing. But in fact, the open ocean is really the largest biome on our planet. The great whales, the world's largest mammals, greatly outweighing even the greatest dinosaurs, were likewise

In the Al Marmum Nature Reserve, filming & documenting Arabian Oryx populations.

A close-up image of 2 Arabian Oryx as they approach to explore me and the crew.

endangered. The great whales have been hunted for millennia by brave men in canoes using nothing more than a handheld harpoon. To begin with, the balance of power was with the whales. Not only did they dwarf their human hunters, but they were able to dive within seconds and escape into the depths of the ocean. In the late 19th and early 20th centuries, the vast majority of people who saw whales in nature were whalers. These were not whale watchers, but whale hunters. They killed for oil and baleen—the stiff, fringed plates hanging from the upper jaw of some whales. The whalers' main targets? Right whales, bowheads, and sperm whales—slower swimmers who would float when harpooned. But blue whales dive deep and swim fast—up to 30 miles an hour fast—faster than wind-powered ships could chase them. Even if whalers had managed to find their mark, without steam-powered winches, they could never have hauled a 200-ton blue whale carcass from the deep. That all changed in the 1870s with Norwegian whaler Svend Foyn. We invented ways of tracking whales down and stabbing them with harpoons that had explosive heads. Factories, some floating, some on land, were built that were capable of processing several giant carcasses in a day. Whaling had become industrialised. From an estimated 350,000 individuals in the pre-whaling years, some 99% of the population was wiped out.

The first whales evolved from land-living creatures. The size of terrestrial animals is limited by the mechanical strength of bone: above a certain weight, bone breaks. Aquatic animals, however, are supported by water so whales can grow much bigger than any land animal. And they do. Their nostrils migrated to the tops of their heads, their forelimbs and tails became paddles, and their hind limbs eventually vanished. For tens of millions of years, they were important members of the complex ecosystems of the open ocean, crisscrossing the seas in their hundreds of thousands. A key problem restricting life in the open ocean is the availability of nutrients. Where conditions are right, plants and animals live in the surface waters and, when they die, they drift continuously downwards as 'marine snow'. Where nutrients are not freely available, the surface waters of the oceans can be almost sterile. Just as land plants need fertiliser as well as sun and water, so do phytoplankton, the photosynthesising foundation of the ocean food web, need nitrogenous compounds in the sunlit surface waters if they are to thrive. There are places in the ocean where the decomposed marine snow is stirred and carried upwards by the currents flowing over submarine mountains and ridges, and here the phytoplankton-and hence fish populations-can flourish. But the rest of the open ocean would remain a vast, blue desert were it not for the whales. They are so big that when they dive to feed in the depths or rise to the surface to breathe, they create a great stirring of the water around them. That helps keep nutrients near the surface. And when they defecate, the waters around them are also greatly enriched. This 'whale pump', as it is often termed, is now recognised as a significant process in maintaining the fertility of the open ocean. Yet although dolphins and Cetaceans are still being hunted to this day, yet animals like whale's and dolphin's excrements alone are full of nutrients these are eaten by bird, and later carried away to land to fertilize the soil for good vegetations. So, despite whales living a lot far from us and we don't get to see them, their lives are somehow touching ours.

The ocean of the Holocene needed its whales to remain productive. In the twentieth century, men killed close to 3 million of them. More than 330,000 blue whales were slaughtered in the Southern Ocean alone in the first half of the twentieth century. Whales cannot withstand such a level of hunting for long. Given the chance, they are very long-lived. Sperm whales can live for 70 years. The females are not sexually mature until they are nine. Their pregnancy lasts for over a year and they give birth only once, every three to five years. As the industrial whalers became more and more efficient, they selected the largest animals when they had the choice, for they were the most profitable. The whales were unable to give birth fast enough to replace their dead.

However, In the late 1960s, an American biologist, Roger Payne turned from recording the ultrasonic sounds of bats to investigating claims from the US Navy that there were songs in the ocean. The Navy had set up listening stations for Soviet submarines and, as well as the signature sound of propellers, they were detecting strange, almost musical serenades. Payne discovered that the chief source of these songs were the 5,000 or so humpback whales that were still alive at the time. His recordings revealed that humpback songs are long and complex, and of such low frequency that they can carry for hundreds of kilometres through the water.

Humpbacks living in the same part of the ocean, learn their songs from each other. Each song has its own distinct theme on which each individual male will invent his own variations. These change over time. Whales, you might say, have a musical culture. Payne released his recordings on vinyl discs in the 1970s, and they became hugely popular, transforming the public's perception of whales. Their mournful songs were interpreted as cries for help. An anti-whaling campaign began with a few passionate supporters and rapidly developed into a mainstream activity. Now, it appears that most, if not all, whale species are beginning to regain their numbers.

But, unfortunately - and perhaps even more tragically - the most pervasive and insidious threats to the natural world presently are those that humans have generated accidentally. They're not that simple to fix. The Industrial Revolution, which would eventually sweep the globe, had begun. The smoke and pollutants emitted by coal-fired machinery wreaked havoc on the countryside and suffocated the environment. Few people thought that such gases would ultimately modify the chemical makeup of the atmosphere to the point that the entire planet's climate would be changed.

However, that process has begun and is now progressing at a breakneck pace, causing chaos.

All life on Earth, and human civilization, are sustained by vital biogeochemical systems, which are in delicate balance. However, our species – due largely to rapid population growth and explosive consumption – is destabilizing these Earth processes, endangering the stability of the "safe operating space for humanity." Humanity is already existing outside the safe operating space for at least four of the nine boundaries: climate change, biodiversity, land-system change, and biogeochemical flows (nitrogen and phosphorus imbalance).

Unfortunately for us, climate change represents just one of nine critical planetary boundaries, which the imprudent actions of our species risk dangerously destabilizing and overshooting. In the mid-2000s, Johan Rockström, founding director of Sweden's Stockholm Resilience Centre, gathered an international, interdisciplinary team of scientists to unite behind a single goal: define the boundaries for a "safe operating space for humanity" on Earth. They asked themselves: what are the safe operating limits of our planet, and what changes can we force on it before we trigger rapid, catastrophic environmental harm?

In 2009, the center published the Planetary Boundaries Framework, which outlined nine key processes, influenced by humanity, that threaten the stability of the entire Earth System. These are: climate change, biodiversity integrity (functional and genetic), ocean acidification, depletion of the ozone layer, atmospheric aerosol pollution, biogeochemical flows of nitrogen and phosphorus, freshwater use, land-system change, and the release of novel chemicals (including heavy metals, radioactive materials, plastics, and more).

Together, the stability of these nine processes is essential to maintaining the Earth's atmosphere, oceans and ecosystems in the delicate balance that has allowed human civilizations to flourish. However, these are also the processes that human activities have impacted most profoundly.

The researchers then estimated a limit for just how much human activities could exploit and alter each of these processes before the global system would pass a tipping point — a threshold beyond which we risk sending the Earth spiraling into a state that hasn't been experienced for the entirety of human existence, bringing extreme change that could crash civilization and endanger humanity.

However, the experts warn, these limits are estimates: what we don't know is how long we can keep pushing these key planetary boundaries before combined pressures lead to irreversible change and harm. Think of humanity, blindfolded, simultaneously walking toward nine cliff edges, and you gain some sense of the seriousness and urgency of our situation.

Since 1880, the global temperature has risen by 1.3 degrees Celsius, and the oceans have warmed as a result of the climatic change, rising approximately 3 inches since 1992. But climate change alone isn't much of a big deal, it is when joined with biodiversity loss, these are enormous catastrophes. Sadly, these 2 aren't the only problems facing our planet. The first fully synthetic plastic was manufactured in 1907, since then plastic has found its way onto land and beneath the waves, due to this the oceans are losing fertility, and every plastic ever made still exists on earth. The plastic we have released into the environment sadly never decomposes, but after many years they degraded into smaller microplastics, but until they get to this stage they kill many animals, and this is so severe that 100 million marine animals die each year from plastic waste alone.

On the 11th of April 2022, for the very first time, I was lucky enough to get hands on, with one of the most extraordinary yet

Planetary Boundary Model

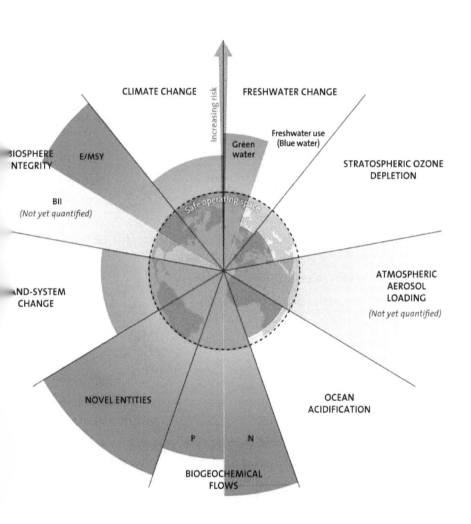

endangered groups of animals on earth. A creature whose ancestors roamed the earth each more than 100 million years ago. It was a juvenile Female green sea turtle. You have to be very lucky to see one near shore without diving, yet even luckier to catch one in a shore. As the waves crashed along the shore it had left seashells dispersed along the shoreline. The sand had felt warm under the feet of several individuals walking on the shore where the sand had met the waves. I have a habit of looking for wildlife in those shadows, and over the years I have come across nearly all species of marine animals. I walked in the water, which covered me till my knees and there beneath the waves, there appeared a very odd-looking rock, one with crescent shaped arms pointing out. Upon closer inspection it appeared to be a resting turtle. Unprepared I passed my phone whose light aided me in finding the turtle to my father and went to catch it. I eagerly moved my hand closer to it until I quickly got a grip on its slippery, smooth, heart-shaped shell, covered with barnacles and with a blend of different colors, including, brown, olive, gray, or black. When one holds these creatures specially a small one, they might assume that it might not be so strong, but this turtle was stronger than I imagined and in order to have a proper grip, I held it's shell with two hands. Once out of the water and on the sand, I noticed it's head had an enormous cut, possibly caused by close contact with a predator or a boat. I had also been able to remove all the barnacles from it's shell. Although Most barnacles do not hurt sea turtles, as they are only attached to the shell or skin on the outside. Others though burrow into the skin of the host and might cause discomfort and provide an open target area for following infections. Excessive barnacle cover can be a sign of general bad health in a turtle, and later I covered those spots along with the wound on the head with Engemycin Spray. Turtles are ancient important creatures in our oceans, not only do they keep sea grass beds in shape, but they also reduce the numbers of jellyfishes by eating them, no matter how venomous.

Jellyfishes, were among the earliest creatures to appear in our oceans and they have remained fairly unchanged for the past 500 million years. In order to catch food and deter predators, these simple creatures have an extraordinary defence, they sting! Jellyfish are transparent and made up of 95 percent water and one of their most fascinating parts is their stinging cells. Located on their tentacles, jellyfish's stinging cells are called cnidocytes. They are small compartments that house a mini needle-like stinger. When an outside force triggers a stinger, the cell opens, letting ocean water rush in. This causes the stinger to shoot out into whatever triggered the action; once it's there, venom is released. All of this happens within a millionth of a second. Though the venom of most jellyfish is not harmful, some can be deadly. For example, the Indo-Pacific box jellyfish—or sea wasp—releases venom that makes the heart contract. There is an antidote, but the poison acts fast, so someone who is stung must seek medical attention immediately. The box jellyfish has Up to 15 tentacles that grow from each corner of the bell and can reach 10 feet in length. Each tentacle has about 5,000 stinging cells, which are triggered not by touch but by the presence of a chemical on the outer layer of its prey. They have developed the ability to move rather than just drift, jetting at up to four knots through the water. They also have eyes grouped in clusters of six on the four sides of their bell. Each cluster includes a pair of eyes with a sophisticated lens, retina, iris and cornea, although without a central nervous system, scientists aren't sure how they process what they see.

Despite being the most dangerous of all jellies they are eaten by sea turtles. As hatchlings, loggerheads and greens are omnivores, but as they transition into adulthood, the former become carnivores while the latter herbivores. Flatbacks feed on seaweeds and shrimps, among others, and hawksbills usually favour sea sponges. Kemp's ridleys are meat-eaters, but olive ridleys are classified as omnivores, munching on sea cucumbers, fish, and various plants. Today, however, we shall be focusing on leatherbacks, who are often known as gelatinivores, devouring gelatinous prey such as jellyfish wherever they go.

Among the seven species, leatherback sea turtles are the largest, with a study showing that they could grow up to 640 kilograms in weight despite their specific jellyfish diet. As jellyfish are 95% water (which amounts to only 5 calories), leatherbacks usually consume up to 16,000 calories of the invertebrate, which is roughly 73% of their body weight. Among their favourite types of jellyfish to eat are lion's manes and moon jellies, and they are usually found well deep in the depth of the ocean, seeing that leatherbacks can swim in high latitudes. These sea turtles tend to experience this high amount of consumption during the summer, before making a 9,000 miles migration journey in search of nesting beaches.

How do leatherbacks exactly feed on jellyfish and how are they capable of doing so? As humans, we are familiar with the venom jellyfish release when stinging an enemy. The venom comes from specialised cells called nematocysts and when made in contact with the human skin, the stung one gets could be awful and at times even fatal. The Blue blubber jellyfish in UAE for example, will cause the region or multiple regions to itch very severely once in contact with its tentacles. Sea turtles, however are reptiles, and their scales can protect them from these venoms. They are also blessed with spine-like projections called papillae which line down leatherbacks' esophagus from the mouth which help them pierce and break down their prey once ingested.

However, if you have dived in the sea or ocean, you will see that a plastic bag resembles a jellyfish very much, and if this plastic can fool us, it can do so for the animals as well, when an animal eats plastic, it

During a search at night, I came across an injured Juvenile green sea turtle. Its shell was covered with barnacles which I was able to remove and later released the Turtle back to the wild. (Jumeirah Beach, April 11, 2022)

does remove the feeling of hunger, but as the animal feels full, it will not feed and the plastic within it cannot be digested, and so the animal starves to death, sea turtles. However, face a different problem, the same papillae that allow them to swallow jellyfishes with ease, now trap the plastic and the sea turtle is unable to breathe. Once the animals die, however the plastic is released back into the environment to kill more wildlife. I have seen plastic all around, it is found even in the most remote places, from the sea to land! Yet we must not question the intelligence of animals when they eat plastic, but be astounded by how we have poisoned our oceans, and how this poison has blended into the environment.

Plastics are present in every aspect of society. We sleep on plastic-filled pillows, brush our teeth with plastic toothbrushes, type on plastic keyboards, drink and eat food from plastic containers—impossible it's to go through a day without coming into contact with some form of plastic.

Due to the industrialization of the manufacturing process, some materials derived from animals were becoming increasingly hard to find by the middle of the 19th century. Elephant extinction was imminent if the demand for ivory, which was used in everything from piano keys to pool cues, persisted. Some turtle species, whose shells were used to make combs, met the same end.

With numerous inventions for new semi-synthetic materials based on natural substances like cork, blood, and milk, inventors quickly tried to address this environmental and financial problem. One of the first was cellulose nitrate, which was created by dissolving cotton fibers in nitric and sulfuric acids before mixing them with vegetable oil.

This new substance was created in 1862 by chemist-artisan Alexander Parkes, who was born in Birmingham. It was a cheap and colorful alternative to ivory or tortoiseshell and is regarded as the first manufactured plastic.

This new plastic has revolutionized consumer goods and culture by making items like combs affordable to many more people.

The threat of plastic pollution is relatively recent. Even though the widespread use of plastic only started after World War II, its mass has already surpassed that of both terrestrial and marine animals combined twice over. 60% of all plastic ever produced had already been converted to waste as of 2015, with a sizable portion of that waste ending up in the ocean. Between 86 and 150 million metric tonnes (MMT) of plastic are estimated to have accumulated in the oceans by this point, although estimates vary greatly.

Today, anyone can simply stroll close to the shore and discover various types of plastic within a short period of time. While I was strolling along the shore of Al Mamzar Beach, a similar thing happened to me. All along the seashore, large crowds can be seen. During this time of year, these people visit the beach to relax. At the same time, kids play in the sand as lifeguards stand back and observe. However, amidst all of those people, I noticed something very odd. It appeared white and rectangular from a distance. However, as you drew nearer, the silhouette started to resemble a rather large fish; it was about 4 feet long. Tetraodontidae was the family of the fish that washed up on the shore. Although the sun had caused its left side to bleach, it was immediately obvious that this creature was a starry puffer when looking at its head. These puffers have bodies that are uniformly spotted with black spots and skin that varies in color from white to grey. They are protected from ferocious predators by a highly toxic poison called tetrodotoxin, which is found in their ovaries and to a lesser extent in their skin and liver. It becomes toxic as it ingests bacteria that contain toxins. Starry puffers, like porcupinefish, can inflate their bodies by ingesting air or water to ward off potential adversaries. But the fish's teeth were undoubtedly this specimen's most eye-catching feature. Strong jaw muscles have allowed the teeth on pufferfish to fuse together to form a structure resembling a beak. Even though pufferfish have strong jaws that can open crabs and crush snails, this constant feeding grinds down their teeth. To make up for this, their teeth continually grow, just like the teeth of rodents. Sea urchins, of which there are two varieties in Mamzar—the long-spined sea urchin and the short-spined sea urchin—might be one of their favorite diets. I had previously observed these remarkable puffers feasting on long-spined sea urchins on a dive. How did they do that without suffering discomfort or harm? Nobody is sure. Yet a single starry puffer managed to consume an entire long-spine sea urchin in under 10 minutes. Crushing and chewing the test of the urchin part by part, without a single going to waste.

However, a stomach examination while preserving the fish revealed that it had consumed plastic, as microscopic fragments had overwhelmed the digestive system.

Once plastic enters the water, it is extremely difficult to remove it due to the difficulties in collecting it and the persistence of plastic in the environment. Additionally, after entering the ocean, plastic keeps disintegrating: macroplastics turn into microplastics, and microplastics turn into nanoplastics, making recovery much less feasible.

The mass of microplastics in oceans and beaches will more than double between 2020 and 2050, even if all inputs of plastic pollution into the ocean were to stop today.

Field and laboratory research have shown that plastics - and the chemical contaminants they are connected with - can move further up the marine food chain when consumed by marine creatures and tragically, everywhere I go—from the most biodiverse ecosystems to the wildest places, from deserts to oceans—I see plastic. I frequently come across dead fish and immature cuttlefish on Mamzar Beach alone.

It's small comfort to discover that the starrypuffers are not alone. There are at least 180 kinds of marine creatures known to eat plastic, ranging in size from microscopic plankton to enormous whales. A

to Bottom) Dead Adult Starry Puffer washed on Al Mamzar Beach, possibly dead due to Plastic
umption. Wild specimens may grow to be one of the world's largest puffers, reaching heights of over 3
They feed on shelled organisms able to crush them with their powerful beaks, they also eat long spine
rchins. The Specimen had many different types of plastic within including Bottle cap fragments. 15
mber 2022.

third of the fish caught in the UK have plastic in their intestines, and this number includes fishes that we frequently eat. It has also been discovered in other creatures, including mussels and lobsters. In summary, creatures of all shapes and sizes are eating plastic, and there is a lot of it since 12.7 million tonnes of it enter the sea each year.

This enormous amount has certain unintended consequences, like the predominance of plastic use. For instance, in zooplankton, where their feeding appendages are made to handle particles of a specific size, it correlates with the quantity of minute plastic particles in the water. "Food must be present if the particle falls within this size range.

The tentacled, cylindrical organisms known as sea cucumbers creep around the ocean floor, collecting dirt into their mouths to extract nutritious material. Like zooplankton, sea cucumbers don't seem to be picky about what they consume. Given the distribution of plastic in the sediment, these bottom-dwellers can eat up to 138 times as much plastic as would be predicted.

While the size and accessibility of plastic particles may just make them simpler for sea cucumbers to consume than other types of food, there are signs that plastic eating is a more active process in other species. This diet seems to be popular with animals. We must recognize how animals view the world in order to comprehend why they find plastic to be so alluring.

Animals' sensory and perceptual capacities are extremely different from ours. They vary, sometimes for the better and sometimes for the worse, but they are always different.

One reason is that animals simply confuse plastic for known food items; for instance, it's been suggested that delectable fish eggs are what plastic pellets mimic. However, as humans, we are skewed by our senses. Scientists must attempt to understand how animals see the world in order to understand their love of plastic.

While humans are predominantly visual beings, many marine species, especially albatrosses, rely heavily on their sense of smell when they are out hunting. According to research the smell of plastic may attract certain fish and seabird species. Researchers specifically claimed that the chemical signal coming from plastic was dimethyl sulfide (DMS), a substance known to draw foraging birds. In essence, algae develop on floating plastic, and when that algae is consumed by krill, a significant source of marine food, it produces DMS, luring birds and fish that eat the plastic rather than the krill they were after.

We shouldn't assume anything while analyzing the attractiveness of plastic, not even in terms of eyesight. Similar to humans, marine turtles mostly rely on their eyesight to find food. They are believed to be able to see UV light, which would make their vision very different from ours.

Older turtles like soft, translucent plastic over their more indiscriminate younger counterparts. It is believed that turtles mistake plastic bags for tasty jellyfish.

The use of plastic is also assumed to be influenced by color, however species-specific preferences may exist. Young turtles choose white plastic, whereas shearwaters, a kind of seabird, favor red plastic.

There are additional senses that animals employ in addition to sight and smell to locate food. Many marine creatures, including dolphins and toothed whales, hunt using echolocation. Numerous sperm whales and other toothed whales have been discovered dead with stomachs full of plastic bags, automobile parts, and other human waste. Since echolocation is known to be highly sensitive, it is possible that these things were mistaken for food.

The reality is that all of these creatures are expert hunters and foragers, with senses fine-tuned by millennia of evolution to target what is frequently a very small spectrum of prey items. There is a misperception that these animals are unintelligent and merely consume plastic because it is around them. They have inadvertently fallen into the "food" category during that period.

Because there is something for everyone in plastic. In addition to appearing like food, it also smells, feels, and sounds like food. The issue is that our trash attracts a wide variety of animals because it comes in so many different shapes, sizes, and colors.

The Qudra Lakes are without a doubt the wildest location in the United Arab Emirates, if someone were to ask me. The lakes there, while being man-made, have drawn a variety of unusual animals, including migrating birds to endangered Ethiopian hedgehogs. Despite the fact that the government has placed dustbins around the reserve, people still do not use them, and plastic is all over the place. Every time I go there to gather some specimens and admire the native wildlife, there are usually traces of dead animals, including different-aged gazelles and other types of birds.

Black swans stand out with their brood throughout the winter months as the lake sparkles brightly during the day, but as night falls, the scene changes. As is routine, I search for birds and specimens throughout the day. In the desert, one may typically locate animal bones beneath the Ghaf. The majority of smaller species, however, hide throughout the day and seek shelter; they only emerge at night. There are several lakes in Qudra, but I often go to the flamingo lakes because I am so familiar with it. My family normally sits at the lake when we go camping, but I usually go around the area, starting in the deserts. There are Ghaf trees spread everywhere, and despite my best efforts to cover as much ground as possible, something exceptional always surprises me. The first time I went to the Qudra Lakes, it appeared like there wasn't much there other than a few black swans and greater flamingos relishing the water. Nevertheless, I also explored the harsh Qudra Desert that lay beyond the lake. I first encountered a dead gazelle that had maybe been dead for a few months. A little distance later, behind a huge ghaf tree, I discovered a very adult Arabian gazelle's skeleton and two small owl pellets on the opposite side. Soon after, I felt the entire tree begin to tremble. Out of dread, I sat down. To my astonishment, a big Arabian Eagle owl flew out of the tree. Perhaps the pellets were from the same owl since, after dissecting them, two years later, I discovered two Lesser Jerboa skulls, a few arabian darkling beetle shells, and some unusual-looking bird toes.

However, on my subsequent visits, I discovered more carcasses, including a grey heron and several gazelles of different ages that had possibly succumbed to an illness or plastic intake.

But if you've ever been to a desert, you know that it's an entirely different environment at night than during the day. The first night I spent in Qudra was shrouded in such total darkness that I was only able to see as far as my outstretched palm. Most of the time, being in the desert at night is a sensory-depriving experience; it is as dark and silent as a cave at midnight. There is an expected abundance of life. The desert is alive, but largely in ways that are invisible to the human eye. Surprisingly, at night, Arabian gazelles start to move closer to the lake than they do during the day, when they are dispersed around the desert and only visible from a distance. They get stunned when you shine a direct torch at them, and you can then gently go closer to them. In one case, for instance, I came so near to a newborn gazelle that I could have captured it; it had gorgeous gleaming eyes and miniature little legs. However, it escaped. Another time, I was so close to an adult that I thought the closer I got, the more likely it would be to ram me with its horns. The Arabian gazelle is classified as a vulnerable species. It has remarkable adaptations for living in the desert. In the summer, the coat is short, shiny, and sleek, reflecting the majority of solar radiation. From their droppings to their tracks, gazelles leave behind unmistakable indications both during the day and at night. But what really breaks one's heart is the knowledge that many also die. Death is undoubtedly a natural part of life. For example, on a small research expedition in December, I came across a recently deceased arabian gazelle. It may have been dead for only a few days or at most a week, but it was still a very sad sign. I also saw two other gazelles that day, and yet the presence of dead animals in an ecosystem is crucial for maintaining its stability. In order to examine the gazelles' carcasses more closely, I restrained myself and put on protective gear, including gloves and a mask. When the carcass was examined more closely, a wide variety of decomposers, including blowflies (Chrysomya albiceps) and carcass beetles, could be seen. Despite the carcass having a nasty and strong stench combined with a tint of sickening sweetness, I was curious to examine the biodiversity around the body. These blow flies and carcass beetles were quite numerous in the Anal area and head region, and despite having a region. I had been looking more closely at the anal region, where the majority of decomposers were concentrated, when I noticed a white shine from a foreign object inside the gazelles. With my forceps in hand, I reached out to grab the edge of the strange material and gently pulled it out. To my shock, it turned out to be a piece of polyethylene plastic bag.

There is no doubting that the world in which we live is seriously flawed. There is seldom a day that goes by without news of another record-breaking hurricane, wildfire, or drought. We are becoming aware that our ecosystems are disintegrating. The carcass beetles are often seen between January and June. Carrion, such as dead camels, oryx, gazelles, and other dead animals found in the desert, is the principal food source for adults and larvae. These extraordinary decomposing machines once agitated will retract legs when agitated in order to defend itself. Their antennae have a vast surface area, that makes them good corpse detector. An adult may use their antennae to seek out a carcass while flying. I've had carcass beetles in the past, and they helped me preserve animal bones & Skulls. As a result, I've seen how in nature these beetle larvae dig into plants or the actual carcass to pupate. The ones I raised in captivity, on the other hand, pupated by nipping and digging into styrofoam. Without oxygen and carbon dioxide, Earth cannot exist. These decomposers are necessary for the gaseous movement. Decomposers degrade dead materials, converting the carbon that has been stored there into carbon dioxide and oxygen as they go.

The presence of plastic in practically every living thing nowadays extends beyond gazelles. By taking samples from 16 beaches in Dubai, it was possible to examine microplastic pollution in beach sediments for the first time. The silt included 0.33 mg/g and 59.71 items/kg of microplastics, while 63.67% of the samples were polyethylene and 32.94% were polypropylene. The impact on the oceans would be greater. Microplastics are present in high numbers in oyster beds off the coast of the UAE; in 51% of the oyster samples analyzed, the particles were between 0.1mm and 5mm in size. Averaging 101.2 particles per kilogram of oysters and 191.7 particles per kilogram of dry weight of oyster-bed sediment, the levels of microplastics differed significantly among the locations.

Currently, our oceans contain 5.25 trillion macro and micro bits of plastic, with 46,000 pieces per square mile and a total weight of 269,000 tonnes. Plastic is everywhere around us—on land, in the water, and even in our food—and some of it even blends in rather nicely with the surroundings. It's possible that the sand you walk on at the beach has plastic particles in it as well. These microscopic, sand-colored fragments are known as "toxic sponges" because they draw chemical poisons and other pollutants to their surfaces. These unappreciated "pre-production plastic pellets," sometimes known as "nurdles," are the basic component of all of our plastic goods. The small beads can be produced from polymers such as polyethylene, polypropylene, polystyrene, and polyvinyl chloride. The density of the pellets and whether they are in freshwater or saltwater will determine whether they sink or float when released into the environment from plastic plants or when delivered around the world as raw material to companies. Only a little attention is needed, and upon closer examination Nurdles, which frequently superficially resemble sand grains, usually grow to be somewhat bigger and have uniform, spherical forms. Nurdles are particularly appealing to seabirds, fish, and other marine creatures because of their size and frequently transparent color, which can make them appear like fish eggs. However, there are also indirect effects from microplastics in the sand, which can alter the sand's properties like warmth and permeability and influence creatures like sea turtles that lay their eggs on beaches. The turtle hatchlings will be male if the eggs are incubated below 27.7° Celsius (81.86° Fahrenheit). Consequently, the hatchlings will be female if the eggs incubate at temperatures higher than 31° Celsius (88.8° Fahrenheit).

The desert, on the other hand, is a natural setting with a stable climate, wild animals that live there and graze, and a region where natural plant growth occurs. All community members who use it for camping, sightseeing, family get-togethers, and safaris must pay it attention and care. Today, Plastic may be found everywhere if you travel into the desert. People don't seem to care, which is ironic given that what we discard doesn't actually vanish.

According to 2008 research, hundreds of camels have perished in the UAE over the previous ten years as a result of the intake of plastic. About 300 of the 30,000 camels examined by personnel from Dubai's Central Veterinary Research Laboratory since 2008—either in the field or in a lab—died as a result of polybezoars, lumps of indigestible plastic debris. Accordingly, one in every 100 camels that pass away in the United Arab Emirates does so because they ate plastic debris that people had left behind when camping or otherwise polluting.

Today You can't just say, "Please don't litter," since it is no longer effective. They must be punished before anybody will even consider it because they will stop once they feel it in their pocket. But Microplastic has gone beyond nature it also within us! Every week, people consume plastic equal to one credit card. For the first time, scientists have found evidence of plastic pollution in the blood of humans, with over 80% of those who were examined having the microscopic particles. The finding demonstrates that the particles can move around the body and can settle in organs.The effect on health is still undetermined. However, because air pollution particles are already known to penetrate the body and cause millions of premature deaths each year, experts are concerned. Microplastics have been shown to harm human cells in the laboratory.

The microscopic particles have been discovered in the faecel matter of both newborns and adults, and people have long been known to breathe them in as well as absorb them through food and water. The researchers examined blood samples from 22 anonymous, healthy adult donors and discovered plastic particles in 17 of the samples. PET plastic, which is frequently used in beverage bottles, was present in half of the samples, and polystyrene, which is used to package food and other items, was present in the other third. The substance polyethylene, which is used to make plastic carrier bags, was present in one-fourth of the blood samples. A recent study discovered that red blood cells' ability to carry oxygen may be hampered by the attachment of microplastics to their outer membranes. The particles have also been identified in pregnant women's placentas, and in pregnant rats, they quickly move through the lungs and into the fetuses' hearts, brains, and other organs. Microplastics were discovered in 11 cases after tissue samples from 13 surgical patients were collected. Polypropylene, a material used in bottles and pipelines, and PET were the most prevalent particles.

The small particles were already known to be ingested by humans through food and water, as well as through breathing them in. It is also known that individuals exposed to high quantities of microplastics have fallen ill.

The oceans are the world's biggest habitat. In addition to climate change and plastic pollution, we are depleting our seas at a rate that will prevent them from ever recovering. The oceans shape the earth and make up more than 70% of its surface, while 97% of our planet's livable space is found beneath its tremendous depths.

Globally, between 0.97 and 2.7 trillion wild fish are thought to be caught annually. Nevertheless, people also go and take marine life in their own ways.

One particular experience from around 8 years ago that I can still clearly remember is going to the Haft Barm-e Kudian. The name Haft Barm, which translates to "7 Lakes," refers to a collection of year-round and seasonal lakes spread across a 70-acre area 65 kilometers west of Shiraz. The average depth of the lakes fed by the snowmelt waters that feed these lakes is between 3 and 15 meters. These lakes are completely full in the winter, but only the two largest are present in the summer and fall.

An elusive ancient creature resides in the two permanent lakes. one that can reach a length of 12 inches and has robust armor. I was skeptical when I first heard about and saw images of this beast that my relatives, who went and captured them there, gave to me. These bottom-dwellers devour decaying stuff, therefore, in order to catch them, we set up a trap net with chicken bones and flesh within it as bait. We inflated our portable orange boat and travelled to the depths where these crustaceans are prevalent in order to set the traps. Once there, we positioned the traps next to some common Reed and waited for two hours. It was already nightfall by the time we finished pulling the nets. We had captured five or six juveniles. The juveniles we had caught were narrow-clawed crayfish (Pontastacus leptodactylus), and no one could have ever imagined that they would grow to be up to 12 inches long. However, Large adults, were not seen.

Although the rocky, muddy region where they inhabit is the ideal location for such crayfish to breed, visitors who camp here nevertheless catch and consume these creatures. I last visited the same lake in the summer of 2022, and I was horrified to see how much pollution and rubbish had been left behind. There were two pieces of plastic near the water on every single step. As you proceeded, it was impossible to miss the crayfish shells that the campers here had killed. The lake itself smelt like a dump and rotting fish. The shells of crayfish, lobsters, and crabs contain a substance called astaxanthin that, under certain lighting circumstances, may absorb blue light and give the impression that the shell is red. The crustacyanin, a membrane that is concealed inside the lobster's shell, is where the pigment is safely kept when the animal is alive. The pigment is unable to freely flow since it is confined inside the membrane due to the lobster shell's extreme packing. Thus, the crustacean typically appears in such subdued shades of dark blue or green. When a crayfish crab is dropped into boiling water, its body chemistry alters because the pigment, astaxanthin, separates from the membrane, crustacyanin, giving the crayfish that deep crimson color.

As the cockroaches of the sea, crayfish are not only the decomposers of their environment but may also be considered allogenic ecosystem engineers since they alter physical habitats through burrowing activities and the removal of macrophytes that serve as refuges for aquatic creatures. However, the majority have been eaten, and because of pollution, many juveniles may be seen lying dead close to the river. I looked everywhere and walked all around the lake for about an hour without seeing any live crayfish, and each time the pollution and death grew more obvious. Atlast, just as I was about to give up, however, I notice a live juvenile. I caught it and took a few measurements; this was a small three or four inch crayfish. As I examined the crayfish, I was astounded by the crayfish's many hues, which included a light blue button, orange-red legs and claw tips, and a greenish blue body overall. Later, the crayfish was released, and I hope that this will aid in reviving the populations. However, I brought a few samples of the shells, claws, and juveniles I found that were deceased for further research.

The life in the ocean is also doomed. We have been fishing in the earth's oceans for a very long time, but it wasn't until the 1950s that large, commercial fleets first sailed into international waters. Fishing in completely unexplored seas initially produced abundant catches. But in only a few years, the nets being dragged into any one region were nearly completely empty. The fleets then continued on.

Plastic is a massive pollution problem, especially in our oceans. Here a critically endangered Hawkbill sea Turtle is nibbling on a plastic bag. (©Rich Carey/Getty Images)

A little penguin trapped in a plastic net. The bird if not freed would have suffocated to death. (©Tsvibra/Getty Images)

All animals are affected by plastic, Here a whale shark filter feeds in polluted waters, ingesting plastic. (©Rich Carey/Getty Images)

Two Indian Women sort out plastic bottles for recycling. (©Mumtahina Tanni/Pexels)

Myself as I collect Carcass beetle specimens from a recently deceased Male Arabian gazelle. These beetles carried I size and shape and were concentrated in the head and anal region of the gazelle. December 2022.

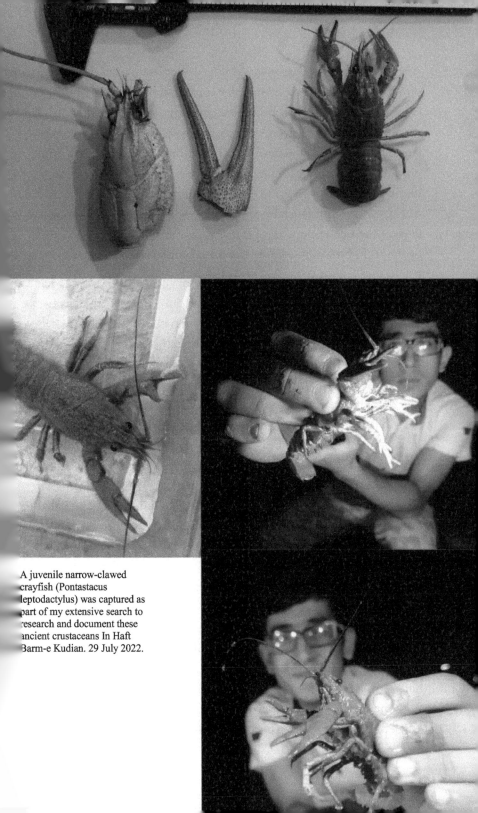

A juvenile narrow-clawed crayfish (Pontastacus leptodactylus) was captured as part of my extensive search to research and document these ancient crustaceans In Haft Barm-e Kudian. 29 July 2022.

After all, wasn't the ocean a seemingly limitless expanse? You can observe how one area of ocean after another almost lost all of its fish stocks by looking at data on captures through time. By the middle of the 1970s, only the waters surrounding eastern Australia, southern Africa, eastern North America, and the Southern Ocean were truly productive. By the beginning of the 1980s, fishing had become so unprofitable on a worldwide scale that nations with sizable fleets had to support them financially, essentially paying the fleets to overfish. 90% of the huge fish in all of the world's waters had been eradicated by the end of the 20th century thanks to human activity.

Simply go to a fish market today and compare the fish sizes to what was available only 16 years ago, and you can surely see the change. Targeting the biggest, most valuable fish in the ocean is extremely harmful. It eliminates not just the largest individuals within a group but also the fish at the top of the food chain, such as tuna and swordfish. Size is important in fish populations. The majority of fish that dwell in open water continue to grow. A female fish's mass affects her ability to reproduce. Egg production is disproportionately higher in large mothers. Therefore, by getting rid of all the fish beyond a particular size, we get rid of their best breeders, and populations rapidly start to decline. There are no longer any large fish in places that are heavily fished. In the hunt for fish, we have created nets that are pushed through the water, drift on the currents, encircle a shoal, and are subsequently dragged inward at their base, are flung into the sea from above, and sink and scrape the seabed. We have now overfished several of our coastal waterways as a result. However, lost or abandoned nets and hooks that are left in the water continue to destroy nature by entangling fish, sharks, sea turtles, whales, and other species. In fishing nets every year, dolphins, whales, seals, and turtles are among the more than 650,000 marine species that die or suffer harm. Animals frequently become entangled and perish in nets that fisherman are actively using. If a sea turtle or whale is trapped or tangled, it drowns if it can't get to the surface.

It is a reckless practice to remove entire populations of fish from the open ocean. Food chains in the ocean function quite differently from those on land. There may only be three links in a chain, from grass to wildebeest to lion. There are frequently chains in the ocean with four, five, and more connections. Microscopic phytoplankton are consumed by barely perceptible zooplankton, which is then consumed by little fry, which are then consumed by a series of fish increasing in size with bigger and bigger mouths. At a baitball, we see an extended chain that is self-sustaining and self-regulatory. If a certain species of medium-sized fish goes extinct because people love eating them, those lower down the food chain may become overabundant, and those higher up may suffer because they are unable to consume the plankton. The hotspots' brief, perfectly balanced bursts of life grow less frequent. The nutrients that fall from the ocean's surface waters and slide downward to linger in the darkness below represent a net loss to the surface community over thousands of years. The wide ocean begins to perish as the hotspots start to disappear. Every year, there are fewer fish to be caught, in addition to the fact that we must feed more people. Even just before our time, in the late nineteenth century and the early twentieth century, records and accounts depicted an ocean that we wouldn't recognize now. Nothing more sophisticated than cotton hooks and nets were used for fishing by our not-so-distant ancestors. With technologies that would make them gasp, we struggle today to capture anything edible. Nowadays, there are fewer fish in the water. Because we have no firsthand knowledge of the ocean's past richness or its future riches, we have come to anticipate less and less from it.

Let's head back and explore Mamzar Beach's depths. Al Mamzar has a remarkable diverse animal population, including stingrays, crabs, echinoderms, and several unique fish species. These waters often make their hidden animals known at night, each time bringing a fresh surprise. The rocky area where we go is a hotspot for wildlife; it is here that some unexpected creatures always appear. At the end of the summer nights, needlefish petrol the waters looking for potential prey. They are especially attracted to light and shiny objects and that's how we saw one. On one of our visits in October 2022, the tide was back like never before. The same day, because of our natural curiosity, Zayaan and I wore our water shoes and ventured beyond those slippery rocks. A few times, we came dangerously close to falling, but soon the first sign of life emerged—a short-spined sea urchin. These amazing echinoderms can dig by biting through rock because of their strong mouth parts, which also give them the ability to conceal themselves during the day. Their name comes from the fact that their skeletons (tests) are coated in small spines. Sea urchins have been dubbed the marine equivalent of porcupines. Sea urchins depend on their long spines, similar to a porcupine's quills, to keep hungry predators away from them. In actuality, the name of the sea urchin comes from the Old English for the spiny hedgehog. In addition to biting and eating their meal, sea urchins also use a device known as Aristotle's lantern to scrape algae off of rocks and other surfaces. The mouth device has the ability to slide from side to side and retract within the urchin's body. It consists of five rigid plates that join together to form a beak. The plates may become worn from the scraping; as a result, sea urchin teeth sprout to replace those that are lost. The animal's mouth is on the bottom of its body, and waste is expelled via the anus at the top. They maintain the ocean floor by consuming algae and decaying organisms. However, I was aware that the tides had retrieved so much that I might easily get my hands on a long spine sea urchin.

The majority of sea urchins may be picked up without injury, but the long-spined sea urchin's toxic, sharp spines can pierce human flesh and break off. However, someone with little expertise can also grip a sea urchin with a long spine. Zayaan carried the torch as I looked for long spine sea urchins once we entered the deeper areas with our torches. We proceeded on, and when I put my hand to the first dark spot, it was only a little crevice. As we searched for sea urchins between my legs, a huge upside-down jellyfish came by and startled us. When I went to retrieve a long spine sea urchin for the second time, the water was up to my chest. I stretched out between two rocks, thinking that this would also be an empty spot, but as soon as my hand extended down, I was in agonizing pain, so I quickly pulled my hand out of the water. For over 15 minutes after being stung by a long-spined sea urchin, I experienced excruciating pain that felt almost like a needle revolving through my finger. Zayaan stared at me in horror as I put out my hand; my finger was scarlet, and the puncture wound with the fractured spine within was clearly apparent. After the pain faded, I returned and dragged two long spine sea urchins out of the water with a stink. Later, after catching around six of them and holding them for a closer examination, we shone a light on the rocks, and the entire area turned pitch-black from the sea urchins' swarm. The spines can extend up to 30 cm in length in exceptionally large individuals, although they typically develop to be 10 to 12 cm long.

On coral reefs, this species typically inhabits depths of 1 to 10 meters. Individual urchins that are unable to find a suitable crevice will live in more exposed conditions. However, they may frequently squeeze themselves in one crevice so that just their spines are visible. Individuals that have managed to discover a crevice typically wander about a meter from it at night while eating. However, their spine is what truly stands out. When examined under a microscope and contrasted with that of a short spine sea urchin, we can observe how well-adapted long spine sea urchins are to defending themselves. A spine sample taken from a long spine sea urchin has a thin, crystal-like spine that is visible under a microscope. It resembles a weapon with backward facing barbs all over the spine, so if one went it, it would lock itself and would be impossible to get out.

The long spine sea urchins, Diadema antillarum, experienced mass mortality in 1983, with more than 97% of the urchins dying. This mass mortality affected the whole Caribbean faunal zone, extending as far south as South America and north to the Bahamas. Since then, foliose macroalgae have taken over several Caribbean reefs. This prevents coral development and has accelerated the scleractinian corals' continuous demise. Additionally, it has a detrimental overall impact on coral reef resilience, which includes a system's capacity to withstand changes brought on by disturbance events and recover from them. Recent research conducted in Discovery Bay, Jamaica, and other areas seems to indicate a significant resurgence of Diadema and strong reef regeneration. Many of the Diadema unexpectedly lost their attachment to the substrate during the crisis, started losing their spines, and died a day or two after these observations. Since then, divers have observed Diadema urchins in other parts of the Caribbean experiencing the same fate. The richness of the marine life on the coral reefs suffered greatly when the sea urchins died from an unidentified sickness. Due to a lack of food and shelter, the fish and other creatures dwelling on the reefs saw a fall in population as a result of the luxuriant algae growth that resulted. Several small countries that relied on their reefs' natural beauty to draw tourists suffered from the decline in coral reef biodiversity. The diminished influx of visitors put these nations' economies under pressure because tourism accounted for a significant portion of their income.

The repopulation of Diadema antillarum is frequently hampered by low densities, predators, and waves from strong storms. Urchins release fluid during fertilization to signal other urchins to respond by releasing their eggs and sperm in a process known as mass reproduction. There is a greater possibility of fertilization when there are more gametes accessible. However, in places with low populations, a small number of sea urchins could not be sufficient to start fertilization. There is still a significant probability that predators will eat the young after fertilization. Urchins may be washed from their habitat during severe storms and perish as a result of the passage of water. With additional study and volunteers, it may be feasible to help the sea urchin population thrive.

It is still early in the study of the species Diadema antillarum. It is possible to raise the urchins in a lab before moving them. The number of urchins on the reef may increase by releasing the adult individuals back into the environment. The construction of artificial reefs can also help the population flourish because materials like concrete can promote coral growth and provide the urchins greater hiding places from larger fish and other predators. Urchins can be moved to other, low-density reefs while there are still some locations with a high urchin density. It appears that the transition back to coral-dominated reefs and away from algae-dominated reefs is feasible with the use of these techniques and volunteer labor. Since adult algae contain toxins that kill Diadema, it is vital to remove the majority of them from the region where they will be relocated.

Meanwhile, marine life was also unravelling in the shallows. Coral cities that stretch for kilometers, some as powerful as the Great Barrier Reef, contain life that can only be imagined and are very beautiful and colorful. I recall my first dive on a coral reef, even though I was quite young. Exploring a coral reef is fundamentally unlike any wildlife experience I have had on land. You are liberated from the grip of gravity the instant you dive in. By flicking one of your foot fins, you may travel in any direction. A vast, varied, and multicolored area of coral extends under you before dissipating into the ocean. It is as broad and diverse as a city seen from the air. As you concentrate, you realize that it is home to a cast of characters that is nothing short of amazing, including colorful fish, tiny cuttlefish, sea anemones, lobsters, crabs, translucent shrimp, and a variety of other creatures you never knew existed. Except for those standing next to you, they are all incredibly attractive and show no signs of being bothered by your presence. Soon enough, you could come upon a coral with a very strange appearance and a pure white tint. The pristine white branches, feathers, and fronds of this may at first appear to be beautiful—they like intricate marble sculptures—but you quickly realize that it is actually heartbreaking. What you are seeing are the remains of deceased creatures, or skeletons. The brain coral specimen I had gathered had perished as a result of the same terrible circumstance. Tiny animals called polyps, which are linked to jellyfish, construct coral reefs. Their basic bodies are little more than a stalk with a stomach on top, surrounded by a ring of tentacles, and a mouth. The mouth closes while the polyp digests its catch before opening again for its next meal. The tentacles include stinging cells that spear passing microscopic prey and carry it into the mouth. In order to shield their fragile bodies from voracious predators, these coral polyps construct calcium carbonate walls. They eventually grow into enormous stony structures, with each species developing its own style of architecture. Together, they expand into massive reefs. The Great Barrier Reef, located off of northeastern Australia, is the biggest of them all and is visible from space. Coral reefs rival rainforests in terms of their biodiversity. Similar to the wealth of options for life found in the jungle, they too exist in three dimensions. However, their inhabitants are far more vibrant and noticeable. Corals' vibrant colors aren't caused by polyps but rather by zooxanthellae, symbiotic algae that live inside coral cells. Like other plants, they have the ability to photosynthesise. In this way, the coral polyps and the algae that live inside them benefit from having both plant and animal characteristics. The joint venture receives sunlight during the day, which the algae use to produce sugars that provide the polyps up to 90% of the energy they require. The polyps continue to gather prey at night. While the polyps continue to construct their calcium carbonate walls upwards and outwards, preserving the colony's location in the sunshine, their algae partners continue to absorb the nutrition they need to execute their jobs from these meals. Warm, shallow oceans that lack nutrients have been converted into oasis of life thanks to this beneficial connection. But it is a delicately balanced one. The corals were stressed and ejected their algae, exposing the bone-white of their calcium carbonate skeletons, which was the source of the bleaching. Without their algae, the polyps diminish. The reef quickly transforms from a wonderland to a wasteland as seaweeds colonize the area and suffocate the coral skeletons. The origin of this bleaching was formerly unknown. For a while, scientists were unaware that bleaching frequently took place in areas where the water was fast rising. Climate scientists have long warned that burning fossil fuels will cause the planet to warm up by releasing greenhouse gases like carbon dioxide into the atmosphere. It was recognized that these gases trapped solar energy close to the Earth's surface, warming the globe in a process known as the greenhouse effect.

The Arctic summer sea ice extent has decreased by 30% during the previous 30 years, according to satellite photos. In some places, the Arctic is warming up to seven times faster than the rest of the planet. Glaciers were disappearing at the quickest rates ever seen in various places of the planet. The summer thaw was also quickening. The ice melts more quickly when the temperature of the air and the seas lapping at the edge of ice floes rises. The whiteness near the poles of the planet Earth recedes as the ice melts. The dark oceans are now absorbing more heat from the Sun, which has a positive feedback effect and hastens the thaw even faster. There was a lot less ice back then than there is now when the Earth was last this warm. The thaw begins slowly with a lag. However, once it starts, it will be hard to stop. The migratory birds are being most negatively impacted by the changing environment; on one occasion, I encountered a Red-necked Phalarope (Phalaropus lobatus) that was in its winter plumage and had suffered from heat stroke. This bird may have become lost since it generally stays away from human settlements and spends its time in open water. Sadly, the bird soon passed away, serving as a sharp reminder of the countless lives that are being lost as a result of our planet's warming.

Our planet needs ice. Algae grow on the underside of sea ice, sustained by the rays of sunlight that pass through it. The algae are grazed by invertebrates and small fish. They in turn are the basis of the food chains in both the Arctic and Antarctic, some of the most productive seas in the world, providing sustenance to whales, seals, bears, penguins and many other bird species. We too benefit from this productivity. Each year millions of tonnes of fish are caught in both the far north and far south, and sent to markets all over the world. Warmer summers in the polar regions lead to longer periods without sea ice. This is disastrous for polar bears since they need the northern sea ice as a platform to hunt seals. They idle around the Arctic beaches throughout the summer, kept alive by their fat stores, while they wait for the ice to form again. Scientists saw a troubling tendency as the time without ice became longer. Females that were pregnant were now giving birth to smaller cubs because they had run out of resources. The summer may become somewhat longer one year, but the cubs born that year may be so little that they won't be able to survive their first arctic winter since they will be so young. Then the polar bear population as a whole will collapse. These kinds of turning points are common in the intricate natural systems. A threshold is often crossed without much notice. It starts off with abrupt, drastic alterations that stabilize at a brand-new, changed condition. It might not be feasible to reverse that point; too much may have been lost, and too many components may have become unstable. Only by keeping an eye out for warning signs—like polar bear babies growing smaller—recognizing them for what they are, and acting quickly, can such a calamity be averted.

However, I think that the alarming loss of our planet's biodiversity is the sole cause of the extreme increase in climate change. Reading the WWF Living Planet report is one method we may see this decline. Globally, the state of nature is deteriorating at speeds not seen in millions of years. The natural world has reached its breaking point as a result of how we produce and use food and energy as well as the obvious disregard for the environment that is ingrained in our present economic model.

The COVID-19 virus is a clear illustration of how we have lost touch with nature. It has brought to light the intricate relationship between nature, human health, and well-being as well as the grave threat posed by the unparalleled loss of biodiversity to both human and environmental health. We need to respond to nature's emergency. Not only is it necessary to protect the tigers, rhinos, whales, bees, trees, and all the other beautiful diversity of life that we cherish and have a moral obligation to cohabit with, but disregarding it also endangers the health, wealth, and future of almost 8 billion people. In the last several decades, land-use change—primarily the conversion of pristine natural ecosystems (forests, grasslands, and mangroves) into agricultural systems—has been the most significant direct driver of biodiversity loss in terrestrial systems, while overfishing has affected a large portion of the seas. These trends have been largely fueled since 1970 by the world's population doubling, a fourfold increase in the global economy, and a tenfold increase in trade. Globally, climate change has not been the main cause of biodiversity loss to this point, but it is expected to overtake the other causes in importance in the next decades. Climate change adversely affects genetic variability, species richness and populations, and ecosystems. Loss of biodiversity can thus have a negative impact on the climate; for instance, deforestation increases the atmospheric abundance of carbon dioxide, a significant greenhouse gas. The decline of biodiversity affects not just the environment but also development, the economy, international security, ethics, and morality. The fulfillment of the majority of the UN Sustainable Development Goals, including eradicating poverty and ensuring the security of food, water, and energy, will be hampered by the ongoing loss of biodiversity. Biodiversity has significant economic value, which should be recognized in national accounting systems; it is a security issue in that the loss of natural resources, particularly in underdeveloped developing countries, can lead to conflict; it is an ethical issue because the poorest people who depend on it are harmed, further exacerbating a world that is already unequal; and it is a moral issue because we humans should not destroy the living planet.

I will however base these living planet reports by my own experiences over the past few years. We will move from our oceans to land. My first experience in a rainforest, was a very enriching one. An ancient part of land that felt enchanted. From far a rainforest just seems green, but it is once you enter inside that you understand that a part from being an oxygen supplier, forests are also hotspots of biodiversity. As we entered inside, just on the doorstep of the forest the first thing we happened to spot during the day was a small orange snake, hardly 12 cm long, slithering under the leaves. Soon enough, we were transformed by the sheer abundance of life, most of which were sound of birds high, beyond sight in the forest canopy. Yet it was the world beneath our feet that was sure to transform my perspective of life as I knew it. This experience of looking at the soil in detail, happened when I took a look at a mammal skull under a tree. In order to find the rest of the bones I dug the soil, and it was here that a whole of Megafauna like worms and Mesofauna like small Isopods that fed on the leave of trees. I was with my grandfather, and the forest was located on and around a mountain. Yet the soil sustained more like that just worms, a 30 min walk from where I saw that skull, We found a huge hole in the walls of the hill, it was clearly dug by a big animal. Upon shining a light in that hole, 2 huge red eyes glowed. This experience would scare away any wondering person, but as a young naturalist when I was just 12, I was beyond curios, but I didn't even have to fear, cause nearby to that hole, we found an Indian crested porcupine quill, the same of which, I still have in my natural history collection. Soil hosts one of the largest reservoirs of biodiversity on Earth: up to 90% of living organisms in terrestrial ecosystems, including some pollinators, spend part of their life cycle in soil habitats. The variety of soil components, filled with air and water, create an incredible diversity of habitats for a myriad of different soil organisms that underpin our life on this planet.

Besides food production, soil biodiversity provides a vast range of ecosystem functions and services, including soil formation, the retention and purification of water, nutrient cycling, the degradation of some soil contaminants and the regulation of greenhouse gases, as well as sustaining plant, animal and human health. Without soil biodiversity, terrestrial ecosystems may collapse. We now know that above- and belowground biodiversity are in constant collaboration. A few miles from the porcupine hole, there was a gap between the forest, a road, it was built by the locals there, the trees in which they had cut down still lied on the side of the sandy dry road, and a little further a gruesome sight, it was strange that on the other side of the road to my left, there was a dead cow, half bone, have flesh and skin. To the south most of the forest had been cut and burned to create pastures. In the daytime cattle browsed in remorseless heat bouncing off the yellow clay and at night animals and spirits edged out onto the ruined land. Farming is the biggest issue that our planet's forests face. Methane is Produced naturally in wetlands, rice paddies, soil bacteria, and cattle intestines. In 1980s atmosphere methane levels rose 11%. Over a century each methane molecule in the atmosphere traps 30 molecules times more heat than each carbon dioxide molecule. The Amazon rainforest is one of the places badly impacted by farming. For generations, the vast area of forest, often referred to as the 'lungs of the Earth', naturally absorbed carbon dioxide in the air.

However, according to the experts, it is now emitting almost one billion tonnes more carbon dioxide annually than it can take up. The Amazon basin as a whole contains roughly half of the world's tropical rainforests, while the research only included the Brazilian forests, which account for around 60% of that total. Because of its richness and capacity to produce rain and humidity, the Amazon rainforest is well known across the world. The release of carbon from a rainforest so huge are largely driven by fires set by developers deliberately burning down the trees to clear agricultural land for the grazing of cattle or the growing of soy beans. The immense forestland, commonly referred to as the "lungs of the Earth," has naturally absorbed carbon dioxide from the atmosphere for eons. However, during the past 40 years, the Amazon rainforest has shrunk by 17% as a result of the natural terrain being turned into agricultural land. The woods have dried up as a result, which may lower their ability to store carbon and increase their susceptibility to fires. They discovered that new growth could only be responsible for eliminating around 0.5 billion tonnes of the carbon dioxide that is typically created by fires each year. They make up more than 10% of total animal biomass in the Amazon rain forest.

By controlling atmospheric gases, natural ecosystems may change temperature, wind patterns, and precipitation. Half of the rainfall in the enormous Amazonian rain forests is self-generated. The water supply is reduced to a corresponding degree as the woods are cleared. According to mathematical simulations of the cycle of precipitation and evaporation, there is a critical level of vegetation beyond which it is impossible for trees to persist, permanently transforming most of the large river basin into scrubby grassland. The pall might then move south, drying off areas of Brazil's fertile agricultural interior. The substances that made up the wood and tissue are partially transformed into greenhouse gases during the clearing of forests. Then, when forests develop again, an equal number of the elements are drawn back into solid form. Between 1850 and 1980, there was a net global loss of tropical forest cover, which added between 90 and 120 billion metric tons of carbon dioxide to the atmosphere, not far behind the 165 billion metric tons produced by burning coal, oil, and gas. Together, these two processes have increased the amount of carbon dioxide in the atmosphere by more than 25%, paving the way for both global warming and an increase in sea level. Methane, the second-most significant greenhouse gas, has increased by roughly double during the same time, with 10 to 15 percent of the rise attributed to tropical deforestation. If 4 million square kilometers of the tropical regions were replanted in forest, in other words an area half the size of Brazil, all of the current buildup of atmospheric carbon dioxide from human agents would be canceled. Additionally, methane and other greenhouse gases would not rise as quickly. Organisms are responsible for creating the world's soils. Rocks are broken down by plant roots, creating the majority of the grit and pebbles in the substrate. But soils are more than just pieces of broken rock. They are intricate ecosystems made up of a wide variety of plants, small animals, fungus, and bacteria that are all carefully balanced and circulating nutrients as solutions and microscopic particles. A healthy soil literally moves and breathes. Its microscopic balance supports both croplands and natural ecosystems. The term "ecosystems services" itself has a mundane ring, similar to that of "waste disposal" or "water quality control." But if even a tiny portion of these auxiliary creatures vanished, human life would be significantly shorter and less pleasurable. The fact that we disregard and sometimes despise the creatures whose life support our own is a failing in our species.

Another identical sign may be found further along Russia's Arctic coast. Walruses mostly eat clams, which only thrive on a few specific Arctic seabed areas. In between fishing sessions, they haul themselves out onto the sea ice to rest. But those resting places have now melted away. They must swim to the beaches on faraway shores instead. There are only a few suitable places As a result, tens of thousands of Pacific walrus, or two thirds of the species, congregate on a single beach right now. Crushingly overcrowded, some clamber up slopes and find themselves at the tops of cliffs. Their vision is quite weak while they are out of the water, but they can clearly smell the sea down below at the base of the cliff. So they attempt the shortest method to get there. It is difficult to forget the sight of a three-ton walrus falling to its doom. It is not necessary to be an expert in nature to recognize when something has drastically gone wrong.

Our impact is now truly global. Our blind assault on the planet is changing the very fundamentals of the living world. Average global temperatures on Earth rose nearly 1 degree celsius between 1880 and 2012. This is now the status of our planet. We are extracting over 80 million tonnes of seafood from the oceans each year and have reduced 30 per cent of fish stocks to critical levels. Almost all the large oceanic fish have been removed. We have lost about half of the world's shallow-water corals and major bleachings are occurring almost every year. Our coastal developments and seafood farming projects have now reduced the extent of mangroves and seagrass beds by more than 30 per cent. Our plastic debris has been found throughout the ocean, from the surface waters to the deepest trenches. There are currently 1.8 trillion plastic fragments drifting in a monstrous garbage patch in the northern Pacific, where currents cause the surface waters to circulate. Four other garbage patches are forming on similar gyres elsewhere in the oceans. Plastic is invading oceanic food chains and over 90 per cent of seabirds have plastic fragments in their stomachs. No beach on the planet is free of our waste. Sharks and rays are important to the health of our oceans, yet they have become increasingly valued for their meat, for parts used for their purported medicinal properties (e.g. manta and devil ray gill plates), or for use in dishes such as shark fin soup. The global abundance of 18 of 31 oceanic sharks and rays has declined by 71% over the last 50 years. This collapse in their abundance reflects an increase in extinction risk for most species. By 1980, nine of the 31 oceanic sharks and rays were threatened. By 2020, three-quarters (77%, 24 species) were threatened with an elevated risk of extinction. For example, the oceanic Whitetip Shark has declined by 95% globally over three generation lengths, and has consequently moved from Vulnerable to Critically Endangered on the IUCN Red List.

Freshwater systems are as threatened as marine. Freshwater environments host a rich biodiversity, including one-third of vertebrate species. Freshwater is also essential to our survival and well-being 49 in domestic use, energy production, food security, and industry. Although fresh water covers less than 1% of the planet's surface, more than 50% of the human population lives within 3km of a freshwater body. This human proximity can be a threat to freshwater species and habitats, including many biodiversity hotspots, via pollution, water abstraction or flow modification, species overexploitation and invasive species. Because freshwater environments are highly connected, threats can travel easily from one location to another.

Around 20% of the freshwater fish species in the world are either extinct or in catastrophic decline. In several tropical nations, the situation is on the verge of becoming critical. Only 122 of the 266 species of lowland peninsular Malaysia's freshwater fishes were found in a recent search. Evolutionary biologists are well-known for the adaptive radiation of cyprinid fishes that happened only in Lake Lanao on the Philippine Island of Mindanao. In three genera, up to 18 endemic species were formerly recognized; a recent search turned up just three species, which represent one of the genera. Overfishing and competition from recently imported fish species have been blamed for the decline.

In the summer of 2022, while visiting Iran, I went to a naturally occuring spring in the Shiraz Kudion district. This spring had more than halved over the previous 30 years because of climate change. The entire area was covered in common reed, and the waterways were alive with fish and, upon closer observation, many moving snails and shrimps. Locals refer to this location as the Spirings of Beyza. I managed to catch a young freshwater turtle there, but the real find was a population of freshwater crabs, which must have been present here for a very long time and helped shaped the environment. The first few crab remnants I noticed were claws and legs, but shortly I discovered a living one. However, as soon as I tried to get a closer look, it retreated into its burrow. I took a quick glance around before kneeling in the water. The water was once up to five meters deep here, according to the locals, but now it is only knee-deep or less. After searching for two days, I eventually located two of those crabs—a male and a female. The larger male was the first crab I discovered and photographed since it was stranded and had nowhere to hide. As I was taking measurements and recording a video, I also caught the smaller female as she was slowly making her way away. I then compared the two side by side. Apart from observing the color of the body or the size of the claws, it is not very difficult to determine a crab's gender. The simplest yet most effective approach to do so is to look at the underside of the animal. Females have larger abdomens because they need more room to deposit their eggs, whilst males may be distinguished by their smaller, triangular abdomens. Freshwater crabs are crucial in the breakdown of nutrients from organic debris that wash into streams. However, few studies have examined the precise effects of these detritivores' interactions with one another and the leaf litter on ecosystems.

At an experiment, the amount of leaf litter was compared across enclosures with and without crabs in Monteverde, Costa Rica. It was discovered that crabs' manipulation and eating of leaves had a greater influence than their consumption of other detritivores and shredders, as seen by the quicker rates of disintegration in their enclosures compared to those without them. The crab actions that had the most effects on leaf litter were studied in further detail in a laboratory environment. The crabs were brought to aquariums from Monteverde, Costa Rica, along with unfiltered stream water and common subcanopy tree leaves. It was discovered that aquariums containing crabs had substantially more leaf mass than the aquariums without. Additionally, they used video records and visual observations to see how the crabs used their claws to grip and tear the leaves, which helped in ingestion. At the conclusion of the experiment, they saw that the leaves in the crab-filled tanks were split up into several pieces, while the leaves in the crab-free aquariums were still intact. Given their prevalence in tropical streams, these results imply that crabs play a significant part in aiding in the processing of the debris that builds up in neotropical streams. A river near Bushehr also had similar-looking freshwater crabs, and their populations were encouraging. These other crabs however where light green in color and lived in the base of a fast flowing river.

We have interrupted the free flow of almost all the world's sizeable rivers with over 50,000 large dams. Dams can also change the temperature of the water, drastically altering the timing of fish

ter searching for two days, I eventually captured a male freshwater crab, and shortly after a smaller
nale.

I approached most burrows the crabs retreated deep into these burrows in which they had excavated, and
nin they were safe from predators.

migrations and their breeding events. We not only use rivers as dumping grounds to remove our litter, but load them with the fertilisers, pesticides and industrial chemicals that we spread on the lands they drain. Many are now the most polluted parts of the environment to be found anywhere on the globe. We take their water and use it to irrigate our crops, and reduce their levels so severely that some of them, at some point in the year, no longer reach the sea. We build on flood plains and around river mouths, and drain the wetlands to such an extent that their total area is now only half of what it was when I was born. Our assault on freshwater systems has reduced the animals and plants that live in them more severely than those in any other habitat. Globally, we have reduced the size of their animal populations by over 80 per cent.

The largest freshwater mollusk fauna in the world is found in the United States, where mussels and gill-breathing snails are particularly abundant. The introduction of foreign mollusks and other aquatic creatures, pollution, river damming, and other factors have all contributed to the long-term, sharp loss of these species. Twenty percent of the remaining mussel species are endangered, and at least 12 species have gone extinct over their entire geographic ranges. Extirpation of local populations is common, even in areas where extinction has not yet taken place. Originally, the Lake Erie and Ohio River system supported large populations of 78 distinct species; today, 19 of them are extinct, and 29 are uncommon. In the past, the Tennessee River in Alabama's Muscle [sic] Shoals was home to 68 different kinds of mussels. Their shells were designed specifically for riffles or shoals, which are narrow streams with sand or gravelly bottoms and swift currents. 44 of the species were wiped off when Wilson Dam was built in the early 1920s, impounding and deepening the water. In a related phenomenon, pollution and impoundment have worked together to wipe out 30 species and two genera of gill breathing snails from the Tennessee and neighboring Coosa rivers.

Due to their propensity to specialize for life in small environments and their inability to travel swiftly from one location to another, freshwater and land mollusks are typically threatened with extinction. The idea is chillingly illustrated by what happened to the tree snails on Moorea and Tahiti. The snails, a little adaptive radiation in a single small area, consisting of 11 species in the genera Partula and Samoana, were recently wiped off by a single type of alien carnivorous snail. It was grand-scale foolishness, the result of two desperate errors made by persons in positions of power. The first was the introduction of the giant African snail (Achatina fulica) as a food source to the islands. The carnivorous snail (Euglandina rosea) was then introduced to manage the Achatina once it had multiplied to the point where it was a pest. Euglandina itself multiplied astronomically, moving 1.2 kilometers forward every year along a front. Along the way, in addition to the enormous African snail, it also ate every local tree snail. On Moorea, the last remaining wild tree snails went extinct in 1987. The identical scenario is currently taking place on adjacent Tahiti. Additionally, due to Euglandina and habitat loss, the whole unique tree-snail genus Achatinella in Hawaii is under peril. The remaining 19 species are in jeopardy, and 22 are extinct.

The most catastrophic extinction episode of recent history may be the destruction of the cichlid fishes of Lake Victoria. Nearly all of the important ecological niches for freshwater fish were filled by 300 or more species that descended from a single ancestor species. The Nile perch was first introduced as a sport fish in 1959 by British colonists. The population of native fish has been greatly decreased, and some species have been eradicated, by this enormous predator, which can reach lengths of about 2 meters. Over 50% of the endemics are anticipated to be eradicated eventually. The perch has an impact on the entire lake environment in addition to the fish. The plant life grows and decomposes as the algal-eating cichlids disappear, reducing oxygen in the deeper water and hastening the extinction of crustaceans, cichlids, and other types of life.

Sometimes there are distinctive freshwater habitats in valleys. I saw this while on a trip to the Boraq Valley, also known as Tang-e Boraq in the Iranian Eghlid area. We arrived here in the late afternoon, there was six of us, and we had packed our camping gear, and now we had to locate a path up the mountain close to a cave. We began our trek at the mountain's foot and worked our way up. It was an arduous climb, but the landscape was breath-taking. However, at first, the presence of humans and their inquisitive attitude disrupted the journey. However, as we climbed higher, the influence of humans almost completely vanished. We stumbled a few times along the way as the sun progressively set and the route grew more difficult to ascend. Nevertheless, we eventually arrived at our destination. When we arrived at the targeted place, it was already dark. We immediately set up camp, and I began exploring inside the cave with a head lamp. Water dripped from the roof, and pools of water had been formed on the cave's floor, there were tiny crustaceans and shrimp-like creatures living in some of the smaller crevices. Soon after, I noticed a frog enjoying the puddles in the cave. It was extremely well hidden, but just as I was going to take a few measurements and hold it in my hand, I heard a startling noise. At first it sounded like people screaming but then soon later golden eyes surrounded us, these sounds were not that of a human, but of a canine. These were a pack of golden jackals, nocturnal canines looking for potential prey, during the day it was impossible to see them, but The golden jackal's coat varies in color from a pale creamy yellow in summer to a dark tawny beige in winter. It is smaller and has shorter legs, a shorter tail, a more elongated torso, a less-prominent forehead, and a narrower and more pointed muzzle than the Arabian wolf.

The golden jackal can exist in a variety of settings due to its omnivorous diet, tolerance of arid circumstances, and ability to eat a wide variety of foods. The jackal can trot over considerable distances in quest of food because to its long legs and lean frame. It has been seen on islands without freshwater, where it may survive for long periods without drinking. There were six of us on the expedition, and each of us worked in pairs to search for combustible plants to use as fuel for our fires. While my father searched for wood and other items, I searched for animals, but each time the jackals' cries became louder. Every hour one of us had to be on patrol for safety reasons and to keep our fire from burning out, which prevented me from sleeping since, in any case, my desire for adventure and curiosity kept me awake in such a beautiful natural setting. During the day, though, there simply is no indication on those jackals, they seem to melt into the ground. With such unusual species, however, people have left their imprint, and the water in Tang-e Boraq's spring, rivers, and water bodies has more than halved over the previous 15 years, according to locals. However, plastic also makes an appearance here. In one area, I noticed a huge truck tire next to the river; how it got there is a mystery. This valley is indeed beautiful, but I can't begin to imagine how enchanting it must have been in the past. I've heard stories of a time when the water descended from the mountain and the entire area was a fruitful, lush terrain rich in biodiversity, but today there are just a few pockets of water left, acting as many of these species' final refugee. However, we were forced to end the trip since one of our crew members fell while descending down a cliff and suffered terrible injuries. It may be easier to visualize than to tell how he slid and how his toe nail came off.

Mountains have been getting drier and dryer over the years, and there was considerably less life there than in earlier years, as far as I can recollect. As a result of the extreme weather and challenging terrain, desert mountains themselves have a very limited variety of life. Mountain hiking is one of my favorite outdoor activities, and whenever I visit my cousins, we almost always go hiking. One of them, whose name is Sina, is just one month younger than me; his brother, Sepehr, is two years younger. We normally prepare our equipment the night before and go for the mountain in my cousin's backyard about four in the morning, just before the sun comes up. We have to trek for over 30 minutes before we get at the mountain's foot, and by that time the sun has already begun to rise. There is a man-made path that hikers can use to reach the top of the mountain, which bears the name Derak. But in addition to hiking, we also came to seek for some animals. As a result, I suggested that we take a different route, one that no people use. It was risky, but with little work and a lot of climbing, we succeeded. Although the risk of falling was quite great, we were driven to climb even higher by the natural beauties we encountered as we had to traverse an ocean of pebbles that frequently slid beneath our feet. From a distance, we could make out a few mountain gazelles and a little flower spider on a shrub. By the time we stopped, it was midday because the rest of the trail required special climbing gear, so we rested at the top and took in the view and what lay beyond the horizon. However, we had no idea how much more difficult and perilous the journey down would be than the way up. Our weight now posed a challenge and risk as we slowly descended due to the downward force of gravity. I was the first person in line, then sina, then Sepehr. Suddenly, Sina quickly reached out with his left arm and grabbed Sepehr as he was about to fall while slipping off a rock. Sina finally caught Sepehr, though, and things quickly got out of hand. Rocks began to slide under our feet, and we began to descend the mountain by what we called "rock skating." It was a risky method, but we had no choice because there were no brakes. Once we reached the bottom safely, we did need new pants because the friction from the rocks had torn our old ones. Now that I think back on it, it seems like a comical incident.

Forests too have been terribly affected. Currently, we remove more than 15 billion trees annually. There are now half as many rainforests as there once were. Beef production is the main cause of ongoing deforestation, which is twice that of the next three worst cases combined. Cattle pastures take up 170 million hectares of land in Brazil alone, which is an area seven times the size of the United Kingdom. There used to be a lot more rainforest there. Soy is the

second driver. Around 131 million hectares are needed to grow soy, mostly in South America. As the forest is reduced, the proportion loss of species gets closer but never quite reaches the percentage loss of forest area. Not only will the world's forest cover disappear in the following thirty years, but also about half of the forest species. Thankfully, this presumption is overstated. Some of the plants and animals that live in rain forests have extensive geographic ranges. Therefore, the rate of species extinction is lower than the area loss. So, if the rainforest area is cut in half, there will be a larger than 10% but less than 50% loss of species. However, it should be noted that this percentage range just represents the loss anticipated as a result of the area impact, and it is still rather little. A few species in the remaining patches will also go extinct due to rifle-shot extinction, which refers to the hunting of endangered species of flora and animals such the New Zealand mistletoe and the Spix's macaw. Others will be wiped off by novel illnesses, foreign vegetation, and animals like feral pigs and rats. As the patches get smaller and more vulnerable to human intrusion, that secondary loss will get worse. The combined strength of these extra damaging factors in all environments is unknown. Only the bare minimum can be inferred with certainty in the case of tropical rain forests—a 10% extinction rate with a half in area.

If the current rate of environmental damage continues, a 20 percent extinction in all forms of world biodiversity is very likely. This includes the most abundant of all creatures - insects. Globally, the number of insects has decreased by a quarter in just 30 years. This proportion is significantly greater in areas where pesticide usage is widespread. According to recent research, Puerto Rico has lost over 90% of the mass of the insects and spiders that live in the canopy, while Germany has lost 75% of the mass of its flying insects. The insects are by far the most diverse group of all living species. Many are pollinators, vital components of many food systems. The main elements preventing populations of plant-eating insects from turning into plagues are those who hunt. However, arthropods are present everywhere; all they need is a chance. When I went to Tang-e Boraq, there was a place where the rock had been worn by water, and it was big enough for me to get inside. I brought my cousin with me so we could photograph what we saw; this little cave appeared first lifeless and terribly gloomy. However, the cave's ceiling was home to a variety of animal species, and the walls were covered with a variety of spider species, from cellar spiders to cave spiders. How these creatures managed to survive in the fast-moving water is a mystery in and of itself. The other end's exit was partially blocked by a boulder, so we had to lay down in the icy spring water and crawl our way out, like soldiers. However, when we eventually left, we were covered with moths and spiders, and some were also in our hair.

34 percent of the 10,290 insect and other invertebrate species were categorized as vulnerable or endangered in western Germany, the former Federal Republic, in 1987. In England, the percentage was 17 percent of 13,741 insect species, while in Austria it was 22 percent of 9,694 invertebrate species.

The wild is now being replaced by us. Today, agriculture is practiced on half of Earth's fertile area. We have overused it a lot of the time. We overgraze it, burn it, overburden it with inappropriate crop kinds, and pesticide-spray it, killing the soil invertebrates that give it life. We also overdo it with nitrates and phosphates. Many soils are losing their topsoil and transforming into hard, sterile, and empty ground from lush ecosystems teeming with mushrooms, worms, specialized bacteria, and a variety of other tiny species. Rainwater drains off it like it would a pavement, which adds to the excessive flooding that now regularly engulfs the interior regions of many countries that engage in industrial farming. On our globe now, domesticated birds make about 70% of the total bird population. Chickens make up the largest bulk. We consume 50 billion of them annually worldwide. At any given time, there are 23 billion living chickens. Many of them are given soy-based feed made from land that has been cleared of trees. Even more startling is the fact that 96 per cent of the mass of all the mammals on

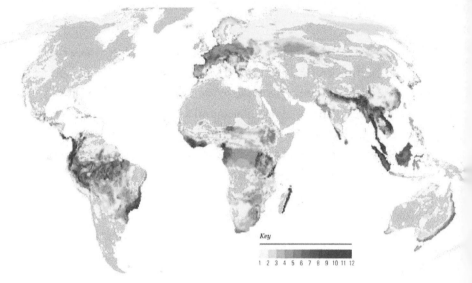

Global hotspots at risk

The relative importance of each pixel across species and threats as measured by the number of times a pixel falls into a hotspot region for any taxon or threat. Hotspot regions are defined as locations containing highest 10% of number of species at risk from each major threat and taxonomic group.

Source: Harfoot et al. (2022) (©WWF living planet report)

Projected loss of terrestrial and freshwater biodiversity compared to preindustrial Period

Biodiversity loss with increasing global warming. The higher the percentage of species projected to be lost (due to loss of suitable climate in a given area), the higher the risk to ecosystem integrity, functioning and resilience to climate change. Colour shading represents the proportion of species for which the climate is projected to become sufficiently unsuitable that the species becomes locally Endangered (sensu International Union for the Conservation of Nature, IUCN) and at high risk of local extinction within a given area at a given global warming level. Source: Source: Figure 2.6 in Parmesan et al. (2022) 11, based on data from Warren et al (2018) (©WWF living planet report)

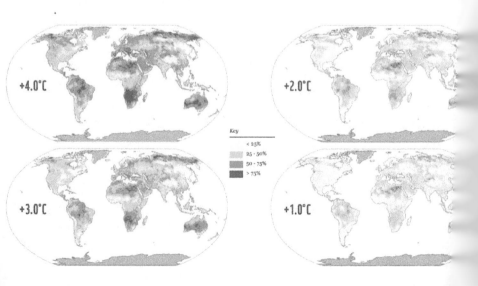

Earth is made up of our bodies and those of the animals that we raise to eat. About one-third of the overall mass is made up of our own mass. Domestic animals, namely cows, pigs, and sheep, account for little more than 60%. The remaining 4% are made up of all the wild animals, including mice, elephants, and whales. 1.47 trillion Every day, methane is produced by cows alone in amounts of over 150 billion gallons. Cows burp every 90 seconds, which accounts for 95% of their greenhouse gas emissions. Environmental damage caused by methane is estimated to be 25-100 times greater than that caused by carbon dioxide.

Despite the world's alarming loss of biodiversity, nature can still be found in unexpected places, including within our cities. We must remember that nature is us, and we are nature, and that no matter how far we live from the wilderness, it touches us in unexpected ways. Demodex folliculorum mites live a secretive life beneath our skin, only emerging at night to mate on our foreheads, noses, and nipples. Despite their success, their days as independent parasites may be numbered. D folliculorum is carried by roughly 90% of people and is most abundant in the wings of the nose, the forehead, the ear canal, and the nipples. They live a harmless life, feasting on the sebum naturally secreted by cells in the pores, and are likely to have been present since childhood, having been passed down from our mothers during birth or breastfeeding. You may not believe they exist until you see them under a microscope for yourself! Every night, these tiny arachnids come to the skin's surface to mate, and if you have a simple light microscope at home, you can see them by putting tape in a few spots on your face and waiting in the dark for a few hours. The landscape will astound you when you remove the tape and examine it under the microscope.

Nature is all around us, and we are part of it. Unfortunately, due to inbreeding and gene loss, these Demodex face mites are becoming extinct, which is bad news. The first genome sequencing study of these mites appears to have caught them in the process of transitioning from external symbionts to internal symbionts, completely dependent on us for survival. This process may eventually lead to their extinction.

This gene loss has resulted in a drastic decrease in the number of cells in adult mites, which is most likely the first evolutionary step on their path to adopting an entirely symbiotic lifestyle within our tissues. The more they adapt to us, the more genes they are likely to lose, until they are completely reliant on us. With no opportunity to gain additional genes from less closely related mites - they don't appear to transfer between adult humans during close physical contact - the mites' isolated existence and resulting inbreeding may have eventually set the mites on a path to evolutionary extinction. If this happens, it could be bad news for us as well because they are associated with healthy skin, so if we lose them, you may experience skin problems.

To protect life, we must first comprehend its significance, role, and operation. According to what is widely regarded as the most accurate estimate of life on Earth, humans coexist with up to 8.7 million distinct forms of life on the planet. The Holocene has been one of the most stable periods in our planet's history; for ten thousand years, the average temperature has not changed by more than one degree Celsius, and the rich and thriving living world around us has played an important role in this stability.

However, the Holocene saw significant advances in human knowledge and technology, which can and are being used to understand the changes we see, predict their implications, and prevent or mitigate the harm they may cause to the Earth and to us. Paleontologists are working to better understand planetary change. Paleontologists are learning more about how upcoming environmental change will affect life on Earth because many fossils contain information about previous climates and ecosystems.

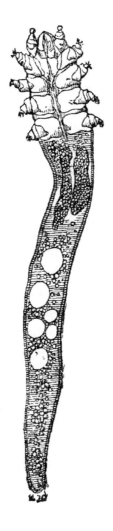

I remember being about 5 years old, visiting a seaside in a place called Buhshehr in Iran, with family and relatives, and there my grandfather's brother brought out of nowhere an enormous sea snake, which he had caught while it was washed ashore, from the picture taken back then, the snake's species isn't obvious, but this could very well be a Persian gulf sea snake (Hydrophis lapemoides). Sea snakes are among the most venomous of all snakes, and seeing one up close reminded me how Nature's beauty can be deadly. But my mission to raise awareness and conduct research did not appear out of nowhere; it was triggered by an animal I had not seen in over ten years. The Iranian tortoise (Testudo graeca zarudnyi) can be found in Iran's harsh arid deserts. This well-armored heavy reptile is one of the desert's longest-living creatures, and it is well adapted to the harsh environment. A charismatic creature whose life has an impact on nearly all other creatures in the ecosystem, its nest, which it digs with its powerful legs, provides protection for itself and others. When I was about 7 or 8, I saw one of these while driving home with my grandfather. It was crossing the road, and I had no idea it would be the last time I saw one; they are endangered and only seen in reserves. Poaching, pet trade, and habitat destruction were the causes of their decline. Since then, I've been spreading awareness, hope, and support for the natural world, as well as conducting research on its wondrous creatures.

The Holocene was the best time for humans to dominate the world, but we have left it behind, and our impacts have given this new epoch a new name, Anthropocene, after us, the age of humans. We are now the world's dominant force for change. Our activities have an impact on three-quarters of the land surface and two-thirds of the ocean. The ice on our poles is melting. There is 40% less Arctic sea ice cover in the summer than there was in 1980.

Things we take for granted are disappearing as the Earth's biodiversity declines. Clean air and water, the food we eat, the soil in which it grows, a stable climate, and productive seas. The nine planetary boundaries that provided balance to our world and the opportunity to dominate it are becoming unbalanced. We are on the verge of entering a danger zone in which irreversible and self-amplifying change could push the entire planet away from the desired equilibrium. The sad thing is that we are not only throwing one problem at nature, but many, ranging from climate change to biodiversity loss, plastic pollution to poaching, acidification of the oceans to the introduction of invasive species.

We need to urgently ramp up mitigation actions to avert a dangerous rise in global temperatures beyond 1.5°C, and to help people adapt to the climate change we are already experiencing. We need to restore nature and the environmental services it provides – both the tangible provision of our clean air, fresh water, food, fuel and fibre; and also the many intangible ways in which nature contributes to our lives and well-being.

However, not all species are impacted by climate change. In the northern temperate and boreal zones of North America and Europe, beetles and moths that attack forests are producing more generations annually due to the extended growth season and greater winter survival. The high Arctic and the Himalayan highlands are experiencing the emergence of new illnesses as a result of the widespread movement of insects and worms that spread disease in both wildlife and humans. The term "positive climate feedback" refers to the way that warming is altering ecosystems' functioning and setting in motion ecological processes that eventually lead to more warming. Increased wildfires, tree mortality brought on by drought and insect outbreaks, peatlands drying up, and thawing tundra permafrost all result in higher CO_2 emissions when dead plant matter decomposes or burns. As a result, systems that have historically been reliable carbon sinks are beginning to change into new carbon sources. These natural processes will become irreversible once they hit a tipping point, causing our world to continue warming at a very rapid pace. This would be a catastrophe for humanity as well as for a large portion of the species on our planet and is one of the largest threats from "overshoot" of the globally agreed-upon thresholds for hazardous climate change.

This will not be our first mistake; we have previously caused environmental disasters, the majority of which were caused by human error and a lack of planning and foresight, as seen in Pripyat, Ukraine. This city contains all of the facilities that humans have built to live a happy and comfortable life—all of the elements of our man-made habitat. There are 160 towers, each built at a specific angle to a well-planned grid of roads. The tallest towers stand nearly 20 stories high and are topped with a massive iron hammer and sickle, the town's creators' emblem. During a busy construction period in the 1970s, the Soviet Union built Pripyat. It was the perfect place to live for nearly 50,000 people. Despite this, no one currently lives in Pripyat. Its structures and accessories are so familiar that you know their demise cannot be due to the passage of time. We humans, alone on Earth, have the power to create and then destroy worlds. On April 26, 1986, the nearby Vladimir Ilyich Lenin Nuclear Power Plant's reactor number 4, now known as 'Chernobyl,' exploded. The exact number of deaths caused by the event is still unknown, but estimates range in the hundreds of thousands. For the next 20 thousand years, the zone was declared uninhabitable. This may appear to be the worst environmental disaster in human history. Unfortunately, this is not the case. For much of the last century, something else has been surfacing everywhere, all over the world. Not just one unintentional accident, but a damaging lack of care and understanding that affects everything we do. It didn't all start with a single explosion. A single instrument cannot detect its fallout. It took hundreds of studies conducted all over the world to confirm that this is indeed happening. Its consequences will be far more severe and could eventually lead to the destabilisation and collapse of everything on which we rely. The spiraling decline of our planet's biodiversity is the true tragedy of our time. There must be enormous biodiversity on this planet for life to truly thrive. Only when billions of different individual organisms make the most of every resource and opportunity they come across, and millions of species live lives that intertwine to sustain each other, will the planet run efficiently.

It has only been in the last few decades that we have realized that our world was inherently unsustainable. But now that we know this, we have a choice. We could go on living our happy lives, raising our families, and occupying ourselves with the honest interests of the modern society that we have built, while ignoring the disaster that was waiting on our doorstep. Or we could change.

In earth history, Every hundred million years or so, after all those painstaking selections and improvements, something catastrophic happened–a mass extinction. For different reasons at different times in the Earth's history, there had been a profound, rapid, global change to the environment to which so many species had become so exquisitely adapted. The Earth's life-support machine had stuttered, and the miraculous assemblage of fragile interconnections which held it together had collapsed. Great numbers of species suddenly disappeared, leaving only a few. Each time, nature has collapsed, leaving just enough survivors to start the process once more. The last time it happened, it is thought that a meteorite over 10 kilometres in diameter struck the Earth's surface with an impact 2 million times more powerful than the largest hydrogen bomb ever tested. It landed in a bed of gypsum, so, some think, it sent Sulphur high into the atmosphere to fall across the globe as rain sufficiently acidic to kill vegetation and dissolve the bodies of plankton in the surface waters of the oceans. The dust cloud that arose blocked the light from the Sun to such a degree that it may have reduced the rate of plant growth for several years. Flaming remnants of the blast may have showered back to Earth, causing firestorms across the western hemisphere. The burning world would have added carbon dioxide and smoke to the already polluted air, warming the Earth through a greenhouse effect. And because the meteorite landed on the coast, it initiated colossal tsunamis that swept across the globe, destroying coastal ecosystems and sending marine sand significant distances inland. It was an event that changed the course of natural history–wiping out three-quarters of all species, including anything on land larger than the size of a domestic dog. It ended the 175-million-year reign of the dinosaurs. Life would have to rebuild. For 66 million years since then, nature has been at work reconstructing the living world, recreating and refining a new diversity of species. And one of the products of this rebooting of life was humanity.

We have made the human age a regret for the planet, and rather the end of humanity. Five mass extinctions have occurred in Earth's 4.5 billion-year history; the most recent was the event that ended the dinosaur era, when a meteorite impact caused a catastrophic change in the earth's conditions. The same thing is happening now, but at a faster rate; we are the dinosaurs, and our actions are the meteorite.

Many might think these harsh conditions are caused by climate change, but I say it Is due to the loss of biodiversity, cause if we had a healthy thriving biodiversity, that would be able to capture our impacts. We are losing terrestrial and aquatic life across the globe.

Each kind of plant and animal living there in an ecosystem is linked in the food web to only a small part of the other species. When one species is eradicated, another one multiplies to take its place. When several species are lost, the local environment begins to clearly deteriorate. The nutrition cycles' pathways get blocked, which reduces productivity. More biomass is either washed away or is buried under dead plants and slowly decomposing, oxygen-starved muck. As the most suited bees, moths, birds, bats, and other specialists disappear, less skilled pollinators take over. Less seeds are dispersed, and fewer seedlings grow. As herbivore populations drop, so do their predator populations. Even though it may seem similar on the surface, life continues in an ecosystem that is degrading. No matter how awkwardly they manage it, there are always species that can recolonize the underdeveloped region and utilize the static resources. If given enough time, a new species combination—a reconstructed fauna and flora—will restructure the ecosystem in a way that moves resources and energy a little more effectively. Since the species is suited to penetrate and rejuvenate only such defective systems, the atmosphere they create and the makeup of the soil they enrich will match those found in analogous ecosystems in other regions of the planet. They do this because they produce more offspring and get more energy and resources. However, the existence of sufficient species to fulfill that particular function is necessary for the world's fauna and flora to have the capacity to heal. They too may enter the endangered species red zone. Our planet has changed. The world's population has grown from 2.3 billion to 7.8 billion since 1937, while the amount of carbon dioxide in the atmosphere has gone up from 280 to 415 parts per million and wildlife has plummeted from 66% to 35%.

A change in the atmospheric carbon has always been a challenge for earth, it was a feature of all 5 mass extinctions. In previous events however, it had taken volcanic activity up to 1 million years to produce enough carbon from within the earth to trigger a catastrophe, by burning millions of years of living organisms all at once as coal and oil, we had managed to do so in less than 200 years. This increase in greenhouse gases would result in the warming of the planet. Nevertheless 'Greenhouse gases' are crucial to keeping our planet at a suitable temperature for life. Without the natural greenhouse effect, the heat emitted by the Earth would simply pass outwards from the Earth's surface into space and the Earth would have an average temperature of about -20°C. A greenhouse gas is called that because it absorbs infrared radiation from the Sun in the form of heat, which is circulated in the atmosphere and eventually lost to space. Greenhouse gases also increase the rate at which the atmosphere can absorb short-wave radiation from the Sun, but this has a much weaker effect on global temperatures.

The biosphere barely accounts for around one part in ten billion of the earth's mass when all creatures are taken into account. It is dispersed over a surface area of half a billion square kilometers in a layer of soil, water, and air that is kilometer thick. No sign of the biosphere could be detected with the naked eye if the planet were the size of a regular desktop globe and its surface were seen edgewise from an arm's length distant. However, life has fragmented into countless species, the basic units, each of which plays a distinct role in respect to the total.

The battle between an enormous diversity of species, each weighing almost little, for a vanishingly small amount of energy, is what defines life. Only 10% of the sun's energy reaches the surface of the planet; this percentage is fixed by green plants during photosynthesis. In the process of moving from one creature to another in the food chain, the free energy is subsequently substantially reduced; only around 10% is transferred to the caterpillars and other herbivores that consume the plants and bacteria. The spiders and other low-level predators who consume the herbivores receive 10% of that (or 1% of the original). The top carnivores are the only ones that are devoured, aside from parasites and scavengers, and they receive 10% of the leftover from the warblers and other middle-level carnivores that eat the low-level carnivores. Due to their position at the top of the food chain, top carnivores like eagles, tigers, and great white sharks are bound to be large and uncommon. They always balance on the brink of extinction because they consume such a little proportion of life's available energy, and they are the first to suffer when the ecosystem in which they exist begins to deteriorate. By observing that species in the food chain are organized into two hierarchies, one may quickly learn a lot about biological variety.

The first is the energy pyramid, which is a simple result of the law of declining energy flow as stated: a sizable portion of the sun's energy incident on earth goes into the plants at the bottom, tapering to a little portion for the giant predators at the top. Biomass—the bulk of living things—makes up the second pyramid. Plants make up the vast majority of the physical mass of the living world. Scavengers and other decomposers, such as bacteria, fungi, and termites, account for the second-largest portion of the food chain. In exchange for returning degraded nutrient chemicals to the plants, they collectively extract the last trace amounts of fixed energy from dead tissue and waste at every level of the food web. The biomass of the plants decreases with each level above it until you reach the top predators, who are so rare that even catching a glimpse of one in the wild is remarkable. Let me emphasize it. Everyone passes by a sparrow, a squirrel, or even a dandelion without batting an eye, but seeing a peregrine falcon or a mountain lion is an unforgettable experience. Not merely due to their size (compare them to a cow) or viciousness (compare them to a house cat), but also because they are uncommon.

We have to keep in mind that Our planet is Vulnerable, we have to realize that our home is not limitless, there is an edge to our existence, by thinking such it becomes clear that we are ultimately bound by and reliant upon the finite natural world around us, my generation , realized the impacts that we had on our planet. We have overfished 30% of fish stokes to critical levels, 10 to 40% of the fish caught are bycatch, this is a huge impact on global biodiversity, and many species are simply fished to extinction. We cut down over 15 billion trees each year, we have cut down 3 trillion trees across the world, half of the world's rainforest have already been cleared. We breathe in what trees breathe out, and they breathe in what we breathe out we are nature, by damming, polluting and over extracting rivers and lakes we have reduced the freshwater populations by over 80%. We are replacing the wild with the tame. Half of the fertile land on earth is now farmland. 70% of the mass of birds on earth are domestic birds. We account for over one third of the weight of mammals on earth, a further 60% are the animals we raise to eat. The rest from mice to whales only make up just 4%. The planet can't support billions of large meat eaters. We may be eating meat thinking we would be as strong as an ox, forgetting an ox itself eats grass. There simply isn't the space.

My uncle, Hamed
Khaledi, about to release a
beached the Persian Gulf
snake back into the wild.

My grandfather's brother,
Faramarz Khaledi, an
expert snake catcher,
holding onto a Persian
Gulf snake.

Remember if the natural world collapses, we collapse. This is now our planet, run by human kind, for human kind.

We are facing the collapse of the living world, the very thing that gave birth to our civilizations. It is now code red for humanity, the past 5 years have been the hottest years on record since 1850, In just 50 years, humanity has wiped out 68 % of global wildlife populations. 9/10 of us breathe unhealthy air. The amazon rainforest now emits more CO2 than it absorbs. The emissions amount to a billion tonnes of carbon dioxide a year. The giant forest had previously been a carbon sink, absorbing the emissions driving the climate crisis, but is now causing its acceleration, researchers said. Most of the emissions are caused by fires, many deliberately set to clear land for beef and soy production. But even without fires, hotter temperatures and droughts mean the south-eastern Amazon has become a source of CO2, rather than a sink. Growing trees and plants have taken up about a quarter of all fossil fuel emissions since 1960, with the Amazon playing a major role as the largest tropical forest. Losing the Amazon's power to capture CO2 is a stark warning that slashing emissions from fossil fuels is more urgent than ever.

Every moment we delay means an increase in how much warmer our planet will get, we can already feel the disasters, a global heatwave is devastating our lives, and many are losing their lives in floods. In the UAE alone we had the heaviest rain that resulted in flooding after 30 years. The conditions will continue to worsen until something would be done, and that is, if it wont be too late. Our planet is already 1.3 degree celcuis warmer, we tipping point is at 1.5 degree Celsius. The CO_2 released from the burning of fossil fuels is accumulating as an insulating blanket around the Earth, trapping more of the Sun's heat in our atmosphere. Actions carried out by humans are called anthropogenic actions; the anthropogenic release of CO_2 contributes to the current enhanced greenhouse effect.

The forces of nature and the planet not need to be put in order. They are already in order.It is now for us to put ourselves in union with this order. No species has ever had such a control and dominance on the world as us. That lays upon us a great resposivbiliy, and it doesn matter whether we like it or not. We must ask ourselves not what nature can do for us, but what we can do for nature, and not stand there saying we hav 10 or 20 years left, but to take action now, like we have no time, because we actually don't, and act in a away like our lives depend on it, cause it actually does. We are one coherent ecosystem. The natural world isn't just a question of beauty, interest or wonder. It's the essential ingredient; the essential part of a human life is a healthy planet.

More than 32,000 species are threatened with extinction. This include 41%of amphibians, 26% of mammals, 14% of birds , 30% of sharks and rays, 33%of coral reefs and 28% of crustaceans. I had believed from a very early age that the most important knowledge was that which brought an understanding of how the natural world worked. As Dr Jane Goodall says, "Only if we understand, will we care. Only if we care, will we help. Only if we help shall all be saved." The International Union for Conservation of Nature and Natural Resources (IUCN), which produces the Red Data Books, divides wildlife into one of the following categories: Rare, Extinct, Endangered, and Vulnerable. The following modifications drove their decline: 73% of species have had their physical habitat destroyed. 68% of species have been displaced by introduced species. 38% of species have had their habitats altered by chemical contaminants. 38% of species exhibit hybridization with other species and subspecies. 15% of species are over farmed (These numbers sum up to more than 100% since many fish populations are affected by many agents.) When habitat destruction is seen as include both the physical loss of acceptable habitats and the chemical closure of habitats, it is discovered to be a significant cause in more than 90% of cases. The rate of extinction has continuously increased over the past forty years due to a confluence of all these variables.

We have not been present in the past 5 mass extinctions, but now we are a part of the 6th one, not only a part of it, but the reason of its happening. Scientist have reached the conclusion that the 6th mass extinction has begun!

CHAPTER III

Rewilding Our Planet

> A grain in the balance will determine which individual shall live and which shall die - which variety or species shall increase in number, or which shall decrease, or finally become extinct.

Charles Darwin

According to the most recent scientific understanding, the living world is headed towards a tipping point and eventual collapse. In fact, it has already begun to do so and is predicted to do so at an accelerating rate, making the consequences of its decline both larger in scope and more significant as they develop one after the other. Everything on which we have grown to rely—all the services that the ecosystem of the Earth has traditionally given us without charge—could start to deteriorate or stop working altogether. More than just real estate flooding, more powerful storms, and summer wildfires would be brought on by it. The quality of life for everyone affected by it as well as for future generations would be drastically decreased. Our most precious but least valued resource is BIODIVERSITY.

Restoring biodiversity gives us more allies in the battle against other environmental issues, such as climate change. Our planet's biodiversity, though, continues to be shrouded in mystery. There are several issues that may be resolved by the living world around us. In a remote Andean region, a rare beetle perched on an orchid may emit a chemical that treats pancreatic cancer. The world's salty deserts might receive green cover and feed from a Somalian grass reduced to twenty plants. There is no way to evaluate this treasure trove of the wild other than to acknowledge its size and its uncertain future.

There is debate in research on the connection between stability and biodiversity. We know that variety increases the ability of the ecosystem to retain and preserve nutrients from a few significant studies of forests. The distribution of the leaf area is more consistent and uniform among different plant species. The more plant species there are, the wider variety of specialized leaves and roots there are, and the more nutrients the vegetation as a whole can absorb from every nook and cranny at every hour throughout all seasons, the more there are to go around. The orchids and other epiphytes of tropical forests, which directly collect soil from mist and airborne dust otherwise destined to blow away, may have achieved the greatest reach of biodiversity anywhere. In other words, an ecosystem that is supported by a variety of species is less likely to fail.

We cannot be certain since most types of creatures lack the necessary natural histories, and there haven't been many tests on ecosystem breakdown. But consider the possible outcomes of such an experiment. The precise results at each stage would be hard to anticipate if we were to systematically destroy an ecosystem by eliminating one species at a time, but one basic outcome appears certain: the ecosystem would eventually collapse. The majority of biological communities are held together by system redundancies. Many times, two or more biologically similar species coexist in the same region, and any one of them can more or less replace the niches left vacant by the extermination of others. But ultimately the resilience would be lost, the effectiveness of the food webs would deteriorate, the flow of nutrients would slow down, and one of the components that had been eliminated would turn out to be a keystone species. If it went extinct, other species may follow, and their loss might have a significant impact on the habitat's physical makeup. Nobody is certain of the identities of the majority of keystone species since ecology is still a developing field. Sea otters, elephants, Ants and coral heads come to mind when we think of the organisms in this important category, but they could just as easily include any of the tiny invertebrates, algae, and microorganisms that swarm in the substratum, which also contains the majority of its protoplasm and moves the mass of nutrients.

The decline of biological variety, in my opinion, is the major issue of our time. It is fundamentally different in quality yet has environmental spoliation as its primary cause. The loss cannot be recovered, but its pace can be reduced to prehistorically low levels. At least a balance in the birth and death of species will have been restored, even if what is left is a less biotic planet than the one mankind inherited. Additionally, there is a positive aspect that is distinct from the reversal of physical deterioration: just trying to solve the biodiversity crisis offers enormous advantages never before experienced, as saving species requires close study, and learning them well necessitates using their traits in creative ways.

This understanding of the practical utility of wild species is the result of a New Environmentalism revolution in conservation thought during the past 20 years. There is no longer an ideological conflict between environmentalists and developers, with the exception of few areas of ignorance and prejudice. Both believe that a declining environment leads to a reduction in health and prosperity. They are also aware that it is impossible to extract important items from extinct creatures. Over time, the economic benefit of depleting wildlands will be far higher if they are mined for genetic material as opposed to being destroyed for a few extra board feet of timber and acres of cropland. The revival of other businesses, such as forestry, farming, medicine, and others, can benefit from salvaged species. The wildlands are like a magic well: the more knowledge and benefits are extracted from them, the more there will be left over for future extraction.

In order to give the free market's invisible hand a green light, researchers are racing to find strategies that will allow them to extract more revenue from natural areas without destroying them. The primary focus has shifted from species to the ecosystems in which they reside, and this revolution has been mirrored by another, closely related shift in biodiversity thinking. Star species like pandas and redwoods are still highly valued, but they are also seen as the ecological "umbrellas" that safeguard their habitats. In contrast, the ecosystems, which house hundreds of less noticeable species, are given similar worth, which is sufficient to justifiably support a significant effort to maintain them, with or without the star species.

We have enough biodiversity to go around, and if we work together to help it regain control, we can jointly address the climate and environmental issues facing our world. As a pointer to the birthplace of our soul, the green prehuman earth is evaporating, but it is also the riddle we were selected to answer. Every year, it becomes tougher to return. 99% of all creatures that have ever existed are now extinct. The survivors of all the radiations and extinctions in the course of geological history make up the fauna and flora of the current world. All living things, whether they are young or elderly, are direct descendants of the creatures that existed 3.8 billion years ago. They are living genetic archives that preserve evolutionary events over a vast amount of time through the use of nucleotide sequences. In combination, organisms are even more remarkable. Take the blossom out of its hiding place, shake the soil off the roots into your cupped hand, and magnify it for a close look. The black soil is teeming with thousands of different bacterial species, nematodes, mites, springtails, enchytraeid worms, and algae. The handful may just be a tiny portion of one ecosystem, but thanks to the genetic makeup of its inhabitants, it is more ordered than the sum of all the planets' surfaces. It is an example of the life power that governs the world and will do so whether or not we are here.

We must learn to share the Earth's limited resources more fairly as well as how to live within them. We still have a lot to learn about the living world, yet it has already provided us with a vast amount of resources. Only 5,000 of the 220,000 species, or less than 3 percent, of the world's flowering plants have had their alkaloids studied, and even those studies have been few and random. Due to the species' widespread planting and ongoing research into its purported antidiuretic properties, the anticancer potential of the pink periwinkle was just recently recognized. A cousin of mahogany and a native of tropical Asia, the neem tree (Azadirachta indica) is seldom recognized in the developed world. According to a recent research by the U.S. National Research Council, the Indian population values the species. Millions have used neem for millennia to clean their teeth, treat skin conditions with neem-leaf juice, drink neem tea as a tonic, and place neem leaves in their beds, books, grain bins, cabinets, and closets to ward off pesky insects. The tree has been referred to as the "village pharmacy" since it has treated so many various types of aches, fevers, infections, and other problems. Neem is believed to have amazing properties by the millions of Indians, and now scientists all around the world are starting to believe they may be correct.

Many plants, especially those in the Cucurbit family, are constantly at battle with leafminers, microscopic insect larvae that eat leaves from the inside out. They appear in the earliest phases of plant development. Just as plants change how they defend themselves throughout time, leaf miners too must adapt. As a result, adjustments are performed and the leaf miners become immune to upcoming circumstances. Some plants have leaves that taste bitter. These leafy greens' defensive mechanism against insects is precisely what gives them their bitter flavor. Some species of leaf miners have adapted to withstand little amounts of these harmful substances. The leaf miners have had to evolve defenses over the last 14 million years to acclimate to the harsher poisons of the plants. I frequently assist my grandfather in planting new vegetables in his garden, and I had spotted these leafminers in the pumpkins we had previously planted. Vegetable leafminers, which are the maggot larvae of a tiny black and yellow fly, were the specific kind of leafminer that afflicted these pumpkins. Leaf miners started to develop on the pumpkin plants that we had planted extremely early. They leave behind black tracks that are the larvae's waste products and tunneling wounds. The areas that these insects mine dry up and perish. Serpentine mines, which are made up of narrow, winding, white trails, or blotch mines, which are wide and whitish or brownish in color, are the terms used to describe the majority of leaf-miner burrows or tunnels. Using her toothed ovipositors, the mature female fly makes holes in the leaf where she will deposit her eggs. A female leaf miner may lay up to 160 eggs in just 13 days. However, before an egg is placed, the female tastes the chemicals coming off the leaf to determine which section has the least poisons or which part holds the most of the nutrients. The larvae burrow into the tissue of the mesophyll. The larva makes an incision, often in the top leaf surface, after three moltings, and then falls to the ground where it pupates. Only the damaged leaves need to be manually removed by gardeners. Insecticides aren't very successful against leaf miners since they are hidden inside the leaf, beneath the epidermis, and might harm helpful pest predators like wasps, spiders, and ladybugs. As a result, leaf miner populations have grown significantly. Neem oil was then sprayed on the leaves in order to successfully get rid of them. This completely altered the pumpkin plant, and the leafminers disappeared very quickly.

The chemical skills of organisms are exceptional. In some ways, they are all better than all the chemists in the world at creating useful organic chemicals. Each type of plant, animal, and microbe has experimented with chemicals through millions of generations to fulfill its unique demands. Each species has undergone an enormous number of genetic mutations and recombinations that have had an impact on its metabolic machinery. The niche that the species fills exactly determines the unique class of chemicals in which it became a wizard. Once it has penetrated the skin, the leech, a vampire annelid worm, needs to continue drawing blood from its prey. The anticoagulant hirudin, which medical researchers discovered and use to treat hemorrhoids, rheumatism, thrombosis, and contusions—conditions where blood clotting can occasionally be unpleasant or dangerous—comes from its saliva. Blood clots that pose a risk to skin grafts are easily broken apart by hirudin.

The development of a second chemical to stop heart attacks came from the vampire bats of Central and South America's saliva. While limiting its action to the region of the clot, it unclogs blocked arteries twice as quickly as conventional pharmacological treatments.

But nature also aids in our defense against viral invasions. When COVID 19 silenced the planet in 2018, nature once more assisted in restoring our stability. One ancient critter that lived in the seas off the Atlantic coast was crucial in the fight against COVID-19. Hundreds of thousands of horseshoe crabs scramble onto beaches all throughout the mid-Atlantic region of the United States each spring to deposit their eggs, led by the full moon. It is a vital tool for drug firms to use in ensuring the safety of human medications. This is due to the fact that the milky-blue blood of these animals is the sole naturally occurring source of limulus amebocyte lysate, a compound that may identify an endotoxin-detection contaminant. Endotoxin is a form of bacterial toxin that can be fatal if it gets into vaccinations, injectable medications, or other sterile medicines like replacement knees and hips. These crabs are used by all pharmaceutical businesses in the globe. Your mind is blown when you consider how dependent we are on such a premitive creature. Pharmaceutical firms seize 500,000 Atlantic horseshoe crabs annually, bleed them, and release them back into the water, where many of them perish. The species has declined in the area over the past several decades as a result of this practice and overfishing of crabs for fishing bait.

Biologists calculated that 1.24 million crabs hatched in Delaware Bay in 1990, a major area for egg-laying and a key gathering site for the businesses. That number fell to 333,500 by 2002. The 2019 study estimated 335,211 Delaware Bay spawning crabs, which is roughly the same as it has been in prior years. Horseshoe crabs have several peculiar characteristics and have remained mostly unaltered for hundreds of millions of years. These critters, despite their name, are more closely related to spiders and scorpions than they are to crabs. They have nine eyes total, including two complex and seven simple ones. Blood from horseshoe crabs reacts with endotoxin, causing amebocytes to coagulate and solidify into a mass. These amebocytes, which are a component of the ancient immune system of the crab, are capable of spotting fatal bacterial contamination in the vast variety of medications intended for infusion into human blood. Since its discovery, workers have been bringing the helmet-shaped animals in large numbers. They then extract blood from a vein close to the heart before being released back into the water. The copper in their hemocyanin, the oxygen-transporting protein, Is what gives them their blue blood.

The procedure looked sustainable in the 1980s and the early 1990s. Only 3% of the crabs they bled were said to have perished, according to the pharmaceutical business. The crabs were abundant, according to population studies, and conservationists did not place much significance on the species. But things started to change in the early 2000s. Annual counts of horseshoe crabs during the spawning season indicated lower numbers, and a 2010 research discovered that up to 30% of the bleed crabs ultimately perished—ten times as many as initially thought. Conservationists are keeping an eye on the effects on the animals that depend on horseshoe crab eggs as essential food sources. Due in part to fewer horseshoe crab eggs, sport fish that were formerly abundant, such striped bass and flounder, have drastically decreased in abundance in the area. Another kind of reptile that depends on this seasonal feast is the endangered diamondback terrapin. Some of the extinct species turn out to be keystone species when extinction spreads, bringing down other species and causing a chain reaction in the demographics of the survivors. Losing a keystone species is comparable to unintentionally running into a power line with a drill. It makes all of the lights go out. These services are crucial for the welfare of people.

Humans are not from other planets; we coevolved with the rest of life on this one. It is foolish to assume that biodiversity can be lost forever without endangering humans when most types of creatures still go by unnamed, and scientists only have a foggy understanding of how ecosystems function. Field research demonstrates that the quality of ecosystem services decreases as biodiversity decreases. Records of stressed ecosystems show that the fall can be sudden and unpredictable. Emotion is what distinguishes humans from machines. We have little understanding of our actual essence, of what it is to be human. Our ignorance of our origins is the main contributor to this intellectual failing. We did not travel here from another planet.

As a species that developed alongside other species, humanity is a part of nature. The more we identify with the rest of life, the more rapidly we will be able to understand the roots of human sensibility and get the information necessary to establish a lasting morality and sense of chosen course. The idea that humans may thrive separately from the rest of the living world has just recently come into existence. A mind-boggling variety of living forms existed in close touch with " primitive " cultures. Fewer than a million people lived as hunter-gatherers during the start of the Holocene, before farming was developed. This way of life was sustainable and in harmony with the environment. At the time, there was no other choice available to our ancestors. Our options expanded and our relationship with nature altered as farming became more widespread. We started to see the natural world as something we could tame, control, and use. Without a question, this new way of living gave us amazing benefits, but with time, we lost our equilibrium.

We need to reverse that transformation now, all these years later. Our only option is to live sustainably once more. We now number in the billions, nonetheless. We can't possible go back to living like hunter-gatherers. We also wouldn't want to. We need to find a brand-new sustainable way of living that restores harmony between the natural and contemporary human worlds.

The biodiversity loss we have triggered won't start to change into biodiversity gain until then. Only then will the Earth become again wild and revert to normal. In order to navigate the path to a sustainable future, we already have a compass. The purpose of the planetary boundaries model is to steer us in the proper direction. According to the planetary boundaries idea, there are nine planetary boundaries within which mankind can expand and flourish for many more generations.

The nine mechanisms that control the stability and resilience of the Earth system were discovered in 2009 by a team of 28 globally known scientists under the direction of former center director Johan Rockström. Quantitative planetary boundaries were proposed by the scientists, within which future generations of humans can evolve and flourish. It becomes more likely that crossing these lines would result in significant, sudden, or permanent environmental changes. Since then, the concept of planetary limits has attracted a great deal of attention in research, politics, and practice By addressing greenhouse gas emissions wherever they occur, the nine planetary barrier warns us that we must stop climate change quickly and ideally begin to reverse it. We need to stop using fertilizers excessively. The transformation of natural areas into agriculture, plantations, and other developments must be stopped and reversed. It also alerts us to the other issues we need to be aware of, like the ozone layer, freshwater use, chemical and air pollution, and ocean acidification. If we do all of those actions, biodiversity loss will start to slow down, stop, and then begin to reverse itself.

There are nine planetary boundaries: climate change, ocean acidification, loss of stratospheric ozone, disturbance of the nitrogen and phosphorus cycle, alteration of land use, loss of biodiversity, rise in aerosols in the atmosphere, and introduction of new organisms into the biosphere. These are the forces that keep the Earth as we know it in balance.

However, human activity has led to the crossing of four of the nine planetary limits. The four are: changed biogeochemical cycles, climatic change, loss of biosphere integrity, and changes to the land system (phosphorus and nitrogen). The scientists refer to two of these as "core boundaries": climate change and biosphere integrity. Both of these "fundamental barriers" would need to be significantly altered in order to "push the Earth System into a new state." Crossing a line raises the chance that human actions might unintentionally make the Earth System far less hospitable, harming efforts to fight poverty and worsening human wellbeing in many regions of the world. The evidence from science indicates that these nine systems and processes

185

control the resilience and stability of the Earth System, or the interactions between the land, ocean, atmosphere, and living things that collectively create the circumstances on which human societies depend.

If left unchecked, it is predicted that most drivers would provide less to nature's contribution to people and will accelerate the effects of climate change and biodiversity loss during the following decades. The Paris Agreement's goal of limiting global warming to 1.5°C will involve quickly bending the curve of greenhouse gas emissions to achieve net zero by the middle of the century in order to prevent severe effects. It will also be necessary to stop the degradation of all ecosystems and the decrease of natural ecosystems in order to reverse the global biodiversity reductions by the middle of the century, as predicted by the post-2020 Global Biodiversity Framework. We have too many obvious answers for the challenges we need to tackle. Finding the correct response is the tricky part.

. There isn't a scientific issue that is more crucial to mankind right now, in my opinion. Given that we know so little about variety in the first place, biologists find it challenging to even quantify the hemorrhage. The least understood and localized of all biological processes is extinction. We don't see the final butterfly of a particular species being grabbed from the sky by a bird or the last orchid of a particular species being destroyed in a far-off mountain forest by the fall of its supporting tree. We learn that a certain animal or plant is near extinction or may even be extinct. When no individuals are found there after several years of searching in the last location where they were found, we declare the species extinct. In the course of existence, humans—50-kg mammals and members of the primates, a group known for their rarity—have multiplied one hundred times faster than any other terrestrial species of equal size. Humanity is environmentally abnormal by every imaginable standard.

The nine planetary boundaries and the evidence provided in the Living Planet Report are both clear. As a result of the strain humans are putting on the environment, it is becoming increasingly difficult for the natural world to deliver essential services, such as mitigating and adapting to climate change. The most vulnerable people are at the greatest risk due to our devastation of the environment, which also makes us more susceptible to pandemics. Although there is still time, action must be taken quickly. There are many options, but I'm going to base my choice on how we can REWILD the planet, which may be broken-down as an acronym. The word REWILD may be broken down into 6 words; each 6 , a distinct solutions.

ng a study of microbial organisms in Qudra Lake waters and a small skin sample from a cuttlefish.

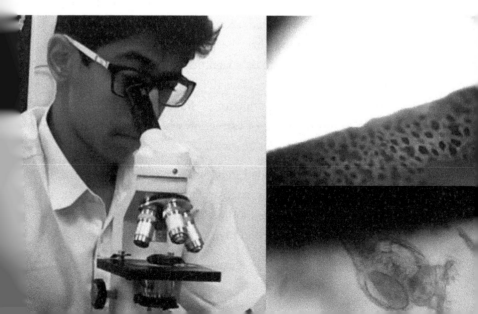

Regeneration

The destruction of our planet's biodiversity is our biggest global issue. This is due to the fact that biological diversity is our strongest ally in the battle against climate change, making it harder to combat the issue the more biodiversity we lose. Helping to regenerate the wildlife that is alive today is the first step toward Rewilding the world, hence the letter "R" in the word.

If we are to turn the tide on nature loss and protect the natural world for present and future generations, we must set a worldwide target of reversing biodiversity loss to ensure a nature-positive society by 2030. It must serve as our north star, just as our efforts to combat climate change are directed by the desire to keep global warming to 2°C, ideally 1.5°C. Everyone can take action to ensure a nature-positive world this decade, which will be measured by an increase in the health, abundance, diversity, and resilience of species, populations, and ecosystems. These actions can also be adopted nationally, and eventually globally, to urgently transform our relationship with nature. Positively, momentum is increasing. More than 90 world leaders have signed the Leaders' Pledge for Environment, promising to stop the loss of biodiversity by 2030, and the G7 has expressed its desire to ensure a future where nature is valued. In order to create a wild world, we must first give our devastated areas a chance to recover. The sad hallmark of our period has been the destruction of natural environments to the point that a significant percentage of plant and animal species—certainly more than 10%—have already gone extinct or are doomed to an early extinction. Many of the "living dead," however—those on the verge of extinction who will eventually perish even if just left alone—can yet be saved.

If natural habitats are expanded in addition to being maintained, the number of species that may survive can be brought back up the logarithmic curve that relates biodiversity to area. There will come a day when scientific understanding will enable even more. The production of synthetic faunas and floras, which are collections of species deliberately chosen from various regions of the world and transplanted into poor environments, might also be considered a return to biology's Eden.

By increasing the geographic ranges and population numbers of a few selected species, they merely contribute to local diversity. However, finding the safe guidelines for biotic synthesis is a very intellectually adventurous endeavor. If the attempt is successful, locations that have already lost their natural biotas can be transformed again into diverse, stable environments. In a way, the wasteland can rebirth as a wilderness. Priority should be given to saving species that are already extinct in the wild and are being kept in zoos and gardens. They can persist as orphan species in foster habitats when transplanted into synthetic or underdeveloped biotas. They may not have access to their old house, but they will recover security and independence. They will pay us back by fulfilling one requirement of wilderness: allowing us to relieve them of the responsibility for their care and visit them on our own terms. How much of the world's biodiversity we can anticipate bringing with us out of the bottleneck fifty or one hundred years from now is the final and most important question. Let me make an educated estimate. We will lose at least one-fourth of the species on Earth if the biodiversity problem is mainly neglected and natural ecosystems continue to deteriorate. We could limit the loss to 10% if we react with the knowledge and technology we now have. . Biodiversity should be protected by the law if it is recognized as an irreplaceable public resource.

Because we want the global economy to flourish forever, we have come to this point of desperation. But nothing can expand indefinitely in an universe that is finite. Individuals, communities, and even environments all have a phase of growth before entering maturity. Once they are mature, they could flourish. Things don't always need to get bigger to flourish. When they develop into viable entities, a single tree, an ant colony, a coral reef community, or the entire Arctic ecosystem, all endure for a considerable amount of time. They develop to a certain degree, at which time they maximize opportunities by leveraging their newly acquired positions in a sustainable way. They progress from the log phase of exponential development, past a peak, and into a plateau. And that steady plateau phase can go on forever because of how they interact with the living world beyond. That is not to suggest that a wild society that has reached a plateau does not alter. Tens of millions of years ago, the Amazon was formed. It has thrived in one of the planet's premier locations over that period, covering nearly the same area of land with its extensive closed canopy as it did until recently. Its soil's nutritional content and the quantity of sunlight and rain it has gotten may have remained essentially consistent throughout. But throughout that period, the species in its living community will have undergone tremendous change. There will always be winners and losers in any given year, just as teams will change their positions in a sports league table or share values on a stock exchange.

Allowing wildlife to recuperate in peace and letting that area of the wilderness recover from impact are both necessary for the world to regenerate. The world's largest and most diversified tropical forest, for instance, is the Amazon. More than 500 Indigenous Peoples (IP) tribes reside there. Nearly 20% of the fresh water in the world is contained in the Amazon River system, and Indigenous Territories physically cover 2.37 million square kilometers of the Amazon basin. By storing approximately one third (32.8%) of the region's above-ground carbon (28.247 million tonnes), Amazonia Indigenous Territories have made a substantial contribution to the prevention and adaptation to climate change. The Amazon area is now approaching a potentially catastrophic tipping point as a result of both impacts and dangers spreading into our territory. According to scientific research, the total rate of deforestation and forest degradation must be between 20 and 25 percent to reach the tipping point. According to data, 26% of the Amazon is experiencing advanced disturbance, which includes deforestation, frequent fires, and forest degradation. This is not a hypothetical situation; rather, the region is now undergoing an ongoing degree of devastation with catastrophic local effects and unfavorable global consequences for climate stability. However, if we let Amazon heal on its own, it can do so quickly, it just needs the space to do so.

My youth was spent in the beautiful desert landscapes of the UAE, where I was born and raised. I have witnessed the regrowth of wildlife in the deserts of the United Arab Emirates, which are home to some very fascinating species. The UAE is dedicated to preserving and protecting the state's vast biodiversity in order to save vulnerable species from extinction. Natural reserves are being established with the goal of promoting ecotourism while also enhancing the country's ecology and protecting its species. We must return to the Qudra lakes in order to comprehend this. The Al Marmum Reserve includes the Qudra lakes, which are home to some unique animals. I'm not talking about just gazelles or birds, though; I'm talking about something more unexpected and remarkable. For the first time ever, my family and I went camping in Qudra Lake one night while winter was just getting started. As usual, I had a torch in hand and was searching for animals. I immediately heard a weird sound, like chips or biscuits being crunched, but there was no one nearby. I followed the hand-like footprints and sound tracks. I immediately discovered its owner. This was the creature that was the inspiration for the film Sonic. Well, it was an adorable desert hedgehog (Paraechinus aethiopicus). Its silvery-shiny hair , and its back was covered with tiny spines served as protection against predators. I remained still for a time to take in this little creature's beauty.

Then I realized that the crunching sound was coming from a little cricket that it had managed to catch and was gorging on. Members of this species reportedly relax along rocks and cliffs throughout the daytime. As a result, they are protected from raptor birds when they are sleeping. Their spines provide minimal protection while they are resting since they sleep on their sides. Despite their charming appearance, they are actually some surprisingly solid predators who hunt at night. I can honestly state that this experience was a lucky one because these hedgehogs hibernate during extended cold spells, waking up sometimes to forage for food. Maybe this was one of those nights for foraging. Due of the insufficient insulation provided by their spines, these periods of hibernation may be essential. The startling part about this is that these adorable animals have a high tolerance for snake and insect venom, which is thought to be 30 to 40 times higher than that of a rodent of comparable size. This shields them from poisonous or stinging prey while they hunt. The hedgehog sensed danger as soon as I had my hands on it, and as a result, its muscles tightened and pulled the skin around its body's, causing its spines to protrude in all directions. I took a good look, put it down, and continued to pay close attention. It gently started to reveal itself, first with the nose and shortly after, its little feet. It then began to circle us before returning to a Heliotropium kotschyi plant. When I started to head back to camp, just as I was ready to conclude that the night couldn't possibly be much more interesting than this, I discovered yet another creature in my path.

Locals refer to these spiders as Yamel Al Aqrab, and It is among the only few endangered spider species, I am aware of. With ten legs, it has a menacing appearance. However, if you looked closely, you would see that these two front legs are actually pedipaps rather than actual legs. They have enormous, strong jaws that can be up to one-third the length of their bodies. They utilize them to trap their prey, then use a saw or chop to reduce them to pulp. This was a camel spider (Gelodes arabs). It was moving extremely quickly, maybe a bit startled by my light, but it soon disappeared into the bushes. Although there have been significant conservation measures, it is not permitted to capture camel spiders since they are still thriving. Additionally, several protected areas have been established, aiding in the preservation of appropriate habitat and mitigating disturbance.

r a nice cricket meal, the desert hedgehog (Paraechinus aethiopicus) runs around in search to find more
and in this image, it's running towards the camera.

enile baby gazelle as it rests under a Ghaf tree at night. It was only a few metres away from me as I
ed it from a short distance.

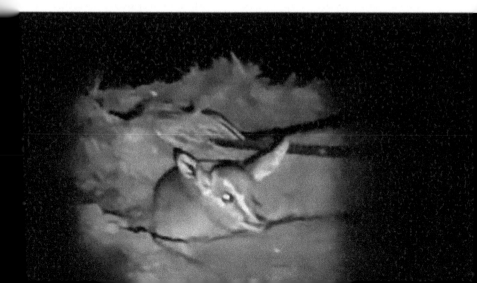

The species are continuously monitored by the Environmental Agency of Abu Dhabi both inside and outside the protected zones. It is really a difficult emotion to describe and goes beyond gladness to see all these local animals prospering here. Efforts to reduce carbon emissions in the atmosphere may become more crucial as the world strives to achieve net zero emissions.

Planting trees is one method since plants breathe in atmospheric carbon dioxide and transform most of it into the solid form of their tissues when they produce nutrition using energy from the sun. Harvesting some of those trees and stabilizing the carbon contained in wood by burning it under low oxygen circumstances (a process called pyrolysis) to produce a charcoal-like substance, biochar, may be even more successful than merely planting new forests. This may be applied to soil and may last for hundreds of years before decomposing and releasing its carbon. Additionally, it can increase the nitrogen content of the soil and other soil qualities like water retention, thereby enhancing agricultural output and crop resistance to climate change. A fairly simple method for removing greenhouse gases is biochar. It differs from other, more expensive methods like direct air capture in that it is relatively affordable, simple to use, and not dependent on highly developed technology.

The ghaf tree, which is indigenous to the United Arab Emirates and was declared as the national tree in 2008, has lately being investigated by researchers in the UAE for its potential as a source of biochar. The ghaf tree, which is widely known for its capacity to withstand severe environments and whose roots may reach depths of tens of meters in quest of water, can be found both in the Arabian deserts and on the Indian subcontinent. Researchers at Zayed University in Abu Dhabi's College of Natural and Health Sciences examined biochar made from a tree's leaves, roots, and branches. They were curious about the biochar's capacity to adsorb carbon dioxide, which is one of the benefits it has for reducing climate change. Adsorption is the process by which substances keep molecules on their surface. It was discovered that certain biochar made from ghaf trees was more effective at adsorbing CO_2 than biochar made from rice husks, coconut shells, carrot peels, or wheat flour.

But in order to repair our world, we must also regenerate the oceans, which are its greatest habitat. Two-thirds of the planet's surface is covered by the ocean. Because of its enormous depths, it has a higher percentage of livable space. Therefore, the ocean plays a unique role in our movement to rewild the earth. We can simultaneously accomplish three things we urgently need to do by assisting the marine ecosystem in its recovery: absorb carbon, increase biodiversity, and increase our food production. It begins by collaborating with the sector of the economy that is now causing the most harm to the ocean: fishing. The world's largest natural harvest is fishing, therefore if we manage it properly, it can continue since there is a shared interest: the more fish there are and can be consumed, the healthier and more biodiverse the marine ecosystem is. So why isn't it functioning right now? We overfish some areas and species. Our waste is too great. We employ crude fishing methods that devastate the ecology. The worst of all is that we fish everywhere.

First, coastal waterways should be divided into a network of no-fish zones. There are currently more than 17,000 marine protected areas, or MPAs, in existence. However, these make up less than 7% of the ocean, and many MPAs still allow for some sorts of fishing.

Due to the way fish reproduce, it is essential that a healthy section of the ocean be never harvested. Individual fish are allowed to become older and bigger in no-fish zones. Additionally, larger individuals have disproportionately more offspring. They subsequently replenish nearby waterways that are fished.

Due to the UAE's extremely rigorous restrictions against overfishing and illicit fishing, several exceptional fish species, including whale sharks and groupers, flourish in its seas. I previously discussed a sea urchin field research at Mamzar. The tide was quite low that day, as I had previously indicated, and as I was searching for urchins, I noticed a peculiar brown oval-shaped structure between two rocks very close to the coast. On closer examination, spots could be seen. I immediately yelled and called Zayaan to grab his net; I had never called someone in this way before. Zayaan quickly arrived with his net and didn't know what to expect, and then to our shock we were fortunate enough to catch this monster fish. This fish was an orange-spotted grouper, or hamour as it is known locally. Due to the Mamzar's protection, this fish had developed into a massive female, which I was able to grasp in my hands. As an apex predator with razor-sharp teeth, it was obvious that it was known for its aggression. The fact that all Orange-spotted Groupers are female at birth is quite unusual. However, if there aren't enough males in the area, some females start to transform into males around the age of 4. After taking a few pictures, Zayaan and I let the fish back into its habitat since we were running out of time and just a little bit more out of the water and the fish would not have made it. Despite the fact that this grouper species is almost extinct owing to overfishing, I still have faith in it because of the protection!

When fishing limitations are first implemented, fishing communities frequently rebel against them, but after a few years they will begin to see the benefits. At the very tip of Baja California in Mexico is the Marine Protected Area of Cabo Pulmo. Due to severe overfishing in the 1990s, the fishing industry consented to marine experts' recommendations to designate more than 7,000 hectares of their coastline as a no-fish zone. The immediate years after the MPA's opening in 1995 are regarded by the locals as the most difficult years they have ever experienced. The Mexican government provided food coupons to the fishing families since they caught so little fish in the nearby seas. Fishermen were frequently tempted to disobey the law because they could observe increasing shoals in the MPA. The only thing keeping them from giving up was the community's confidence in the marine scientists. Sharks first returned to Cabo Pulmo after roughly ten years. They were signs of recovery to the elder fisherman

is Orange-spotted Grouper was trapped within a small pocket of water, so we captured it and after a few
le samples, released it back into the deeper waters.

Left to right) Magnified View of a long spine sea urchin spine when in contact with human skin.

since they recognized them from their youth. After just 15 years, the no-fish zone's marine life had grown by more than 400% to a level comparable to reefs that had never been fished, and fish shoals had started to expand into the nearby seas. The town also had a tourist attraction just outside their door, and the fisherman caught more fish than they had in years.

The MPA model functions because it prevents us from engaging in behavior that we should never have started, namely, depleting the ocean's primary fish populations. Due to the fact that no-fish zones boost fish populations overall, the capital keeps growing, generating more and more interest and fish for the net. Fishing becomes simpler, resulting in less wasteful bycatch, reduced use of fossil fuels at sea, and the ability to stay ashore when the seas appear rough. According to estimates, no-fish zones covering a third of our ocean would be enough to allow fish populations to repopulate and provide us with fish in the long run. The greatest areas for these MPAs are the ocean's nurseries, including rocky and coral reefs, underwater seamounts, kelp forests, mangroves, seagrass meadows, and saltmarshes, where marine creatures find it easiest to reproduce. It is no accident that these are also the locations that will aid us most in achieving our second major goal, carbon capture. Currently, saltmarshes, mangroves, and seagrass meadows alone take from the atmosphere the equivalent of around half of all of our transportation-related emissions.

If these ecosystems are preserved in no-fish zones, they will recover and allow for more fishing. Additionally crucial is the method of fishing. A more intelligent approach to fishing is required, one in which huge, predatory fish like tuna are captured with pole and line and where harmful seabed dredging is prohibited. Trawl nets should also incorporate emergency escapes for non-target species. Our major fish populations require continual observation, and we must exercise self-control to maintain yields that are sustainable. If all international waters were declared no-fish zones, we would turn the open ocean from a place depleted by our relentless chase into a flourishing wilderness that would add more fish to our coastal waters and support us all in our attempts to trap carbon via its diversity.

By creating some new natural ocean sanctuaries, we can aid in the recovery of our seas. Mangroves and coral reefs are examples of this. Mangroves are distinct marine forests. They serve as a significant biodiversity reservoir, sustain coastal populations' daily needs for food and fuel, support commercially significant fisheries, and provide cultural services including ecotourism, education, and spiritual values. Another important natural response to climate change is mangroves. They help with mitigation by sequestering and storing "blue carbon" in their flooded soils at concentrations that are higher than those of many other ecosystems. Mangroves also aid in the adaptation to climate change since some of them can extend their surface area and keep up with sea-level rise thanks to their entangled above-ground roots, which act as a wave buffer and sediment trap. This resilient tree serves as a natural wind break, shielding us from tidal surges and purifying the nearby waters.

As a WWF leader of change, I accepted an invitation to help Emirates Nature WWF plant 2,000 mangrove plants, so I teamed up with them. Our planting location was Khor Al Kalba, which is close to the oman border and is at the further end of the emirate of Sharjah. This was a part of the Priceless Planet coalition's effort to restore 100 million trees worldwide by 2025, with 50,000 mangrove trees being planted in the United Arab Emirates alone.

Mangroves are plants that can survive in water that is up to 100 times saltier than most other vegetation. Despite being flooded twice a day by the ocean tides, they survive. The floods alone would drown the majority of trees even if this water were fresh. We had a goal of planting grey mangrove seedlings (Avicennia marina). Mangroves are able to survive in such harsh environments because to a unique collection of evolutionary adaptations.

must extract freshwater from the sea First is their extraordinary ability to cope with water. Saltwater can kill plants, so mangroves must extract freshwater from the sea water that surrounds them. Many mangrove species survive by filtering out as much as 90% of the salt found in sea water as it enters their roots. Some species excrete salt through pores in their leaves. To test this I myself tasted these leaves by licking their surface, and it was actually really salty, similar to taking a teaspoon of table salt and putting it on your tongue. A third strategy used by some mangrove species is to concentrate salt in older leaves and bark, so when the leaves drop or the bark sheds the stored salt goes with them. Second is their ability to extract freshwater. Like desert plants mangroves store freshwater in thick succulent leaves, a wavy coating on some mangrove species seals in water and minimizes evaporation. Small hairs on the leaves of other species deflect wind and sunlight which reduces water loss throught the tiny openings where gas enter and exit during photosynthesis, these openings are the stomata. On some mangrove species the stomata are on the underside of the leaf, away from the sun and the wind. Third adaptation is the way they breathe. Some mangroves like the grey mangrove grow pencil like roots that stick up out of the dense wet ground like snorkels, I had to watch my step to not step on them as I moved around. These beathing tubes called pneumatophores allow mangroves to cope with the daily floodings by the tide. They also broaden the base of the tree and stabilize the shallow root system in the soft loose soil. These roots apart from providing structural support also play an important role in providing the trees oxygen for respiration. Oxygen enters the mangrove through lenticels, thousands of cell-sized breathing pores in the bark and roots, lenticels close during high tide thus preventing mangroves from drowning. Yet the importance of mangroves comes from their ability to provide a sanctuary for juvenile fish species. Here I saw different species of creatures, one of my most favorite to observe was the fiddler crabs. Here male fiddler crabs dance, by moving their larger claws, they tap those claws on the sand which is double adapted to attract females while fighting off other males. However, there is a lot of competition around. The larger more larger clawed males have more chance to get the females. Mangroves are home to many fish species, species like barracudas and tarpons find shelter among the mangroves as juveniles. An estimated 75% of the commercially fish caught spend some time in the mangroves or depend on the food webs that can be traced back to these coastal forests.water that surrounds them. Many mangrove species survive by filtering out as much as 90% of the salt found in sea water as it enters their roots. Some species excrete salt through pores in their leaves. To test this I myself tasted these leaves by licking their surface, and it was actually really salty, similar to taking a teaspoon of table salt and putting it on your tongue. A third strategy used by some mangrove species is to concentrate salt in older leaves and bark, so when the leaves drop or the bark sheds the stored salt goes with them. Second is their ability to extract freshwater. Like desert plants mangroves store freshwater in thick succulent leaves, a wavy coating on some mangrove species seals in water and minimizes evaporation. Small hairs on the leaves of other species deflect wind and sunlight which reduces water loss throught the tiny openings where gas enter and exit during photosynthesis, these openings are the stomata. On some mangrove species the stomata are on the underside of the leaf, away from the sun and the wind. Third adaptation is the way they breathe. Some mangroves like the grey mangrove grow pencil like roots that stick up out of the dense wet ground like snorkels, I had to watch my step to not step on them as I moved around. These beathing tubes called pneumatophores allow mangroves to cope with the daily floodings by the tide. They also broaden the base of the tree and stabilize the shallow root system in the soft loose soil. These roots apart from providing structural support also play an important role in providing the trees oxygen for respiration. Oxygen enters the mangrove through lenticels, thousands of cell-sized breathing pores in the bark and roots, lenticels close during high tide thus preventing mangroves from drowning. Yet the importance of mangroves comes from their ability to provide a sanctuary for juvenile fish species. Here I saw different species of creatures, one of my most favorite to observe was the fiddler crabs. Here male fiddler crabs dance, by moving their larger claws, they tap those claws on the sand which is double adapted to attract females while fighting off other males. However, there is a lot of competition around. The larger more larger clawed males have more chance to get the females. Mangroves are home to many fish species, species like barracudas and tarpons find shelter among the mangroves as juveniles. An estimated 75% of the commercially fish caught spend some time in the mangroves or depend on the food webs that can be traced back to these coastal forests.

Despite its significance, mangroves continue to be deforested at rates of 0.13% year due to aquaculture, agriculture, and coastal development. Along with other natural stresses like storms and coastal erosion, many mangroves are also damaged by overuse and pollution. Mangroves cannot easily be replaced after they have disappeared. Mangroves may grow again in their original habitats, but it might be challenging or even impossible when the ground erodes and the sea's tides and currents change the shoreline. Loss of mangroves entails loss of ecosystem services for coastal populations, loss of habitat for wildlife, and in certain cases, loss of the land on which coastal settlements are based.

Thankfully, mangrove destruction has significantly decreased since the 1980s, and by 2070, there are feasible scenarios in which the global mangrove area may stabilize or even grow. Seedpods begin to develop while still attached to the tree and are prepared to take root as soon as they fall. One mangrove may grow up to 2 feet in a single year and can swiftly establish itself in the fragile soil of tidal mudflats if a sprout falls during low tide. Over 35% of the mangroves have already been gone, largely as a result of habitat loss brought on by coastal development.

The latter would need intensive mangrove restoration, but when done successfully, such measures may restore essential ecological services that enhance livelihoods and lessen climate change. Mangroves must be regenerated. They play a significant role in the history of the UAE. Thanks to the founding father of the UAE, His Highness Sheikh

Zayed bin Sultan Al Nahyan, who recognized the value of mangrove trees and launched a huge forestation program that considerably expanded the quantity of these trees, they now cover up to 155 square kilometers of the UAE's coastline. I have planted approximately 8,000 trees, of which 2,000 were planted in khor al-kalba with the assistance of Emirates Nature WWF by myself and volunteers. While desirable, ambitious restoration goals are sometimes difficult to convert into actual results. Mangroves must be protected and restored further if global climate, biodiversity, and livelihoods are to continue improving.

A conversation with Arabella Willing, Senior Manager of Conservation Outreach & Citizen Science at Emirates Nature WWF, about the importance of mangroves. (©Emirates Nature WWF)

Mangroves are extraordinarily hardy trees, we had the aim to plant 2,000 trees. Zayaan & I planted nearly 20 mangroves each, our hands at the end were too tired. (©Emirates Nature WWF)

The team had to cross a muddy region and walk for some time to reach the planting hotspots. (©Emirates Nature WWF)

With the help of Emirates Nature WWF we planted 2,000 mangrove plants. Here I stand preparing to film for the documentary, the magic of mangroves.

(©Emirates Nature WWF)

Evolution

Our planet is a complex ecosystem, and natural selection and species adaptation have created the wonderful environment that is home to 8 billion humans today as well as other animals that share the planet with us. But evolution brought us to this point, therefore in order to survive in this constantly changing environment, both we and our society must begin to evolve. The second phase toward rewilding the planet is called evolution, thus the second letter "E" in the word.

We must be prepared to evolve our civilization in order to allow wildlife to flourish in our cities as we allow nature to regenerate. The fundamental issue with biodiversity is how little consideration is given to biological riches. This is a serious strategic mistake that will be regretted moving forward. The potential for enormous untapped material riches in the form of food, medicine, and comforts exists in diversity. As a result of millions of years of localized development, the fauna and flora are just as much a part of a nation's legacy as its unique linguistic and cultural characteristics and should thus be of national interest. The number of people on earth has surpassed 5.4 billion, is expected to increase to 8.5 billion by 2025, and may plateau around 10 to 15 billion by the middle of the century. There will soon be much less space for the majority of plant and animal species due to the extraordinary rise in human biomass and the emerging countries' rapidly increasing material and energy demands.

The reduction of economic expenses while also minimizing extinction rates is possible, at least in theory. The more different kinds of life are utilized and preserved, the more productive and secure our own species will be. The smart choices made by our generation in support of biological variety will benefit future generations. Environmental issues are inherently moral. They call for eyesight that can see both the near and beyond ranges of time at once. What is currently beneficial to people and civilizations might easily turn bad in ten years, and what appears to be wonderful over the coming decades could devastate future generations. The creation of a sustainable economy is the primary emphasis of environmental economists. They want to alter the system so that global markets benefit people and the environment in addition to maximizing profits. Many of them have great expectations for the kind of growth they refer to as "green growth," which has no detrimental effects on the environment. Green growth may be achieved by making products more energy-efficient, by converting harmful activities into clean ones that have little or no impact, by promoting development in the digital industry, which has a minimal impact when fueled by renewable energy sources, or by any combination of these. The proponents of green growth cite a history of invention waves that have periodically revolutionized humankind's potential.

The natural environment around us may serve as the finest inspiration for the evolution of our cities, thus we must imitate it. So that we may open the doors for wildlife to return, we must change our cities and our methods of living. Finding more efficient ways to farm is the best approach to efficiently provide a chance for wildlife. The fact is that we must stop expanding our industrial farms if we want to stop biodiversity loss and live sustainably on Earth. In fact, if we want to enable nature to start healing, we need to intentionally decrease the amount of land we occupy in order to make room for the wild.

The single largest direct driver of biodiversity loss over the Holocene has been the conversion of natural habitat to agricultural as humans extended its area. Only around 1 billion hectares of the earth's surface were cultivated in 1700. Our cropland now spans just under 5 billion hectares, which is about equal to the combined areas of North America, South America, and Australia. This indicates that we presently reserve more than half of the planet's habitable territory exclusively for ourselves. Over the past three centuries, we have destroyed seasonal forests, rainforests, woodlands, and scrub, drained wetlands, and fenced in grasslands in order to acquire the additional

4 billion hectares. In addition to being one of the main contributors to greenhouse gas emissions, habitat degradation is also one of the main drivers of biodiversity loss.

The carbon content of soils and land plants worldwide is two to three times more than that of the atmosphere. We have so far released two-thirds of this historically stored carbon through the cutting down of trees, burning of forests, dredging of wetlands, and plow-over of untamed grasslands. Farmland is easy to overlook and mistake for a natural scene, yet it is actually highly unnatural. Wild environments have evolved to be self-sufficient. In an ecosystem, plants work together to collect and preserve all the essential components of life, including water, carbon, nitrogen, phosphorous, and potassium. They accumulate organic matter in their soils, lock away carbon, and develop more complex structures and biodiversity through time.

Farmland in the modern, industrial era is significantly different. We give it what we deem necessary while taking away everything else. When adding fertilizer to deficient soil, we occasionally go so far as to make the soil hazardous to soil microorganisms. If there isn't enough, we bring water in from somewhere else, which decreases the amount of water in natural systems. If any other plants are present, we use herbicides to eradicate them. We use insecticides to get rid of insects that are stifling the growth of our crop. We typically remove all the plants at the end of the growing season and turn the soil over, exposing it to air and sunlight and reducing the soil's carbon supply. For years, we keep herds of animals on pastures until the grasses have used up all of their reserves. In order to reduce the overuse of land, we must farm efficiently and start to green some areas of our cities. By doing so, we give animals the chance to establish a new home and, in turn, a new connection with us.

In the Netherlands, there was a great desire for families to be self-sufficient and have enough land to cultivate their own food in the 1950s as a result of the traumas of the Second World War. The farms were passed down to the next generation in the 1970s, and they industrialized the farms by using items that were becoming more widely accessible at the time: fertilizers, greenhouses, machines, pesticides, and herbicides. Families mastered the art of increasing productivity, and each farm eventually became specialized in one or two crops. However, when their children took over at the turn of the 2000, some of them set out with a new goal: to keep raising yields while lessening their negative effects on the environment. In order to heat their greenhouses with renewable energy, the new, youthful owners built wind turbines or drilled geothermal wells deep into their fields. In order to maintain the greenhouses at the ideal temperature while minimizing water and heat loss, automatic climate-control systems were installed. They started to utilize their own greenhouse roofs to collect all the rainwater they required. To minimize input and loss, they grew their crops not on soil but rather in gutters filled with nutrient-rich water. Instead of using insecticides, they carefully released natural predators, allowing domestic bee populations to pollinate the crops without risk.

The high-tech method is costly to implement, though. Smaller-scale and subsistence farmers won't benefit from it, but huge food production businesses, who control a large portion of the world's acreage, may find it motivating. For these farmers, there are efficient, low-tech methods that have been shown to increase productivity and lessen impact in many global contexts. By adding carbon-rich organic matter back into the topsoil, regenerative farming is a low-cost method that can restore most farms' depleted soils.. They gradually stop using fertilizers. After harvest, they plant a variety of "cover crops" to protect the soil from direct sunshine and rain and to return nutrients to the soil through the plant roots. To ensure that the soil is never depleted, they rotate crops in a single field over time utilizing a cycle of up to ten distinct crop plant species, each of which requires a particular profile of nutrients from the soil. Crop rotation also lessens insect infestations, allowing for a reduction in the need for pesticides. The farmers may even intercrop, planting many crops in the same field in alternate rows so that they nourish the soil rather than deplete it. These methods will ultimately restore depleted soil, do away with the need for fertilizers entirely, and extract carbon dioxide from the air and put it back into the soil. Around half a billion hectares of fields have been abandoned owing to depletion worldwide, especially in the world's poorer countries. They could be able to return to being productive land with the aid of regenerative agriculture, which would also store an estimated 20 billion tonnes of carbon.

We must start by simply converting our cities into urban wildlife sanctuaries in order to enable the repopulation of animal populations. Ras Al Khor Wildlife Sanctuary is located in the marshes not far from the busy city of Dubai. It's incredible that tens of thousands of birds may be found in a location so near to the city. Although fish, crabs, and animals all use this vast reserve as a breeding site each year, it is the flamingos who steal the show in the winter. If you look closely, you could see other colorful bird species within the mass of pink feathers, such as grey herons, great egrets, reef herons, cormorants, black-winged stilts, sandpipers, and ospreys.

I went to the Ras Al khoor Wildlife Sanctuary for the first time with Zayaan and Mayank Ramchandani, a wonderful environment enthusiast who had introduced us and informed us about this sanctuary. The fact that wildlife thrives even outside of the refuge is simply astonishing. The Jujube Lappet moth (Streblote siva), which thrives on sidr trees, produces large numbers of eggs, or caterpillars in the nearby trees. I had trapped and raised about 100 eggs and caterpillars throughout the winter, which I eventually released back into the environment. However, the Ras Al Khoor wildlife reserve is where the real gems may be found. Fish species range from mangrove red snapper to short-nosed tripod fish, while mammals include from Arabian Red Fox to the Cape Hare. However, the Ras Al khoor nature reserve is most known for its birds than than its crustaceans, mammals, reptiles, or fish. The birds are the sole accessible area to see birds from various parts of the sanctuary. We had a short walk to the flamingo lagoon entrance of the sanctuary, and on the way there, we could observe western ospreys flying overhead, patrolling the area. But when we first arrived, there were maybe 100 greater flamingos here greeting us. The Dubai Municipality has made enormous efforts to safeguard and maintain this sensitive ecosystem's biodiversity. Three birding hides have been constructed, and the marsh has been fenced off from the general public. About 470 species of animals and 47 different types of plants may be found in Ras Al Khor.

However, the main draw to this reserve is the greater flamingos. We were there to film a documentary called Earth our living planet, and it was the first time I had ever been able to observe flamingos up close. The biggest flamingo species, known by the Arabic name Fanteer, is represented by these birds. But they make quite a noise within the sanctuary. They communicate by honking loudly, and the adult flamingo can recognize its chick's call. Throughout the breeding season, they only deposit one egg. About six years ago, I had collected one egg. It was discovered floating in the water in one of the lakes in al Qudra, spoiled with a hole in the shell. It has a really tough shell, but sadly this one was decaying, so I preserved it because you don't get to see how a flamingo egg looks every day, and of course to spread awareness.

The security at the flamingo hide was gracious enough to let us remain for more than an hour because we needed to record for the documentary. When we sat there watching the flamingoes, I made notes of my observations and took in the scenery as sometimes fighting flamingoes appeared. The day only got better when the security asked the park rangers to feed the flamingos while we were there. Within a few minutes, a ranger arrived, stepping out of his Toyota wearing long waterproof boots. He then moved amongst the group of flamingos with four bags of prepared brine shrimp and threw the meal there. The security reports that the flamingos appear to recognize their feeders. When the brine shrimp hit the water, the flamingos' heads turned upside down and they started to feed with their bent beaks, which are known as "bills." This is also why they are one of the few terrestrial animals that are "filter feeders." With the use of their bills, flamingos are able to filter feed, which involves scooping up a mouthful of water and prey while separating or filtering out undesirable elements like dirt and seawater. Their beaks are lined with several intricate rows of horny plates that, like those of baleen whales, are employed to squeeze food from the water. The Greater Flamingo's filter captures insects, mollusks, and crustaceans up to an inch long. However, the Lesser Flamingo possesses a filter that is so thick that it can separate out single-celled plants with a diameter of two hundredths of an inch in diameter. The pink colouring of flamingos is a result of the food they consume. Flamingos are grey when they are young and progressively turn pink as they age due to the colors in the organisms they consume, such blue-green and red algae and brine shrimp. The Ras Al Khoor Wildlife Sanctuary is a remarkable location and a source of inspiration for the existence of wildlife in urban areas.

We also need to alter how we catch different fish species if we want to let marine life take over our shores and oceans. Aquaculture, or the growing of fish, oysters, and other mollusks in artificial ponds or, in the case of mollusks, on the surfaces of support racks erected in estuaries, has the greatest potential for increasing output. Fish consumed by people worldwide account for more than 90% of the total catch, which is taken from wild animals in their native habitats. Even though advanced aquaculture techniques are available and fish in particular have been raised in ponds and other enclosed facilities for 4,000 years, this archaic business persists.

With fish aquaculture, we have essentially doubled our catch. Aquaculture has the potential to help lower the worldwide demand for wild seafood where it is needed, but up until now, our industrial approach has been plagued with unsustainable practices. To make space for fish farms that cling to the beach, coastal ecosystems including mangrove swamps and seagrass meadows have been cleared.

A behind-the-scenes shot with friend and Nature enthusiasts Mayank Ramchandani, and Zayaan Qureshi, as we head towards the Ras Al Khoor Wildlife Sanctuary.

A ranger as he empties a bag full of brine shrimp in the water for flamingos to eat at Ras Al Khoor Wildlife Sanctuary.

The farm, which consists mostly of fish, prawns, and clams, is usually tightly packed, and infections are widespread. As a result, farmers are frequently forced to apply antibiotics and disinfectants, which can subsequently spread the disease into the surrounding saltwater. We remove hundreds of millions of tonnes of baitfish from the ocean, starving wild fish populations, which is just as harmful to the environment as overfishing. Predatory fish like salmon have been nourished on this food source. The farms may generate enormous amounts of effluents, which leak from the enclosures and end up in the nearby water. Farm fish regularly escape, wreaking damage on the delicate ecosystems of foreign seas. To its credit, the marine aquaculture industry is reacting to all of these problems with best practices. These producers demonstrate the future of sustainable fish farming. Many of their fish pens are miles offshore to take advantage of stronger currents, and they are dispersed widely over the ocean to lessen their impact. The fish there are vaccinated to prevent antibiotics from getting into the water and are grown at much lower densities to decrease illness.

Insect protein from urban farms that breed billions of flies on the food waste of coastal towns is given to predatory fish, who are also fed on oils from agricultural crops. The fish farms are multi-leveled, with cages of sea cucumbers and urchins—both of which are prized delicacies in Asia—hanging below the fish pens and feeding on their dropping waste. There are ropes adorned with edible seaweed fronds and mussels hanging around the pens, all of which benefit from any leftover food and garbage that is carried away from the pens by surface currents.

It is mind-blowing to think of how small people around the world's coasts may use these sustainable techniques to expand their access to food and revenue from the sea while causing little environmental harm. In the distant future, ocean farmers may establish themselves just offshore along your local shores. They could also be accompanied by ocean foresters. The wide, brown fronds of kelp, the fastest-growing seaweed on the planet, may grow up to half a meter in length in a single day. It flourishes in nutrient-rich, chilly coastal waters, generating enormous underwater forests with astounding levels of biodiversity. Sea urchins frequently attack the forests, and when predators like sea otters that eat the urchins have been eradicated, whole kelp forests have been destroyed. But with our assistance, we may rebuild these forests and gain a great deal as a result. The kelp's upward growth would support invertebrate and fish populations and, most importantly, enable it to absorb massive amounts of carbon. According to experiments, each dry tonne of kelp has the same amount of carbon dioxide as one tonne of air. The kelp might be harvested responsibly as it expands and used as a fresh supply of biofuel. The re-established kelp forests would not be in competition for space with us or the terrestrial wildness, unlike bioenergy crops on land. We start to venture into uncharted terrain when paired with CCS technology, which absorbs carbon dioxide as the kelp is digested. When that happens, our electricity generation can actually reduce atmospheric carbon.

Last but not least, we may progress by using public transportation more often instead of private cars, which is far more effective. The annual carbon dioxide emissions from a typical passenger automobile are around 4.6 metric tons. One bus or subway can carry more passengers, which reduces emissions. In order to allow the creatures who depend on silence for their survival to live in cities, we must also create better, more silent vehicles like electric ones. This includes creatures that employ echolocation, such as bats, who are typically disturbed by the constant noise of our automobiles. They generate ultrasound, or sound waves at frequencies exceeding human hearing. The objects in the bats' habitat reflect the sound waves that the bats generate. When the bat hears the sound, it can determine how far away its victim is. By capturing bat sounds with sophisticated microphones and recording equipment, scientists and managers may identify and analyze different species of bats. Humans are able to see and hear the bat cries in their translated versions. For various objectives, bats can alter their sounds. Their social, eating, and searching calls vary. Each type of bat also has a distinctive call pattern. In addition to being unable to utilize their skills effectively owing to the noise of human automobiles, some bats are also awakened during the winter from their hibernation, which causes them to starve to death due to a shortage of food.

Welcoming Wildlife

It's time to get ready for the wilderness to return as our cities will start to change and resemble the natural environment. The wonderful world will begin to develop within our cities and transforming them into fantastic refuges for the wild. This is W, the third letter of the word.

The few remaining woods, grasslands, marshes, forests, and rain forests on Earth are in reality priceless. We can't live without the environmental services they provide. We must prevent losing the biodiversity that they support. Biodiversity is something that we should be valuing if we want to build a secure and healthy planet. Since a habitat performs better at carbon absorption and storage when it is more biodiverse, increasing biodiversity will naturally maximize that process. What would the world be like if landowners were encouraged to enhance biodiversity wherever and however they can and it was fairly valued? It would be enchanted. Natural grasslands, pristine ponds, old-growth temperate forests, and primary rainforests would all of a sudden become the most valuable properties on Earth! Finding ways to utilize pristine wilderness without compromising its biodiversity or capacity to sequester carbon would be encouraged. Such actions are taken, in fact. It would be authorized to engage in sustainable logging, which involves selectively felling and carefully removing trees at rates that reflect a forest's natural turnover, since this has been demonstrated to protect biodiversity.

Numerous earnings are generated when biodiversity begins to rebound. Ecotourism may generate large revenue for wild areas without having a big negative impact since it allows us all to experience the treasures that are being conserved. In fact, future tourism might be more dispersed the more wilderness there is. There would also be a strong motivation to develop and revitalize all of the regions that border pristine nature. Local and indigenous groups that reside in and near our wildest places would be the greatest candidates to spearhead these efforts. Experience with conservation projects has demonstrated that local communities must be actively included in the planning process and must immediately benefit from increased biodiversity for positive change to endure over the long term.

The return of the animals would be beneficial to us psychologically as well as financially. We are aware that one of the most important elements assisting individuals in managing the stress of the COVID-19 pandemic has been time spent outside. This is a really crucial point because it clarifies how having a connection with nature may improve our mental health and provides us with valuable guidance on how to make the most of these advantages for our overall wellbeing. Evidence now demonstrates that one of the factors contributing to nature's beneficial effects on our wellbeing is the nature of our interaction with it. Researchers refer to the ideal connection as "connectedness." The term "connectedness" describes how humans interact with and perceive the natural world. Feeling a deep bond or emotional tie to our natural environment is a sign of having a strong connection with nature. According to research, people who have stronger connections to nature tend to be happier overall and are more inclined to believe that their lives are valuable. Nature may inspire a variety of good feelings, including serenity, joy, and creativity. It can also help people focus.

Given enough room, the wilderness will rebound where biodiversity growth and carbon capture are rewarded thanks to the advantages of something known as the trophic cascade. The most well-known instance was observed in Yellowstone National Park when wolves were reintroduced there in 1995. The massive herds of deer would spend hours perusing the bushes and saplings that grew in the river basins and gorges until the wolves returned. That ceased when the wolves showed around, not because they were eating a lot of deer but rather because they scared off all the deer. The deer herds' routine was altered. They no longer stayed in the open for very long and were constantly moving. The trees came back after six years, sheltering the water and allowing fish to congregate out of sight. On the bottoms and sides of the wide valleys, aspen, willow, and cottonwood thickets grew. Bison, beavers, and forest birds all saw population growth. Because the wolves also targeted coyotes, rabbit and mouse populations flourished, leading to a rise in fox, weasel, and hawk populations. Finally, due to their ability to scavenge the remains of wolf killings, even the bear population increased. They gorged themselves on the berries of trees and bushes in the fall that would never have produced fruit otherwise.

Governments that recognize the genuine importance of nature and its contribution to stability and well-being are increasingly considering the return of the wild as a viable policy alternative. By the end of this century, the incentives are all in place to create a world that is far more wild than it was at the start. According to a 2019 research, the regrowth of trees may potentially absorb up to two-thirds of the carbon emissions that are still present in the atmosphere as a result of our actions. Rewilding the earth is within our power, and it is unquestionably a worthwhile endeavor. Restoring biodiversity would help stabilize the earth by doing what it does best: creating natural places all across the planet.

Reducing trash is one important method to welcome animals, and this too may be accomplished by imitating nature. In nature, the leftovers from one phase are used as the ingredients for the next. In cycles involving several species, all components are recycled, and practically everything is ultimately biodegradable. Researchers exploring the potential of a circular economy are attempting to improve our societies' efficiency and rationality. The key to the circular thinking is to envision a manufacturing model in which raw materials are viewed as nutrients that must be recycled, exactly as nutrients are in nature, as opposed to the existing take-make-use-discard approach. Then it becomes obvious that humans are basically caught up in two separate cycles. Food, wood, and clothing made of natural fibers are all examples of things that decompose naturally and are thus a part of a biological cycle. Anything not is engaged in a technological cycle, including plastics, synthetic materials, and metals. It is necessary to recycle the raw materials used in both cycles, such as titanium or carbon fibers.

In particular, plastic poses a significant threat to animals; I have personally observed it everywhere. In 2021, on a research trip to the Qudra lakes I examined a few bird populations. I encountered a wide variety of birds, from greater flamingos to small king fishers. However, as I approached a group of shoveler ducks who were resting, I discovered something strange. All except one of the birds took off when I approached. When I got closer to the female northern shoveler (Spatula clypeata), she was clearly intoxicated, so I put on my gloves and mask. After that, I captured the animal and brought it to camp; the weak female was unable to even lift her head. Active charcoal can be used as a treatment. When consumed, activated charcoal binds to toxins in the digestive tract and stops them from being absorbed into the body. Despite our efforts, the bird still passed the charcoal and showed no signs of improvement. The following day, it died. I preserved it and looked inside its gut to see why, regretfully discovering plastic. This female, which has been preserved, raises awareness of the effects of plastic on nature today.

The manufacturers of products made of plastics, synthetic materials, and metals could design them to last rather than only function for a short time. They may create parts that are simple to remove, disassemble, reassemble, and update. For components to be produced by many suppliers and switched, manufacturing would need to become much more standardized. Some others think that the cyclical method would lead to new customer-company interactions in which customers simply rent televisions and washing machines from manufacturers, just like they do now with phone handsets, but with a lot higher focus on mending and recycling. Both cycles would gradually eliminate from the economy any materials or chemicals that cannot be recycled or are essentially harmful to the environment. The most notable of them are the synthetic hydrofluorocarbons (HFCs) that are today found in air conditioners and freezers all over the world. These would add the equivalent of 100 gigatonnes of carbon dioxide to the environment as greenhouse gases if they were released from machines at the end of their useful lives.

The goal is to eliminate all forms of pollution, including oil slicks, hazardous gas emissions from industrial chimneys, burning rubber tires, and floating pieces of plastic in the ocean. The wastefulness of today may possibly be eliminated in such a world. Our landfills may transform into open-cast mines for businesses that are paid well to extract nutrients for the circular economy. The ocean's gyres of microplastics might be collected and blended to create ocean farmsteads. A rising number of people think that by altering how we utilize our resources, humans will eventually imitate nature's cyclical process and eliminate waste.

Environmentalists used to view cities as the scourge of the earth, choked with pollution and energy-guzzling traffic, with their residents' insatiable need for goods and resources leaving a soiled trail around the globe. However, they have grown to understand that the urban environment has a lot of promise for sustainability because of the large population concentrations in cities. City planners are becoming more adept at making their communities welcoming to bikes and pedestrians. They might incorporate effective, low-carbon public transportation.

There is a surprising animal living in Dubai's Jumeriah Village Circle. There is a little desert landscape that surrounds JVC. Once during the day, I went exploring these areas close to Al Khail Road, and what I saw genuinely startled me. There, I discovered canine-like footprints. At first, one may assume the prints belong to a dog that was probably out for a walk, but eventually, more certainty about the presence of Arabian red foxes emerged. These canines had dug several holes in the sand and constructed dens for themselves all around that area. Since no one really travels through such areas, foxes there live in peace. The

Arabian Red Fox can adapt to any habitat, even urban settings, and is widespread across the United Arab Emirates (UAE). Where do these foxes acquire their food is one question. Well, I just so chance to come upon a chicken carcass that was probably stolen by foxes from the homes nearby. They eat fish, birds, rodents, certain desert flora, and even carrion as part of their diet. However, they are most active at night, so I went back there then. There were no evidence of them, but they have a keen sense of smell and hearing, so maybe they heard me approaching. I reasoned that perhaps foxes used to live in this area before JVC was created, but what about all the evidence—the chicken, the dens that weren't obstructed by sand, and the skull I subsequently discovered? However, a week after that encounter, I had the opportunity to witness one Arabian red fox at nighttime as it was crossing the street close to the area where I had first noticed those indications.

I had previously seen Arabian red foxes on a beach in Jebel Ali when camping with my family and searching the ocean for crabs and cuttlefish. Suddenly, two foxes appeared out of nowhere and approached within a few meters of me while they were devouring a dead crab. As I tossed the food we ate for the foxes, who did not fear us, they approached us from a distance of a few meters. However, when the sun rose, they vanished. At the Qudra lakes during the day, of course, was another occasion when I observed an Arabian Red fox. The common Red Fox and the Arabian Red Fox have a similar coloring. It has a brownish-pale red color, yet it is more suited to desert living than its parent species. The abdomen is white, while the neck is black. Reddish-colored lower legs, ears, and a bushy tail with a white tip are all present. Compared to the Red Fox, it has significantly smaller body and much bigger ears. In order to protect its feet from burning on the scorching desert sand, it also possesses fur between its toes. I had for the first time gone far further into the Qudra desert, close to the road. Once more, I found corpses beneath the ghaf trees in this location, including a dead duck under one of the tree with peculiarly formed branches. I took the duck's skull because it was the only part that had been preserved, and I left the tree by crouching under a branch that had an unusually formed circular passageway. I tipped my head and passed under it, and as I moved a few meters further, I turned. A duck shouldn't have ventured this far from the water, therefore there must be another explanation. Soon after, I sneezed, and an Arabian red fox fell on its side from the branch I had been passing through. I attempted to pursue it, but my legs gave up. It may have been startled by my sneeze because it quickly fled. Even while I still consider what may have happened if the fox had landed on me as I went beneath that very branch, I eventually learned why the duck was actually there. Cities have the potential to develop and support magnificent biodiversity.

Making a city as green and pleasant as possible is one of the best strategies to draw people there. Urban plant life has been found to cool cities, purify the air, and enhance the mental health of city people in addition to offering areas for recreation. Cities are embracing nature as a consequence by expanding parkland, creating avenues, and promoting green roofs and walls covered in plant cascades. 100 hectares of new green space are now being added to the walls and rooftops of Parisian buildings. To absorb seasonal flooding and provide residents more natural space, wetlands are being constructed along the edges of municipal rivers in a number of Chinese cities. With a goal to convert half of its land into natural areas and improve the quality of life for Londoners, the city has proclaimed itself the first National Park City in the world. Singapore is a city-state that aspires to become a city enclosed in a garden. All new development is required to restore any lost vegetation on the ground with an equivalent amount of vegetation above ground. As a result, the city boasts hundreds of structures made particularly to be covered with vegetation, including a hospital that attributes improved patient recovery rates to the greenery. Singapore has converted 100 hectares of prime land on its shoreline into a water reservoir and garden with

a grove of 50-meter artificial supertrees that power themselves with solar panels, irrigate the gardens with the water they have collected, and filter the air. Singapore is connecting all of its parklands with green corridors.

Oriental pied hornbills groom their black-and-white plumage and nibble on fruit with their curled bills at the housing development directly across from the mall. Although the huge bird with the characteristic casque on its beak is difficult to miss, they were an uncommon sight in Singapore for over a century. The first known sighting of wild oriental pied hornbills since they disappeared from Singapore in the late 19th century was on Pulau Ubin in 1994. One of the Nature Society Singapore (NSS) members who first saw the birds was Dr. Ho Hua Chew, a long-time conservationist. It was an exciting experience to see a comeback for such enormous forest species, as the bird is a beautiful species that was previously thought to be extinct in Singapore.

The National Parks Board (NParks), Wildlife Reserves Singapore (WRS), and researchers who work on the Singapore Hornbill Project installed nest boxes in trees for the birds to breed in order to attract visiting birds from nearby nations to settle here and rear their young. The preservation of Singapore's biodiversity in an urban environment is a movement that has developed gradually over the past few decades. Otters also started to return to Singapore as a result of the river cleanup, which also focused on giving residents access to clean water. Otters had been absent in Singapore for a few decades, but when the river was made more aesthetically pleasing for humans, all of a sudden they appeared.

A large portion of Singapore's wildlife remains concealed in the few remaining patches of woodland near the city's center, while certain species, including small-clawed otters, still live on the north-east islands. There are numerous species here. One of them—the freshwater crab species Johora Singaporensis, which is unique to Singapore—

famously appeared on a list of the top 100 most endangered species in the world. Only a few hills in this area have fast-moving streams, where its limited population of a few hundred may be discovered. They are only found in Singapore. Therefore, if they are lost here, the entire world's population is lost. More than 100 crabs were returned into the environment as a result of a coordinated effort by NParks, WRS, and NUS in 2015 to rescue the pebble-sized crustacean. According to NParks, effective breeding programs and translocations have probably led to an increase in the crab population in recent years.

However, because to the species' restricted habitat options, its future is still uncertain. Currently, ecological research is being conducted to look at potential dangers to the species in the wild, such as drought and stream acidity that may be caused by climate change.

Over the years, other initiatives to protect important species, such as the Singapore freshwater crab, sea turtles, and native flora like the Singapore ginger, have also been established. Because the forests are too small, the majority of forest animals will experience a drop. However, by working to connect the various forest pieces by building corridors we can help the wilderness. He cites the 2013 construction of the Eco-Link, an animal highway, as one of Singapore's most significant conservation initiatives since it links the Bukit Timah and Central Catchment Nature Reserves, which were split apart by the Bukit Timah Expressway (BKE) in 1986.

Nature and people can coexist. We can flourish and cooperate with nature if we have the correct techniques. I came upon a factory during my travels to Iran in the summer of 2022. I was there with my grandfather, who owns the property with my uncle. The factory, which mostly constructs electrical meter boxes, is situated next to a mountain that is surrounded by desert and is home to some unusual wild species. The staff members here have gained experience working with animals. Many scorpions from the mountains would descend at night and be caught by the employees to be released back into the mountains when they went for a hike.

The moment I personally saw an Indian mongoose family's reliance on the factory workers was my happiest moment. Six individuals are allegedly living beneath a tiny cabin, starting with only a male and female. The employees relax in this hut, and they dump their leftover lunch food into a barrel there. This food is not being thrown away; rather, it is being provided for the mongooses. Normally nocturnal animals, they are now used to people and may be seen feeding during the day by hopping into barrels. So I put up a camera trap to get a close-up shot of this. It was amazing to watch the mongoose gently emerge from its hiding spot behind the cottage and leap onto the barrel's lid. It then carefully surveyed its surroundings before jumping into the barrel and starting to eat. However, as soon as it heard a faint sound, it leaped out and dashed back to the cottage.

Saving biodiversity is straightforward if we learn to work and act like nature; all we need is the will to do it. According to my own experience, wildlife may be found anywhere; all it takes is a little window of opportunity for them to emerge and thrive.

Innovation

We must start using our technology once more if we want to have the living world around us. There are amazing advancements coming that will imitate nature even better. This makes the letter I in the word Rewild.

The most intelligent beings to have ever walked the earth are us. The discoveries we discovered helped us overcome all of our issues and provided us the chance to rule the globe. The first was the introduction of water power in the eighteenth century, which allowed mills to operate machinery that greatly enhanced a company's production. After that, we began using fossil fuels and steam power, which not only sparked an industrial revolution in manufacturing but also led to the development of railways, ships, and finally airplanes that could swiftly transport people and goods throughout the world. The next three waves came. The early twentieth century's electrification, which gave rise to telecommunications, the 1950s space age, which oversaw a consumer boom in the West, and the digital revolution, which gave rise to the internet and brought a vast array of smart gadgets into our homes. All of them have drastically altered the globe and boosted the economy. Many environmental economists believe that the sustainability revolution, the sixth wave of innovation, is almost here. Entrepreneurs and inventors will prosper in this new world order by creating goods and services that have a lesser environmental effect. Of course, we are already seeing the beginnings of this: inexpensive solar energy, low-energy light bulbs, plant-based burgers that taste like meat, and sustainable investing.

In essence, the entire living universe runs on solar energy. Three trillion kilowatt hours of solar energy are annually captured by plants, phytoplankton, and algae on Earth. That is over 20 times more energy than humans consume. And they take it straight from the sun, encapsulating the energy in carbon-based organic compounds. Animals and humans alike spend a lot of time attempting to capture a share of this industry. For 3.5 billion years, the activity of life on Earth has been centered on the acquisition and distribution of the Sun's energy as well as the subsequent cycling of carbon between the atmosphere and the living world. But in the process, we have quickly released into the atmosphere carbon that has been in the atmosphere for millions of years. It was a potentially terrible thing to have done. By itself, carbon dioxide is a harmless gas that is comparatively inactive. With each breath, we exhale it. However, it is a greenhouse gas, which means that it serves as a blanket in the atmosphere, trapping heat at the Earth's surface. The ability of it to warm the Earth increases with its concentration. Additionally dissolving in water, carbon dioxide has the effect of raising the ocean's acidity.

We are now left with no choice but to alter the way we provide our activities with energy. However, we don't have much time to do this. 2019 saw 85% of the world's energy coming from fossil fuels. Hydropower, which has a minimal carbon footprint but is only available in a few places and has the potential to seriously harm the environment, accounted for less than 7%. Just over 4% was provided by nuclear power, which is likewise low in carbon but is undoubtedly not without hazards. The Sun, the wind, the waves, the tides, and the heat from deep inside the Earth's crust—the so-called renewables—are the power sources we should be using, yet they currently only account for 4% of our capacity. We have fewer than ten years to transition to renewable energy from fossil fuels. The global temperature has already risen by 1°C since pre-industrial times.

Our carbon budget, which sets a ceiling on how much carbon we can still add to the atmosphere in order to keep global warming below 1.5 degrees Celsius, will be reached by the end of the decade if present emissions rates continue.

Humanity will always be grateful to this generation if we manage to switch to renewable energy sources at the rapid speed necessary. After all, we are the final generation with a realistic chance to make a difference and the first to properly comprehend the situation. Above all else, we humans are the most amazing problem solvers.

We must once more draw inspiration from nature, from a creature that lives inn warm coastal places all around the world serving as one example. We can easily overlook an upside-down jellyfish when at the beach. Until lately, I was unaware of how magnificent they are. While out on a walk on Mamzar Beach, I came across a dead upside-down jellyfish. Using forceps and a pair of scissors, I detached a little portion of the creature's bell and tentacles, putting it in a test tube until I got home. The specimen was placed under the microscope. I was amazed by what I discovered within. Dinoflagellates that live inside the jelly's tissues in a symbiotic relationship are what give the jelly its brownish hue. The jelly allows its algae to photosynthesize by lying on its back, exposing it to the sun. The jelly's arms have the largest concentration of these zooxanthellae algae, although the bell also contains some of them. 90% of the jellyfish diet is made up of the photosynthetic byproducts of the algae. The remaining 10% is made up of aquatic debris. These jellyfish have several mouths as well. To swiftly capture and ingest food, they have a primary mouth and up to 40 secondary mouths on their arms. The upside-down jellyfish is a filter feeder that draws planktonic food in by pulsing its bell.

The ability to produce electricity from the Sun, wind, water, and the inherent heat of the deep Earth is now well understood by the energy business. The issue with storage persists. The development of battery technology is still insufficient. Additionally, renewable energy sources are not as effective as they should be to fully meet the needs of transportation, heating, and cooling. On these cases, we have to work around the issue by bridging our flaws with short-term solutions.

The majority of experts concur that the most challenging issue to overcome will be air transportation. Although hybrid, completely electric, and hydrogen aircraft are being developed, airlines intend to include carbon emission offsets in ticket pricing until those aircraft are

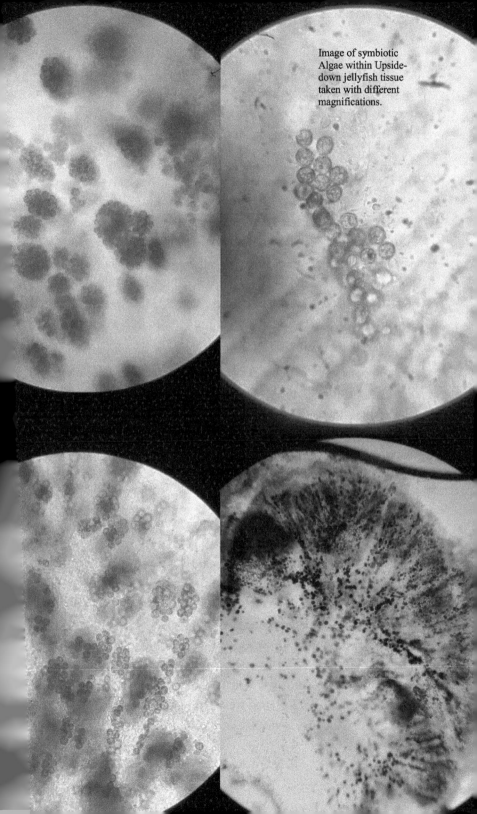

Image of symbiotic Algae within Upside-down jellyfish tissue taken with different magnifications.

available commercially. To make sure that all of these repairs are as temporary as feasible, we must put in a lot of effort. Given the short amount of time we have before exhausting our carbon budget, any prolonged use of fossil fuels eventually necessitates deeper, more drastic reduction in emissions elsewhere.

The cost of renewable generating per kilowatt has already fallen to levels that compete with coal, hydropower, and nuclear power, and it is getting close to the cost of gas and oil as a result of the scaling up of solar and wind power. Renewable energy sources are also far less expensive to handle than other types of power. An energy industry dominated by renewable sources is predicted to save billions of dollars in operating expenses over the next 30 years. Many observers think that just making renewable energy more affordable will cause it to quickly displace fossil fuels.

According to some commentators, the introduction of autonomous cars will revolutionize the transportation industry. They anticipate city inhabitants would stop owning cars in a few years and will only order a car when necessary. All of these vehicles would be electric, self-charging with green energy, and maybe controlled directly by the automakers, encouraging the whole sector to increase productivity and dependability.

Is this a fantasy? It's not necessary to be. At least three countries presently produce 100% of their power without utilizing fossil fuels: Iceland, Albania, and Paraguay. Another eight countries generate less than 10% of their power from coal, oil, and gas. Rapidly growing nations have a unique chance to innovate and catch up to many Western nations thanks to the energy transition and the broader sustainable revolution. One country that has embraced the revolution is Morocco. Nearly all of its energy at the turn of the century came from imported oil and gas. Today, a network of renewable power facilities, including the biggest solar farm in the world, provide 40% of its domestic energy demands. It is paving the way for a promising and reasonably priced kind of energy storage known as molten salt technology, which utilizes table salt to store solar heat for many hours, allowing for the usage of solar power into the night.

By the middle of this century, we could pull off a miracle and switch to a clean energy society. There is one more cause for optimism in this regard: the chance that we may deliberately take some of the carbon we have released into the atmosphere and lock it back out of harm's way as a planet-saving bridge while we introduce renewable energy. Politicians and corporate leaders who need to extend the time period for the phase-out of fossil fuels find this carbon capture and storage, or CCS, to be quite appealing. There are filters that catch some of the carbon as it leaves fossil fuel power plants, towers of fans that pull it directly out of the air, bioenergy power plants that recover greenhouse gases as the crop is digested, and facilities that inject the carbon deep into the earth where it is protected from the elements.

Some geoengineers put up more radical suggestions, like using bacterial and algal blooms for agricultural purposes, fertilizing the ocean with iron, pumping CO_2 to the ocean floor, and obscuring the Sun with dust in the upper atmosphere. Although some of them may potentially function and others might be feasible on a large scale, they are currently relatively little understood and run the danger of having unanticipated negative effects. We have a far better technique of trapping carbon, and the rewilding of the earth will take massive amounts of carbon from the air and store it away in the growing wilderness.

30% of the sun's heat is reflected away by clouds, deserts, woods, snow, and seas. By releasing substances into the stratosphere, such as sulphur dioxide, we may increase the amount of solar energy that is reflected back into space. The ground underneath would cool as less solar energy entered the lower atmosphere. Aerosol injection into the stratosphere is the name of this procedure. Long explored, the idea is comparable to what happens when a big volcano explodes. Sulfur dioxide would need to be introduced into the stratosphere at low latitudes in order to cool the Earth using this approach. The material would then be dispersed by the winds, slowly moving towards the pole of the hemisphere it was discharged into, thus creating a reflecting shield. The release would cool the whole planet if it were administered at low latitudes in both hemispheres.

Beyond the fields, a new generation of farmers are increasingly growing food in areas that we already use for other purposes. The technique of cultivating food for profit in urban areas is known as urban farming. Urban farmers increasingly cultivate food on roofs, in abandoned structures, below ground, on office window ledges, down the outer walls of city buildings, in shipping containers on brownfield sites, and even above parking lots, shading the vehicles below. The farms often utilize hydroponics, low-energy lighting, and climate control to optimize growth conditions and reduce the amount of soil, water, and fertilizers needed. Urban farms not only make efficient use of unused space but also are situated close to where their consumers are, which significantly reduces transportation emissions. Vertical farming is a significant expansion of this strategy, where layers of various plants, frequently salad crops, are stacked one on top of the other, lighted by LEDs driven by renewable energy sources, and supplied with a nutritional medium via feeder pipes. Although expensive to set up, vertical farms offer benefits. They increase a hectare's output by up to 20 times. They are not affected by weather fluctuations, and they may be kept free of pesticides and herbicides in enclosed facilities.

Additionally, we can start to grow trees in new and interesting ways. Commercial forest harvesting has been perfected by forestry engineers, but restoring those forests or creating new ones still relies heavily on human labor, utilizing a shovel and a bag of seedlings. Drone seed delivery might change all of that and end up as a typical tool in the forester's toolbox, reducing the ongoing labor scarcity for the taxing task of physically planting trees in sometimes tough and isolated terrain. By swiftly creating new forests, restoring timber-harvested regions, reseeding in fire-devastated zones more quickly, and reaching hard-to-reach locations, the use of drones to spread seeds might contribute to the cooling of the globe.

Seed must first be gathered, cleaned, and sifted by skilled workers before aerial seeding can begin. For the seeds of each species to effectively germinate, a separate pre-treatment could be necessary. Others won't sprout until they've been through a forest fire, passed through an animal or bird's intestines, or endured two periods of sub-zero temperatures followed by thawing into spring-like conditions. To withstand being blasted pneumatically into the ground from a height by a drone, pre-treated seeds need to be enclosed in a protective shell. To enclose the seed, clay pellets or gel packs are frequently utilized. Some businesses add chilli to the capsule to make it unpleasant for foragers who are skilled at gathering food, such as squirrels, or for passing birds, who may quickly kill the likelihood of the seed ever maturing.

Learning

Understanding the planet is the first step towards rescuing it. Before we can come up with practical solutions, we must first comprehend the issues and how nature works. We must begin learning. Thus, the letter L becomes the fifth letter in Rewild.

To begin with, we must redefine environmental issues so that they better represent reality. The ongoing rise of human populations has pushed the deterioration of the physical environment to an unlivable state, the well-known syndromes of toxic pollution, ozone layer loss, climate warming from the greenhouse effect, and the depletion of arable land and aquifers. If we are determined enough, we can stop these tendencies. I have been bringing awareness to many issues throughout the world ever since I started. Understanding our world is crucial because only when we can care, and only when we start to care, are we capable of saving it. Since the beginning, I have helped bring people closer to nature by making documentary films and sharing podcasts with you like the nature talks, which feature expert lectures on how we can all rescue the earth.

The free movement of organisms and the uninterrupted flow of the natural processes that support life on Earth are referred to as ecological connectedness. This interconnectedness is broken by habitat fragmentation across land, air, and water, which poses a worldwide danger to biodiversity preservation and the biological processes that support the biosphere. The three main ways that habitat fragmentation affects nature are through habitat deterioration and destruction. First off, it lowers the quantity and quality of habitat overall. Additionally, it makes habitat sections seem more isolated from one another. Last but not least, it intensifies edge effects along the edge of a fragmented habitat, for instance by increasing the frequency of abrupt changes from natural to changed environments. reestablishing ecological links throughout the landscape The fragmentation of ecosystems caused by habitat loss and degradation poses a serious danger to ecological connectedness. As a response to this, connection conservation is quickly becoming a viable option for reestablishing species migration and the flow of natural processes.

Realizing that there is life all around us is the greatest approach for us to understanding our world and its biodiversity. Just take a stroll at night and scan the grass at a neighboring park; you may see a variety of insects, arachnids, and even slugs there. I have a lot more examples to share. Zayaan and I have been friends for almost 6 years, and it was I, who first introduced him to nature and encouraged his desire to experience nature. Our first, brief experience took place in a typical park. But here, we encountered a variety of species that went well beyond anyone's expectations. Elegant rhinoceros beetles were the first insects we saw. Strong insects that can carry 80 times their own weight and have armor that is very strong. It would be like me lifting eight elephants. The populations of rhino beetles declined in number and the size of their horns as we watched over the following years. This indicated that the soil's fertility was diminishing. When I initially took Zayaan there, he was astonished by the animals he saw, including earwigs, slugs, and eventually a radiated wolf spider. Zayaan was arachnophobic and dreaded spiders up close and far away. After exhausting it for a bit, I was able to hold the speedy female in my palm. Zayaan was astounded by how calm these spiders could be, and with minor persuasion, he took the spider into his own hands. His fear of spiders has now vanished.

We need to start surveying the world's flora and wildlife in order to understand biodiversity. When it comes to diversity, scientists are almost completely in the dark. They know very little about the number of species on earth or where they are located; more than 99 percent of their biology is still a mystery. The approach that has the best chance of success is a mixed one that aims to create a comprehensive inventory of all species on Earth, but it does so over a fifty-year period and at various levels or scales in time and space, from hotspot identification to a global survey, audited and readjusted at intervals of ten years.

Progress could be evaluated and new courses might be determined when each decade came to an end.

Emphasis would be put on the hotspots that are known or suspected right away. There are potential for three levels. The first is the RAP strategy, named after the prototype Rapid Assessment Program developed by the Washington-based conservation organization Conservation International. Its goal is to protect the world's biodiversity. The goal is to analyze understudied ecosystems that might be regional hot spots quickly—within a few years—in order to provide emergency suggestions for more research and action. The region that is being attacked is quite small, such as a single valley or solitary mountain. It is essentially difficult to classify the whole fauna and flora of even a small endangered environment because the categorization of the great majority of creatures is so little understood and because there are so few specialists available to perform additional investigations. Instead, a RAP team is assembled from specialists in what are known as the "elite focus groups"—organisms like flowering plants, reptiles, mammals, birds, fish, and butterflies—that can be quickly inventoried and act as stand-ins for the surrounding biota.

The Neotropical Biological Diversity Program of the University of Kansas and a group of other North American universities established it in the late 1980s. This technique is known as the BIOTROP approach, and it represents the next level of inventory. In contrast to RAP, which focuses on identifying brushfires of extinction at specific locations, BIOTROP conducts more systematic exploration across large regions thought to be key hot spots or at the very least to contain several hot spots. The bigger objective is to establish research stations around the region that encompass various latitudes and altitudes in addition to identifying key sites. Starting with a few targeted species, the job begins. As enough samples are gathered and specialists in the groups are enlisted to analyze them, the scope of the study extends to less well-known groups like ants, beetles, and fungi. The species inventory is being expanded as further studies of rainfall, temperature,

and other environmental factors are conducted. The most significant and well-equipped of the stations are thus expected to develop into hubs for extensive biological research, with experts from the host nations taking on leading positions. They may also be used to educate scientists from other nations.

The third and final step of the biodiversity survey is finally reached. The description of the living world will progressively come together to provide a fine-grained picture of global biodiversity from inventories at the RAP and BIOTROP levels in various regions of the world, together with monographic investigations of one group of species after another. Even with ongoing effort, knowledge will inevitably develop faster because it will create its own economies of scale. As new strategies for gathering and dispersing specimens are developed, and access to information processes is enhanced, the cost per species registered into the inventory decline. For instance, entomologists can perform the process backward, gathering plant specimens in addition to the insects they collect, while botanists can collect insects living on the plants they study while also identifying these hosts. The complete environments may be tested for groups like reptiles, beetles, and spiders, and the samples can then be given to experts on each group in turn. The knowledge amassed by biodiversity surveys at all levels becomes an increasingly potent magnet for other fields of inquiry as time goes on. The imagination is sparked by field manuals and illustrated treatises, and networks of technical knowledge entice geologists, geneticists, biochemists, and others to the project. The majority of the activities should be concentrated at biodiversity centers, where new research is being planned and data is being obtained.

Geographic Information Systems, a collection of layers of data on terrain, vegetation, soils, hydrology, and species distributions that are electronically registered to a common coordinate system, are an example of a functional technology. Gap analysis is the name given to the mapping when it is used to study biodiversity and endangered species. Gap analysis can show the efficacy of current parks and reserves, despite being unfinished. It can be used to assist in resolving more general inquiries about conservation techniques. It will be necessary to conserve certain land parcels as protected areas. Others will be chosen as the ideal locations for extractive reserves, buffer zones utilized for restricted hunting and part-time agriculture, and for land Systems for Geographic Information Geographic information systems link layered data sets to incorporate information on the physical and biological surroundings. These can be used, together with the declaration of natural reserves, to manage the landscape in a way that safeguards threatened species and ecosystems. The clever arrangement of woodlots, hedgerows, watersheds, reservoirs, and artificial ponds and lakes may nonetheless support ecological variety at high levels in landscapes that have been largely humanized.

Master plans will incorporate the preservation of species and races in addition to economic efficiency and aesthetic appeal. The layered data may also be used to define "bioregions," which are geographic entities like watersheds and forest tracts that connect related ecosystems but frequently span regional or even international boundaries. A full study of the earth's enormous stocks of biological diversity may seem unattainable with so few individuals ready to undertake it. Even the least effective, antiquated techniques may be used to process 10 million species in 50 years. A systematist would need to put in around one million person-years of work if they collected 10 species every year at a conservative pace that included field excursions for collection, laboratory examination of specimens, publishing, and time off for holidays and family obligations. The work would take up 25,000 professional lifetimes, assuming scientists had a 40-year lifespan of active life.

By using new methods that are now widely used, systematic work may be expedited significantly. The taxonomic identifications and locations of individual specimens are recorded using the Statistical

Analysis System (SAS), a series of computer tools that are already in use at thousands of institutions throughout the world. Other computer-assisted methods, such as phenetics, automatically compare species across a wide range of attributes using unbiased metrics of similarity. Others aid in the cladistics approach, which is used to determine the most plausible family trees of species. Insects and other minute species are now more often illustrated thanks to scanning-electron microscopy. In the future, image scanning technology will be able to rapidly identify species while identifying specimens that belong to new species. Biologists are also near to achieving electronic publishing, which will enable desktop computers to access descriptions and analysis of specific groups of species. The databases allow for the layering of every other type of biological information about a species, including its ecology, physiology, economic applications, status as a vector, parasite, or agricultural pest. Gene maps and DNA and RNA sequences can be included. A computer database containing all known DNA and RNA sequences as well as associated biological data is made available by GenBank, the genetic-sequence bank, according to its charter. It had amassed 35 million sequences by 1990, spread over 1,200 different plant, animal, and microbial species. With the introduction of better sequencing techniques, the pace of data access is rising quickly.

A variety of strategies may be used to preserve biodiversity, but not all of them will be successful. Consider one that futurists frequently bring up in conversation. Let's say we failed in our efforts to protect the environment and all natural ecosystems were allowed to disappear. Once genetic engineers have figured out how to put life together from basic chemical molecules, may new species be generated in a lab? It is unlikely. There is no guarantee that living things can be created artificially, at least not ones that are as sophisticated as flowers, butterflies, or even amoebae. Even with this divine ability, only the easiest portion of the problem would be resolved. The technicians wouldn't be aware of the background of the extinct life they were

I have long been preserving animals and plants. Presenting a female shoveller duck specimen at The Westminster School, Dubai. April 2022.

mpty Exhibition with different student art exhibits and a giant tree as the centrepiece of the exhibition.

attempting to mimic as they worked. The many mutations and events of natural selection that put billions of nucleotides into the now extinct genomes are unknown, and can only be inferred in minuscule bits.

They would need close attention, just like the zoos and botanical gardens that were created on top of them. But is it possible to revive extinct species using the DNA that is still present in fossils and museum specimens? Once more, the answer is no. A 2400-year-old Egyptian mummy and magnolia leaves preserved as rock fossils 18 million years ago have both had portions of their genetic codes decoded, although they only make up a small percentage of the entire genetic code. Even that portion has become completely jumbled. Cloning these species, or a mammoth, a dodo, or any other extinct life, would be comparable to trying to piece together a massive book in an unfamiliar language without using your hands. So why not collect tissue samples from every species that is still alive and freeze them in liquid nitrogen? Later, they may be cloned to create whole creatures. The technique is effective for some microorganisms, including spores from fungus, bacteria, and viruses.

Numerous bigger animals may be similarly stored in nitrogen sleep, at the very least as fertilized eggs, to be raised later and grown into full beings. Even little pieces of undifferentiated tissue can be encouraged to grow and mature normally. For creatures as complicated as frogs and carrots, it has been done. Tens of millions of species must reside in the new Noah's ark, the cryotorium, where they would sleep. An enormous effort including hundreds of species, the majority of which are yet unknown to science, would be required to preserve the content of even one threatened habitat, such as a mountain ridge forest in Ecuador. Only a limited portion of each species' genetic diversity could be practically covered, even when done at the species level. There would be a huge variety of naturally existing genetic strains lost unless the samples reached in the millions. When the time comes to reintroduce the species to the wild, the ecosystem's physical foundation, such as its soil, special nutrient composition, and precipitation patterns, will have changed, making restoration unlikely. At best, cryopreservation is a last-minute effort that could save a few rare species and strains that would otherwise perish.

The preservation of seed banks, in which seeds are dried and stored for extended periods, is one that benefits a variety of plants. The banks are maintained cool (often around - 20°C), but not in liquid nitrogen to keep them suspended in time. The method has been shown by botanists to be efficient for maintaining the majority of crop species strains. A hundred or more nations maintain seed banks, and they continue to grow through exchanges and new expeditions for gathering seeds. Around 50,000 plant species, or up to 20% of all plant species, have "recalcitrant" seeds, which cannot be preserved in the usual ways. Even if seed storage for all plants could be mastered, which is improbable in the near future, the effort of gathering and caring for thousands of endangered species and races would be enormous. The current seed banks' combined efforts barely cover a hundred species, and even those are sometimes poorly documented and have questionable survival rates. Another issue is that if exclusive dependence were placed on seed banks and the species subsequently went extinct in the wild, the bank survivors would be deprived of their symbiotic partners, who cannot be kept in cold storage, such as root fungus and insect pollinators. The majority of the symbionts would become extinct, making it impossible to reestablish the saved plant species in the wild. Other ex situ techniques rely more realistically on growing and reproducing captive populations. Across 1,300 botanical gardens and gardens exist around the globe, many of which house plant species that are vulnerable to extinction or are extinct in the wild.

However, we may learn about the species we are familiar with from the museums across the world. The best and most efficient approach to introduce people to nature is through museums. I firmly believe that museums contain the solutions to the disappearance of our planet's biodiversity and that, when taken to a museum, many people,

With the wonderful team of students, staff and teachers, who made this amazing exhibition come true. In front of us is my specimen exhibit and the cardboard pangolin.

especially the youth, may experience and comprehend nature like never before.

Over the years, I've gathered and conserved more than 200 specimens of both flora and animals. April of 2022, we coordinated an annual art show with The Westminster School Dubai. We gave it the name "my world." Ms. Rukhsana Choudhary, the head of arts, and I created this exhibition with the main objective of bringing attention to the devastating loss of biodiversity in our planet. There were more than 200 participants, representing a range of ages, educational levels, and talent levels. everyone on a mission to use their creativity to safeguard the earth. Over the course of the two-week spring break, the art department, faculty, and students worked many hours to complete this exhibition. It was a magnificently shown fusion of art, science, and nature. The most trafficked animal on earth was represented by a near life-size African pangolin, which took a few students and I approximately a week to construct after some tries and errors. This pangolin's scales had to be cut out of recycled cardboard one at a time and put on the inner metal wire skeleton. Each work of art there had a narrative quality and related what we had just seen in some way. Young students' depictions of indigenous cultures in paintings and sketches could be seen in one area. This served as a stark reminder that if ecosystems are gone, people who live there would also lose their homes—forest dwellers, for example. But as soon as you walked inside the show, you were greeted by a giant tree that acted as the centerpiece and particular emphasis on both life and forest fires on either side of it. It amply demonstrated how a small fire may extinguish all life, yet a mere tree can sustain a large range of species. Its construction was made from wood and wires and afterwards coated in recycled paper to mimic a tree's trunk and leaves.

The base of the tree was struck by an ocean wave constructed of plastic bottles, whose shape was created by a thick steel wire, and under the tree were objects that depicted oil spills. As a reminder that we may all be nature's heroes, omnipresent superheroes like Spider-Man, Iron

Man, and others could be seen standing strong throughout the show. Together we hold the power to change this world's fate, to be our planet's sustainable superheroes; with spiderman's sense of responsibility, black panther's determination, iron man's sense of judgment, and wonder woman's drive towards attaining hope and victory, together we will learn, heal and move on. They were made using a time-consuming procedure that yielded spectacular results, using wires as its foundation and recyclable plastic, cotton, and tape. On the stage, there was a kiosk displaying student-drawn book and magazine covers as well. There were three things that struck out: the David Attenborough portrait, Greta Thumberg's book cover, and the cover of the book you are currently reading.

But from everyone's perspective, the exhibition's focal point—three tables connected by a few display stands, on which my specimens were displayed—was the largest and most eye-catching sight. When I was eleven years old, I often came across dead animal specimens in the field, most of which had died due to human activity. My outstanding collection of more than 200 animal and plant specimens that I have gathered over the years was shown in this exhibition which gave more than 5,000 children a new level of connection to nature. The interest and reluctance to leave this sign was endearing. told the children the tales of the majority of my specimens, ranging from the common pheasant that was shot to the poisoned shovelnose duck. I utilized the specimens to inform both adults and children about the dangers facing the world's biodiversity. to introduce children to nature in a way they had never done before. The kids were in wonder as they saw the creatures for the first time, and possibly the last time in their lives. You could soon sense their increasing concern for the environment and their passionate desire to learn how to save the earth.

More than 90% of the species of fungus, insects, and other tiny creatures on Earth are unknown to biologists. Even with the species that have been saved, they have no method to guarantee a representative sampling of genetic diversity. If it is even conceivable, they have no clue how to put ecosystems back together using rescued species. Not to mention how pricey the entire procedure would be. Ex situ approaches will preserve a few species that would otherwise be beyond hope, but the preservation of natural ecosystems is the light and the path for the world's biodiversity. Finding the world's hot spots and safeguarding the overall environment they contain must be the main strategy for conservation. Because even the most iconic species are only the representatives of thousands of less well-known species that coexist with them and are also vulnerable, entire ecosystems are the preferred targets. Any natural ecosystem that shrinks in size also has fewer species that can reside there permanently. In other words, even if all of the remaining habitat were to be protected going forward, certain species are destined to go extinct. The vast majority of species of microbes, fungus, and insects are not well recognized, therefore it stands to reason that the Endangered Species Act has failed to catch them as they have been sliding through the gaps. As ecosystems are more understood, less obvious endangered species will be discovered, increasing the likelihood of conflicts.

The hot areas will become clearer when biodiversity surveys are upgraded. As additional local ecosystems are identified, the greatest priority for conservation may be given to those areas. This implies that they will typically be put aside as inviolate reserves. Warm spots, places that are less endangered or have fewer species that are unique to that area, can be allocated for partial development, with core preserves concentrating on endemic species and races and buffer strips around the preserves preserved largely natural. It is possible to properly plan agricultural landscapes and harvested forest tracts to support endangered species and races. When taken all at once and delivered properly, these steps will work. But whether or not vulnerable species are kept in reserves, the Endangered Species Act or a comparable law is also required to act as a safety net for them in all situations.

Finally, population management can be used to reach a compromise in the rare instances where the electorate finds the costs unbearable.

This includes moving the species to neighboring habitats that are favourable for it, reintroducing it to areas outside the conflict zone where it was previously extinct, or, if all else fails, banishing it to botanical gardens, zoos, or other ex situ preserves. The area-species relationship that controls biodiversity demonstrates that maintaining already-existing parks and reserves won't be sufficient to conserve all the species that call them home. Currently, just 4.3 percent of the earth's land area is protected by law; this protection is split between national parks, research facilities, and other types of reserves. These pieces indicate newly decreased habitat islands, whose faunas and floras will continue to decline until a new equilibrium is found, which is frequently at a lower level. Most of the surviving high-diversity ecosystems and more than 90% of the remaining land surface have undergone changes. The bulk of the terrestrial species on the globe will either be wiped out or put in grave danger if the disturbance persists until the majority of the natural outside reserves are swept away. Additionally, even the current reserves are in danger. Timber thieves operate on their margins, poachers and illicit miners invade them, and developers discover methods to partially convert them. Therefore, we should work to increase reserves from 4.3 percent to 10 percent of the land surface in order to encompass as many undisturbed ecosystems as we can, with the world's hot places receiving priority.

We must start incorporating all of these into the educational curriculum in order to make all of them achievable. People will begin to care and take action for the environment if they are given a thorough awareness of their local fauna. All these new farming techniques must be taught to Farmers. As we learn more about and develop a greater awareness of the living things that inhabit our globe, the entire world may alter. Even though we may believe we know a lot, we actually don't. This was visible during the art display. It was regrettable that so many kids were unaware of what a pangolin was.

Discontinue

We have now reached a stage when almost everything we do negatively impacts the environment. Therefore, we need to stop doing those things that are bad for the environment. As a result, the word "Rewild" has the letter "D" as the last letter.

In the future, what we eat will matter more than how much. Again, nature has an explanation. Herds of Arabian gazelles spend most of their days munching on tree leaves in the Qudra Desert. In order to achieve this, they must spend energy finding the ideal trees and biting off and chewing through the tough, outer edges of the branches to get at the food within. They exclusively consume the leaves at ground level, occasionally standing on their two feet to reach the upper leaves. They expend additional energy as heat while the leaves are being digested in their stomachs, and the majority of the fiber in the leaves and branches goes through their bodies completely undigested and is ejected as feces. Like all animals that consume plants, gazelles can only utilize a part of the solar energy that is stored in the food they consume. Between plants and herbivores, there is inefficiency and an energy loss. Which explains why antelopes and cows must spend the majority of their days feeding. The food chain also experiences energy loss between herbivores and carnivores. The previously widespread in Arabia Arabian leopard may have hunted the gazelles. They looked for chances to do so throughout most of the day. In most cases, they won't succeed in catching their victim even after starting a chase. Furthermore, even if they are successful, they will only be able to take advantage of a small fraction of the energy that the gazelle has taken in from the leaves. The gazelle will have already used the most of its energy by moving around in search of Ghaf trees, engaging with other herd members, and in fact keeping an eye out for and dodging the Leopard. Furthermore, the gazelle's bones, tendons, skin, and hair contain energy reserves that the leopard would ordinarily overlook since he only eats the animal's flesh. The quantity of creatures we see in the wild may be explained by the energy loss that occurs as we move up the food chain. Large predators can't possibly be widespread according to the law of nature.

Humans are neither herbivores nor carnivores. We are omnivores, with the anatomical capacity to digest both plants and animals. A sizable area of land is needed for the production of each piece of meat served at our table. Currently, 4 billion of the 5 billion hectares of agriculture in the world—nearly 80% of all farmland—is utilized for the production of meat and dairy. This amount would span both North and South America. Surprisingly, there is no cattle at all in a large portion of this area. It is devoted to crops like soy, which is sometimes cultivated in another nation solely for use as animal feed for cattle, poultry, and pigs. Therefore, the true amount of area that cattle needs may go unnoticed. Beef is by far the most environmentally harmful of all the meats in terms of production damage. Despite making up only 2% of our calories and nearly a quarter of the meat we consume, 60% of our acreage is used to raise beef. Pork and poultry production need less land per kilogram than beef production. Simply put, it won't be possible for everyone in the future to expect to eat as much beef as those in the world's richest countries do right now. On Earth, we don't have enough space to achieve that. It is widely believed that in the future, we will need to switch to a diet that is primarily plant-based and contains far less meat, especially red meat. This will improve our health and reduce greenhouse gas emissions in addition to reducing the amount of land we require for farming. According to studies, cutting back on meat consumption might reduce heart disease, obesity, and various cancers mortality rate by up to 20% by 2050, saving the global healthcare system a trillion dollars.

However, many people's culture, traditions, and social lives heavily revolve around consuming meat and caring for animals. Additionally, hundreds of thousands of people across the world make their living by producing meat, and in many places, there is now no substitute. How will we get from our current situation to a lifestyle mostly reliant on plants? Indeed, I've noticed that I've progressively quit eating meat in recent years without making any dramatic decisions. I won't claim that it was very intentional or even that I feel good about it, but I was shocked to discover that I don't miss it. My entire family no longer consumes meat. To meet this change, the whole food business is creating new strategies. The biggest fast-food chains and grocery stores are all currently experimenting with alternative proteins—foods that resemble meat and dairy products in appearance, texture, and flavor, but without the negative effects of livestock production on animal welfare or the environment. It's now fairly simple to discover plant-based substitutes for foods like milk, cream, chicken, and hamburgers. Some of these substitutes are remarkably accurate replicas of the original foods and can provide all the nutrients we require.

According to estimates, just half of the land we presently farm—an area the size of North America—could provide enough food for all of humanity. And it would be incredibly useful because we need all of that land immediately. It is the location of our most significant initiatives to boost biodiversity and trap carbon. And the farmers, who will be most impacted by the "clean, green revolution" taking place all around them, will play a crucial role.

Additionally, we must eliminate poaching and shooting wild creatures. All of the food we require is already here. A species' biodiversity will be further harmed if its members are removed. We have brought numerous creatures, including rhinos, elephants, tigers, and pangolins, dangerously close to extinction by hunting them for their scales, horns, skin, and other valuable parts. We must start realizing that the majority of the species we murder for purported medicinal reasons serve no actual medical function. If true and they really serve therapeutic reasons, it would be ideal to preserve the fingernails and hair of the eight billion people on the planet and utilize, store, and sell those. Animal horns and scales are formed of the same components that produce our fingernails, and hair, a protein called keratin.

ve always been a supporter of biodiversity. Here I stand speaking with a caretaker of a Burmese
ion at the Green Planet Dubai.

I'll never forget my first trip to the Qudra lakes because in addition to the incredible nature I observed, I also witnessed an animal die in front of my very own eyes. We must travel through the Al Qudra road to get to the Qudra lakes. As my father drove the car, we observed a brown bird with spots in the sky. As we drew closer to the bird, I watched it abruptly lose consciousness and fall to the ground. Soon after, my father stopped the car, and I took the bird inside. This was a female ring-necked pheasant (Phasianus colchicus). At first, we thought it had been struck by a car, but then I noticed that its abdomen was bleeding profusely. Despite my best efforts to stop the bleeding by wrapping it in tissue and a bandage, the bird's wound was too deep, and 15 minutes after we first saw it, it passed away in front of me. The pheasant had been wounded with an air rifle, and I had to remove the bullet from its abdomen while preserving the pheasant.

The bullet is still with me because it serves as a constant reminder that once we have a species on our target, there is nowhere on earth where it can hide from the effects of people.

We must immediately halt all deforestation worldwide and, through trade and investment, assist those countries who have not yet cleared their forests so they may profit from these riches without sacrificing them. It is simpler to say than to accomplish. The idea of protecting wild lands is significantly different from that of protecting wild waters. No one is the owner of the high seas. On the other hand, we live on land. It is divided up into billions of different-sized plots that are owned, purchased, and sold by a wide range of diverse business, government, local government, and private parties. Markets determine its worth. The main issue is that there is currently no method to estimate the value of the services that wildness and the environment, both locally and globally, provide. On paper, an oil palm plantation is worth more than 100 hectares of standing rainforest. Destruction of wildness is therefore justified.

Additionally, by importing invasive species, we have been eliminating biodiversity. Native plants and animals may go extinct as a result of invasive species, which compete with native species for scarce resources, and disrupt ecosystems. A former pet that was released into the wild or escaped was most likely the first Burmese python discovered in the Everglades in 1979. Burmese pythons have been connected to severe animal population decreases in Everglades National Park. The isolated southernmost areas of Everglades National Park, where pythons have been maintained for the longest, have seen the most drastic losses in native species. Another well-known invasive species in Australia is the cane toad. The cane toad, which was first brought from Hawaii and released in Queensland as a biological control for sugar cane beetle pests.. When consumed, cane toads can kill local predators because they are poisonous at every stage of their life cycle—as eggs, tadpoles, toadlets, and adults. In the Northern Territory and Queensland, cane toads have been blamed for the decrease and extinction of a number of native predator species, notably the northern quoll. In the western North Atlantic, lionfish have emerged. Since lionfish are well-liked by aquarists, it is conceivable that repeated releases from aquariums into the wild are what led to the invasion. Today, lionfish may be found living in the warm ocean waters of the wider Atlantic on reefs, wrecks, and other forms of habitat. Lionfish have very few predators outside of their home region as adults and consume mostly fish. According to research, a single lionfish living on a coral reef can lower the recruitment of local reef fish by 79%. Lionfish eat on the same food that snapper, groupers, and other local species of significant economic importance generally ingest.

I've seen invasive species in the UAE as well; in Dubai, house crows have horrible effects on local wildlife and humans. One of the most invasive bird species in the world, the house crow is found in over 25 countries in the Indian Ocean region, the Arabian Peninsula, and Southeast Asia. Development, public hygiene, biodiversity, tourism, and transportation are all negatively impacted. I've had dealings with them in the past. While I was unaware of their negative effects on the environment, I saved a chick by climbing and placing it back in a tree. In addition to attacking people during the mating season, they also devour numerous native bird eggs and chicks. However, I've also heard that some of these crows in deserts would target baby gazelle and take their eyes out. We need to start introducing native fauna, not invasive species, and we need to start eradicating them.

Finally, we need to put an end to the locations where animals are abused and hurt for financial gain. Examples of these sites include circuses, some zoos that don't offer the correct habitat for the animals, and tourist attractions that focus on overusing animals like Asian elephants. The best way to enjoy wildlife is In their natural habitats.

When we consider , all of them are possible. The planet may be rewilded. We can all come up with our own ideas, so it is not simply these ones that I have talked about. The biodiversity will begin to recover through rewilding the earth. The world is changing, and we must gradually prepare for it. As buyers, it is our responsibility to compel sellers to hear from customers that they will not purchase from them until they have a sustainability strategy covering the whole supply chain of the goods they are selling.

Behind the scenes while recording a speech for COP26

The Path to Save the Planet

I was born during a period when we had lost a significant portion of our planet's biodiversity and are still losing it. We are all currently residing in the Anthropecene, often known as the Human Era. However, at this time when biodiversity is rapidly disappearing, I am fortunate enough to have the opportunity to explore the natural world.

I have visited unexpected locations that, shockingly, were teeming with life. On the other hand, I have also visited locations where there was an abundance of life, but it had almost completely disappeared. This definitely isn't a good time.

One of them happened when I visited my grandfather's garden this year. It is situated in the midst of a desert, miles away from any real civilisation. Six years ago. When the plants were watered, small juvenile Perrin's green toads (Bufotis perrini) emerged from the ground. Just 6 years later, their numbers, which had previously reached 20 in the garden alone, had decreased to just 2 adults. Just 6 years prior, the garden was considerably morewild. This is a desert-dwelling nocturnal amphibian t+++++++++++hat emerges at night to eat everything it can fit in its mouth, including insects. Toads provide significant benefits for both humans and ecosystems. As prominent predators of insects and other invertebrates and a source of food for fish, birds, mammals, reptiles, and other amphibians, they play a crucial role in ecological food chains. Toads have a unique technique of releasing their poisons, and it is thought that they are all toxic. Depending on the species, it can exude a variety of milky alkaloid compounds known as bufotoxins, which function as neurotoxins to ward off predators. The parotid glands secrete this chemical. The most harmful components of its venom are steroids with digoxin-like properties. The majority of patients experience gastrointestinal symptoms such as; nausea, vomiting, and abdominal pain. Many anuran amphibians, particularly the common toads, secrete bufotoxin, a fairly strong poison (genus Bufo). Bufagin, which has cardiac effects akin to those of digitalis, bufotenine, a psychedelic, and serotonin, a vasoconstrictor, are all detectable components of the milky fluid. The presence of an amphibian in a location has significant relevance, which is the most crucial factor. These species' semi-permeable skin allows them to breathe and absorb certain nutrients, thus it stands to reason that toxins and pollution have a significant impact on them. Therefore, if you find one somewhere, it means the area is clean and healthy.

The Chytrid fungus is the largest danger to all species of frogs and toads, other than chemicals and pollution. The fungus targets the keratin-containing areas of a frog's skin. Frogs have trouble breathing because they utilize their skin for respiration. The fungus also weakens the neurological system, which alters the behavior of the frog. It is brought on by the fungus Batrachochytrium dendrobatidis (Bd). Over 200 species of frogs and other amphibians have either declined or gone extinct as a result of the illness.

The worst feeling for me is leaving a beautiful habitat, learning about a species, or distantly seeing a wild animal and wondering whether this is the last time I will ever see these things.

An elite group of geologists first proposed the word "Anthropocene" in 2016. What for geologists was a word generated by scientific procedure is today, however, a dramatic reflection of the terrible transformation that we are currently facing for many people. We have developed into a powerful global force that is having an impact on the entire world. In reality, the Anthropocene may terminate with the final extinction of human civilization and prove to be a very limited phase in geological history. It is not necessary. A new and sustainable interaction between humans and the environment may emerge with the onset of the Anthropocene.

There is still hope for the planet, despite the loss of biodiversity. I've saw it happen. Populations have recovered since 1982, when commercial whaling was outlawed internationally. Amazing progress has been achieved by humpback whales. There are currently thought to be 135,000 swimming the seas. Due to their low global population of about 5,000–15,000, blue whales are still regarded as endangered. They continue to be highly enigmatic, and their environment is still endangerdanger. There are limits to the ocean. Another notable case was the return of the Arabian Oryx to the deserts of the United Arab Emirates. Cactus finches and geckos, formerly believed to be extinct on the Galapagos Islands, made a comeback ten years after an invasive rodent species was eradicated. Biologists who recently visited the Rabida and Pinzon islands in the Galapagos to track animal recovery claim that both the geckos and finches are now "thriving" in their respective environments. The rhino population in Zimbabwe has recovered, with over 1,000 rhinos present for the first time in three decades, including 614 black and 415 white rhinos. This information comes from the African Rhino Specialist Group of the International Union for Conservation of Nature's Species Survival Commission. According to conservationists, the increase of rhinos in Zimbabwe is evidence that efforts to conserve them have been effective.

We have lost many species over the history of humanity, all of which have been lost due to the impacts of humanity. The northern white rhino for example has been a famous example of how we kill animals without realizing the problems that will come. Now only 2 females are left, In Kenya's Ol Pejeta Conservancy, Najin and Fatu live under continuous guard against poachers. The last male, Sudan, passed away on March 19, 2018, essentially eradicating the whole subspecies. Since they have existed for millions of years, rhinos have been an important part of their environment. They play a significant role in shaping the African environment since they consume vast amounts of vegetation. This helps maintain a healthy balance in the ecosystem and benefits other creatures.

The estimated timing of insect evolution is 450 million years ago. however, we know that flying insects most likely first appeared 400 million years ago. Before the emergence of flowering plants, there were no bats, birds, pterosaurs, or other flying creatures in the sky before insects. Because so much of what makes the Earth that we live on unique has been fashioned over hundreds of millions of years of insect evolution, it may be difficult to fathom a world without insects. From the moment we get up until the moment I'm speaking to you now, insects have really had a role in that. Whether it was in the clothing we wear or the food we consume, there are many things that insects do that we kind of take for granted. The vast majority of people are unaware of the crucial ecological responsibilities that so many different insects play. They are the primary plant pollinators. Insects pollinate over 85% of the world's blooming plants. They do decompose organic matter returning nutrients to their environment. Several animals rely on them as a major source of food. Our biosphere is basically structured by them. Knowing the history of insects is like knowing the history of the Earth.

When I was a kid, I recall that if you drove out on a highway or freeway, your windshield and the front of the car would be covered in insect spatter. It just doesn't happen anymore, And that is merely a straightforward way for us to comprehend the decrease in the actual-the bulk, the quantity of insects around us. But it's also the diversity. You need variety, even if you have a huge number of insects. To create a healthy environment, several species must coexist peacefully. We are losing that, unfortunately.

While we frequently discuss rescuing the environment, the reality is that we must take these steps in order to rescue ourselves. The wild will come back, with or without us. The ruins of Pripyat, the city that had to be abandoned when the Chernobyl nuclear reactor exploded, provides a less dramatic example of this. The abandoned city has been overrun by a forest in the 34 years following the evacuation. The bricks were torn away by ivy and the concrete was crumbled by shrubs. Poplar and aspen seedlings have broken through the pavement, and the weight of the gathering vegetation has caused the roofs to droop. The gardens, parks, and avenues are now covered in 20-foot-high oak, pine, and maple tree canopies. The wilderness has reclaimed the area.

Image captured using a camera trap of an Indian Mongoose carefully scanning the surroundings before entering the barrel to eat.

Observing a Perrin's green toad (Bufotis perrini), as it emerged after heavy rain the previous night.

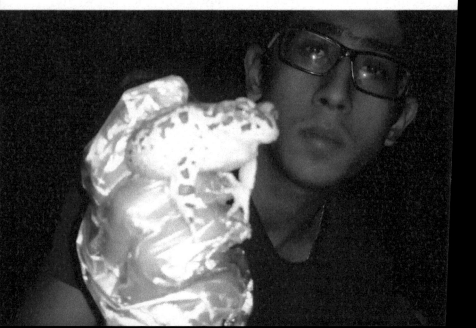

A refuge for creatures that are uncommon elsewhere has been established on the territory that includes the town and the destroyed reactor. Using video traps set up at the town's windows, biologists captured footage of healthy fox, elk, deer, wild boar, bison, brown bear, and racoon dog populations. A few members of the almost extinct Przewalski's horse species were released some time ago, and their numbers have since grown. Even wolves have settled in the region, safe from the hunters' firearms.

We still have time to make reparations, control our influence, reorient our growth, and regain our natural equilibrium as a species. The will is all we need. The next few decades provide a last chance for us to create a secure home for ourselves and rebuild the rich, healthy, and beautiful planet that our ancestors left for us. Our future on the earth depends on each and every one of us performing our part in the Rewilding Program. In every aspect, nature may inspire us. For instance, a bird doesn't learn to fly overnight. Birds don't just fly; they have to go through many obstacles, crash, and then get back up.

While our past has been recorded, our future is still up in the air and in our control. This is about rescuing ourselves, not just protecting the environment.

The natural world will repopulate in that time. And as it does, it will restore the stability and effectiveness on which we rely. Fish biomass in certain ocean locations that have been protected from fishing has increased by almost 400% in just a few years. Forests, marshes, meadows, and mangroves will regrow wherever we allow space. We have now demonstrated that it is feasible to stop deforestation. In recent decades, we have done that. With forests, we were able to attain 20% of our coverage, and as of right now, that number is 50%. The natural plants will sequester carbon once more when they regrow, assisting us in our fight against a changing climate. Animal seed-spreaders and pollinators will reappear.

At the poles, sea ice may begin to form once more. Our supply networks' reliance on the weather may return to its regular patterns. Our world is capable of rewilding. Increasing diversity and stability as a result.

Choosing what is best for both the immediate and long-term prospects is a difficult assignment that sometimes seems contradictory and calls for information and ethical standards that are, for the most part, still unwritten. Thus, the study of biodiversity is both a scientific endeavor, a subfield of pure biology, and an applied one, a subfield of biotechnology and the social sciences. Similar to how biomedical studies draw from biology at the level of the cell and molecule, it draws from biology at the level of whole organisms and communities. Biodiversity studies focus on the health of the planet's biological ecosystem and its fitness for the human species, as opposed to biomedical studies, which are concerned with the health of the individual person.

The key to a balanced and healthy life is the balance of giving and receiving. We can achieve a more balanced life when humanity as a whole is able to give back to nature at least as much as we receive and pay off our debt. To make the most impactful improvements, it will require the participation of every country, particularly those with the largest ecological footprint. For sustainability to be successful, it must be implemented globally, not just by some nations. It's easy to focus on what we stand to lose when considering sustainability, but it also brings many benefits such as clean air and water, affordable energy for all, safer and more peaceful cities, and a reduction in our dependence on coal and oil. We can also improve the health of our oceans by giving up fishing rights in certain areas, which will aid in the fight against climate change and provide more wild seafood. Additionally, eating less meat will improve our health and fitness and make food more affordable. A route to sustainability exists. A brighter future for all species on Earth may result from following this route. We must REWILD the world!

A speech during the UAE National Day about how we can unite to save wildlife at Al Nakheel JVC.

5 Park Road, Richmond, Surrey TW10 6NS

19.8.22

Dear Erfan Firouzi,

thank you for your letter and all you and your pupils have done to awaken people to the pressure facing our planet and what must be done to save it.

Best wishes

from David Attenborough

267

THE YEAR THE EARTH CHANGED

——————◆•◆——————

My speech at TEDx

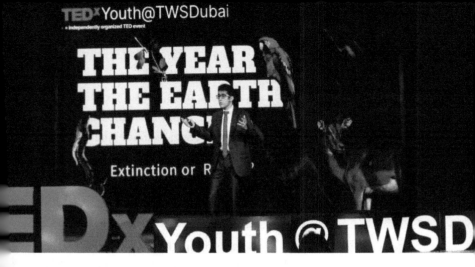

What you are hearing is the sound of the native wildlife, in the UAE's

Desert, the calm, tranquil feeling we all get is not a coincidence, we all evolved In such ecosystems, with sounds of Flamingoes for example, insects, or gazelles indicating the possibility of the resources we needed for survival, ecosystems and biodiversity today still hold the key to life today, but now all of us are used to the hustle and bustle of the cities in which we live, and one of the greatest consequences of this is that we are broken off the natural world, and if we lose that sense, we have lost one of the most important things in our lives.

I as a young boy grew in 21st century, back in 20s not all knew about biodiversity loss. It is Now I realize that the earth back then was much more biodiverse, just in 17 years, the world has transformed, Earth is losing 1.2 trillion tons of ice each year, The seas have risen about 8- 9 inches. Just in a decade we have made some 160 species disappear from the phase of earth. I mostly had my adventures with my grandfather, he told me stories about the abundant diversity of life back in his childhood, and so this was the root of my love for nature. I had unique adventures, spending my time chasing butterflies, catching frogs, or sometimes having very rare visits from the local wildlife, from scorpions, to snakes, from hedgehogs, to Flamingoes, and I vividly remember the time of my first visit to a rainforest, emerged in the amazing sounds of wildlife, just seeing trees or walking past trees, restores your minds and bodies, that's the magic of trees, and when you're in a forest you can feel it, go on breathe!

At some point, some 10 years ago, I helped a wild Iranian tortoise cross the road, never did I realize that this was the first and last time, I saw one, now endangered, and this was among first signs of change. The living world that gave stability to our planet was disappearing. The animals I used to find became rarer, you had to dive deeper in the oceans to find sea urchins, and you had to move deeper in the desert to see an Arabian gazelle. As we lose species what we no longer have is the capacity of the natural world, to provide the services we need to function.

When I first started researching some 8 years ago, people referred to me as young sir David Attenborough, nature boy and animal expert. I never imagined that I would one day stand here among you all speaking about threats like biodiversity loss or climate change! People often ask me, "You research and catch these animals, aren't you scared?" Well I am scared up to a point, but what makes me really scared is living in a world where you can't find those creatures!

What is happening around the world currently and what will happen in the future is more severe than the nuclear explosion at Chernobyl. Over 100,000 people were evacuated in less than 46 hours and were never able to return. The zone was declared uninhabitable for the next 20,000 years. If we do not change our actions, scientists predict that in 80 years, the planet could be four degrees

aring my experiences with the
dience and a shot Video I had taken
Arabian Oryxes, during a visit to
Marmoon Nature Reserve.

TWS Radio / TEDx)

of me and my grandfather in
orests of Mazandaran.
g the untouched wilderness.
Radio / TEDx)

warmer, resulting in numerous extinctions and making large parts of the Earth uninhabitable. The sixth mass extinction has begun!

We're in the middle of a great species extinction; we're losing biodiversity everywhere and we're burning fossil fuels very, very fast.

Actually how is it possible that the most intelligent species to ever walk the earth, is knocking down its only home?

We must keep in mind that the natural world is a parallel world which exists alongside us and which is the basis of our own lives. They are living these lives all around us whilst we carry on with our lives, and we never see it, we basically need to think like a tree or an animal. I can tell you that life exists in the most unexpected places and if given the chance it will surely recover.

Now we must choose our path..... The next big thing is of our choice? What will you choose?

A path that will lead to a planet doomed, Plagued with diseases, unreliable weather, and the onset of sixth mass extinction, or would you go on the path of eternal existence, one where we work with nature and the healthier our planet would be.

The amazing thing here is, that unlike an avenger movie where 1 hero exists, in this story we all can be heroes, the future is ours to write, if I can make earth a better place, so can you, if you can, we all can.

We must REWILD the world - An Acronym that could be the Next Big Thing in my point of view. Let me throw some light on it -

This is what REWILD MEANS TO ME! This can be a story of humans as they lead the whole planet to an amazing recovery and we have shown we can do it!

I witnessed The Arabian oryxes returning to the UAE's deserts, from a herd of just 160 in 2007, there are now more than 6900 individuals, the largest wild population in the world.

Perhaps, the best proof of nature's ability to recover can be seen at the site of one of our greatest disasters, Chernobyl. The truth is, without human intervention, the natural world will rebuild. In the 30 years since the evacuation of Chernobyl, despite the radiation, there has been a remarkable recovery. Within a decade, vegetation began to germinate, and as the forest established itself, animals began to appear. This is powerful evidence that no matter how grave our mistakes, nature will ultimately overcome them. Honestly, there is no species as clever and innovative as Homo sapiens. Let's live up to that name, let's open the doors to the future and witness the next big thing ourselves. What path will you choose?

Age on Humans

Animals lost to
History because of us

EXTINCT ANIMALS

LOST TO HISTORY DUE TO HUMAN ACTIVITY

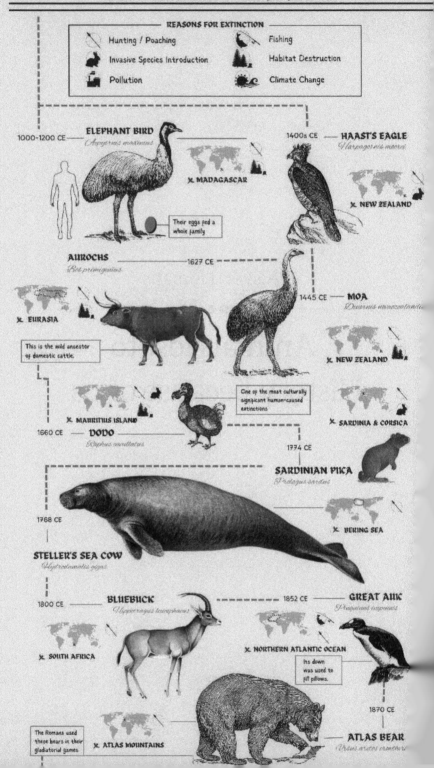

REASONS FOR EXTINCTION

- Hunting / Poaching
- Invasive Species Introduction
- Pollution
- Fishing
- Habitat Destruction
- Climate Change

1000-1200 CE — **ELEPHANT BIRD**
Aepyornis maximus

✗ MADAGASCAR

Their eggs fed a whole family

1400s CE — **HAAST'S EAGLE**
Harpagornis moorei

✗ NEW ZEALAND

AUROCHS ———— 1627 CE ————
Bos primigenius

✗ EURASIA

This is the wild ancestor of domestic cattle.

1445 CE — **MOA**
Dinornis novaezealandiae

✗ NEW ZEALAND

One of the most culturally significant human-caused extinctions

✗ MAURITIUS ISLAND

1660 CE — **DODO**
Raphus cucullatus

✗ SARDINIA & CORSICA

1774 CE

SARDINIAN PIKA
Prolagus sardus

1768 CE

✗ BERING SEA

STELLER'S SEA COW
Hydrodamalis gigas

1800 CE — **BLUEBUCK**
Hippotragus leucophaeus

———— 1852 CE ———— **GREAT AUK**
Pinguinus impennis

✗ SOUTH AFRICA

✗ NORTHERN ATLANTIC OCEAN

Its down was used to fill pillows.

The Romans used these bears in their gladiatorial games

✗ ATLAS MOUNTAINS

1870 CE

ATLAS BEAR
Ursus arctos crowtheri

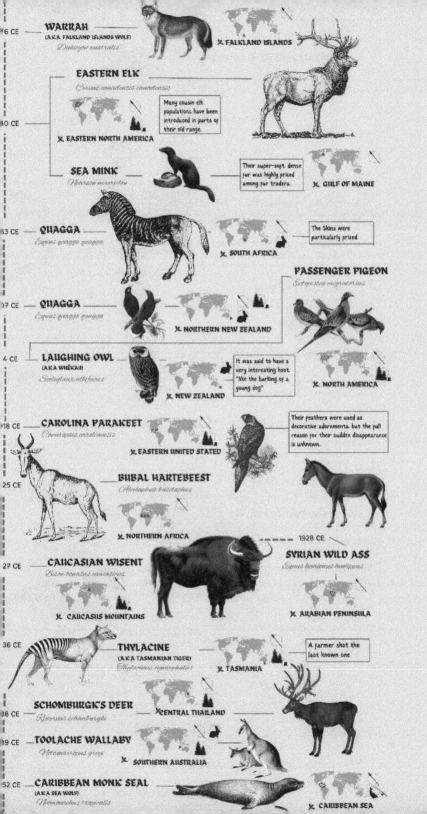

WARRAH
(A.K.A. FALKLAND ISLANDS WOLF)
Dusicyon australis

6 CE

✗ FALKLAND ISLANDS

EASTERN ELK
Cervus canadensis canadensis

40 CE

Many cousin elk populations have been introduced in parts of their old range.

✗ EASTERN NORTH AMERICA

SEA MINK
Neovison macrodon

Their super-soft, dense fur was highly priced among fur traders.

✗ GULF OF MAINE

QUAGGA
Equus quagga quagga

83 CE

The Skins were particularly prized

✗ SOUTH AFRICA

PASSENGER PIGEON
Ectopistes migratorius

QUAGGA
Equus quagga quagga

07 CE

✗ NORTHERN NEW ZEALAND

LAUGHING OWL
(AKA WHĒKAU)
Sceloglaux albifacies

4 CE

It was said to have a very interesting hoot, "like the barking of a young dog"

✗ NEW ZEALAND

✗ NORTH AMERICA

CAROLINA PARAKEET
Conuropsis carolinensis

18 CE

Their feathers were used as decorative adornments, but the full reason for their sudden disappearance is unknown.

✗ EASTERN UNITED STATED

BUBAL HARTEBEEST
Alcelaphus buselaphus

25 CE

✗ NORTHERN AFRICA

CAUCASIAN WISENT
Bison bonasus caucasicus

27 CE

1928 CE

SYRIAN WILD ASS
Equus hemionus hemippus

✗ CAUCASUS MOUNTAINS

✗ ARABIAN PENINSULA

THYLACINE
(AKA TASMANIAN TIGER)
Thylacinus cynocephalus

36 CE

A farmer shot the last known one

✗ TASMANIA

SCHOMBURGK'S DEER
Rucervus schomburgki

38 CE

✗ CENTRAL THAILAND

TOOLACHE WALLABY
Notamacropus greyi

39 CE

✗ SOUTHERN AUSTRALIA

CARIBBEAN MONK SEAL
(AKA SEA WOLF)
Neomonachus tropicalis

52 CE

✗ CARIBBEAN SEA

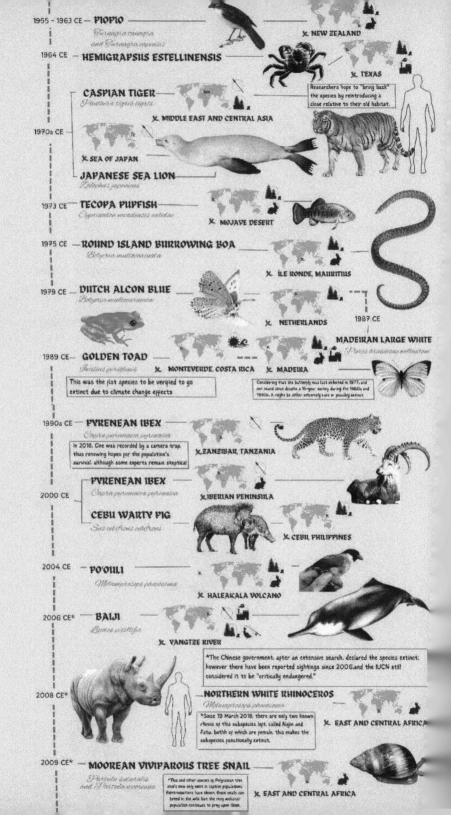

1955 - 1963 CE — PIOPIO
Turnagra tanagra and Turnagra capensis
✕ NEW ZEALAND

1964 CE — HEMIGRAPSUS ESTELLINENSIS
✕ TEXAS

Researchers hope to "bring back" the species by reintroducing a close relative to their old habitat.

CASPIAN TIGER
Panthera tigris tigris
✕ MIDDLE EAST AND CENTRAL ASIA

1970s CE

✕ SEA OF JAPAN

JAPANESE SEA LION
Zalophus japonicus

1973 CE — TECOPA PUPFISH
Cyprinodon nevadensis calidae
✕ MOJAVE DESERT

1975 — ROUND ISLAND BURROWING BOA
Bolyeria multocarinata
✕ ÎLE RONDE, MAURITIUS

1979 CE — DUTCH ALCON BLUE
Bolyeria multocarinata
✕ NETHERLANDS
1987 CE

MADEIRAN LARGE WHITE
Pieris brassicae wollastoni

1989 CE — GOLDEN TOAD
Incilius periglenes
✕ MONTEVERDE, COSTA RICA   ✕ MADEIRA

This was the first species to be verified to go extinct due to climate change effects

Considering that the butterfly was last collected in 1977, and not found since despite a 15-year survey during the 1980s and 1990s, it might be either extremely rare or possibly extinct.

1990s CE — PYRENEAN IBEX
Capra pyrenaica pyrenaica
✕ ZANZIBAR, TANZANIA

In 2014, One was recorded by a camera trap, thus renewing hopes for the population's survival, although some experts remain skeptical

PYRENEAN IBEX
Capra pyrenaica pyrenaica
2000 CE
✕ IBERIAN PENINSULA

CEBU WARTY PIG
Sus cebifrons cebifrons
✕ CEBU, PHILIPPINES

2004 CE — PO'OULI
Melamprosops phaeosoma
✕ HALEAKALA VOLCANO

2006 CE* — BAIJI
Lipotes vexillifer
✕ YANGTZE RIVER

*The Chinese government, after an extensive search, declared the species extinct; however there have been reported sightings since 2006,and the IUCN still considered it to be "critically endangered."

2008 CE* — NORTHERN WHITE RHINOCEROS
Melamprosops phaeosoma
✕ EAST AND CENTRAL AFRICA

*Since 19 March 2018, there are only two known rhinos of this subspecies left, called Najin and Fatu, both of which are female, this makes the subspecies functionally extinct.

2009 CE* — MOOREAN VIVIPAROUS TREE SNAIL
Partula suturalis and Partula mooreana
✕ EAST AND CENTRAL AFRICA

*This and other species of Polynesian tree snails now only exist in captive populations. Reintroductions have shown these snails can breed in the wild, but the rosy wolfsnail population continues to prey upon them.

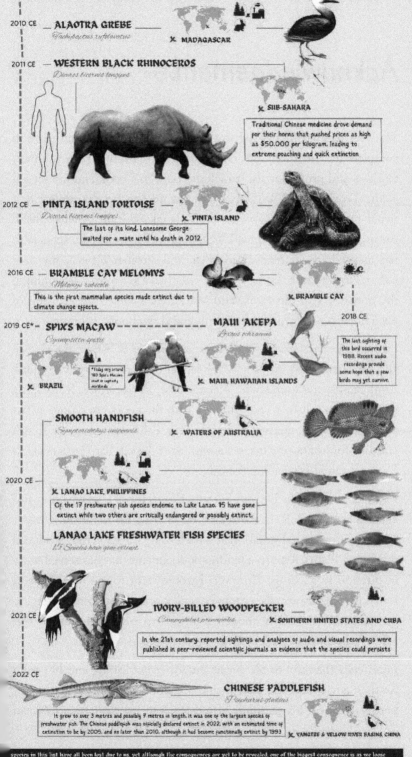

2010 CE — **ALAOTRA GREBE**

Tachybaptus rufolavatus

✗ MADAGASCAR

2011 CE — **WESTERN BLACK RHINOCEROS**

Diceros bicornis longipes

✗ SUB-SAHARA

Traditional Chinese medicine drove demand for their horns that pushed prices as high as $50,000 per kilogram, leading to extreme poaching and quick extinction

2012 CE — **PINTA ISLAND TORTOISE**

Diceros bicornis longipes

✗ PINTA ISLAND

The last of its kind, Lonesome George waited for a mate until his death in 2012.

2016 CE — **BRAMBLE CAY MELOMYS**

Melomys rubicola

This is the first mammalian species made extinct due to climate change effects.

✗ BRAMBLE CAY

2018 CE

2019 CE* — **SPIX'S MACAW**

Cyanopsitta spixii

✗ BRAZIL

*Today only around 160 Spix's Macaws exist in captivity worldwide.

MAUI 'AKEPA

Loxops ochraceus

✗ MAUI, HAWAIIAN ISLANDS

The last sighting of this bird occurred in 1988. Recent audio recordings provide some hope that a few birds may yet survive.

SMOOTH HANDFISH

Sympterichthys unipennis

✗ WATERS OF AUSTRALIA

2020 CE

✗ LANAO LAKE, PHILIPPINES

Of the 17 freshwater fish species endemic to Lake Lanao, 15 have gone extinct while two others are critically endangered or possibly extinct.

LANAO LAKE FRESHWATER FISH SPECIES

15 Species have gone extinct.

IVORY-BILLED WOODPECKER

Campephilus principalis

✗ SOUTHERN UNITED STATES AND CUBA

2021 CE

In the 21st century, reported sightings and analyses of audio and visual recordings were published in peer-reviewed scientific journals as evidence that the species could persists

2022 CE

CHINESE PADDLEFISH

Psephurus gladius

It grew to over 3 metres and possibly 7 metres in length. It was one of the largest species of freshwater fish. The Chinese paddlefish was officially declared extinct in 2022, with an estimated time of extinction to be by 2005, and no later than 2010, although it had become functionally extinct by 1993

✗ YANGTZE & YELLOW RIVER BASINS CHINA

species in this list have all been lost due to us, yet although the consequences are yet to be revealed, one of the biggest consequence is as we loose ... es what we also loose is the ability of the natural world to recover and as biodiversity is lost , our planet looses its stability and balance. The list ... t look enormous but the reality still remains hidden, there might be many more species gone extinct and many that could have been lost, that are not ... even discovered. We are loosing biodiversity the very key to the stability and balance of our world, it was biodiversity that allowed us to dominate the ... d, and yet we are also loosing time to act. The more species lost the more out of balance our planet gets and the further the chain of life breaks, which ... urselves are a part of l

Acknowledgements

The year the Earth changed was a project that took several years to complete and involved the help and contributions of many of my teachers and professionals. It includes both this book and my speech at the TedxYouth@TWSDubai. The inspiration for the project first struck me when I was preparing my Tedx talk with Ms. Anvita Zutshi, the organizer of TedxYouth@TWSDubai and my beloved teacher who has assisted me in many initiatives, and Arsalan Firouzi, my dear father. I'm grateful to both of them. They had a key role in determining the framework of this book, and Ms. Anvita oversaw the creation of my TEDx speech, which greatly influenced the book's contents.

I would especially like to thank Emirates Nature WWF for the chance and for recognizing me as a WWF leader of change. I want to thank Amit Banka, the founder of Wenaturalist, in particular, for helping me along the way by recognizing me with the people of nature award in 2021 as the young storyteller of the year. I also want to thank Tanith Harding for honouring me as the winner of the Global Youth Award's Environmental Leadership Award.

I want to thank Mike Barrett, Executive Director of Conservation and Science at WWF-UK, in particular, for sharing his insightful analysis of the environmental situation and for leading the team that produced the Living Planet Report, a landmark document that has served as an inspiration to all of us. However, I would want to specifically thank Johan Rockström and the group that collaborated with him to develop the planetary boundary model. During this pivotal period in our history, their work has provided important insights.

I am really thankful to Shirley at BlueRose Publishing and her team for their advice and also to everyone of them to help me in getting my book published. My gratitude also extends to my close friend Zayaan

Qureshj, who joined me while I explored the living world and who has listened this book several times. A special thank appreciation also goes out to my wonderful grandpa Mohammad Khaledi, my uncles Hamed and Ali Khaledi, for helping me with the majority of my projects and research, which ranged from Indian mongooses to freshwater crabs.

Additionally, I would want to express my thanks to the UAE leaders for all they have done and are doing to preserve the country's nature and cultural history for young people like me to enjoy and discover.

Additionally, I want to express my gratitude to Sir David Attenborough for encouraging my work in a letter he sent after the Art Exhbition and doing all in his power to protect and raise awareness about our planet. I've always looked up to and admired him.

This project has brought a wide range of emotions in me. The reality of our planet's situation right now is really concerning. I've been deeply worried after learning the most recent information about our problems. The fact that I frequently wonder if the animals I've observed will return or disappear at the end of an adventure is the most distressing. Contrarily, it is heartening to see how much our creative minds are currently working to comprehend and, ultimately, address the difficulties we confront. My greatest wish is that we, the brilliant minds, will soon unite and be in a position to shape the course of history.

References

Chapter I

1. The exact number of mass extinction events depends upon at what point you determine a large extinction event to be 'mass'. Typically, geologists talk of five mass extinction events before present, in order, the Ordovician-Silurian event of 450 million years ago (Ma), the Late Devonian event (375 Ma), the Permian-Triassic event (252 Ma), which was the most extreme extinction event with up to 96 per cent of marine and 70 per cent of terrestrial species disappearing, the Triassic-Jurassic event (201 Ma) and the Cretaceous-Paleogene event (66Ma) which ended the age of the dinosaurs.

2. There are a number of theories concerning what brought about the end of the age of the dinosaurs. The proposal that it was largely due to the impact of a meteorite on the Yucatan Peninsula was viewed as radical when first suggested but, with increasing evidence, including, most recently, deep-rock drilling in the Chicxulub crater in 2016, it has become the most widely supported theory. For a good recent account of this evidence, see Hand, E. (2016), 'Drilling of dinosaur-killing impact crater explains buried circular hills', Science, 17 November 2016, https://www.sciencemag.org/news/2016/11/updated-drillingdinosaur-killing-impact-crater-explains-buried-circular-hills.

3. The important role of whales in distributing nutrients is just now coming to light. Whales transport nutrients laterally, in moving between feeding and breeding areas, and vertically, by transporting nutrients from nutrient-rich deep waters to surface waters via faecal plumes and urine. It is estimated that the capacity of animals to move nutrients away from patches where

it is concentrated has decreased to about 5 per cent of what it was before industrial whaling. See Doughty, C.E. (2016), 'Global nutrient transport in a world of giants' https://www.ncbi.nlm.nih.gov/pmc/articles/PMC4743783/. For a localised study in the Gulf of Maine, see Roman, J. and McCarthy, J.J. (2010), 'The Whale Pump: Marine Mammals Enhance Primary Productivity in a Coastal Basin', PLoS ONE 5(10): e13255, https://doi.org/10.1371/journal.pone.0013255.

4. Eukaryotic cells are widely estimated to have evolved between 2 and 2.7 billion years ago, so roughly 1.5 billion years after the origin of life; https://www.scientificamerican.com/article/when-did-eukaryotic- cells/. Multicellular life evolved just over half a billion years ago, roughly 1.5 billion years later; https://astrobiology.nasa.gov/news/howdid-multicellular-life-evolve/.

Chapter II

1. Estimates on remaining wilderness are based on data and extrapolations from Ellis E. et al (2010), 'Anthropogenic transformation of the biomes, 1700 to 2000 (supplementary info Appendix 5)', Global Ecology and Biogeography 19, 589–606.

2. The logs of all the communications of the Apollo missions are available via the NASA website, and make fascinating reading: https://www.nasa.gov/mission_pages/apollo/missions/index.html.

3. The website www.globalforestwatch.org is a useful resource online that aims to chart all change in global forest cover. There are difficulties in doing so. Plantations can appear to be natural forest from space, whereas they are in fact very low-diversity habitats in comparison. The Global Forest Biodiversity Initiative https://www.gfbinitiative.org/ is attempting to more

accurately chart the biodiversity of forests. One of its lead members, Thomas Crowther, recently assessed the global tree total and estimated its depletion at our hand. See 'Mapping tree density at a global scale', Nature 525, 201–205 (2015), https://doi.org/10.1038/nature14967.

4. In 2016, the IUCN estimated that the Borneo orangutan numbered 104,700 individuals. This represents a decline from an estimated 288,500 individuals in 1973. They predict a further decline of 47,000 individuals by 2025; https://www.iucnredlist.org/species/17975/123809220# population.

5. A study of the world's fishing catch data was conducted by researchers in 2003 and revealed the startling rate at which our fishing effort reduced the largest fish in the sea. See Rupert Murray's film The End of the Line for an interview on this research, or the paper, Myers, R. and Worm, B. (2003), 'Rapid Worldwide Depletion of Predatory Fish Communities', Nature 423, 280–3, https://www.nature.com/articles/nature01610.

6. People in UAE eating one debit card worth of plastic a week: https://www.khaleejtimes.com/environment/uae-people-eat-one-credit-card-worth-of-plastic-a-week-say-researchers?_refresh=true

7. Evaluation of microplastics in beach sediments along the coast of Dubai, UAE. https://doi.org/10.1016/j.marpolbul.2019.110739

8. Microplastic in oyster samples in UAE: https://www.thenationalnews.com/uae/environment/2022/04/15/microplastics-found-in-half-of-oyster-samples-tested-at-five-sites-off-uae-coast/

9. Statistic and data about camels consuming plastic in UAE: https://www.thenationalnews.com/uae/environment/uae-

recycling-hundreds-of-uae-camels-have-died-from-eating-plastic-bags-study-shows-1.1117788

10. Further detail about how plastic pollution affects camels: https://plasticoceans.org/plastic-is-killing-the-camels-of-dubai/

11. Details of microplastic in human breastmilk: https://www.theguardian.com/environment/2022/oct/07/microplastics-human-breast-milk-first-time

12. Plastic particles descovrery in human organs :

https://www.theguardian.com/environment/2020/aug/17/microplastic-particles-discovered-in-human-organs

13. Microplastic found in tissue and lungs of living people : https://www.theguardian.com/environment/2022/mar/24/microplastics-found-in-human-blood-for-first-time

14. Detail on te plastic particles found in human lungs https://www.theguardian.com/environment/2022/apr/06/microplastics-found-deep-in-lungs-of-living-people-for-first-time

15. The study and discovery of microplastic in human blook https://www.oceancare.org/en/stories_and_news/plastic-in-human-blood/

16. More information on the microplastic discovery in human blook can be viewed: https://www.theguardian.com/environment/2022/mar/24/microplastics-found-in-human-blood-for-first-time

17. WWF impacts of plastic pollution on marine life: https://wwfint.awsassets.panda.org/downloads/wwf_impacts_of_plastic_pollution_on_biodiversity.pdf

18. How plastic came to dominate the world today: https://www.sciencemuseum.org.uk/objects-and-stories/chemistry/age-plastic-parkesine-

pollution#:~:text=Belgian%20chemist%20and%20clever%20
marketeer,phenol%2C%20under%20heat%20and%20pressur
e.

19. Sea cucumber feeding on microplastic: https://doi.org/
10.1016/j.jembe.2008.09.007

20. Why do Marine Animals Eat plastic:
https://www.bbcearth.com/news/why-marine-animals-cant-
stop-eating-plastic

Chapter III

1. The status of extinct and vulnerable fish species in North
America is reviewed by Jack E. Williams et al., "Fishes of
North America. Endangered, Threatened, or of Special
Concern: 1989," Fisheries (American Fisheries Society),
14(6):2– 20 (1989); R. R. Miller et al., "Extinctions of North
American Fishes During the Past Century," Fisheries,
14(6):22–38 (1989); and Jack E. Williams and Robert R.
Miller, "Conservation Status of the North American Fish
Fauna in Fresh Water," Journal of Fish Biology, 37(A):79–85
(1990). I am grateful to Karsten E. Hartel for sharing his
unpublished analysis of data pertaining to species decline.

2. For an up-to-date assessment of the impact of fishing subsidies
worldwide, see Sumaila et al (2019), 'Updated estimates and
analysis of global fisheries subsidies',
https://doi.org/10.1016/j.marpol.2019. 103695; WWF
(2019), 'Five ways harmful fisheries subsidies impact coastal
communities', https://www.worldwildlife.org/stories/5-
waysharmful-fisheries-subsidies-impact-coastal-communities.

3. On the high rate of extinction of freshwater fishes, see
Diamond, and Walter R. Courtenay Jr. and Peter B. Moyle,
"Introduced Fishes, Aquaculture, and the Biodiversity Crisis,"
Abstracts, 71st Annual Meeting, American Society of

Ichthyologists and Herpetologists, no pp.; and Irv Kornfield and Kent E. Carpenter, " of Lake Lanao, Philippines: Taxonomic Validity, Evolutionary Rates and Speciation Scenarios," in Anthony A. Echelle and Irv Kornfield, eds., Evolution of Fish Species Flocks (Orono: University of Maine Press, 1984). The total of 18 species accepted in the classical accounts of the Lake Lanao cyprinid species flock may be excessive, even though the Maranao people of the region recognize all of them. Some of the species may instead be morphs of very plastic species, as I described for the Mexican cichlid and arctic char in Chapter 7. However the matter is judged taxonomically, the adaptive radiation of the Lanao cyprinids is extreme for a single lake, and it has been almost completely erased during the past fifty years. The fate of the Lake Victoria fishes is described by Christopher G. Barlow and Allan Lisle, "Biology of the Nile Perch Lates niloticus (Pisces: Centropomidae) with Reference to Its Proposed Role as a Sport Fish in Australia," Biological Conservation, 39(4):269–289 (1987); Daniel J. Miller, "Introductions and Extinction of Fish in the African Great Lakes," Trends in Ecology and Evolution, 4(2):56–59 (1989); and C. D. N. Barel et al., "The Haplochromine Cichlids in Lake Victoria: An Assessment of Biological and Fisheries Interests," in M. H. A. Keenleyside, ed., Cichlid Fishes: Behaviour, Ecology and Evolution (London: Chapman and Hall, 1991), pp. 258– 279.

4. The UN's Food and Agriculture Organisation (FAO) publishes the most comprehensive review on the marine and freshwater fish sector every two years, entitled The State of World Fisheries and Aquaculture. Find the 2020 edition here: http://www.fao.org/state-of-fisheriesaquaculture.

5. The decline of freshwater mollusks is documented in The IUCN Invertebrate Red Data Book (Gland, Switzerland:

International Union for Conservation of Nature and Natural Resources, 1983).

6. The Moorean tree snails have been the subject of classic studies of microevolution by Henry E. Crampton and Bryan C. Clarke. The snails' total destruction in the wild is described by James Murray, Elizabeth Murray, Michael S. Johnson, and Bryan Clarke, "The Extinction of Partula on Moorea," Pacific Science, 42(3,4):150-153 (1988); I am grateful to Bryan Clarke for supplying additional unpublished details on the episode. The loss of the Hawaiian tree snails is documented in The ICUN Invertebrate Red Data Book (1983).

7. Two leading bodies are dedicated to reporting on the state of the planet. The Intergovernmental Panel on Climate Change (IPCC) is the best source of information on the consensus of current and forecast climate change (www.ipcc.ch). The Intergovernmental Platform on Biodiversity and Ecosystem Services (IPBES) is the best source of information on the state of biodiversity (www.ipbes.net). For those interested in the concept of tipping points, a helpful review is McSweeney, R. (2010), 'Explainer: Nine "tipping points" that could be triggered by climate change', available at https://www.carbonbrief.org/explainer-nine-tipping-points-that-couldbe-triggered-by-climate-change.

8. For a detailed account of this work and its implications, the very readable Rockström, J. and Klum, M. (2015), Big World, Small Planet, Yale University Press, is recommended.

9. The threatened plant species of the United States are counted by Linda R. McMahan, "CPC Survey Reveals 680 Native U.S. Plants May Become Extinct within 10 Years," Plant Conservation (Center for Plant Conservation), 3(4):1-2 (1988). The species already extinct were tabulated by Michael O'Neal and other CPC staff members in 1992 (personal

communication). The account of the Puerto Rican endemic Banara vanderbiltii is based on John Popenoe, "One of the World's Rarest Species," Plant Conservation, 3(4):6 (1988).

10. The latest study by the IPBES (2019) suggests that the current rate of extinctions is tens to hundreds of times the rate of the average over the last 10 million years, and the average rate of vertebrate species loss over the last century is thought to be up to 114 times higher than the background rate. See https://ipbes.net/global-assessment.

11. A catalogue of threatened and endangered habitats is provided in The IUCN Invertebrate Red Data Book (1983).

12. The reduction of coral reefs by both natural and human-caused stress is reported in "Coral Reefs off 20 Countries Face Assaults from Man and Nature," New York Times, March 27, 1990; Peter W. Glynn, "Coral Reef Bleaching in the 1980s and Possible Connections with Global Warming," Trends in Ecology and Evolution, 6(6):175–179 (1991); and Leslie Roberts, "Greenhouse Role in Reef Stress Unproven," Science, 253:258–259 (1991).

13. The effects of climatic warming on biodiversity are predicted by Robert L. Peters and Joan D. S. Darling, "The Greenhouse Effect and Nature Reserves," BioScience, 35(11):707–717 (1985); Andy Dobson, Alison Jolly, and Dan Rubenstein, "The Greenhouse Effect and Biological Diversity," Trends in Ecology and Evolution, 4(3):64–68 (1989); and Robert L. Peters and Thomas E. Lovejoy, eds., Global Warming and Biological Diversity (New Haven: Yale University Press, 1992). The account given here is drawn from these sources and from my "Threats to Biodiversity," Scientific American, 260(9):108–116 (1989).

14. A key source of data on bleaching events and coral reef loss is the US government's NOAA Coral Reef Watch, https://coralreefwatch.noaa.gov, which uses satellite data together with geographical information systems to monitor sea conditions across the world. For more detail, I'd also recommend the Global Coral Reef Monitoring Network reports: https://gcrmn.net/products/reports/.

15. The expected impact of the rise in sea level on biodiversity is examined by Walter V. Reid and Mark C. Trexler, Drowning the National Heritage: Climate Change and U.S. Coastal Biodiversity (Washington, D.C.: World Resources Institution, 1991).

16. The UN's Food and Agriculture Organization produces frequent reports on the state of global agriculture and food production. One of its keystone reports is its Status of the World's Soil Resources from 2015, which laid out the chief concerns over the sustainability of modern, industrial agriculture: http://www.fao.org/3/a-i5199e.pdf.

17. The account of the fragility of tropical rain forests is drawn from "The Current State of Biological Diversity," in E. O. Wilson and F. M. Peter, eds., Biodiversity (Washington, D.C.: National Academy Press, 1988), pp. 3–18; from Christopher Uhl, "Restoration of Degraded Lands in the Amazon Basin," ibid., pp. 326–332; and from T. C. Whitmore, "Tropical Forest Nutrients: Where Do We Stand? A Tour de Horizon," in J. Proctor, ed., Mineral Nutrients in Tropical Forest and Savanna Ecosystems (Boston: Blackwell Scientific Publications, 1990), pp. 1–13.

18. Accounts of the record 1987 destruction of Amazonian forest are given by Mac Margolis, "Thousands of Amazon Acres Burning," Washington Post, September 8, 1988; Marlise Simons, "Vast Amazon Fires, Man-Made, Linked to Global

Warming," New York Times, August 12, 1988; and "Amazon Holocaust: Forest Destruction in Brazil, 1987–88," Briefing Paper, Friends of the Earth (London, 1988).

19. The estimates of annual tropical deforestation rates in 1989 were taken from the report by Norman Myers, Deforestation Rates in Tropical Forests and Their Climatic Implications (London: Friends of the Earth, 1989). They are based on data assembled country by country. Myers provides a summary of his study in "Tropical Deforestation: The Latest Situation," BioScience, 41(5):282 (1991). He defines tropical moist forests, roughly equated with tropical rain forests, as "evergreen or partly evergreen forests, in areas receiving not less than 100 mm of precipitation in any month for two out of three years, with mean annual temperature of 24-plus degrees Celsius, and essentially frost-free; in these forests some trees may be deciduous; the forests usually occur at altitudes below 1300 metres (though often in Amazonia up to 1,800 metres and generally in Southeast Asia up to only 750 metres); and in mature examples of these forests, there are several more or less distinctive strata." In late 1991 the Food and Agriculture Organization of the United Nations released a preliminary report ("Second Interim Report on the State of Tropical Forests") that independently conforms to the assessment by Myers. The authors estimate that in 1981–1990 tropical forests were being removed at a rate of 170,000 square kilometers per year. The figure is 20 percent higher than Myers', but the FAO measurements included removal of thinner forests than those considered by Myers, as well as high bamboo stands. More precisely, forests were defined as collections of trees or bamboos with a minimum of 10 percent crown cover associated with wild floras and faunas and relatively undisturbed soil conditions. The extent of prehistoric forest cover is reviewed in Peter H. Raven, "The

Scope of the Plant Conservation Problem WorldWide," in David Bramwell, Ole Hamann, V. H. Heywood, and Hugh Synge, eds., Botanic Gardens and the World Conservation Strategy (New York: Academic Press, 1987), pp. 20–29. The history of estimation of tropical deforestation rates from the 1970s to Myers' 1989 report is evaluated by J. A. Sayer and T. C. Whitmore, "Tropical Moist Forests: Destruction and Species Extinction," Biological Conservation, 55(2):199–213 (1991). They conclude that deforestation grew worse during the 1980s. They doubt that extinction was greatly increased as a result, but they make no reference to many of the data and models in the literature.

20. During the COVID-19 pandemic, the IPBES (2020) made clear the link between emergent viruses and our degradation of the environment in a guest article; see https://ipbes.net/covid19stimulus.

21. Species extinction from loss of rain forest: projections similar to the ones I have made globally were obtained independently by Daniel S. Simberloff for plants and birds in the American tropics, "Are We on the Verge of a Mass Extinction in Tropical Rain Forests?," in David K. Elliott, ed., Dynamics of Extinction (New York: Wiley, 1986), pp. 165–180. Simberloff projects that with a halving of the original rain forest, expected by the end of this century (parallel to but not the same as cutting in half the amount left at this moment), 15 percent of the plant species—about 13,600 in all—will become extinct. If forests are saved only in existing parks and reserves, 66 percent will suffer extinction. For birds of the Amazon Basin, the figures are 12 and 70 percent respectively.

22. The C40 cities organisation is a network of the world's megacities committed to addressing climate change. It is a good source of information on how urban areas are likely to

be affected by global warming, and how responsible cities are tackling the issues they face. See https://www.c40.org.

23. Information on the natural origins of medicines used in the United States is provided in Chris Hails, The Importance of Biological Diversity (Gland: World Wide Fund for Nature, 1989).

24. An authoritative account of pharmaceuticals harvested from plants, including a complete list of the 119 substances used in pure form, is provided by Norman R. Farnsworth, "Screening Plants for New Medicines," in E. O. Wilson and F. M. Peter, eds., Biodiversity (Washington, D.C.: National Academy Press, 1988), pp. 83-97. Additional perspectives are provided by D. D. Soejarto and N. R. Farnsworth, "Tropical Rain Forests: Potential Source of New Drugs?," Perspectives in Biology and Medicine, 32(2):244-256 (1989).

25. The properties of the neem tree are described in Noel D. Vietmeyer, ed., Neem: A Tree for Solving Global Problems (Washington, D.C.: National Academy Press, 1992).

26. An account of leeches and the anticoagulant they produce is given by Paul S. Wachtel, "Return of the Bloodsucker," International Wildlife, September 1987, pp. 44-46. A news report of the new anticoagulants from vampire bats and pit vipers was published in Science, 253:621 (1991).

27. The list of pharmaceuticals derived from plants and fungi is drawn from Hails, The Importance of Biological Diversity; D. D. Soejarto and N. R. Farnsworth, "Tropical Rain Forests: Potential Source of New Drugs?," Perspectives in Biology and Medicine, 32(2):244-256 (1989); and Margery L. Oldfield, The Value of Conserving Genetic Resources (Sunderland: Sinauer, 1989). An impressive number of Amerindian natural products, few of which have been investigated to date, are

described by Richard E. Schultes and Robert F. Raffauf, The Healing Forest: Medicinal and Toxic Plants of the Northwest Amazonia (Portland: Dioscorides Press, 1990).

28. The potential of wild plant and animal species is detailed in the previously cited studies by Margery Oldfield, Norman Myers, and the authors in Biodiversity, as well as in Hails, The Importance of Biological Diversity. Inca agriculture is described in Hugh Popenoe, Noel D. Vietmeyer, and a panel of coauthors, Lost Crops of the Incas (Washington, D.C.: National Academy Press, 1989).

29. The descriptions of wild animal species as potential food sources are based on Little-known Asian Animals with a Promising Economic Future, ed. Noel D. Vietmeyer (Washington, D.C.: National Academy Press, 1983); Oldfield, The Value of Conserving Genetic Resources; Neotropical Wildlife Use and Conservation, eds. John G. Robinson and Kent H. Redford (Chicago: University of Chicago Press, 1991); and Microlivestock, ed. Noel D. Vietmeyer (Washington, D.C.: National Academy Press, 1991).

30. The role of tropical deforestation in the buildup of atmospheric carbon dioxide has been analyzed by many authors; the sources used here are Richard A. Houghton and George M. Woodwell, "Global Climatic Change," Scientific American, 260(4):36-44 (April 1989), and R. A. Houghton, "Emission of Greenhouse Gases," in Myers, Deforestation Rates in Tropical Forests, pp. 53- 62.

31. Bryan G. Norton's assessment of the option value of species is given in "Commodity, Amenity, and Morality: the Limits of Quantification in Valuing Biodiversity," in Wilson and Peter eds., Biodiversity, pp. 200-205. General aspects of economic analysis are explained by other authors in the same volume, including Nyle C. Brady, J. William Burley, Robert J. A.

Goodland, and John Spears. They are also treated by Harold J. Morowitz, "Balancing Species Preservation and Economic Considerations," Science, 253:752–754 (1991).

32. In thinking about economic and moral foundations of conservation, I have been informed by the writings of ethical philosophers, including David Ehrenfeld, The Arrogance of Humanism (New York: Oxford University Press, 1978); Bryan Norton, "Commodity," and Why Preserve Natural Variety? (Princeton: Princeton University Press, 1987); Peter Singer, The Expanding Circle: Ethics and Sociobiology (New York: Farrar, Straus, and Giroux, 1981); Holmes Rolston III, Philosophy Gone Wild: Essays in Environmental Ethics (Buffalo: Prometheus Books, 1986), and Environmental Ethics: Duties to and Values in the Natural World (Philadelphia: Temple University Press, 1988); Alan Randall, "The Value of Biodiversity," Ambio, 20(2):64–68 (1991); and the authors of The Preservation of Species: The Value of Biological Diversity, ed. Bryan G. Norton (Princeton: Princeton University Press, 1986).

33. The discussion of the conservation ethic is based in part on my Biophilia (Cambridge: Harvard University Press, 1984). The general definition of ethic comes from Aldo Leopold, A Sand County Almanac and Sketches Here and There (New York: Oxford University Press, 1949).

34. The definition of biodiversity studies given here and a discussion of its ramifications were presented in Paul R. Ehrlich and Edward O. Wilson, "Biodiversity Studies: Science and Policy," Science, 253:758–762 (1991).

35. The three-level approach to surveying global biodiversity was developed in collaboration with Peter H. Raven.

36. The RAP search for hot spots is described by Sarah Pollock, "Biological SWAT Team Ranks for Diversity, Endemism," Pacific Discovery, 44(3):6–7 (1991).

37. The use of Geographic Information Systems to map ecosystems is described by J. Michael Scott et al., "Species Richness: A Geographic Approach to Protecting Future Biological Diversity," BioScience, 37(11):782–788 (1987). On a much broader scale, essentially the same method has been applied by Eric Dinerstein and Eric D. Wikramanayake to assess reserves and parks in Asia and the western Pacific, in "Beyond 'Hotspots': How to Prioritize Investments in Biodiversity in the Indo-Pacific Region," Conservation Biology, 7(1): 53–65 (1993). Techniques for mapping endangered species are given by many authors in Larry E. Morse and Mary Sue Henifin, eds., Rare Plant Conservation: Geographical Data Organization (New York: New York Botanical Garden, 1981).

38. The employment of landscape design to enhance biodiversity has been widely discussed. Summaries of key topics are provided in separate chapters by Bryn H. Green, Larry D. Harris (with John F. Eisenberg), and David Western, in Western and Mary C. Pearl, eds., Conservation for the Twenty-First Century (New York: Oxford University Press, 1989).

39. The concept of bioregions, dating back to the 1800s and developed in modern form by Raymond F. Dasmann, Peter Berg, Charles H. W. Foster, and others, is reviewed in C. H. W. Foster, Experiments in Bioregionalism: The New England River Basins Story (Hanover: University Press of New England, 1984), and "Bioregionalism," Renewable Resources Journal, 4(3):12–14 (1986).

40. The shortage of systematists is cited in my "The Biological Diversity Crisis: A Challenge to Science," Issues in Science and Technology, 2(1):20-29 (1985), and "Time to Revive Systematics," Science, 230:1227 (1985).

41. The progress of GenBank in recording DNA and RNA sequences is described by Christian Burks et al., in Russell F. Doolittle, ed., Molecular Evolution: Computer Analysis of Protein and Nucleic Acid Sequences (New York: Academic Press, 1990), pp. 3-22.

42. The concept of chemical prospecting was developed by Thomas Eisner during the late 1980s and presented in "Prospecting for Nature's Chemical Riches," Issues in Science and Technology, 6(2):31-34 (1990); and "Chemical Prospecting: A Proposal for Action," in F. Herbert Bormann and Stephen R. Kellert, eds., Ecology, Economics, Ethics: The Broken Circle (New Haven: Yale University Press, 1991), pp. 196-202.

43. The status of microbial preservation is described in "American Type Culture Collection Seeks To Expand Research Effort," Scientist, 4(16):1-7 (1990).

44. Seed banks are reviewed by Erich Hoyt, Conserving the Wild Relatives of Crops (Rome and Gland: International Board for Plant Genetic Resources, etc., 1988); Jeffrey A. McNeely et al., Conserving the World's Biological Diversity (Gland and Washington, D.C.: International Union for Conservation of Nature and Natural Resources, World Resources Institute, etc., 1990); Joel I. Cohen et al., "Ex Situ Conservation of Plant Genetic Resources: Global Development and Environmental Concerns," Science, 253:866-872 (1991)

45. The National Collection of Endangered Plants is the subject of a report in Plant Conservation, 6(1):6-7 (1991).

46. The performance of zoos and other captive-animal facilities in maintaining diversity is described by William Conway, "Can Technology Aid Species Preservation?" in Wilson and Peter, Biodiversity, pp. 263–268; and by Colin Tudge, Last Animals at the Zoo (London: Hutchinson Radius, 1991)

47. The number of species of mammals facing extinction and requiring rescue is from Michael E. Soulé et al., "The Millennium Ark: How Long a Voyage, How Many Staterooms, How Many Passengers?," Zoo Biology, 5:101–114 (1986). William Conway is quoted on the limits of zoos by Edward C. Wolf, On the Brink of Extinction: Conserving the Diversity of Life (Washington, D.C.: Worldwatch Institute, 1987).

48. A pioneering set of recommendations to save tropical ecosystems was advanced in 1980 by Peter H. Raven et al., Research Priorities in Tropical Biology (Washington, D.C.: National Academy Press, 1980). A review of ongoing efforts is provided by the authors in Wilson and Peter, Biodiversity; by McNeely et al., Conserving; by Janet N. Abramovitz, Investing in Biological Diversity: U.S. Research and Conservation Efforts in Developing Countries (Washington, D.C.: World Resources Institute, 1991); and by Kathleen Courrier, ed., Global Biodiversity Strategy (Washington, D.C.: World Resources Institute; Gland: World Conservation Union; New York: United Nations Environment Program, 1992).

49. The provisions of the Endangered Species Act of the United States, as well as those of international regulatory protocols, are reviewed by Robert Boardman, International Organization and the Conservation of Nature (Bloomington: Indiana University Press, 1981); by Michael J. Bean, The Evolution of National Wildlife Law (New York: Praeger,

1983); and by Simon Lyster, International Wildlife Law (Cambridge, Eng.: Grotius, 1985).

50. The progress of ecosystem restoration in the United States can be followed in issues of Restoration and Management Notes, published by the University of Wisconsin Press since 1982. A recent account of prairie renewal and the general hopes and misgivings of restorationists is provided by William K. Stevens, "Green-Thumbed Ecologists Resurrect Vanished Habitats," New York Times, March 19, 1991. The creation of new dry tropical forest in Costa Rica's Guanacaste National Park is described by Reid et al., Bankrolling Successes.

51. Useful information on the status of Marine Protected Areas is to be found at Protected Planet: https://www.protectedplanet.net/marine. It is important to note that at present not all protected areas are effectively managed. Indeed some estimates suggest only about 50 per cent of them are true, effectively run MPAs.

52. The history of animal-species introduction into new environments is reviewed by Paul R. Ehrlich, "Which Animal Will Invade?," in Harold A. Mooney and James A. Drake, eds., Ecology of Biological Invasions of North America and Hawaii (New York: Springer, 1986), pp. 79-95.

53. For more on the effectiveness of coastal ecosystems in capturing and removing carbon, and the efforts under way to restore mangroves, saltmarshes and seagrass meadows for this purpose, see https://www.thebluecarboninitiative.org/. To see more detail on design of Marine Protected Areas, this is an interesting read from Australia: https://ecology.uq.edu.au/filething/get/39100/Scientific_Principles_MPA

54. Examples of studies that link greater biodiversity with a greater capacity to capture and store carbon in ecosystems include Atwood et al (2015), which demonstrates that, when top predators were removed, carbon capture and storage in saltmarshes in New England and in mangrove and seagrass ecosystems in Australia was reduced due to the rise of herbivores, https://www.nature.com/articles/nclimate2763; Liu et al (2018) found that tree species richness in subtropical rainforests in China increased the capacity of the forest to capture and store carbon, https://royalsocietypublishing.org/doi/full/10.1098/rspb.2018.1240; and Osuri et al (2020) found that natural forests were better at capturing and holding on to carbon than plantations in India, https://iopscience.iop.org/article/10.1088/1748-9326/ab5f75.

55. For a vivid account of the ways in which humankind uses land, see the presentation created by the research and data project, Our World in Data: https://ourworldindata.org/land-use.

56. The technology of Bioenergy with Carbon Capture and Storage (BECCS) is currently under investigation as a method of removing carbon from the atmosphere whilst generating heat or electricity. If it proves to be a scalable option, it could help reduce the pressure of bioenergy crops that compete for space with food production or natural habitats. The advantage of using kelp as a bioenergy crop is that a restored kelp forest is a high-biodiversity habitat that grows at such speed it can withstand regular but well-managed harvesting.

57. Two leading sources of information on regenerative agriculture are Regeneration International (https://regenerationinternational.org) and Burgess, P.J., Harris, J., Graves, A.R., Deeks. L.K. (2019), Regenerative Agriculture: Identifying the Impact; Enabling the Potential,

Report for SYSTEMIQ, 17 May 2019, Cranfield University, Bedfordshire, UK, https://www.foodandlandusecoalition.org/wpcontent/uploads/2019/09/Regenerative-Agriculture-final.pdf.

58. For a presentation on how much of the world's land we would need in order to feed the world population with the average diet of a given country, see https://ourworldindata.org /agricultural-land-by-globaldiets. Data on meat consumption around the world can be found at https://ourworldindata .org/meat-production#which-countries-eat-themost-meat.

59. The leading reports in recent times have been The Planetary Health Diet and You by the EAT-Lancet commission (2019), see https://eatforum.org/eat-lancet-commission/the-planetary-health-dietand-you/, and the FAO's Sustainable Diets and Biodiversity review (2010), see http://www.fao.org/3/a-i3004e.pdf.

60. For Yellowstone National Park's own account of the wolf recovery and its effect on biodiversity, see https://www.nps.gov/yell/learn/nature/wolf-restoration.htm

61. Ariel E. Lugo has spoken on behalf of exotic species in expanding local biodiversity. While conceding the high risk of introductions and the need to remove elements that endanger native fauna and flora, he notes that most such species are naturalized without creating ecological problems. "Exotics appear to do best in human-disturbed environments. Exotics can provide food and fiber without causing ecological havoc. For example, when managed properly, certain exotic trees grow well in highly degraded lands where they contribute to soil rehabilitation and reestablishment of native species." "Removal of Exotic Organisms," Conservation Biology, 4(4):345 (1990).

62. The marine environment poses particular difficulties in assessing populations of fish stocks and monitoring the activities of fishing vessels at sea, both of which are needed to ensure sustainability. These issues are being grappled with by existing certification schemes but are not yet fully resolved.

63. The Stockholm Resilience Centre is a guiding light in Earth system science and thinking on sustainability. It was behind the planetary boundaries model and works to advise governments on environmental policy. See more at https://www.stockholmresilience.org/.

64. Figures on both fishing catch and aquaculture production are reported regularly by the UN's FAO in their State of World Fisheries and Aquaculture. The 2020 edition can be found here: http://www.fao.org/state-of-fisheries-aquaculture.

65. The UN's Convention on the Law of the Sea is the presiding international treaty on the world's use of the ocean. It is currently being amended for the first time in decades, and many people are working hard to ensure that sustainability is at the heart of its refreshed contents. If we get these changes right, it could transform humankind's relationship with the ocean. For more information, see https://www.un.org/bbnj/.

66. The greater attendance of people at zoos and aquariums than at professional sporting events (football, baseball, basketball, ice hockey) is cited in Directory of the American Association of Zoological Parks and Aquaria, ed. Linda Boyd (Wheeling, West Virginia: Ogle Bay Park, 1990–91).

67. Tropical rainforests are in many cases ancient ecosystems. A good overview of their history and how they function can be found in Ghazoul, J. and Sheil, D. (2010), Tropical Rain Forest Ecology, Diversity, and Conservation, Oxford University Press.

68. The innate affiliation of human beings with the natural world is elaborated in my Biophilia (Cambridge: Harvard University Press, 1984). The imagery of the serpent was drawn from Balaji Mundkur's masterful The Cult of the Serpent: An Interdisciplinary Survey of Its Manifestations and Origins (Albany: State University of New York Press, 1983). The concept of the idealized living place as a biological adaptation was developed by Gordon H. Orians, "Habitat Selection: General Theory and Applications to Human Behavior," in Joan S. Lockard, ed., The Evolution of Human Social Behavior (New York: Elsevier North Holland, 1980), pp. 46–66; and "An Ecological and Evolutionary Approach to Landscape Aesthetics," in Edmund C. Penning-Rowsell and David Lowenthal, eds., Landscape Meanings and Values (London: Allen and Unwin, 1986), pp. 3–22.

69. This comes from The Dasgupta Review: Independent Review on the Economics of Biodiversity, due out in late 2020. This review will present a powerful argument for valuing the environmental services of nature more appropriately within a modern economy. See https://www.gov.uk/government/publications/interim-report-the-dasgupta-review-independent-review-on-the-economics-of-biodiversity.

70. Excellent histories of wilderness in the human imagination, especially in Europe and America, have been presented by Roderick Nash, Wilderness and the American Mind (New Haven: Yale University Press, 1967); and by Max Oelschlaeger, The Idea of Wilderness: From Prehistory to the Age of Ecology (New Haven: Yale University Press, 1991).

71. More information on Impacts of Invasive lion fish. See fisheries.noaa.gov/southeast/ecosystems/impacts-invasive-lionfish#:~:text=Lionfish%2C%20which%20are%20native%20to,the%20cause%20for%20the%20invasion.

72. Detailed study off how mental health is affected by nature can be seen https://www.mentalhealth.org.uk/our-work/research/nature-how-connecting-nature-benefits-our-mental-health#:~:text=Nature%20can%20generate%20many%20positive,particularly%20lower%20depression%20and%20anxiety.

73. Detail on UAE wildlife and what UAE is doing to save many species can be viewed https://www.ead.gov.ae/ & https://www.moccae.gov.ae/en/knowledge-and-statistics/biodiversity.aspx

74. How Singapore is living with its wildlife and urbanizing . https://www.channelnewsasia.com/singapore/singapore-wildlife-conservation-city-in-nature-reserves-hornbill-1339231

75. Could the UAE's ghaf tree be part of the solution to climate change? Can be viewed here https://www.thenationalnews.com/uae/2022/12/27/could-the-uaes-ghaf-tree-be-part-of-the-solution-to-climate-change/?fbclid=PAAab9bBri-tmjNrkQcb0doqNRFWnFN3jqUST0Hj6nua2LVnXMTLxdghaCEXg

76. Many of the graphs and statistics from this book is taken from WWF living planet report 2022. To see it in detail https://wwflpr.awsassets.panda.org/downloads/lpr_2022_full_report.pdf

77. Horse shoe crabs and their role during COViD 19. See https://www.nationalgeographic.com/animals/article/covid-vaccine-needs-horseshoe-crab-blood

78. How can we cool down the arctic. See https://theconversation.com/what-could-we-do-to-cool-the-arctic-specifically-188626

79. Many scientific names and species Identification found in UAE can be seen in the Dubai desert Conservation reserve website; https://www.ddcr.org/

80. The ways we can plant seeds and trees are a unique way to reforest the world. To learn more : https://eandt.theiet.org/content/articles/2022/01/tree-planting-drones-could-help-restore-the-world-s-forests/#:~:text=But%20how%20effective%20is%20seeding,metrics%20are%20not%20what%20counts.

81. Recent successful Conservation stories. https://abcnews.go.com/Technology/arctic-sharks-caribbean-red-wolves-black-rhinos-best/story?id=95015247